PRAISE FOR NATIONAL BESTSELLING AUTHOR

"Julie Beard strikes gold with a delightful, earthy, and up-
lifting romance that is sure to please. 4½ stars."

—*Romantic Times*

"Experience the passion and pageantry of the Elizabethan
world in this wonderfully entertaining story!"

—Susan Wiggs, author of *The Drifter*

"An unforgettable love story, rich in history, cloaked in
intrigue, full of contrasting settings all bound together by
the vivid, descriptive writing style of this talented author."

—*Rendezvous*

Falcon and the Sword

"A medieval romance at its best. Julie Beard paints a lively and colorful portrait of the 13th century with vivid descriptions, sharp narrative, and an engrossing, original plot. She is at the top of her form and continues to dazzle with stories that speak to the heart and the mind."

—*Romantic Times*

"A sensitive, thought-provoking story with an original plot, fascinating characters, and a vibrant setting. Another best-seller for Ms. Beard."

—*Rendezvous*

"Since her debut . . . Julie Beard has fast become known for her rich, dramatic medieval romances. There is a magical quality to Julie Beard's writing that brings to life a long-ago time of pageantry and legend, yet gives us characters who are living, breathing people to care about."

—*Heart to Heart*

A Dance in Heather

"Lively [and] endearing."

—*Publishers Weekly*

"A nice interweaving of medieval British history, pageantry, and love."

—*Library Journal*

"Every scene is beautifully rendered . . . a nonstop read."

—*Romantic Times*

"Vivid and compelling, the 15th century springs to vibrant life . . . From roistering festivals in ancient castles to teeming life in medieval London, she paints an astonishingly vivid picture of the times; and a bold lord, his fair lady, and their love . . . a memorable read."

—Edith Layton, author of *The Crimson Crown*

"A glorious love story in every sense—alive and vibrant, enthralling, and intriguing . . . I couldn't put it down until the last page."

—*Rendezvous*

Lady and the Wolf

"Fiery passion . . . Ms. Beard captures your imagination from page one of this outstanding tale of the Middle Ages."
—*Rendezvous*

"*Lady and the Wolf* mixes the plague, primogeniture, the Spanish Inquisition, witchcraft, jousts, grave robbing, and some sizzling sex scenes into a brand-new, bestselling, 14th century romance."
—*Chicago Suburban Times*

"A powerful debut novel that sweeps us into the lives of a medieval family . . . A stunning and poignant climax."
—*Romantic Times*

"Beard is writing tales of love and romance that always have happy endings."
—*Chicago Tribune*

Titles by Julie Beard

THE MAIDEN'S HEART
ROMANCE OF THE ROSE
FALCON AND THE SWORD
A DANCE IN HEATHER
LADY AND THE WOLF

THE CHRISTMAS CAT
(an anthology with Jo Beverley, Barbara Bretton, and Lynn Kurland)

The Maiden's Heart

Julie Beard

JOVE BOOKS, NEW YORK

If you purchased this book without a cover, you should be aware that this book is stolen property. It was reported as "unsold and destroyed" to the publisher, and neither the author nor the publisher has received any payment for this "stripped book."

THE MAIDEN'S HEART

A Jove Book / published by arrangement with
the author

PRINTING HISTORY
Jove edition / June 1999

All rights reserved.
Copyright © 1999 by Julie Beard.
Excerpt from *Blue Moon* copyright © 1999 by Jill Marie Landis.
This book may not be reproduced in whole or part,
by mimeograph or any other means, without permission.
For information address: The Berkley Publishing Group,
a division of Penguin Putnam Inc.,
375 Hudson Street, New York, New York 10014.

The Penguin Putnam Inc. World Wide Web site address is
http://www.penguinputnam.com

ISBN: 0-515-12515-6

A JOVE BOOK®
Jove Books are published by The Berkely Publishing Group,
a division of Penguin Putnam Inc.,
375 Hudson Street, New York, New York 10014.
JOVE and the "J" design
are trademarks belonging to Penguin Putnam Inc.

PRINTED IN THE UNITED STATES OF AMERICA

10 9 8 7 6 5 4 3 2 1

*To the memory of Jan "Mathews" Milella,
and Stephanie Walker.
Two loving women whose passion for books
made the world a better place,
and whose absence will always be felt.*

ACKNOWLEDGMENTS

Special thanks to Wendy Gifford and Mary Alice Kruesi for reading and critiquing this manuscript. Thanks, also, to Pat White and Ann Haskel for their friendship. My gratitude goes to Denise Domning for generously sharing her vast knowledge of the Middle Ages. And kudos to John Beard for creating my web site.

The Maiden's Heart

Prologue

You who find this illuminated manuscript, I pray God you do not burn it, for you are holding a sheaf of history in your hands. Yea, I admit my tale is full of what some call heresy and certainly much evidence of man's frailties, but it is so much more than the sinful sum of its parts.

My name is Brother Edmund. I am the one weeping on the ink before it dries as I scratch these words in the parchment with my quill. Sentimentality is not a noble trait in a monk, but I come late to this calling, having lived many years in the world as a man subject to all manner of sin. I joined Treyvaux Abbey and became a Benedictine monk after the death of my beloved wife.

Forgive my intrusion, for you do not want to hear about a gaunt and gray-haired old Benedictine such as myself. But without my skills as an illuminator of manuscripts, you would not be privy to this story at all. I am not so much proud of my role as historian as I am grateful that I can share these events. I have questioned many people, includ-

ing the hero and heroine, to ensure the tale's accuracy. And where necessary, I have used my imagination which, I pray God, you will not find wanting.

You will hear little from me directly as the story unfolds. Like an angel I shall hover over the pages unseen and unheard, except when clarification is required.

A great fable, like a life well lived, is a seamless tapestry that requires no interpretation. God does not trumpet his best creations. Nor does a weaver toil for hours, even years, at the loom for mere applause. No, the creation, whether a man or a work of art, speaks for itself. And so it shall be with this tome over which I've toiled half a lifetime. This chronicle of love.

One

England, 1313

w! God's teeth, man, what are you trying to do?
Kill me? You accursed, damnable knave!''

The roaring voice fairly shook a round, faded
yellow tent at the edge of the tilting yard, giving pause to
more than a few pages and squires scurrying by before the
start of the Round Table. But Sir Hugh de Greyhurst—a
bear of a man—had never cared what anyone thought of
him, and so he let out another string of curses.

"That's my leg, damnation take you! God's wounds!
Don't twist it!''

Brian, the squire kneeling at his feet, merely squinted at
the insults. When the shouting ceased, he opened his eyes
wide and smiled overbroadly as would a cowered mother
trying to placate an unreasonable child, which merely reig-
nited Sir Hugh's explosive anger.

"God curse you, you patronizing knave!'' he shouted.

"Now, now, my lord," Brian said, "you must bend your knee. If you do not do so, and often, you will never have use of this leg again. It grows stiffer by the month."

"Damn you to hell, do not remind me," Sir Hugh muttered. He nearly cuffed the ear of his handsome young squire, but instead balled his mighty hands into fists and pressed them to his forehead.

"Oh, Lord, curse me for a fool," he groaned, wishing anew he could wheel back time and relive that fateful joust six months ago. He had been knocked from his horse and fell badly in a careless charge down the lists, exacerbating an old injury. His opponent, Sir Ranulf Blakely, had rightly claimed Hugh's charger and best armor, the victor's spoils, leaving Hugh to struggle ever since with his second-best armor and a body that would not heal from whatever unseen wound ailed it.

"Dress me," he commanded, lowering his fists to his lap. He sat on a stool, naked save for a billowy shirt, with one leg stretched out straight and stiff.

"My lord, I always have trouble putting on your leggings. If you could just bend your leg . . ."

When Brian looked up and saw the fury blazing in his master's golden eyes, he fell silent.

"Very well, then," the squire said with a beleaguered sigh. "I'll start with the other leg."

"I've been at this too long," Hugh said as they exited the tent a half hour later.

He tried not to grimace as he swung his injured leg out and around with the force of his hips, his mail and plate armor clanking with each awkward step. All his concentration was spent on trying to look natural, which was a difficult task for someone who usually strode with the force of a giant on a rampage.

A stone's throw away, trumpets were blaring as more than a dozen knights began to parade around the tilt yard, displaying their arms on flapping pennons and banners, some catching garters and ribbons from women in the stands to tie on their lances. The crowd responded to the tourniers with a burst of applause and cheers of approval.

In days gone by, the sights and sounds of such a spectacle would mesmerize Hugh—smartly caparisoned horses, snorting and pawing the ground as they carried silver-plated knights; the flushed cheeks of haggard peasants and the lush velvet gowns of rich town merchants eager for the competition; a cool breeze snapping the multicolored banners. But now these familiar sights and sounds merely reminded Hugh that more pain was imminent.

"I'm too old for this, Brian."

"Too old? Nay, my lord, that's not true! You are but thirty years of age. Here's your shield. You're up first on the lists. Sir Roland is your opponent."

By now they had reached the edge of the oblong yard where the jousting would take place. The parade was over.

"Rolly," Hugh said with an easy chuckle. He tugged at the chin of his coif—a mail hood that constrained his full mane of amber, shoulder-length hair—and thrust out his chin, adjusting to the gear. He wouldn't put on his stifling helmet until the last moment. "My old and dear friend Sir Rolly. Pray God I don't crack his head open."

"You'll manage a draw, I'll warrant," Brian mused, retrieving Hugh's horse from a young page. "You two have been on the tournament circuit for nigh on two decades, I hear, and in all that time neither one has ransomed the other or his horse and armor."

"True enough."

Hugh had been among the best of the best of the so-called "iron men." Until recently, he had never been ransomed or lost his armor to an opponent in his fifteen grueling years as a knight errant.

In times gone by his successes had made him wealthy, rich with ransoms from knights he had bested. If he had been any other man, he might have parlayed his wealth and glory into a position of power at court. He might have won favor with the king and received a grant of land to become a baron in his own right. But he was the son of Jervais de Greyhurst, a powerful and ruthless lord who would rather burn in hell than see his disinherited son benefit from the king's benevolence.

And now he was a knight who had been injured once too often. Which was to say that overnight he had gone from a feared and awesome jouster to someone who was useless. Thinking of such ill fortune made his thoughts turn to what might have been.

"Brian, I'd rather be stretched out before a cozy fire with my head in the lap of a woman than waiting here for my turn on the lists. She wouldn't have to be pretty, mind you, and she wouldn't even have to please me. If she would just . . ." He reached a hand out as if to snatch the fantasy from midair. "If she would just comb her fingers through my hair . . . Well, you understand what I'm saying."

Brian held out gauntlets and Hugh thrust his hands into the metal gloves, then tucked his foot in a stirrup. With a heave-ho from Brian and a roar of pain from deep in his soul, which was thankfully muted by the crowd, Hugh swung his right leg over the saddle, sinking onto it in defeat.

"What's so special about women?" Brian said, pretending he hadn't noticed the depth of Hugh's pain. "What good are they? You know we must live by the sword. A home and grandchildren to bounce on our knees is not our lot in life."

At the hard tone of resignation in Brian's normally melodic voice, Hugh looked down at the seventeen-year-old and resisted the urge to tousle his hair in sympathy. "I forget that you are just setting out on the long journey I'm ready to be done with. One day you, too, will long for all that might have been."

Brian, like his sponsor, was a second son. Not the lucky first who would one day inherit the only private chamber and bed in his father's manor. Nor was he the third son who, like many, became a priest or, if rich and powerful enough, a bishop or archbishop. No, he was the second in line and therefore was expected to be a warrior, or in the absence of war, a knight errant and sometime mercenary.

Those who lived by the sword usually died by it at a young age. It was God's way of ridding the world of useless sons who had no property and nothing to offer a woman. For a man was a child in the eyes of the law until he owned his own bed. And so few did in this brutal world. Particularly not men like Sir Hugh de Greyhurst. For even if his older brother died, he would not inherit. He had been disowned. But that was another tale of woe.

"You're up, my lord," Brian said when he heard the shouted orders of the herald.

"I'm first?" Hugh squinted at the other knights. "Isn't there someone younger and more eager to start the Round Table?"

Usually the younger challengers went first, warming themselves up before bouts with the more experienced jousters.

"Oh, well," Hugh sighed. "May as well get it over with."

He accepted the enormous lance Brian handed him. He raised it upright and rested the butt on his mail-covered thigh, then trotted his horse to his end of the lists.

He and Rolly, who sat mounted and ready at the opposite end, acknowledged one another with their usual wry smiles, reminders of shared laughter and good times. They'd drunk more than their share of ale together over the years, even shared a damsel or two—on different nights, of course. They often joked that if one accidentally killed the other, as sometimes happened even though they jousted with blunted lances, the survivor would say a quick Hail Mary and go on to his next opponent, and his next maiden.

While Hugh felt intensely competitive with some knights, such as Sir Ranulf, he did not want to hurt Rolly. Sir Roland Montague was perhaps the only opponent who had never underestimated his intelligence. The others dismissed Hugh as a dumb animal and blamed their own defeats on his brute strength. But Rolly liked to say that Hugh was such a good strategist on the lists that his opponents didn't even know when they'd been outsmarted.

Yes, Rolly was a good friend. So the events that followed seemed particularly shocking and ironic. Hugh could not later recall their exact sequence. All he knew was that in the moment before he and Roland met at thundering speed, a priest leapt between them on a seemingly suicidal mission, cursing them for defying a papal ban on tournaments.

"Fie on you!" cried the mad-eyed cleric from the midst of a windmill of churning horse hooves. "Damn your souls to hell!"

Both horses reared back, sparing the rabid priest. Hugh managed to hold fast, but Rolly fell hard.

"God!" Hugh cried, for even in the mayhem, he could hear the unnatural sound of cracking bones.

"You will not joust in this bishopric!" the priest shouted as Hugh whirled around on his steed. The black-robed man waved a crucifix, his eyes bulging. "The Pope has forbidden you and the new bishop will not allow it!"

Hugh dug his spurs in the bristled hair of his mount's belly; horse and rider leapt forward, coming to an abrupt stop at Rolly's side. When he saw the widening pool of blood that leaked from Rolly's head, Hugh jumped down and shoved the priest aside, pulling off his helmet.

"Out of my way! Rolly! Dear saints, Rolly!"

At the sight of Sir Roland's eyes, once winking with life and kindness, now glassy and wide in a head that was turned backward, Hugh reeled with a painful mix of affection and regret. A broken neck. Oh, God. "Rolly!"

Tugging off his gauntlets, Hugh knelt, ignoring the ripping pain in his leg for which he would later pay a terrible price, and pulled Roland into his arms, fruitlessly searching for any signs of life. Angry at his own stupidity, Hugh gently lowered the body back to the earth and raked his bloody fingers through his tousled hair. Then he turned his rage on the priest.

"You," he growled with such ferocity the cleric went pale.

"Y-y-you see what comes of this sinful act!" the skinny figure sputtered, backing away as Hugh rose with black fury. The priest turned for support to the crowd. "A man has been murdered! This is why the Pope has banned all tournaments."

He now turned to Hugh, who approached with wide strides. "These wicked events force otherwise upright men to commit murder—a mortal sin," he continued with less certainty, taking a step backward for every forward step from Hugh. "Tournaments rob the Holy Father of soldiers in his crusades against the infidels in the Holy Land! They spawn sinful pride in the victors. They—"

"Silence!" Hugh bellowed. "Curse you for your pious villainy! *You* are the murderer!"

Hugh gripped his hands around the priest's cowl and began to squeeze.

"No, Sir Hugh!" cried his alarmed squire, dashing to his side. "Do not choke him to death."

"Let him go!" shouted another.

The other knights gathered timidly around Hugh as he strangled the terrified priest. Silence engulfed them. Though no one wanted to spend an eternity in hell, which is what they would all suffer if Hugh murdered a cleric in their presence, they likewise enjoyed the sight of one of their own having his say against the church. The Pope's ban was widely ignored and detested, for like Hugh, these men had no other way to survive but by fighting one another.

As he choked the priest, an image of Roland's lifeless body filled his vision. Sore regret drained him of his will to fight. Vengeance would not bring Rolly back. Overcome with sorrow and a sense of waste, he loosened his grip, and the priest choked in a desperately needed breath of air. Hugh staggered away.

Like some pagan, he stood before the crowd with blood-streaked hair, eyes wild with incivility. They could not know that he wanted to retch with remorse over his part in his friend's death. God forbid, but the priest was right. Hugh *was* a murderer. No, he wasn't to blame this time, but he had killed other men in jousts. The deaths were accidental and to be expected, even surreptitiously desired, depending on the opponent. But Hugh saw it differently on this brilliant spring day.

Despite the colorful, noble banners, the great helms with peacock feathers and lions carved atop them, and the jewel encrusted swords; despite expensive armor emblazoned with heraldic emblems of lions rampart and bears, and shields striped with colorful chevrons, one truth remained: they were little more than cocks fighting for a blood-hungry crowd. They were animals besting one another.

That was all he had ever been—an animal. Ever since his father had banished him at the age of nine to be raised in the home of an untutored quarry worker, he had been a beast of burden.

Shuddering with this cold realization, Hugh came to one clear conclusion. He looked up with calmer eyes to the blazing sun, which beat on his cheeks day after day with unmatched fidelity, and inwardly vowed that he would never joust again. Never.

And then he said a Hail Mary.

Two

Two days later Hugh sat at a trestle table in a cozy corner of a wayside inn. With a tankard of wine in hand and a full belly, he stared at a roaring fire in an enormous stone hearth, contemplating his uncertain future. The ache of grief over Rolly's death was beginning to dull, making room for other thoughts. But inward reveries evaporated like smoke from the fire when he sensed a half dozen men gather around him, staring at him as if he were a two-headed cow.

"I'm not in the mood for company," he growled. "Not with the likes of you."

Hugh's squire stepped forward and cleared his throat.

"My lord," Brian said, quietly stealing a glance at the others, "you've been silent all night. Your friends grow worried."

"Don't be glum over Roland's death!" said the man standing next to Brian. "You'll be the first one to joust when next we gather together, Greyhurst."

"Is that so, Keath?" Hugh replied with scarcely concealed disdain.

Sir David Keath was ten years younger than Hugh. He sported a mop of curly blond hair, a quick smile, and empty eyes. Like a handful of other knights, Keath had stayed on a few days after the aborted Round Table to take advantage of a local armorer renown for his ability to repair the intricate interlocking loops of chain mail. Tomorrow all the knights, with squires and pages in tow, would move onward in search of their next tournament. All except for Hugh.

"I won't be following you, Sir David," Hugh said.

The small crowd went still. Hugh took a draft of wine, enjoying its bite as much as the uneasiness his decision created amongst his colleagues. "You'll be glad to be rid of me, I'm sure."

"Be rid of you?" Brian said. Panicked and eager to give his master succor, he flagged down a tapster and placed a fresh tankard of wine in front of Hugh. Sitting down on the bench beside him, he whispered, "You can't think of quitting the circuit, my lord. You are just downhearted about Sir Roland's untimely death. Your spirits will rally in no time."

Hugh grinned darkly. "You're wrong. I will never joust again."

"A man must mount up again once he's fallen off a horse, Greyhurst."

The surly voice cut cleanly through the smoke and noise and the men surrounding Hugh parted. Sir Ranulf Blakely pushed his way through the gathering, plunking his drinking horn on the table with a splash. Beneath his hawkish nose he rubbed a hand with courtly elegance. He was both graceful and coarse, a dangerous combination that could disarm and dissect a man in one fell swoop.

Taking measure of Hugh, his sometime friend and ofttime enemy, Ranulf smiled ruefully. The gesture creased the scar that rode down his left cheek like a perpetual flash of lightning.

"You're not quitting on me, are you?" Ranulf goaded. "You haven't even won back your armor and horse from me."

Hugh smiled and swirled the last sip of wine in the bottom of his pewter cup. "Five years ago a comment like that would have been enough to have me challenging you before the night was through." He tossed the wine down his throat and swallowed with an audible sigh. "But I'm too old for this, Ranulf. I deserve better."

"Oh!" the black-haired knight crowed, looking at the others in search of indignation. "He's too good for the likes of us. Did you hear that, men?"

"I didn't say that." Hugh sighed with resignation. No use arguing with Ranulf. His only purpose in life was to distort the truth and destroy all that was good.

Once Hugh had loved a damsel named Lady Alys, the daughter of a simple knight. Though she was of humble means, her beauty was beyond price, the apotheosis of the age: her budding lips were the color of a damask rose, her skin fair, her body slight and her breasts small. More perfect still was her sweet disposition.

After a tournament in her town, she had chosen Hugh out of all the knights to court her, offering with her love the promise of a small parcel of land upon her father's death. She told Hugh she'd chosen him because he had the most trustworthy eyes, and she did not mind that he had not been tutored like the others and did not have land of his own. Though Hugh could not read, she had taught him to memorize love poems and did not laugh when at first he faltered in embarrassment.

But when Sir Ranulf got wind of the budding courtship, he wooed Lady Alys himself with a honeyed tongue and a black heart. Ranulf despoiled her before Hugh could ask for her hand. He would have killed Ranulf for it, but in a stinging reversal, the lady claimed that she'd never loved Hugh and did not want his blood on her hands. In the end, Ranulf left her with a bastard in her belly, and a few months later she died in childbirth.

But for all that, it was Ranulf who had once saved Hugh's life when they were attacked by thieves in a forest. He was not an easy companion to dismiss.

"Any fool can get back up on a horse," Hugh said, leaning back to take full measure of his towering nemesis. "Only a wise man knows when it's time to bid farewell to a useless venture."

"A useless venture." The words burst from Ranulf's lips with a rich laugh as he flung an arm around Keath. "I am happy, dear friends, to say that our livelihood is utterly without merit in the opinion of our once beloved friend, Sir Hugh de Greyhurst."

"What will you do instead?" Keath asked.

Before Hugh could answer, Sir David Connard, a red-haired pudgy fellow adorned in a mud-splattered tunic, staggered to the table, grabbing an edge to steady himself.

"Eh, whas zis we hear?" Connard said. "Whas zis about Greyhurst hanging up his shpurs?"

"Where have you been?" Ranulf drawled at the drunken knight. "At the bottom of an ale vat, you sot? Christ could have returned for the second coming and you'd hear about it two days after all good souls had risen from the earth."

Keath laughed, a jarring staccato rhythm.

"Wha—?" Connard said, wounded, then belched.

Another knight errant, Sir David Shrewsbury, a bald man with an enormous potbelly, joined the circle and began to chuckle for no apparent reason. He swilled some ale and belched as well.

"You make quite a chorus," Hugh said, smothering a smile as he reached for the second tankard Brian had procured. Seeing Connard, Shrewsbury, and Keath—the three Davids, as they were called on the tourney circuit—Hugh realized he'd miss at least a few familiar faces.

"What will you do?" said Shrewsbury.

Hugh swallowed hard, drawing up the courage to give voice to his impossible dream. "I will take a wife."

There was stunned silence.

"A wife!" Brian gasped, reeling back from his master as if he were a plague-ridden leper. "You cannot marry. We have the tournament in France at midsummer. And we're expected in Yorkshire in a fortnight. I was to enter the lists for the first time. Remember, you promised!"

"Brian, peace, lad." Hugh slapped a hand to his cheek and pulled him into a rough embrace. Brian clutched him with an iron grip, the promise of a warrior in the making. Hugh whispered in his ear, "I'm sorry. I am too old a mentor. You need someone who still thirsts for blood. Go your own way if you must. Go. I'm a wounded old bear."

Hugh released Brian and found the other men studying him with far more contemplation than he would have credited.

"Who will you marry, Greyhurst?" Ranulf said, swilling his ale, then licking the foam from his lips. He seemed the most disturbed by Hugh's turnabout, though he hid it well behind his cool slate-colored eyes.

"I can honestly say I have no idea," Hugh said on a long sigh, then gave him a malicious grin. "Though you above all should know that I wouldn't tell you if I did have a lady in mind."

At Hugh's seething tone, Ranulf raised his black brows

and tipped his head in acknowledgment. "Then you are confident in your ability to defy the odds against you. Or you're very foolish. After all, who would take a landless knight as husband? You above all people. An ignorant bear! You're good for nothing other than fighting, and now you can scarcely do that. I've seen you limping about. Who on earth would have you?"

"A half-wit heiress," Keath replied, snorting with laughter into his ale.

"Or a toothless widow," added Shrewsbury, tugging at his girth.

"A pock-marked crone?" said Connard.

The three Davids exchanged looks, then broke into laughter, alternately slapping their knees, holding their bellies, and clutching one another's arm for support. When the boisterous laughter died down, the drunk men belched again, one after another, then turned back to their ale.

Ranulf slid down onto the bench next to Hugh.

"Our friends here may speak the dire truth," he whispered intimately with mock concern. "Have you considered that only a diseased whore would have a man with no dower or property?"

"Go to hell, Ranulf."

"Watch your tongue," Keath warned Hugh, wagging a finger. "Haven't you heard? Ranulf's cousin is Jerome Blakely, the new bishop of Burnham."

Hugh shook his head. "I should have known. The office of bishop requires a black heart. They must run in the family."

Ranulf smiled. "Buy me another cup of ale and I'll see that your soul is absolved of Rolly's murder."

"I don't buy dispensations from the likes of you."

"Then it's you who will burn in hell," Ranulf said with a cheerful chuckle.

"I'll take any help I can get," Shrewsbury said. "I'll buy another round if it will clear away some of my sins. Innkeeper! More ale!" he called out.

"Hear! Hear!" the other two Davids chimed in, clanking their empty tankards together in the air.

"Fair you well, gentle knights." Hugh rose, sketched a short, ironic bow, and started away, trying his damnedest not to limp. Brian scrambled after him.

"Greyhurst, you'll find a horny alewife in the corner over there," Connard called after them. "Mayhap she's needing a husband as well as a good, hard swiving."

Hugh nodded with tolerant humor at the crude jest, but before he could slip gracefully away, he felt a hand grip his shoulder determinedly.

"Are ye lookin' fer a wife, then?" a froggy voice intoned.

Hugh looked down at the man holding him back and saw a few wisps of hair on a shiny bald pate, and below that two nut-brown eyes; lower still was a pug nose and two days' growth of beard all tightly organized in one impish-looking face. It was the innkeeper.

"What did you say?" Hugh replied.

"Are ye lookin' fer a wife?" the man repeated impatiently. He slapped a soiled cloth over his shoulder and put his fists on his waist, arms akimbo. "Well, are ye or ain't ye?"

"Yes." Intrigued, Hugh's gaze narrowed on the peculiar fellow. "Why do you ask?"

"There's one what's looking fer a husband not far from 'ere at Longrove Barony."

The group of knights stilled. The smoky air seemed to thicken. Hugh felt a hitch in his chest, as if he'd been thumped soundly on the back by the hand of fate.

"Tell me more."

The innkeeper shrugged. "What can I say, my lord? A man's got ter make a living."

The impish face suddenly seemed more cunning. Whistling a soft tune, he began to wipe crumbs from the table with his soiled rag.

As Hugh's companions glared at him expectantly, he growled with frustration, then tucked his hand in his girdle, pulling out a well-worn coin.

"Here." Hugh slapped it in the innkeeper's palm, which closed in a flash. "Now that you have my utter attention, tell me who she is."

The knavish man bit the coin, held it in the torchlight, then, apparently satisfied, tucked it in his girdle. He leaned closer to Hugh, as if imparting a great secret, and the other men tilted forward as well, like the crew of a keeling vessel.

Glancing around his audience, he cleared his throat. "She's the daughter of a local baron."

"What is her name?"

The conniving tapster held open his palm for another coin. Hugh shook his head in disgust, but procured a second from his purse, placing it in their host's open hand. "Well?"

" 'Er name is Lady Margrete Trewsbury. A twenty-five-year-old maiden, an heiress wit' land aplenty, a right fine castle, and a manor house, wot I 'ear, and no one 'cept her aging father to tend to 'em."

One of the knights let out a low whistle. The innkeeper puffed out his chest, basking in the attention.

"That's right, my lord, yer lady lives on a wee but right lovely barony south of 'ere on the ole' Roman road, near Tilmon River."

Hugh stroked his chin, hoping the wild pulse in his neck could not be seen by the others. Tamping down a lifetime of hope, he frowned skeptically. "Why hasn't she married before?"

"Because she's a homely hag," Keath volunteered.

"Doubtless," Sir Ranulf snorted. "She must be hideous beyond belief, else some other knight errant would have snatched her hand ere now."

Hugh glared over his shoulder at Ranulf, but quickly turned back to the innkeeper, repeating his question more forcefully, "Why hasn't she married?"

The sly, elfin-faced man held out his open palm and grinned innocently.

Hugh cursed under his breath, but again reached into his pouch for another coin, which he promptly handed over.

"I've no clue why yer lady 'asn't married."

When Hugh pounded the table and let out a growl of frustration, the innkeeper rushed on.

"But I know why she's amarrying now. 'Er father says he's dying an' wants his daughter settled so that she willn't be forced into a match o' the king's choosing. Don't yer know she'll be a piece o' chattel ter trade if she doesn't take a mate afore her ole' man dies."

Hugh's heart began to pound. Could fate finally be shining on him? He pictured the maiden in his mind, hideous as she must be, but then he also envisioned the land—rundown, perhaps, if the baron was ailing, but also full of potential. He saw himself as the lord of his own castle, a baron after all these years of relentless struggle. The very idea was so intoxicating, his skin turned cold. He stifled a shiver and looked intensely at the innkeeper through a haze of smoke being spewed from a nearby spit. Some blasted fool was burning a perfectly fine leg of lamb in the kitchen.

"What does she look like?" Hugh said, trying to keep a quiver of excitement from his voice.

Again, the smiling innkeeper held out an open palm.

"Curse you for your greed," Hugh muttered, but reached into his pouch nonetheless. It was empty. He looked up with chagrin, this time mustering a charming smile. "Look here, goodman, I have no more coins. Have mercy and tell me what she looks like."

The innkeeper frowned at him if he were a hapless corpse in a winding sheet. "A pity then noble knight, but ye'll have ter find out yerself. I run a business, not a hospital fer the poor."

With that, he picked up Hugh's empty tankards and hurried through the crowd to the kitchen.

Hugh raked a hand through his hair, so frustrated he thought briefly of pulling it out by the roots, then surveyed the men, who looked at him expectantly.

"Well?" Keath pressed. "What will you do?"

"Brian," Hugh said tersely. The squire came to his side. "Go to Longrove Barony and make an offer of marriage."

The men exhaled in surprise.

The squire gulped, eyes protruding. "Marriage?"

"G-g-good God, man, you can't marry the wench sight unseen," Shrewsbury sputtered, reaching into his girdle. "I'll give you a pence. Go fetch the innkeeper. Find out what she looks like."

"I'll pitch in as shwell," said the slurring Connard.

"No!" Sir Ranulf gripped Shrewsbury's wrist. "You'll give him nothing. If he is so desperate to marry, let him take his chances. I want to see him drag his arse from here to this so-called barony before he realizes what a fool he's been, and how much he has insulted we noble knights for our livelihoods."

"Keep your money," Hugh declared, accepting the challenge. "I'll take her sight unseen, and with pleasure."

"God's shteeth!" Connard mumbled. "She could be so

loathshome you'll not be able to shred her save in darkness.''

"You mean bed her," Brian said, glaring at the drunk.

"Thas zit!" Connard replied, weaving back and forth.

"I don't care what she looks like," Hugh said.

"You're a desperate man, Greyhurst," Keath said, his youthful face smug with superiority.

"Yes, I am," Hugh admitted. "Just as you will be ten years from now, Keath, when you reach my age and still must wield a sword. If you're lucky enough to live that long. This maiden may look like Medusa herself, and I'd still have her. And I mean to marry her before any of you poor sots realize what you're passing up."

"You'll regret it!" Ranulf called out.

Hugh chuckled as he limped his way through a sea of drunken men. No matter the outcome, he would not regret this daring decision, for it was his and his alone. For once he would claim what he wanted in life, not merely what misfortune God had planned for him.

"Go, man!" he urged his squire, giving him an eager shove. "Make the offer, I command you. For in three weeks' time, I shall claim my wife. And my future!"

Three

Margrete Trewsbury entered Longrove Castle's enormous great hall two steps behind her waddling father and quickly scanned the familiar faces of the vassals seeking justice from the baron. There were a dozen attending hallmote this month.

The men and women included villeins, who were virtual slaves to the estate, and freemen, who worked there by choice, receiving land in exchange for labor. There were also a few merchants who operated stalls down the road in Longrove Village.

Most of their grievances put before Lord Giles today would be petty. But one matter was of such grave importance it could well determine whether Margrete had enough food to feed their household.

Two of the baron's best plowmen had been neglecting work they owed him in his demesnes, tilling a neighboring earl's property instead. The plowmen were clearly breaking their oaths of fealty to Margrete's father. But if Margrete reclaimed the land he had granted them as punishment, she wasn't sure she could find men to replace them, and certainly not in time to sow the spring crops.

"There they are, Father," she whispered in Lord Giles's ear as they proceeded to the dais. "If you look in the second row of benches below the dais you'll see Roger Davis and Henry Morton. Remember I told you about them?"

"What? Eh? You mean the plowmen?" Lord Giles said in a loud, indiscreet voice. He craned his neck for a good look at the men. "Where are they?"

"Over there. But don't stare."

"Greetings! Welcome!" Lord Giles waved and smiled exuberantly at the men.

"Father!" Margrete admonished sotto voce, pulling his arm back down to his side. "You must maintain an air of intimidation or they will never do as you command."

By now father and daughter had reached the dais. The crowd stilled and waited for the baron to call the court into session. When he merely gazed with a childish smile up at the colorful banners that hung from the rafters, mesmerized by the rich reds and blues, Margrete turned to the crowd, taking charge as usual.

"Greetings to one and all. My father welcomes you to his manor court. How many of you have grievances to be heard?"

A half-dozen people stood, most of whom indicated they were content to wait their turn. Not so Sir William MacGregor. He remained standing even after the others sat back down. Margrete did her best to ignore him.

Old MacGregor was a doddering knight with a shrunken spine and, undoubtedly, an enlarged liver, who still paid homage to her father long after he'd outlived his usefulness on the battlefield. In fact he was the only knight who still served Lord Giles. All the others had abandoned Longrove to serve more prosperous and powerful barons.

While MacGregor's loyalty was to be admired, he didn't have the strength to lift a sword let alone defend the castle. In striking contrast, he had no trouble raising tankards of ale, and instead of serving the usual forty days of knight's service, he stayed at the castle year round. During that time, he managed to consume the drink and food portions of a man twice his spindly size, oblivious to Margrete's ongoing battle to stretch the larder from harvest to harvest.

"I'll start, if'n you don't mind," the scrawny old knight said. He smoothed a hand over his bald head, then scratched his fingers over a rough patch of gray hair that grew on his wizened face. "My lord, as you know I have served you faithfully lo these many years. Why, I was at yer wedding, and we are old friends. Yet this week I've been finding meself with naught but one cup of ale at supper."

"Heavens!" Lord Giles said, placing his palms solemnly on the table. "Is that true, William? That's terrible. Why have you not complained before?"

"He has," Margrete offered drolly.

"I have," MacGregor agreed.

"Sir William," she said, trying to cut him off before he launched into a tirade, "I give you all I can spare. You mustn't—"

"And it seems that *someone*," the knight hissed through a half-dozen remaining teeth, glaring at Margrete, "has ordered the servants to ignore my thirsty pleas."

"What a shame," the baron sympathized.

"Sir William," Margrete repeated more forcefully. "Please sit down and wait your turn."

"I was speakin' to yer father," he said indignantly, bracing his rounded shoulders.

"And my father would like for you to sit and wait your turn. Wouldn't you, Father?"

"What? Oh, yes, yes, Daughter, most assuredly."

Margrete turned her focus back to the complaining knight with a contented smile. "You've heard the verdict. Please sit."

She waited until MacGregor took his place, then picked up the list of complaints. "Now what have we here? Martha Brewer is accused of selling her ale before the village ale testers had a chance to drink it. Oh, and I see she's also accused of selling ale that is weak."

William MacGregor popped up from the bench and raised a finger in the air. "I'll have a cup of Martha Brewer's ale even if it's half piss. At least she's not accused of being stingy."

The small crowd burst into laughter. Margrete bit her tongue and raised her eyes from the parchment to glare at him. "*Please*, Sir William."

He sat down with a grudging harumph. Margrete hurried on before the pesky knight could raise another objection.

"Let's proceed directly to the matter of the freemen who have been negligent with their crop duty. Goodmen Morton and Davis, it seems you haven't yet begun to till the fields held directly by my father. You know you will be fined for such slaggard behavior."

The two men stepped forward. Morton was a burly fellow with a wild sprig of carrot-colored hair, and Davis was a slim man with skin as tough as tanned hide who was rarely without a piece of hay between his teeth.

"We ain't slaggards, my lady," Morton said in a gruff voice, nervously fingering his hat in his hands. The orange freckles dotting his beefy face darkened. "We're tending fields for the earl of Ludham and he's paying us handsome like for it, with gold as well as land."

"Look here, you have sworn fealty to my father. You

do not have the right to work for a neighboring baron without his permission.''

Morton set his jaw and frowned. ''Beggin' yer pardon, my lady, but we're freemen, not villeins. Besides, we're also workin' Kilbury Hide, which your father claims as his own.''

''Kilbury Hide? Did you say Kilbury Hide?''

Margrete's natural blush was replaced with a lily-white pallor as the grossness of their betrayal began to register. Kilbury Hide contained some of the richest farm fields in the realm and had once been considered part of Longrove Barony. But the property also bordered the estates held by the earl of Ludham and the bishop of Burnham, and they had laid claim to the hide in recent years as well. The earl had even been farming the territory as if the dispute had been settled.

''You know very well that Lord Richard reaps the benefits of that land, even though it rightfully belongs to this barony. If you do not desist in your service to the earl, my father will be forced to send you packing.''

''Then let him,'' piped in Davis, his lips set in a thin, angry line against the dark hide of his face, the straw between his lips bobbing with each word. ''We'll work for Lord Richard if that's what yer'd like. Gladly.''

''But you have sworn homage to my father!'' Margrete cried out, unable to conceal her outrage. ''Is your word worth nothing?''

''We're loyal, all right. But a man's got to do what's best for 'is family. Lord Richard's a fair lord, like yer sire, my lady. But he pays more. And more'n that, he's got his wits about him.''

A deadly quiet settled in the hall. A few sitting on the benches gasped at the plowman's audacity. Margrete felt the blood drain from her face, turning her already pale complexion a vaguely green shade.

"How dare you say such a thing?" she rasped. "What exactly are you implying?"

"Well, my lady," Morton said, reddening. "It's like this, ye see, Davis didn't mean—"

"Silence!" Her voice rose in a powerful burst to the ceiling. She stood at her place behind the long table. "I will not tolerate such insolence. You are dismissed. Both of you. You are freed from your allegiance to my father. Go work for Lord Richard. We will find replacements for you with no trouble at all."

The plowmen stood stock-still a moment, eyes wide, mouths slack with surprise. Then they turned to one another, sharing a furtive look of relief, and departed.

Margrete watched them go with thwarted frustration and self-reproach. Why had she lost her temper? She could not afford to replace these men. But neither could she tolerate anyone who was bold enough to state the obvious—that her father had the mind of a child. It was an understood secret. One she had been struggling to hide from the king since she was eleven years old.

When the doors to the great hall closed with a bang after the departing plowmen, all eyes turned to Margrete, but no one dared break the silence. That is, until William MacGregor stood again.

"Now, me lady, about me portions of ale. I—"

"Silence, William MacGregor! I've had just about enough of your complaints. Now if you will excuse me, all of you, I've had all I can take of the ingratitude of our vassals. This court is closed. Good day, Father."

With that, she marched out of the great hall, praying her tears would remain dammed until she was out of sight. She hurried across the castle yard past the stables, the dovecote, and the beehives. She strode around the fishpond, careful not to look down, lest she glimpse her own visage in the silvery water. Self-examination was a vanity in which she had never indulged. When she reached the castle chapel, she creaked open the heavy wooden door and inhaled the scent of incense that still clung to the stone walls, though mass hadn't been said here for six months. She could no longer afford to pay the chaplain.

Shutting the door behind her, she sighed away the fierce frustration and impotence that seemed to be aging her before her time. She'd been strong for so long, but how much more could she take?

She dashed a gaze around the cozy little chapel, but took no comfort in it. This was the place to which she always retreated. It was God's world and infinitely better than anything outside the chapel door. But today her strong faith seemed shadowed with travails. She hastened to the altar, dropping her knees onto the marble step. As usual, she began by counting her blessings.

"Thank you, Lord, for these moments of peace. I pray I have not made a terrible mistake letting those plowmen go. But how could I keep them when they were openly questioning my Father's wits? Oh, Lord, I feel like a jongleur juggling too many bean sacks. Where will they fall? And when? How can I—?"

A faint knock snapped her from her reverie. It could only be one person. She sighed with resignation and looked back at the entrance to the chapel, calling out in as patient a voice as she could muster, "What is it, Father?"

The door creaked open and the baron stepped inside. The sunlight beaming behind him illuminated the edges of his fluffy silver beard and shoulder-length hair.

"Don't be upset, child. You should not worry so," Lord

Giles said, his voice gentle and rich. "Matters are not that bad."

"Yes, they are, Papa. We are running out of money. How can we continue to pay scuttage to the king? And I've set aside enough food for this winter, but what about the next? We are in a dreadful state. No matter how strong my faith, I can't imagine how I'll go on as I have."

"Fear not! For I have solved all our problems."

She looked up warily. Her father hadn't made any meaningful decisions in years. "What do you mean?"

"I have found a husband for you."

Margrete's eyes widened. "You've *what*?"

"I've found a husband for you. You'll need one now, Margrete, more than ever. You see, lass, I'm dying."

Four

Margrete shut the door to her father's solar and tugged him by the hand to the hearth, pushing him gently down into his favorite chair. When he sank with a groan, she knelt before him, leaning close, gripping his hands in her own.

"What is it, Father? Why do you say you will die soon?"

He blinked his watery blue eyes and worked his lips silently while he tried to muster an explanation.

"Well . . ." He turned to the yellow flames in the fireplace, unable to face her. "I had another spell."

Her brows drew together. "When?"

"Earlier this week. On Monday."

"Oh, no."

"And Tuesday."

"*What?*"

"And again on Wednesday."

"God's wounds!" she cried softly. "You had three spells and you did not tell me?"

"I did not want to worry you." He stroked her cheek. "And I rallied without you. William MacGregor was there each time and saved me."

William MacGregor had saved her father's life? Margrete frowned with chagrin. "Tell him to have his fill of ale tonight."

Several times over the last few years, Lord Giles had collapsed in some sort of spell, swooning and then passing out. The first time it happened, his skin had turned white and then blue, and he lay so deathlike that Margrete assumed he had died. Out of her mind with grief and furious with God for taking her last living relative, she had raised her arms up in a defiant gesture and pounded her father's chest with her fists, crying out in anger.

Moments later, Lord Giles's eyes had popped open, his color returned, he resumed normal breathing, and he later sat up as if nothing had happened. She quickly realized that a sound blow to the chest had somehow saved his life. Old William, who had watched in wonder that day, had apparently given her father a few lifesaving thumps this week. But what if MacGregor hadn't been there?

"Papa, you must tell me when this happens again. I must know."

"You don't have to know everything that goes on in this barony."

"Yes, I do," she said emphatically. This barony would fall apart without her. Her father was the only one who didn't realize that.

He turned baleful eyes her way. "I've not long to live, child. What will happen to you when I'm gone?"

"Oh, dear heart, I'll manage." She leaned forward and wrapped her arms around his neck, hugging him close as if for the last time. "Don't worry about me."

"You must marry," he whispered in her hair.

"No, Father."

"If you don't," he said, his voice breaking, "the king will force you to marry one of his foul companions."

She recoiled from his arms. "I will never marry a king's man!"

"Once I am gone, you will have no choice. You will be at the mercy of King Edward. Wouldn't it be better to marry someone of your own choosing?"

Acknowledging the unusual soundness of his logic, she looked up guardedly from beneath a lush row of blond lashes. "What husband have you chosen for me?"

He let out a wheezing sigh of relief. "There's my girl. You will like this man."

"Who?" she asked.

"Well, I don't know precisely."

She blinked several times in quick succession. "What do you mean you don't know?"

Lord Giles nervously caressed the carved arms of his oak chair. "His squire's name is Brian. I remember that. Friendly fellow. Charming. But I just can't seem to remember the knight's name."

Margrete rose up on her knees. "You don't even remember his name?"

"Verily, I did not meet him, just his squire."

"What? You agreed to marry me to a man you've never met?" she nearly shouted. "Was his marriage portion so great that you would not even stop to consider his person?"

"Lord, no! He scarcely has a farthing to his name."

Margrete's jaw dropped. She was speechless.

"Now what was his name?" The old man drummed his fingers on his upper lip. "Sir Harold? No, that wasn't it. Sir Hugh! Yes, now I remember. A great knight errant."

"A knight errant!" Margrete stood up, then skittered back in horror. "Oh, Papa! How could you?"

"He'll be able to protect you. That's what is most important."

"Not to me!"

Her father could not even remember the incident that had left her with a deeply imbedded horror of broadswords, and left him with the wits of a child.

The terrible incident had happened when Margrete was eleven; she'd awakened one night in the women's bower to the sounds of thundering horse hooves, clashing swords, and screaming women.

"It's a raid," the others in the bower whispered. "The earl of Ludham is attacking."

Lord Henry had attacked before, but this time one of the victims was the lady of the castle, Margrete's beautiful mother Rosamunde. Young Margrete recognized her cries for help at once. Willow, her nursemaid, tried to press Margrete's ears into her ample bosom to stifle the horrifying sounds, but the lithe child would not be contained and slipped away, dashing through the cold corridors to the great hall.

There she watched in horror as a knight errant raped and killed her mother. Her father arrived too late to save his wife and suffered a grievous blow to the head trying to avenge her death. And though Lord Giles survived, he was never quite the same. Once stern and remote, he became docile, almost childlike in his demeanor, forcing young Margrete, his sole heir, to become the parent.

Shortly after the attack, when her paternal aunt came to stay with them, Margrete learned that Lord Henry's fateful raid had been financed by Edward II, then Prince of Wales. For some political reason Margrete had been too young to comprehend, Edward had supplied the mercenary soldiers who had raped, pillaged, and killed that night.

She had spent the intervening years trying to hide her

father's witless state from others, including Edward, who was now king. She made excuses for Giles's absence from parliament, and since his barony was small he had not been missed. At least not as long as Margrete continued to send gold to the crown in lieu of military service.

But she was running out of gold, and her role as caretaker and mistress of the barony had left her emotionally exhausted. And now, adding to her misery, her naive father had agreed to give her hand in marriage to the very sort of knight who had ruined their lives on that fateful day.

"I will never marry a knight errant!" she rasped, pallid and shaking. "I will tell him you did not know what you were doing when you agreed to such a match."

"Not know what I was doing?" he said, wounded. "Whatever do you mean?"

She could not humiliate him by telling him that he knew little more than the town fool.

"What I mean, Papa, is that I would rather join Treyvaux Abbey and become a Benedictine nun."

"Pshaw!" he waved her off with a gentle chuckle. "Nonsense."

"But it is my dearest wish," she said, desperate now. Didn't he even remember that she had spent five years at Treyvaux, fully expecting to take the veil?

After her mother's death, Margrete's paternal aunt Rowena had taken over as chatelaine of the castle. Realizing the trauma Margrete had endured, Rowena sent her to the abbey with the promise that when she was old enough she would be endowed as a nun. Once again, though, fate intervened. Just a few months before Margrete was to take her vows, Rowena had died, and the burden of Longrove barony had fallen on the younger woman's shoulders.

"Don't you remember, Father? I have always wanted to be a nun."

"No, no, I don't remember," he stammered. Averting his eyes, he waved her off as if she were a pesky fly. "Enough of such nonsense."

"I have learned to read the scriptures in Latin. Abbess Phillipa took special care to teach me."

"A waste of time for a girl," her father muttered, warming his hands over the fire.

"Do not make me marry," she pleaded. "The king can have this land. I want nothing more than a life of prayer."

"No! I want grandchildren. No daughter of mine will become a nun."

"But Papa—"

"Margrete, do not argue with me!" the baron shouted with unexpected clarity and pounded his fist on a table. Two goblets jumped and fell on the wooden surface.

Margrete gasped, staring at the empty cups in amazement, then turned agape to her father, as if someone else had taken his place; someone with wits and resolve; or as if he were his old self, iron-fisted and assured. For one brief moment, he *was* himself, eyes as hard and dark as chestnuts, face flushed with indignation, spine stiff with resolve.

Then his strength withered. He clutched his chest. His face turned ghostly white. His mouth gaped open, but no words would come, and he collapsed into one of his dreaded deathlike states.

"Papa!" she shrieked, dashing to his side. She knelt down and entwined her fingers. Raising them high, she brought her hands down hard on his chest.

Thwomp! The sound was bone-chilling. If he survived, he'd have a terrible bruise. He was still unconscious.

"Damnation!" she muttered, then tried it again. *Thwomp!* Lord Giles choked and drew in air, eyes fluttering open, then he let out a raspy little chuckle.

"Fine," he whispered, nodding as if she'd merely awakened him from a nap, but he could say no more and shut his eyes again.

She pinned him with a wary stare, not quite willing to surrender her state of siege. She couldn't let him die! He was breathing. He would live. For a while. But soon he would die, and she would be alone.

"Good girl," he said in time. "You're such a good girl, Margrete."

"Am I, Papa?" she said on a gush of air. She sagged and dropped her head to his chest, not at all certain that she'd have the strength to rise again. How long could this go on? How much longer could she be strong?

Lord Giles combed a hand over her hair. "Marry him, Margrete. Whoever he is, he'll be a sight better than a friend of the king's."

"Yes," she whispered, righting herself. She would do anything to avoid marrying a man connected to Edward II. Even if it meant marrying a knight errant.

She would agree to marry this stranger, but not before visiting Abbess Phillipa. Margrete was still loath to accept this fate. If anyone could provide her with the grace to accept it, or a miracle to escape it, it was the abbess of Treyvaux Abbey.

Five

argrete dashed out of the keep without a backward glance, heading straight for Treyvaux Abbey. She raced through Long Grove, the stretch of trees that gave the barony its name, until at last she saw the abbey chapel rising out of the morning mists.

The dawning sun gleamed on the looming spires and illuminated the intricate blind arcading along the front of the chapter houses. There were two chapter houses, for everything was mirrored here at this double abbey. There were two cloisters—one for the monks and one for the nuns; and two refectories, two dormitories, two warming chambers, and so on. If you climbed up into a tall tree you would see that the compound as a whole looked like two squared-off hourglasses laying top to bottom.

As Margrete passed through the gatehouse, the nuns in their flowing black gowns and veils and white wimples were exiting from the chapter house after conducting their morning business. Abbess Phillipa led the women in a neat line. Margrete knew the routine and went to the abbess's lodging, knowing that Phillipa would soon be there for a brief respite before attending the Day Office of Tierce.

As she waited, Margrete sat by a window, watching the nuns and monks conduct their daily rituals. Several monks strolled through the cloisters, their somber expressions cradled in black cowls; shiny round tonsures on their heads browned by the sun; hands, bony for the most part, fingering fat rosary beads. Most monks were contemplative sorts, but now and then Margrete would spot a brawny one, usually a former man of the world, whose eyes, when turning up to heaven, flitted like birds eager to be freed from their cage.

She gazed at the passing monks so intently, wondering if they were content, that she did not hear the abbess enter or notice her presence until she placed a hand on Margrete's shoulder.

"Greetings, my child."

"Oh!" She spun around in her chair with a hand over her heart. "Abbess Phillipa! You caught me daydreaming."

"It is good to see you." The fifty-seven-year-old nun held out her arms. Margrete rose and flung herself into the warm wool and the reassuring scent of lavender that clung to the abbess's full bosom.

Phillipa was like a mother to her, and more, for she had nurtured not only Margrete's heart, but her soul as well.

For two painful years after her mother's death, Margrete had not spoken a word, and resumed verbal discourse only after hearing Phillipa lecture young nuns about the perfection of their souls. It was then that Margrete learned that one did not have to expect goodness here on earth. It was already waiting for her in heaven. She had decided then to become a nun. Unlike most noblewomen, who joined convents because they offered freedom from marriage, Margrete felt she had a true calling. But alas, fate had intervened, leaving her to struggle in the world alone.

"What is it, my dear?" the abbess said, gently disengaging from Margrete's fervent hug. "You seem ill at ease."

Margrete chuckled morosely at this understatement. "Indeed, Mother Abbess, the time has come for me to marry. And I cannot bear the thought of it."

She explained her predicament, the words tumbling out in an angry rush. As she spoke, the nun gently nudged her toward a chair by a softly crackling fire. She sat opposite Margrete at a small table and listened with her usual brand of attention.

There was no one quite like Phillipa de Claire. Her posture was as firm and upright as her finely honed spirituality. Unlike many abbesses and abbots, she gloried in her position not because of the power it wielded, or the extra portions of fish it afforded her at mealtime, but because it gave her an opportunity to serve Christ more fully. She believed in God truly and without doubt, and in her presence Margrete believed just as strongly.

Phillipa was tall and big-boned, strong yet feminine. Her soft blue eyes were intense, but she always carried a ready smile to smooth the snap of her quick wit and sharp mind. She was renown in the Catholic church as a great thinker, a fact that caused her male counterpart, Abbot Gregory, endless agitation. And if it were not for her connections to papal authorities in Avignon, Phillipa might well have been pilloried by local clerics for her forthrightness and inquisitiveness.

She was the most extraordinary human being Margrete had ever known. It was the abbess who had taught her to read and write, who had convinced her that a woman is as dearly beloved by God as a man. She impressed upon Margrete that women can aspire to greatness in the church, that a woman's soul can be just as pure as a man's, regardless of what the local priests, who cited ad nauseam scriptures about the wicked Eve and Mary Magdalene might preach.

"Help me, Abbess Phillipa, to find some way to accept my fate," Margrete said, somewhat calmer, after telling her sorrowful tale. "All these years I harbored the hope of returning to your convent. What a fool I was!"

The abbess put her hands in a prayerful pose and pressed them to her thinned lips. Her fingernails were smooth and eggshell pink. "This is my fault. I have encouraged you to learn more than a woman of the world is allowed to know. I told you to read the great religious thinkers who espouse the benefits of chastity and holiness over the duties of marriage and procreation." Phillipa shook her head ruefully. "Your father will not bend on the matter of marriage?"

"No, he cannot be reasoned with. It is a great irony, is it not, Mother Abbess, that because I love God I must follow his commandment to obey my father, even though my father has the wits of a child?"

Phillipa's sharp eyes sparked with warmth and she held an index finger in the air for emphasis. "Ah, but we must have the faith of a child to enter the kingdom of heaven. God is with your father, Margrete, perhaps more than he is with you and me. You must have faith that all will work out in accordance with God's plan."

"You are right," she whispered. "I should have more faith."

Phillipa gave her an approving smile. "Now tell me more of this husband you are to take. Is he as honorable as you?"

Margrete couldn't stifle a doubtful laugh. "I hardly think so, my lady, and in so saying I do not mean to praise myself. He is a knight errant. He lives by the sword. Papa says he took part in that blasphemous Round Table not far from here. He is doubtless a murderer who glories in the pride of victory. For all I know, he may be excommunicated already.''

''Do not judge a man by his need to feed himself,'' Phillipa said sharply, and Margrete looked at her in surprise. ''I do not condone tournaments, my dear, but I cannot judge a man who is forced to fight for a living or else face starvation. And you should not worry about his past sins. There is nothing God cannot forgive. If your husband's soul dwells in darkness, you must share your faith with him.''

Margrete pressed her hands to her face, overwhelmed by the thought of sharing anything with this itinerant warrior. Whenever she imagined the inevitable night of consummation, she could not help but envision the brutal rape of her mother.

''If only there was a way to remain holy in wedlock,'' Margrete said, sighing. ''But a husband demands all of a wife's devotion, sullying her body and stealing the time she'd sooner spend in prayer.''

The distant swell of chanted prayers soothingly filled the air as the abbess drummed her fingers thoughtfully on her chair.

''Perhaps,'' she said, eyeing Margrete with a hint of intrigue, ''there is a way to do your duty to your father and his estate and serve God at the same time.''

''How can these two irreconcilable purposes coexist?''

''Come close, my dear, and let me whisper in your ear, like the Archangel Gabriel. Sometimes these walls have ears. Let no one know this was my suggestion or you will be condemned by your very association with me. There are those even within my own convent who are jealous of my friendship with the Pope and look dubiously upon my books.''

Margrete listened in hushed amazement as the abbess

shared her plan. When Phillipa finished her explanation, Margrete smiled, feeling hopeful for the first time since her father's dreadful announcement.

"How shall I proceed?" she asked the abbess.

"You must first find out if this knight is a good man. His past sins do not matter, but he must be true and honorable. Can you manage that?"

"I-I think so. But why are these qualities so important?"

"Because," the abbess said, rising from the table and rustling in her clothing trunk for some buried object, "what you both must undertake will be very difficult. He will find it a great burden. Especially with a woman like you."

The abbess righted herself and held out a small looking glass. "Have you ever gazed upon yourself?"

Margrete quickly glanced down at her folded hands. "No, it is a vanity in which I have not indulged."

The abbess gently tilted the younger woman's chin up with the touch of her forefinger, gazing into her soul. "Are you afraid of what you will see?"

Margrete's back stiffened at the notion. "I may have many faults, Mother Abbess, but cowardice is not one of them. I am not afraid."

"You should be." The abbess's graying blond eyebrows drew together. "For what you will see in this looking glass will confirm how difficult it will be to do what I suggest."

She held up the mirror, and before Margrete could turn away, she came face to face with herself. She was at first startled by the stranger she saw, then shocked by her visage. And finally, she was indeed fearful.

"Oh, heavenly Father," she whispered.

"Yes," Phillipa said soothingly, gazing at the mirror over Margrete's shoulder. "Now you see how difficult it will be. But it can be accomplished. If you are strong, and if your husband is honorable, my plan will work."

"Do you think so?"

"Yes, indeed." Abbess Phillipa smiled in triumph. "You will be able to live with one foot on earth, and one in heaven."

$\mathcal{S}ix$

The old Roman road that wound from the wayside inn to Longrove Castle was paved, but hazardously deteriorating. The thoroughfare had been paved many times over since the Romans had abandoned the British Isles some eight hundred years earlier. But clumps of grass grew between upturned stones, making the going difficult even for shod horses.

Hugh and Brian managed to keep their balance, riding side by side in silence, each contemplating the drastic measure that Hugh was about to undertake to secure a home and hearth. They kept up a steady pace during the half-hour ride until the castle—gray, ancient, and enchanting—loomed against the horizon.

Hugh reined in with a sharp tug and rose in his stirrups for a better look, blinking in wonder, heart aching with longing for that which he had never before even hoped to possess. And now it could be his. But at what cost?

"What if she's a leper?" Brian blurted in the silence as if he, too, pondered the price of such a gem.

Hugh hesitated, a moment too long to pretend he had not wondered the same. He sank back into his saddle and waved a hand nonchalantly in the air.

"Neighbors would not tolerate a leper," he reasoned as he cleared his throat uncertainly. "She'd be taken care of by some of the monks who tend the lepers far from civilized folk."

"But this barony is isolated. Perhaps neighbors do not know of her condition. Maybe that's why the innkeeper knew so little about her. Maybe that's why the baron never introduced me to her yesterday." Brian's face began to twist with horror at the possibilities. "S'blood, can you imagine!"

"For the love of God, I'll have no more of such speculation. The lady will be my wife. I don't give a damn what she looks like."

"So you say," Brian said with a shiver.

Hugh snapped his head toward his squire, ready to blister him for such impertinence, but all curses stilled when he saw the pity with which Brian regarded him.

"And you'll not say a word about my leg!" Hugh shouted, thrusting a warning finger in the air. "Do you hear? I'll not be turned away because her father thinks I'm a cripple."

"I would hardly call you a cripple, my lord. Your leg will heal now that you're no longer a fighting man."

Hugh glared at his squire, jealous of his youthful optimism. Brian was handsome in a way that made young girls swoon. He had a perfectly straight nose, as yet unbroken by battle, wavy wheat-colored hair, and unusual eyes. One was green, the other blue. Self-conscious about this anomaly, he never stared long at anyone.

When he was a child an old crone had accused him of being the devil's spawn because of the different colors, and he'd barely escaped a burning at the stake. Since then he'd spent a lifetime trying to be normal, outstanding only in imminently acceptable ways. Brian longed to be the best warrior, the most chivalrous and admirably ambitious on the lists. He was drawn to the prettiest and most perfect women. He wouldn't stay long by Hugh's side now that he was giving up the sword for the hearth, that was certain. Life on a small barony would be too dull for such an enterprising lad.

"What do you know of physical weakness?" Hugh growled at him, not without affection. He dusted off his tunic, grimacing at an ale stain splattered down the front. Then he smoothed a hand over half an inch of a grisly beard. "Hell, I should have shaved. I do not look too road-weary for a fine lady, do I?"

Exposing a row of healthy teeth, Hugh rehearsed a broad smile, as friendly as it was pathetic.

"You look better when you scowl, my lord," Brian replied.

"Oh." Hugh's smile faded. "God's teeth, let's get this over with."

By the time they reached the castle, the rusty sun was settling for the night in pillows of purple shadows. A distinct peace hovered around the land.

When knight and squire passed through the gatehouse, castle servants, a few villagers, and one ancient knight gathered around with friendly greetings.

"Look at that, will ye? Now there's a warrior," a young shabbily dressed woman whispered loud enough to be heard.

"A warrior or a giant, Mama?" remarked a child who stood beside her with a dirty gown and a snot-smeared nose.

Brian made introductions and explained their purpose while Hugh quickly scanned the surroundings.

There was a tall stone curtain, crumbling in a few places, that walled in a large bailey. The castle itself consisted of a single tower and a tall, square keep with arrow slits and a few embrasures cut deep in the stone for windows. Beyond the keep lay a small chapel, stable, beehives, a small herb garden, a dovecote, mews, and a fishing pond. Admittedly the estate looked a bit tattered, but to a man without a home, it held great promise. Seeing such cozy abundance, Hugh's earlier sense of longing turned instantly into deep craving. Only reluctantly did he force his attention back to those gathered around.

"My lord, this is Sir William MacGregor," Brian said. The squire pointed with a deferential nod to a wizened old man who sported a tattered and faded surcoat emblazoned with a lion and a stag. His clothing was thirty years old if it was a day.

"Ach, now here's a fine warrior, see?" the whiskery old man said, slapping Hugh's back.

"The honor is mine, Sir William." Hugh bowed his head. "I've come to meet your liege lord, Giles Trewsbury, the baron of Longrove."

"And his wee lass, Lady Margrete, eh?" MacGregor winked and rubbed his knotted hands together as if before a toasty fire. "Watch oot fer that one, laddie. She's a hard one, she is."

Hugh compressed his lips but did not respond.

Brian's brows knitted in concern. "Why, good sir, do you say that?"

MacGregor looked anxiously over his shoulder, then whispered, "She's wont to beat a man aboot the head, that she is."

"A shrew!" Brian discreetly whispered to Hugh behind a raised hand.

"She curses me to no end fer feedin' meself a crumb or two at supper. Downright cruel, that lassie, she is."

"I'm sure the lady will please me well," Hugh said gruffly. "Now where is her father?"

"Ach, he's aboot, here and there. Look for Lord Giles, but do na' gaze upon his daughter if she's in one of her foul dispositions, lest ye turn to stone at the very sight of her."

Brian gulped, and whispered, "Maybe she *is* Medusa."

Hugh glared at his squire. "I'll find the baron myself then if no one knows where he is."

"What ho! Raise the drawbridge! The enemy approaches!" a voice shrieked from the ramparts.

The crowd all turned toward the round tower. Hugh squinted against the gathering darkness at the crowning ramparts, then gaped when he saw what was most certainly a plump old man, wildly waving his hands two stories above the earth, adorned in nothing but the skin God gave him.

"What is this about?" Hugh said. He'd seen no signs of an approaching army.

"Prepare the Greek fire!" the man cried out in warning, flinging his arms this way and that to an imaginary band of warriors. "The enemy has breached the gatehouse. Watch to the south, a siege engine approaches!"

"Lord Giles," Sir William called out through cupped hands. "Coom down at once! Yer new son is here!"

The silver-haired man, not in the least abashed by his absence of clothing, suddenly calmed and looked down at Hugh. His distress turned to glee. "Hail, fellow! Greetings. I've waited a lifetime for you!"

Hugh turned to Brian. *"That's* Lord Giles?"

"I'm afraid so," Brian whispered. "Though he was fully clothed when I met him yesterday and not quite so obviously knotty-pated. I'd recognize that silver hair anywhere."

"I noticed everything *but* his hair," Hugh said wryly.

"My lord," Brian reasoned, "the baron is a man of unusual enthusiasm. Not a bad quality in a man who will be your wife's father, eh?"

When Hugh merely frowned, Brian elaborated. "What I mean to say, my lord, is that not many a baron would offer his inheritance to a second son who has nothing but a sword and a second-rate destrier with which to commend himself. Perhaps it's a blessing if he's a little . . ." Brian diplomatically let his words fall away and tapped his temple with a forefinger, eyebrows raised suggestively.

"Just so," Hugh muttered to himself. "Yes, I see what you mean."

"Here he comes," MacGregor said, waving his friend over as he crossed the yard, having exited the tower. "Lord Giles, this young man has coom for ye daughter."

"Welcome, Sir Harold!" the baron said to Hugh, beaming at him.

"His name is Sir Hugh, my lord, remember? Not Harold," Brian said.

"Ah, yes, yes, Sir Hugh. What a fine husband you will make for my daughter. Come, friend, let me show you the castle you one day will inherit."

The baron started away, unembarrassed by his exposed and portly girth. Hugh hesitated. Was this a madman? Was that why his daughter was for the taking? Perhaps she was daft as well. Hugh's fellow knights errant would howl over this one.

"Come along," Lord Giles said, turning back expectantly. "What is it, my boy?"

"I . . ." Hugh broke off, his conscience warring with his desire to accept the gift of a barony apparently here for the taking. "I . . . well . . . my lord . . . you are naked."

The baron raised his brows innocently and looked down, blinking. "Why, so I am. MacGregor, why didn't you tell me I'd forgotten to dress?"

"I did, mon," the old knight said, pounding a fist into his palm. "A hoondred times if I said it once."

"Hmmmm." The baron stroked his silver beard. "Well, can you spare your cloak, young man?"

Hugh began to remove it. "Of course, my lord. But will it be enough?" He threw the light garment over the baron's shoulders. "Night is falling. You could catch your death of a chill."

"We all have to die sometime, my son," the baron said as they marched away from the others. "We all have to die sometime."

Hugh remembered the stingy innkeeper saying that Lord Giles believed his time was near. And that made the tour of the castle, and all its exquisite features, that much more enticing and bittersweet. Now all Hugh had to do was see the lady herself. He braced himself for the worst.

Seven

By the time Lord Giles and Hugh finished their tour of the castle grounds, the shadows of dusk had conquered the last rays of light. Darkness oozed victoriously into the cracks of the castle's mossy stones, hunkering down around the raptors in the mews, as well as the wild birds on whom they preyed in woods nearby.

The men retired to the lord's solar, and old MacGregor, dressed in his hopelessly soiled and tattered surcoat, followed uninvited, settling on a stool before the roaring fire, chuckling now and again to himself as the very old are wont to do.

Now fully dressed in an old but elegant floor-length burgundy tunic, the baron of Longrove poured three cups of claret, his hands shaking at the task. Furtively he glanced sideways, apparently to see if Hugh noticed.

Hugh pretended not to, putting his hands behind his back and roving to the hearth as he softly whistled. MacGregor looked up at him, working his lips over nearly empty gums.

"I had to slay him, ye see," he explained, tears filling

his eyes. He gripped Hugh's wrist. "Thrust me sword through his heart. But I had no choice. Don't ye see, mon? Don't ye?"

"Yes, of course," Hugh said.

The gentle assurance made the doddering knight smile with relief, and he turned back to the blue and yellow flames, mumbling quietly to himself. Hugh scowled at MacGregor, then at Lord Giles, trying to decide which one was worse off.

Things must be very bleak indeed for Lady Margrete, Hugh thought, concerned for her though they'd never met. She was in a castle full of old and witless men. She needed a younger man to take control. And he was the man to do it, he thought, his chest expanding with a sense of manly purpose.

Lord, this was too good to be true, he thought, looking about him. The intimacy of the moment, of this place, congealed suddenly into intense hope that burned in his chest more fiercely than the fire that blazed before him. He just might make his mark here. He just might wrestle from life some lasting meaning.

"Here, Sir Hugh," Lord Giles said, bringing him a pewter goblet and handing one to MacGregor as well.

Hugh smiled and thanked him, taking a long drink to temper his wild thoughts, enjoying the warmth the wine kindled in his belly.

"You see, my boy," Lord Giles said after he took a swill himself, "I am a good-hearted man. Too much so to be a good baron. My vassals take advantage of my kindness."

"Do they, my lord?"

Hugh wondered if some of the problems at the castle— the obvious neglect—might be due to the baron's state of mind. He was in no position to discipline any laggards, that was certain.

During their tour, Lord Giles had stopped to feed the sparrows, calling each one by name, talking to them, then laughing to himself as if they'd not only answered back with their chirps, but made a jest. He'd slapped his knee and laughed long after the men had wandered on.

"You see," the baron continued, as sober now as he was giddy before, "I've not long to live. I want my daughter married to a strong man who can rule this barony when I'm gone. If you marry Margrete, you will inherit all of this. And until I die, you can live as lord of Longrove Manor, which is not far from here. You see, I want grandchildren. And Margrete, she . . . she . . ."

The baron tugged a hand over his brow, as if trying to wring from it a cogent thought. "MacGregor, what was I saying a fortnight ago about Margrete and the king?"

"Ye didn't say it," the old knight replied indignantly. "*I* did. I said the disagreeable filly needs a husband who is brave and strong, someone who can defend against invaders, who can answer the king's summons, or make enough money off the land to send gold in lieu of knight's service. Ach, I'm getting too old to fight!"

Hugh stifled a smile, wondering if the old soul could still even bear the weight of armor.

"She needs a brave knight," Lord Giles said in conclusion.

"I could be such a man, I avow." With these words Hugh sealed his fate without so much as a kiss.

"Good!" Lord Giles patted him warmly on the back. "I'm glad to hear it. Oh, but there is one small detail I failed to mention, about my daughter. One you might find . . . repugnant."

Hugh's heart began to clamor against his ribs. The fire suddenly felt too hot. He stepped away, bracing himself for the one glaring defect that he knew all along awaited him.

"Out with it then, my lord. I can take the suspense no longer." He turned soberly to the baron. "What about your daughter?"

"How can I put this gently?" Lord Giles said, worrying his fingers together.

"Tell me nothing, man," Hugh said impatiently. "Just *show* her to me and that will tell me all I need to know. Where the devil is she?"

"Here."

Hugh heard the gentle, feminine voice from somewhere behind him. He swallowed the boulder that lodged suddenly in his throat. God, could he have been more indiscreet? When had she entered the chamber? How much had she heard?

He turned slowly, struggling to mend his tattered dignity as he went, and found her standing in the open doorway, holding a single sputtering candle in hand at her waist. The circle of light did not quite reach her chin. Naturally, her face would be cloaked in shadows! The suspense was killing him. He clinched his fists. Was the Creator conspiring to keep her visage from his eyes? Was it so horrible?

"There she is," old MacGregor hissed quietly with a fearful look in his eyes, pointing at her as if a witch had alighted on her broomstick. He clutched Hugh's hand with cold, bony fingers, tugging him down to whisper in his ear. "Watch oot for her, I say, or soon ye'll be bruised upon yer bonny pate."

"A moment ago you were worried for her future," Hugh whispered to Sir William as the baron bustled forward to greet his daughter.

"I look to her future only because she's the daughter of a dear friend. Verily, I still say a girl such as that should know the sting of a whip."

Hugh could not fathom that, based on the naturally sweet

tone of her voice. He righted his posture and frowned at the shadows, straining desperately to make out details while the baron weaved and bobbed anxiously in front of her, whispering to her. Pray God he had told her before now that Hugh was coming!

Lady Margrete wore a veil, apparently with some sort of circlet topping what appeared to be a full skein of golden hair. A few wild strands that clung to her shoulder were illuminated by light from a torch in the hall behind her. He could tell a wimple swathed her neck from ear to ear, but hellfire, he could not make out her features!

"My father says you are curious about me, good sir," she said again in that dulcet voice of hers that made his heart melt and gently silenced the old man with unmistakable strength of will. "What is it you would like to know?"

"Why, the man wants a good look at you!" the baron said, letting loose with a belly-jiggling round of laughter, crossing back to Hugh's side. "Admit it, boy, admit it!"

Hugh reddened from head to toe, for that was exactly what he wanted. He felt uncomfortably like a hostler sent by his master to buy a new horse. Lord, how did Margrete feel? He could only imagine. Thankfully, the chamber was too dark to read her face, or for her to read his.

"Let him have a look, Margrete. Go on, lass. He'll see you look just like my Rosamunde."

At the mention of this name, the room seemed to grow stuffy. Hugh sensed, rather than saw, a frown emanating from the shadows. What had disturbed Margrete?

Lord Giles turned to him. "Rosamunde is my wife. She's gone on a trip to visit her sister. She'll be back any day."

Again, he sensed discomfort from the shadows. Lady Margrete swallowed thickly, or cleared her throat, he wasn't sure which.

"Go on, Margrete, show the man who he will be marrying."

"Very well," she said with a distinct tone of resignation. "I will obey you as I do in all matters, Father."

Lord Giles's chest puffed out with pride at this sign of obedience. "Wait till you see," he whispered to Hugh, overcnunciating each word.

The young lady lifted the candle closer to her face. When its halo of light fully illuminated her features, Hugh gasped.

"Good God!" he whispered. "By the Rood and all that's holy."

His heart began to beat wildly, his head grew light, and his goblet of wine slipped through his slackened fingers, clattering on the stone floor.

He had never seen a more beautiful woman in all his days.

Eight

Hugh didn't know how long he stood there gaping at her, but it was long enough to take measure of every lovely feature. Had he ever seen a more enchanting woman? Perhaps in a dream, when white smoke swirls into the likeness of an angel. But a dream is never satisfying. One always awakens startled to learn it wasn't real, fighting the futile urge to reach out and embrace the tendrils of smoky images as they vaporize.

But Lady Margrete was real. She stood before him now, blinking like a doe, eyes peacock blue and innocent, with strong and forthright cheeks, full and expressive lips, and a delicate nose. And a frown. He wanted to smooth it away with a fingertip. It didn't belong on a face so lovely.

She watched him as well. He saw the judgment in her eyes, the curiosity, the discernment, the slight flicker of her gaze to his mouth, his chest, his legs. Then a blush of self-consciousness tainted her skin.

He stood more erect, hoping she would not see his weakness and find him wanting, hoping against hope she was the sort of woman who didn't care about appearances and that she would have him and he could rest at last. He could be someone of consequence. A man with a future. God willing, a man with children and grandchildren. And with this woman, this exquisite, lovely woman. Could this really be happening?

"Well?" It was Lord Giles who finally broke the laden silence. He looked eagerly between them, eyes bright and childlike. "What do you think?"

Margrete licked her lips and looked at her feet, then pushed past Hugh, trailing a plume of womanly scent, and he noticed for the first time she held two unlit torches at her side.

"The sun has set, Papa. You need more light. Sir Hugh will want to see everything about his new home."

She touched the torches to the fire, and when they sizzled and flamed, she placed them in sconces on the wall.

"Isn't that better, my lord?" she said, turning to Hugh with an open smile.

"My new home," he repeated. "Does that mean you will have me, then?"

"I obey my father's command."

Her voice was lovely and lilting, but he detected a double meaning in her inflections.

"Papa," she added, in an almost patronizing tone, "I think that Goodman Bartholomew wants a word with you in the great hall."

"Very good, very good," he said, tugging at his tunic, which strained against his girth. "I cannot keep up with all the responsibilities that weigh me down, but try I must."

He shook his head in wonder at his own perseverance, then waddled out the door. Margrete stared after him a moment, then turned to MacGregor.

"Sir William, my father doubtless needs your able assistance."

The old Scot rose with a harumph and strode past her at a turtle's gait, muttering all the while. "Damned impertinent filly." At the door he paused and turned back to Hugh. "Just remember, laddie, I warned ye!"

When MacGregor slammed the door behind him, Margrete mustered a patient smile. "They're quite a twosome. My father . . ." Her voice trailed away and she blinked several times, her eyes softening with each bat of her blond lashes. "My father does not have all his wits about him."

Hugh nodded. "I thought not."

"He received a blow to his head some years ago when our castle was attacked by a neighboring baron. I don't think he remembers anything about that night, neither his fall, nor . . ." She paused. "Nor my mother's murder. He still thinks she's away on a visit to my aunt, who is also deceased."

This time it was Hugh who looked to the ground. It seemed the only appropriate gesture when one admitted such a sad thing. And he stared at his mud-splattered boots longer than propriety dictated, for he could well imagine who had committed such a crime upon her mother—a knight errant like himself. Suddenly he felt foolish for coming here. Whatever had made him think this lovely woman would want a wounded old bear with blood on his paws?

"My father does, however, retain a strong need to see me protected. On that matter, his fatherly instincts prevail over his loss of judgment." Her voice warmed with affection, and he looked up to see her perfect lips curling in a wistful smile. "He wants me to marry before he . . . dies. And rightly so."

"If it is right, why have you not done it before? You are

an heiress, and a beautiful one at that. You could have any man you wanted."

She bent down to retrieve the goblet he had dropped earlier. "I did not marry because I did not want to. And though I obey my father, as God has commanded, Papa is not in a position to remember from one day to the next what it is that a young woman should be doing with her life. I managed to stretch the days of my maidenhood into months, and months into years."

She refilled the goblet and handed it to him, glancing up at the last moment with a hint of mischief wreathing her stunning blue eyes.

"So why marry now?" he inquired as he accepted the wine.

"On one matter my father speaks wisely. If I am not married before he dies, then I will be obliged to take a man of the king's choosing. And I would rather die than marry under those circumstances. You see, though he won't admit it, Edward II ordered the attack on my father's castle that night. He killed my mother just as surely as if he'd held the dagger himself."

"Why?"

She shrugged. "I was too young to know when it happened, and afterward my father was too forgetful to remember."

"So though I am unknown to you, I am better than an unknown of the king's choosing."

She looked up at him with a frankness uncommon in women he had known. "Possibly."

"Your father said I might find something about you that is repugnant. What is it?"

She bit her lower lip as she searched for words. "Let me be frank. I will marry you, Hugh de Greyhurst, if you are an honorable man. And I will be a wife to you in all ways . . . save one.''

He blinked hard against the glare of the torches. ''And what way is that?''

''I will not share your bed.''

He stood stock-still, trying to make sense of her words.

''We must remain celibate. You see, I want a spiritual marriage.''

''A *what*?''

''You may have heard of such unions before,'' she hurried on, straightening the room as she spoke, fluffing pillows on the bed, smoothing the covers. ''Couples who aspire to be like Christ join their lives together in holy matrimony but resist the sin of lust. They work together, share companionship, they pray together, they simply do not . . . do not consummate . . . their . . . their union.''

''I've never heard of anything so absurd in all my life!''

''It is *not* absurd!'' She spun around to face him. ''There was a reason Christ was born to a virgin. It is the purest state possible and therefore is more pleasing to God.''

''If everyone thought so then what would happen to mankind? There would be no procreation, no children, no life at all!''

''Then the more quickly our souls would join the host of angels in heaven, which should be the place to which we all aspire.''

Hugh fell silent. Sweat trickled down his chest. He rubbed the spot, feeling weary after his momentary respite from despair. For the love of God, who would have thought such a bizarre condition would rear itself to ruin his only hope of settling down?

''I cannot fathom this, lady.'' He waved her off. ''I am not a priest. I am a warrior with no mind for heavenly matters. You do not want a husband. You want a saint.''

"No!" She pounded her fisted hands against her thighs. A golden lock of hair fell out of her veil and trickled like spun gold over her full and well-hidden breasts. "All I want is to live a holy life!"

Desperation rang in her voice, and the frustration that strained her body, that tightened the tendons in her delicate neck beneath her wimple, made her look like a dove ready to take flight.

"I'm sorry," she whispered, casting her eyes down. "I should not lose my temper."

"You should probably do it more often. Or do you listen to those lying priests who tell you that any utterance that is not a prayer is a sin?"

He pictured in his mind's eye the priest responsible for Rolly's death, and the cleric who had betrayed him as a lad, destroying his once-happy life. "To hell with them, I say. God, I could kill them all."

He picked up a chair and shoved it down with such force that a leg broke. The sound of splintering wood rent the air. Hugh looked down in surprise, then up in time to see Lady Margrete step back with a gasp of fear.

"My lady, forgive me. Sometimes I don't know my own strength."

She did not speak for the longest time, merely stared at him with wide, troubled eyes. Then she turned abruptly to leave.

"Don't go," he said, resisting the urge to lunge after her. "Please, my lady, I was wrong to lose my temper. It has been too long since I've been in the company of a lady. I would never hurt you."

She stopped, hand poised on the door latch, then snatched a deep breath and turned back to face him. Seeing his brawny arms and the muscles that strained against his tunic, she judged him very capable of hurting her.

"You are rightly angry," she said, trying to keep her voice from trembling. "For I have wasted your time. I could never marry a man like you. I loathe swords. I hate killing."

She brushed back the hair that had sprung rebelliously from her veil. "And it was foolish of me to think you could agree to the restriction I am demanding. I can't imagine two people less suited to one another. Can you?"

A frown gathered on his chiseled, tan forehead. His eyes, a curious liquid gold, flashed with disappointment.

"If you say so, my lady."

"I do." She smiled wanly. "Will you at least stay for the evening meal? You have ridden a long way. You and your squire may stay in the great hall tonight. In the morning you can—"

"In here, in here," Lord Giles said as he pushed the door open with a bang. He bustled in, leading a trail of servants carrying pails of hot water. Moments later two pages, grunting from the strain, entered with a round wooden tub. "Put it in the center of the room."

The pages set the tub down as instructed, and the others emptied their pails into it. Steam billowed up from the splashing water.

"There you are," the old man said as he slapped his hands together. "You will enjoy a bath, Sir Hugh, before we feast on roasted hens and sturgeon."

Margrete glanced at Hugh and noticed the covetous look he bestowed on the inviting tub. She was happy to see a bit of pleasure soften his hardened features.

"Please take your time, Sir Hugh," she entreated, breathing easier. "Let your road-weary muscles relax for as long as you wish."

"When I was young," her father said, slapping Hugh on the back, "a visitor considered it an insult if he was not bathed by the lady of the castle herself. It is an old-fashioned custom, but one we adhere to here at Longrove.''

"We *do*?" Margrete turned to him with widened eyes. "Nonsense, Papa—"

"My wife, Rosamunde, will be up momentarily to help you undress."

Margrete sidled over to him and gripped his upper arm with viselike fingers, even as she smiled her sweet smile. "Papa, Mother is not here. *Remember?*"

He turned to her aghast. "Really?"

"Yes, Papa. Mother cannot bathe Sir Hugh."

"Well, then there is only one solution."

Margrete smiled. "That's correct. Sir Hugh can bathe himse—"

"*You* will do it."

She blanched. "Papa—"

"I won't take no for an answer. Obey your father, Margrete. It is God's command."

She closed her gaping mouth at that, and catching sight of a rare gleam in her father's eyes, Margrete wondered just how mad, or cunning, the old man truly was.

Nine

on't be long," Lord Giles said as he started for the door, then paused, looking back at the embarrassed couple with what Margrete could have sworn was a devilish smile. "Unless you *want* to tarry. That's entirely up to you."

"Papa, I . . ." Margrete started after him in protest, but the old man slammed the door nearly in her face and she stopped short, willing her heart to cease its furious gallop. She could resolve this situation logically. She would simply refuse. "Sir Hugh, forgive me, but . . ."

She whirled around, prepared to beg off from this odious duty, but fell silent when she saw that he was already undressing. He was pulling off his tunic, lifting the tattered brown leather, and the cambric shirt beneath it, over his broad shoulders. In the few seconds before his head emerged from the tangle of clothing, as he pulled his arms from his sleeves over his head, she stared in wonder at what the man was revealing—a marvelous tapestry of muscles, a network of sinews and tendons that bulged beneath brown nipples and creamy bronze skin.

The sight was so arresting, Margrete nearly staggered back. The power of the man, the animal-like strength, represented all that was contrary to her contemplative nature. And yet for some reason in the quiet of this room it was not repugnant. Quite the contrary.

When his head reemerged from the tangle of clothing, he caught her gaze and held it a moment, not bothering to mask the leaden disappointment that turned his golden eyes the color of dead leaves in autumn. Clearly, his humor had taken a brittle turn. He looked away and snapped his wrists out of his sleeves. Fully exposed, his chest was an inverted pyramid of entwining muscles. She forced herself to look at safer territory—his face. If she could merely focus on that he would seem like any other unthreatening human, another soul, not a heathen, a vessel of earthly lusts. With some dismay she realized she'd never even imagined what *he* might look like, or how it might affect *her*.

Sensing her disquiet, he turned to her with hands on his hips, glaring down at her over his aristocratic nose. "What, pray you, is the matter? Tell me what troubles you so? Would you deny me even a bath, gentle lady? I have traveled far for naught. Is a bath too much to ask?"

"Of course not," she replied, stung by his implied rebuke. "I would deny you nothing . . ."

His brow rose in feint mockery. Frustrated, she flung her hands up in the air. "Oh, it's pointless. I will leave you be before I expend any more of your good will."

Before she reached the door, he called out in a surly voice, "What is the matter, Lady Margrete? Are you afraid you might realize you desire men after all?"

Bristling, she whirled around. "I hardly think so, my lord."

"Or do you only obey the commands from your father that you *want* to obey?"

"Not at all."

"Oh?" Hugh chuckled jadedly. "I thought he'd ordered you to bathe me." He smirked. "An old tradition."

She tipped up her chin, teeming with indignation. How could these knights errant be so arrogant, so thoughtless of others? She would be damned before she'd let him think that he posed a threat to her chastity.

"I am not in the least afraid of you, Sir Hugh," she said, rolling up her sleeves. "I suggest you hurry and finish undressing before the bath cools entirely."

The irony shimmering on his face turned to grudging admiration.

"By the Rood, you are a courageous woman," he said as he tugged off his breeches and muddied leggings.

"I hardly think it takes much courage to gaze upon the likes of you."

But he proved her wrong. He pulled down his last defense—the braies tightly entwined around his groin and muscular buttocks. He kicked them off his feet and rose to full height.

She never looked down, but she knew what was there. One could not live in a crowded castle without seeing naked bodies now and then. As a child, she had seen squires peel off their masters' armor and drenched underclothing in the great hall following military skirmishes. She'd even helped her mother and servants bathe the bodies of slain vassals. But she had never seen the naked form of a man she had hoped to take as a spouse. Somehow this experience, unlike the others, was chokingly intimate.

"Then again," she muttered, swallowing the great lump that had congealed in an instant in her throat, "perhaps it does take courage to note the differences between men and women."

He blinked against a waft of smoke from the hearth that burned his eyes. "You are honest, too. Fine qualities in a wife. Such a waste."

"Certainly God doesn't think so," she said, making sure her gaze did not go any lower than his bulging chest. "Now will you please get into the water? The temperature will be tolerable by now."

She turned her head in modesty as he stepped in. She knew when it was safe to look again, for she heard water lap over the edges of the tub and slap onto the floor. The hot water penetrated the strewn rushes and herbs, and soon the genteel scent of mint and camomile wafted in the air.

Hugh exhaled a rich and grateful sound, and with her back still turned, she smiled. She wanted him to have gotten something out of this night, if nothing more than a bath. It was a rare treat, and clearly one he was enjoying, if the contented groans emanating from his massive warrior's chest were any indication.

"Is there soap?" he said.

She turned to find him slouched down. Only his head and his brawny knees rose above the water's surface. His hair was wet; moisture dripped from his nose.

"The servants left some on the table." Retrieving it, she pulled a stool to the tub and sat down to begin her work.

Fortunately, the dirt and grit that had been clinging to his body colored the water with a brownish tint and she didn't have to worry about seeing any embarrassing details below the surface.

"I won't even ask when was the last time you washed yourself."

He peeked open one eye and nailed her with a glare. "I do not have the luxury of servants to prepare baths like you, my lady. Besides, baths are unhealthy.''

She let out a soundless laugh. Personally, she cherished cleanliness enough to risk catching a death of a chill. And if he only knew how few servants she had, and how inept many of them were, he would not make it sound as if she lived the life of a queen.

"Are you intentionally growing a beard or are you merely too lazy to shave?"

He shut his eyes and sighed. "I have no time to worry about such details. But a shave would not hurt."

"It depends on who wields the blade." This wry comment earned her a frown from him, but he didn't open his eyes. She smiled to herself and took a knife that one of the servants had brought and lathered up his face with wood ashe soap. Carefully, she began to scrape at the tough bristles of hair, and marveled at what their absence slowly revealed.

His lips were distinctly carved by the artistic hands of God, leaving luscious peaks and valleys of wine-colored flesh. His cheeks were prominent, chiseled by experience. His jaw was square and prominent, as if he didn't say much, but meant whatever he said.

She wiped at his cheeks with the cloth, her knuckles tingling when they brushed his warm skin. She sensed a gentleness beneath his tough hide. Suddenly she thought about his limping gait and realized there was much she didn't know about this man. Why, for example, was she beginning to relax in his presence? On the outside he was rough, but inside . . .

"Sir Hugh," she said as she placed the rag on his right arm and began to scrub. "It's a pity, is it not, that we are so ill-suited to one another? You cannot deny that this barony is a great prize and worthy of some sacrifice."

He peeped open an eye to study her and pushed himself

up a few inches. "There is no denying the value of your offer, my lady."

She moved the cloth over his collarbone, working the soap into a lather against the chest hair that swirled this way and that at the water's surface.

"I'm not asking for much from a husband. Merely that he be honorable."

"By that you mean he must keep his promise to remain chaste?"

At the dubiousness laced through his gruff baritone, she swallowed and nodded.

The hot water enveloped her wrist and forearm as she lowered the cloth down his abdomen. As she did so, she focused on his mouth, noticing for the first time what provocative twists there were at the corners, hinting at some secret waiting to be discovered. He seemed to be studying her mouth as well with half-lidded eyes, for their breaths mingled sweetly, intimately. She leaned forward, like a moth to a flame, not sure what she was doing or why.

Suddenly he snatched his hand around her wrist, stopping her downward progress. The sound of splashing water startled her. She gasped and found his eyes. They were ablaze, burning her without touch.

"Don't," he growled. "You know not what you do."

"I'm bathing you, just as you—"

"You know not what you do! God's wounds, you ask the world of me, lady. Do not go further or you will regret it."

"But I—"

"Leave me."

"But I only—"

"Leave, I beg of you!" he roared.

He tossed aside her hand. Water flew through the air; the rag flopped from her fingers to the floor. He sat up and hunched his shoulders over his knees, looking like a caged animal. "Go, I say!"

Dumbfounded, confused as to the nature of her offense, Margrete stood up, then ran from the room.

When the door whisked shut behind her, Hugh groaned and raked his hands over his wet hair. He looked down at the enormous and humiliating evidence of his attraction to her, then sank back into the cooling water.

Margrete was pacing in the shadows of an alcove down the hall, debating whether to return to Sir Hugh's side or make herself scarce, when she heard the door open with a bang. She stepped from the shadows, prepared to confront him, but when she saw the fierce agony that gripped his body, she shrank back.

He strode down the corridor, swinging one leg out stiffly, fully clothed, with wet hair swept back. So he was fleeing. Well, what had she expected? She could never love such a brute, and he would not be satisfied without conjugal rights. Let him go, then.

Suddenly there was another sound. The wail of a child. The fearful howls grew louder, and a toddling babe stepped into the corridor. Margrete recognized her instantly. She was the chief cook's daughter. But what was she doing in the lord's private chambers? Lost, no doubt, poor child.

Great dollops of tears rushed down her reddened cheeks. Her toothless mouth widened with each grief-stricken sob. Margrete wanted to rush to the child's aid, but decided to wait until Hugh passed by.

He brushed past the girl, unaware of her existence. Then he stopped abruptly, as if he'd run into a wall. He sighed and turned back.

"What is it, little one?" he crooned.

He walked to the child's side and picked her up in his

great arms. He chucked her chin and gave her a sympathetic smile. "It's a cruel world out there, wee one. Don't start crying till it really hurts."

The girl continued to wail, but she clutched his chest for comfort. When she finally quieted, he reached into his tunic and pulled out a bright yellow ribbon.

"This was meant for the mistress of your castle. But you can have it. And perhaps when you grow up and become a pretty damsel you'll remember the first man who gave you a trinket for your heart."

The girl smiled as she reached out for the ribbon. Clutching it in one moist hand, she steadied herself with shivering gasps of breath. Then she looked up into Hugh's face with wonder.

He kissed her forehead. "Farewell, maiden. Now save those tears."

He lowered her to the ground, patted her head, then strode onward.

Margrete shrank further into the shadows, clutching her heart, moved by the giant's gentleness.

"Brian!" Hugh growled at his squire when he reached the stable. "What the devil are you doing?"

"What? Oh, Sir Hugh! I was just telling this young lady about the fine art of . . . jousting."

The squire disentangled himself from an embarrassed young maiden, a black-haired beauty who had apparently already agreed to some sort of assignation. Blast the randy youth for his luck at love.

"Get my horse saddled. Now!" Hugh turned in disgust, and marched in a huff to the castle yard, where he paced while Brian quickly readied their mounts.

By the time the red-faced squire brought him his horse, Hugh's own aching need had dissipated. He'd dressed as soon as he could, certain that there was no hope of marriage to Lady Margrete, and slipped out of the castle without bidding anyone farewell.

God's wounds, he could not be chaste in the presence of such a beautiful woman. It would be agony. Hugh was not a man who lived for pleasure. He didn't rape the wives and daughters of his victims as other mercenaries did, and he no longer thought of lovemaking as a mere act of physical pleasure. It had taken on deeper meaning. It represented the hope of creation. He wanted some kind of legacy. But with Lady Margrete, he would enjoy neither pleasure nor the fruit of his loins.

"Damnation take her for her foolish notions," Hugh growled as he mounted up, wincing when he sank in his saddle. He tossed back a lock of damp hair that had fallen in his eyes and scowled at the stars. What horrible fate written in the heavens had brought him so tantalizingly close to happiness? He squeezed his forehead and sucked in a shivering breath.

"My lord, are you all right?" Brian said as he mounted up.

"Yes," he said through clenched teeth. But it was a lie. That old ache throbbed in his leg, and it spread up through his belly to his head. He had lived by the sword, and it was clear he would die by it, too. Just as his father had predicted.

The last time Hugh had seen him, Jervais de Greyhurst was shouting down at him from a tower of magnificent Greyhurst Castle—the very tower in which Hugh's mother had that morning been imprisoned in shame.

"You will amount to nothing," Lord Jervais shouted at his nine-year-old disfavored son, "for you are too much like your mother, that bitch I called my wife. The faithless harlot. And you, who called yourself my son, was hiding her infidelities from me. God curse you for a traitor! I do wonder now if you are even of my blood.''

The handsome, distinguished, and cruel lord of Greyhurst chewed his words with venom; his face was scarlet with rage. The wind blew his black and gray hair about his broad shoulders. Behind him stood his dutiful first son, Hugh's thirteen-year-old brother John.

Slender, undistinguished, uncomplicated John. He was the perfect son for Lord Jervais. He could be molded like a handful of clay. So different than Hugh, who loved his unfaithful mother despite her adulteries, perhaps because of them, because she had feelings she could not control, unlike her husband who did not seem to have a heart at all.

Like his mother, Hugh was cursed with compassion. He was damned with the ability to forgive. He was burdened with a sense of honesty. In short, he was a perplexing oddity in a world ruled by brutality. Ironically, Hugh was his father's only legitimate son. John had been conceived of an adulterous union. But Hugh, out of loyalty to his dame, would never tell Jervais that.

The one attribute that Lord Jervais found praiseworthy in his second son was his brute strength, which was evident even as a child. And when the great baron of Greyhurst disowned him, Hugh was being condemned even for that.

"Go work in the quarries. Work like a beast of burden!" Lord Jervais shouted, swiping the air with a fist. "By God, I swear you will never own a fief, you worthless knave! You will die young in battle, scraping for food, with no place to lay your head. Mark my words!"

Shaking off the memory, Hugh released the tight hold on his forehead and took in a steadying breath. His father had been right. After being disinherited and spending the rest of his youth fostered by poor vassals, Hugh had amounted to nothing. And this brief brush with fortune was surely a sign that he should resign himself to ignominy.

"Let us quit this place," he said, and tapped the belly of his mount with the spurs he'd earned in battle so long ago.

Brian unexpectedly reached out and grabbed his reins. Hugh's charger tossed back his head with a whinny of complaint.

"My lord, hold fast! Why are we leaving?"

"I cannot marry her!"

"Why not?" Brian looked back at the castle, his face awash in confusion. "I heard the baron say all this was yours for the taking."

Hugh dropped his head, twisting it to the side, swallowing the taste of bile. "You don't understand."

"No, I don't."

"And I don't have to explain it to you."

"No, but one day you'll have to explain to yourself why you are riding away from the best and perhaps last chance you have of finding happiness."

"God's wounds, lad, I should strike you with the flat of my sword for your impertinence." Hugh raked a hand over his damp hair. "She . . . she will marry me but . . . she wants to remain celibate."

Brian's jaw dropped with a snort of disbelief. "Who cares what she wants?" he whispered. "Marry her and then take her as you will. Her father won't care. He clearly wants you here. Lady Margrete will thank you for taking her maidenhead once she learns it's nothing to fear."

"No, God, no!"

"My lord, you can't be so pure-hearted."

"I am not pure! Don't you see? That's the point. I cannot take Lady Margrete's honor. She is the only good thing I have seen in I can't remember how long. This is the right thing to do. We must go now, before I change my mind."

Hugh violently heeled his mount. The charger reared back then bolted forward.

"Wait!" Margrete cried out.

The keen wind whisked the word from the steps of the keep to Hugh's ears. Her voice was so faint he could have traveled on as if he'd not heard it, and that would have been the wisest course to take. But that beggar-child he called hope held out a frostbitten hand for one more scrap, and Hugh could not turn away without searching its pitiful eyes one last time.

"What is it?" he called out in a barely civil tone, then tugged on the reins until his steed stopped and turned a half-circle with impatient steps. Brian reined in belatedly a short distance down the road.

Margrete dashed toward Hugh, and as she closed the distance, the moonlight revealed a face etched in turmoil.

"Don't go," she said, gasping for breath when she reached his side. She reached up as if to grip his knee, but her hand shrank back to her side, and she repeated her entreaty in a humble tone, "Please don't go. I misjudged you."

He blinked hard at the accursed compassion and the painful hope that swelled in his heart. "Do not put me in this unenviable position, maiden. I would help you if I could, but I am not so pure as you. I am not as strong as you."

She looked up, startled. "But you are an honorable man. You prove it with every passing moment we share. I realized when I left you in the solar that you . . . that you might have . . . felt some . . . desire for me. And yet you sent me away. Why? Because you are honorable."

"Even honorable men sin, sometimes brutally."

She laughed with unexpected depth and irony, pressing a hand to her chest. "Even *I* sin. I do not pretend to be a saint. I am only a woman who would live as purely as I can. I know that in our harsh times that is much to ask. Please help me to find some measure of goodness, to assure a place in heaven for myself. And for yourself as well. Surely you have sins to account for. Please, Sir Hugh, don't we both know there has to be something better than what we have? I think you are looking for some contentment also, are you not? You seem . . . weary. I could help you, be a companion, your helpmeet. I . . ."

She fell silent, ran a shaky backhand over her wrought brow.

With a sigh of frustration, he dismounted and squared off before her. "Don't you understand, my lady? You are too exquisite for me to resist."

She looked up timidly, contemplating this dilemma. "Then I will make myself plain," she offered with the faith of a child. "I will wear a hair shirt so you will not *want* to embrace me. I will bind my breasts so my form is without any mark of femininity."

"No, Margrete." He waved her off and began to pace. She followed step for step.

"I will frown and be surly so you will eschew my presence. I will wear dirty clothes so that you will avoid the air about me. I will splatter mud upon my cheeks to hide the pink that blossoms there."

"Margrete, stop!" He turned on her, feeling as if she were desecrating her own image. "You can't."

"I can. And I will. Please, Hugh, my father is dying. He could pass away any day. Then who would I be forced to marry? Some cruel baron who would make a rape out of a first night of consummation? Or someone who would imprison me in my own tower just for the pleasure of denying me any say in my father's barony?"

He thought of his mother, the last glimpse he'd had of her, with her lovely, aging face pressed against the bars of the tower window. He thought of his cruel father, and knew the misery he'd caused her. She'd lived out the rest of her days imprisoned by Hugh's father. And he thought of his own hopes, that no one seemed to care about, that even God had forgotten about.

And then he realized the power that he held in his hands. The power to make a dream come true. Not just for her, but for him as well. His small, impossible dream.

"Very well," he said quietly, looking at the moon. It was perfectly round and stunningly white, full of possibilities and mysteries. Full of purity and all that is eternal.

"What?" she whispered. "What did you say?"

"I said I will be your husband." He turned to her, unsure of whether he should laugh or cry. "Frankly, my lady, I need you more than you need me. I will be your husband. And I will pray to God for the strength to resist you. That is, if I can remember how to pray."

He looked away, embarrassed by the compromises he continued to make in his life, and marched toward the keep, leaving Margrete slack-jawed to stare after him in wonder.

Just when she thought all was lost, she'd found a man who would give her what she wanted most—a spiritual marriage.

But excitement turned to wariness, for she realized as she watched his massive figure stride toward the great hall that there was no way to bind *his* massive chest, no way to douse the musky masculine scent that *he* exuded, no way to make callow the dignified grooves that experience had marked on *his* ruggedly handsome face. She'd seen the specter of temptation when bathing him earlier. For the gentleness of his soul had disarmed her, making her aware in a way that no brute of a man could: She was a woman. Heaven forbid, but she knew at last her sex.

She, too, would pray for the strength to resist her sinful urges.

Ten

Four weeks later, after the banns had been read on three consecutive Sundays at the village church, Margrete and Hugh awoke to greet the day of their wedding—Hugh from his pallet in the great hall, and Margrete from her straw bed in the women's bower.

Her lady-in-waiting had already risen and was doubtless continuing preparations in the great hall for the wedding feast. Thoughtfully, she had let Margrete sleep late. She was just sitting up in bed, trying to shake off the oddest dream when Hugh appeared in the doorway—dressed in a simple russet tunic and leggings, looking harried and grumpy.

"Sir Hugh, what is it?" She drew the sheets closer to her chest. Thankfully she had worn a light gown to bed.

"Lady Margrete, I . . ." His words fell away and he wiped a hand over his face.

"Is something the matter?"

He propped one arm against the arched doorway and

stared at her with disbelief. "Yes, there's something the matter. We're getting married today."

So he was going to back out after all. She steeled herself against a wave of disappointment. "Of course, if you're having second thoughts—."

"No!" he nearly shouted.

"So you're not having second thoughts. What is it, then?"

She went still, waiting for his response, but it was so long in coming that she began to recall her dream. Oh, Lord, she had dreamt about him all night long!

"What is it?" he said, worried himself now. "Are you having second thoughts?"

"No . . . No, I . . . I just remembered I dreamt about you last night."

Would he be surprised to know that she had dreamt of him naked? The image came rushing back to her in potent detail. He was all hot skin and smooth muscles, hard shoulders, narrow hips, animal-like thrusts. She had cried out in her sleep, craving more, never quite satisfied. She was woozy still from the images. And ashamed, on one level. But on another, she was glad to see him in the doorway, excited to know that such a man would be with her evermore, like a forbidden jewel to be admired but never touched.

"What did you dream about?" he said.

She moistened her lips and fought a blush. "I don't remember. I just know you were in the dream."

"I dreamt, too," he replied, then pushed off the door frame and strolled into the bower, roving to an open window and glancing out at the bustling activity in the castle yard below. "Actually, it was a nightmare."

"Then I hope I didn't make an appearance," she said with a soft laugh.

He turned to her with a look of surprise. "You have such a lovely laugh." He scowled. "Is there anything about you that isn't lovely?"

"You make my attributes seem like faults."

"Perhaps they are. Or at least they might seem to be in the eyes of one who will be denied that which other husbands consider a right."

She tipped up her chin, understanding washing over her. "So that's it. Your concerned about . . . conjugal rights."

He laughed bitterly. "Is that what they call it?"

"My lord, if you don't think you can go through with thi—"

"No, it's not me I'm worried about." He pounded his chest with a fist, then waved her off. "Never mind."

She frowned, tilting her head in puzzlement. "You're worried about me?"

"Yes!" He came to her, striding forward as if through a sea of enemy soldiers, then sank down abruptly by her side. He placed his hands on the bed on either side of her legs, which were still tucked under a sheet, and leaned forward, studying her face as if he could read his fortune in it. Her cheeks tingled under the intensity of his liquid-gold eyes.

"Margrete, when I was a boy, before I was sent away by my father, my mother made me swear that I would never beat or imprison a wife. She must have known then what was in store for her. She spent the last ten years of her life a prisoner in my father's tower. How can I bind you in a marriage that isn't really a marriage to a man who represents all that you loathe? Isn't that a form of imprisonment?"

She frowned, trying to comprehend the depth of his chivalry and goodness. Lord, how had she been so blessed with such a husband? Wanting to give him something, wanting to thank him, she reached out and grasped one of his hands, squeezing hard.

"Sir Hugh, you could never imprison me. I have chosen a celibate life. It is I who may be trapping you." She tipped her chin down while her eyes remained fixed on him, taking measure of his intentions. "Have you not thought that *you* are the one who might be unhappy?"

"I will be miserable. No doubt about it. Unless . . ." He withdrew his hand from hers, crossed his arms, and regarded her with a gentle smirk. "Unless this God you believe in so ardently will have mercy and keep me from desiring you."

"He will," she said earnestly. "You must pray for strength."

He gave a cynical chuckle. "No, I won't pray for divine intervention to keep me from your bed. I'll do it myself. I will resist you, Margrete Trewsbury, if it's the last thing I do. Mark my words."

He rose, somehow more at peace. "After all, why would I desire a woman like you?"

She smiled, for it was clear he didn't mean a word of what he was saying. He started for the door, but turned back before he rounded the corner, a wry half-smile dimpling one of his rugged cheeks.

"Margrete, are you *sure* you don't remember what you dreamt of last night?"

Her cheeks flamed red. Had he read her mind? Did he know how erotic her dreams had been? When he sauntered off with a quiet chuckle of triumph, she dressed as plainly as a nun and headed straight for Treyvaux Abbey.

• • •

It was one of those spring mornings when nature is so overwhelmingly perfect that not even the most despondent person can ignore its promise of rejuvenation. Birds chirped and sang from nearby trees, flitting in and around branches exploding with virgin greenery.

In the grove, a few apple trees planted amidst the oaks, elms, and maples bore clusters of red buds eager to burst open and fill the air with sweet-smelling blossoms. Later in the summer, those buds would yield plump red fruit, heated on the surface by the sun, but cool, juicy, and sweet on the inside.

It was in this very grove that Margrete had spent many hours alone as a child and as a younger woman. Now, sadly, duties too often kept her away. But she needed only brush her feet through the dew-laden grass to remember the exquisite solitude she'd found in this soothing, quiet grove.

Here she had mourned the brutal death of her mother, letting the wild wind fill her bruised and aching soul, swirling around in the empty cask that was her self until the cringing images of blood, the shrieks of death, and the loss of innocence blew away.

She would slump down against a tree trunk as nimble and feminine as herself, leaning her head back until all she could see was the profusion of apple blossoms overhead, lush clouds of pink and white, a mollifying bouquet of sensitive flowers that absorbed her grief without a single petal withering in the onslaught.

And here she had prayed, without words, for it seemed that God dwelled in this place. It was God's voice that whispered soothingly on the wind; it was *His* gentle touch that warmed her shoulders, not the sun; *His* embrace that held her tight, not her own arms hugging herself as if for life.

And she would now give all that comfort up for a man.

Her precious few moments of solitude in the grove could be ruled away by a husband. He would be master of every aspect of her life, including her time. But at least this husband would not insist on replacing God's embrace with his own all-too-human and therefore repugnant arms.

Thinking of embraces, Margrete blushed to remember her dreams and rushed on to seek reassurance from the abbess. She found the statuesque and bright-eyed nun at her table, writing by the sunlight that streamed in through an open embrasure.

At her side stood the lanky, assiduous Brother Edmund. His bony shoulders were stooped over her as he observed her work. He kept his hands folded together at his chest, as if in a constant state of prayer.

When the door creaked open, Phillipa looked up and smiled with warmth at her favorite pupil. Edmund's look was more constrained.

"Ah, Margrete, you have been on my mind for days," Phillipa said as she rubbed her reddened eyes. "I was just writing about the struggle in a woman's soul between holiness and worldliness. Brother Edmund has been kind enough to offer to copy and illuminate my treatise on parchment for posterity."

A look of cordiality was exchanged between the nun and the monk.

"That is, if he can steal away the time from his duties to Abbot Gregory," Phillipa added on a teasing note.

"Mother Abbess," Edmund said with a smile of conspiracy, "the less Abbot Gregory knows of our efforts, the better."

When the monk looked furtively at Margrete, Phillipa said, "Do not worry. She is like a daughter to me. You can trust her to keep our secret."

Edmund was one of the few monks who did not shy

away from the abbess. Even some of her own nuns regarded her as an eccentric, if not a heretic, for her championing of women in the Roman Catholic hierarchy.

Every time Abbot Gregory reminded her that it was Eve who caused the downfall of mankind by seducing Adam with an apple, Abbess Phillipa pointed out that it was a woman, the Virgin Mary, who gave birth to Christ, the savior of mankind. When Gregory cited the sins of Mary Magdalene, Phillipa reminded him of Christ's forgiveness of Mary. When the abbot grumbled that a nun, even an abbess, should not be so presumptuous as to write down her thoughts on anything whatsoever, the abbess pointed to the theological contributions of the likes of Abbess Hildegard Von Bingen and the letters that Heloise wrote to Abelard. And if these gentle reminders failed to pacify the curmudgeonly abbot, the politic Phillipa expressed her gratitude that she enjoyed so much support from the Pope, with whom she maintained a correspondence. It was only the Pope's acknowledged respect for Abbess Phillipa de Claire, and the friendship she enjoyed with his likely successor, that kept her from being pilloried by the local clergy for what was perceived as her intellectual arrogance and lack of submissiveness.

It was this magnificent example of womanhood that had so skewed Margrete's hopes for her own life. Brother Edmund's presence here as Phillipa's scribe reminded Margrete of what her life might have been like had she been allowed to join the convent.

Phillipa settled back in her chair, pushing aside her quill. "So, my child," she said with a mother's warmth, "this is your wedding day."

Edmund picked up the papers she'd written, gave a short bow, and excused himself.

Margrete's first impulse, now that they were alone, was

to throw herself at the abbess's feet and beg for strength. But it was time she faced her own destiny with some of the dignity the abbess unfailingly showed.

"All is in order for the wedding, Mother Abbess. The feast has been prepared, and Sir Hugh continues to prove himself an honorable man. I am concerned, though, by dreams that I have been having."

Phillipa frowned as she tipped her chin up. "Oh?"

Margrete crossed her arms, compressed her lips, and felt her cheeks heat with a blush of shame. "I cannot describe them to you, for they are full of all that is sinful."

How could she tell this holy nun that in her dreams Hugh slowly, erotically stripped her of her garments, piece by piece, until she stood naked before him? How could she describe the other sensual vignettes, when he'd rocked over her on some carnal journey; how he'd held her in the aftermath, perspiration from their bodies mingling in an unholy alliance?

"You've dreamt about Hugh in a way that . . ." The abbess tapped her lips thoughtfully as she searched for the right words. "In a way that only lovers would understand?"

Margrete shot her a grateful look. Phillipa understood so much of the world, even though she had been in a convent since her girlhood. She understood all and condemned nothing. That was what made the abbess a spiritual woman, where other nuns were merely full of rote piety.

"Why would I dream of him in such a state when all I want is a spiritual marriage?"

"Perhaps that is not what you want."

"But it is!" Margrete whirled around and began to pace. "I swear it is."

Phillipa smiled without ridicule. "Then your dreams are

merely the work of the devil, making you doubt the devotion you hold in your heart.''

''Are they?''

''Yes, child, have faith that God will lead you down the right path. Follow your heart, not your head, and all will be as God deems it to be.''

''Thank you,'' Margrete replied with a sigh of relief. She hugged the abbess, tilting her head up to touch her cheek to the taller woman's, which was tightly wrapped in a white wimple. ''I knew you would explain everything. God bless you, Mother Abbess. Wish me God's speed.''

''I do, child, I do.''

Margrete gathered herself up and rushed out the door, eager to prepare herself for the day's wedding and festivities.

Abbess Phillipa watched her go with a reassuring smile. But when the door shut behind Margrete, the nun's smile faded, and her eyes clouded with worry. She wondered if she'd done right by suggesting a spiritual marriage to Margrete. For in taking on such a challenge, she would have not only her dreams to contend with, but the disapproval of the new bishop as well.

Eleven

ow that I have appeared as a character in this chronicle, I feel obligated to clarify a point for you pilgrims to this abbey, or to those who find a copy of the tale in far-flung lands. I did not accurately describe myself. I am not slight of frame or gaunt in appearance, as I indicated, but rather short and beefy and my chins number three. Moreover, at the time these events took place I was not aging and wise as I implied. I was, though a widower, relatively youthful and unusually lively for one who is cloistered. I am to this day frequently quick to laugh, though it is frowned upon at the abbey. I cannot say why I was inspired to exaggerate the details of my appearance, except that perhaps I lost myself in the act of creation. Or perhaps I can blame simple vanity. In any event, you are not interested in my shortcomings. Let us return to our story.

Now we come to the wedding. The ceremony at the church door was simple and without incident. The *wedding mass that followed and the subsequent feast appeared to any outsider as flawless events.*

Yet, you lover of faithful hearts, wipe the glass of your reflections clean and you will see grit upon your hands. There is dirt tarnishing every great occasion even though it seems hidden from our eyes. Sir Ranulf Blakely did not know of the blessed event, and so his plans churned on maliciously, gelling as the bright days of spring gave way to sullen hot summer, when greed and malcontent could rot and rule the day.

Ranulf Blakely did not know precisely when Hugh and Margrete were to be married, but he knew it would be soon. He'd followed their courtship from afar, through hearsay and gossip. Hugh had beaten Ranulf too many times on the lists for any of his victories outside the tilting yard to slip by unnoticed.

Granted, Ranulf had injured Hugh on the lists seven months ago, and still held Hugh's armor and charger to prove himself the better warrior. Yet that prize seemed hollow in the end. Ranulf could have beaten him to a bloody pulp and still Hugh would retain that air of perpetual guilelessness that made him so damnably attractive to women and so repulsive to ignoble men. Somehow Hugh de Greyhurst managed to be victorious even in defeat.

Hugh was a fundamentally good person. He was honest and forthright and incapable of deceit, even when he would be better off employing such tactics; even when a little deceit would benefit his good causes. In short, Hugh was all that Ranulf was not.

Ranulf had survived through cunning and intellect which, at the end of a weary day, were sorry companions. He'd bedded more than his share of women, but only by artful and sometimes wicked seduction, never for love. He'd never heard a woman say "I love you, Ranulf," except once at knifepoint in a rare moment of self-pity when he'd drunkenly demanded more than the slaking of his ornery lust. The girl had said it, but not very convincingly.

In truth, Ranulf did not know what love was, and did not even know that he did not know until he'd seen Hugh wooing Lady Alys. That had been years ago. But Ranulf still didn't understand the essence of love. And so when he heard about the simple goodness that was at the very heart of Hugh and Margrete's union, he wanted to destroy it utterly, because he could never have what they had together—respect and bedeviling good fortune.

To prove that Hugh was no better than he, Ranulf decided he would have what Hugh had. Literally, not figuratively. He would have Lady Margrete. And since the wedding was imminent, he would have to work quickly. He hastened to his cousin's castle the moment he heard that the bishop had finally taken up residence in his See.

"My lord bishop and most beloved cousin," Ranulf said as he strode across Bishop Jerome Blakely's solar. He knelt before his kin, waiting for permission to rise.

"Get up, Ranulf. I'm not the damned Pope." Lounging in his ornately carved chair, the fifty-year-old cleric surveyed his cousin's mud-splattered tunic and smiled. "You must have been in a hurry to see me. Either that or you rolled in a pig trough."

Ranulf looked down at his mud-encrusted boots and mustered a charming smile. "You will be happy for my haste when you learn what sped me to your castle." He looked enviously around the richly appointed solar—at the enormous canopy bed littered with richly embroidered silks, the brightly hued stained glass that filled the arched embrasures, the fresh-smelling rushes on the floor, and the tapestries colorfully adorning the walls. "This castle is fit for a king. I wonder what took you so long to take up residence."

"I just returned from Avignon." Jerome stroked his carefully manicured black and gray beard, allowing a prideful smile to adorn his distinguished face. "I'm glad you approve of my new abode. My predecessor had excellent taste."

"Indeed. It gives me great comfort. I'd feared that with your new position you might have finally become a man of faith. I was afraid you might start wearing hair shirts and give away all your worldly possessions. It's good to know the trappings of the office haven't sapped you of your inherited sense of greed."

Jerome barked out a laugh. "Good God, no!"

Ranulf sauntered to a table where a pitcher of mead sweated and gleamed in the torchlight. He helped himself, careless as the rich amber liquid splashed into a finely carved silver goblet. He brought the cold metal to his lips and drank the sweet liquor, like a bee sucking life from a flower. Yes, fate had definitely taken a turn for the better.

"Excellent taste in spirits as well, Cousin."

"You've come for more than a taste of my cellar, Ranulf. What brings you to my fine and enormous castle?" The bishop reached for a plate of figs and popped one in his mouth.

"I come to offer you a share of my prosperity."

"Save your fortune for yourself, Ranulf. As you can see, I have more than I need. And you, who have no property, will need to cling to your money."

Ranulf's grip tightened around the stem of his chalice. Cousin Jerome never missed an opportunity to point out the disparity in their fortunes. "Ah, but I'm feeling generous, Jerome. And I do have something unique to offer. All I ask in return is for your support."

"What are you after?"

"I want to marry a certain lady. Margrete Trewsbury."

Jerome frowned. "Haven't heard of her."

"She's the daughter of a local baron. Contrary to what I once thought, I hear she is beautiful beyond reckoning. And while she has no dowry to speak of, her property would become mine upon her father's death, which is imminent. What I need from you, Coz, is a little interference. She has already agreed to marry another knight."

"Are they betrothed?"

"From what I hear, and the marriage will doubtless happen any day. I hope I'm not too late. I've been waiting for your arrival at Burnham for days."

The bishop waved him off. "I cannot undermine a solemn oath of betrothal."

Ranulf stroked the jagged white scar trailing down his cheek. "You might if there is something in it for you."

Jerome frowned, studying the guts of a half-eaten fig as he chewed, but not jumping to the bait.

"And you might have cause to interfere if there is something odd about the union."

This intrigued Jerome sufficiently to give Ranulf his complete focus. "What do you mean, odd?"

"I'm not sure, but I hear that Sir Hugh is not acting like a happy man about to inherit a barony through his bride. There's something rotten at Longrove Barony." And Ranulf could smell rot like a hound could smell fox.

"What will *I* get out of this for my pains?" the bishop asked, eyeing his cousin with a cynical glint.

"You will have the satisfaction of knowing your own kin will not continue to embarrass you by ignoring the papal ban on jousting. If I am a landed lord, I will no longer want to risk my arse on the lists, will I?"

"There are easier ways to keep you off the lists."

At the hard tone in Jerome's voice, Ranulf's good humor

withered. Jerome Blakely would not be above detaining a man in his tower, even his own cousin.

"More importantly," Ranulf continued, pacing as he spoke, "if I am the lord of Longrove, I will relinquish all claims to Kilbury Hide, a rich stretch of land the See has been fighting over for generations."

"Hmmm," the bishop intoned thoughtfully. "Now that does interest me."

When the door creaked open, he waved in a sallow and gaunt priest dressed in black. "Come in, Father Cedrick. Your timing couldn't be better. What do you know of the Lord of Longrove and his daughter, er . . . ?"

"Margrete Trewsbury," Ranulf offered when Jerome faltered.

"This is my steward," the bishop explained. "He served Bishop Eustace until his death a few months ago. Father Cedrick, this is my cousin, Sir Ranulf Blakely."

The pious-looking priest gave Ranulf a brief, almost disdainful nod, then turned to Jerome. "My lord, you have a visitor."

"It can wait. First tell me about Longrove Barony."

Father Cedrick folded his hands together and raised his brows. "It is a modest barony, but one rich in land. Unfortunately it is poorly run by the current baron. He was on good terms with Bishop Eustace, until fourteen years ago when his wife was murdered. Lord Giles then became reclusive and cut off contact with the bishop and everyone else, it seemed."

"Curious," Jerome said, eyeing Ranulf, whose eyes kindled with reflected intrigue.

"And of course there is the D'Arbereau treasure."

Ranulf's head snapped in the steward's direction. "A treasure, did you say?"

The priest's placid eyes narrowed, as if he'd read in a moment every nefarious thought Ranulf had ever had. "Indeed. It belonged to the late Lady Rosamunde. It was her dowry, which was brought over by one of her Norman ancestors who came with William the Conqueror to this island. It is a cask of jewels, pearls, and gold said to be beyond value."

"Then her daughter, Lady Margrete, can afford a dowry after all," Ranulf snarled. "The conniving little vixen. Apparently Sir Hugh doesn't know he's being taken."

"It is a mystery why the baron hasn't used his wife's fortune to shore up his decrepit barony," the priest said. "Perhaps Lady Margrete has inherited her father's parsimony."

"What of the mother?" Jerome said, now sitting at the edge of his seat.

The priest grimaced. "That's a sad story. Lady Rosamunde was killed when the first earl of Ludham attacked Longrove in a raid. As a matter of fact, Lord Henry died trying to steal the D'Arbereau treasure. Though Lord Giles had kept the dowry secret, Ludham's spies managed to find out about it and, supported by the Prince of Wales, he attacked."

"Did he get his hands on the treasure?" Ranulf said.

"Momentarily. Lord Henry stumbled and fell on his own dagger trying to drag the cask of jewels to his horse. It was said that the D'Arbereau treasure comes with a curse—only the pure of heart can possess it without suffering some bloody peril."

Ranulf stroked his chin. "The pure of heart? What in God's name does that mean?"

"You wouldn't know, would you?" the priest said, his dour lips parting in an ironic half-grin. "No one since Lord Henry has put the curse to the test. Lord Giles often said to Bishop Eustace that riches can rob the young of ambition. He didn't want his daughter to learn of her inheritance until she came of age."

"Well, she surely knows about it now," Ranulf said.

"Too bad this Lady Margrete is already promised to another, eh?" Jerome said tauntingly.

Ranulf smiled, for he knew then that his cousin would help him.

"As I said earlier, my lord bishop, a visitor has arrived. A Prior Anselm from Treyvaux Abbey." When the bishop seemed unmoved, the priest added, "As you know, the abbey sits next to Longrove Barony. The prior might have more to report than I."

The bishop's face brightened. "In that case, send him in."

Moments later, the prior entered and knelt before Jerome with effusive greetings. The pale monk had keen, busy eyes, thick shoulders and an odd-shaped skull, unflatteringly exposed by the bald circle on the top of his head.

"My lord bishop, I thank you for seeing me so quickly. May we speak in private?"

His eyes darted toward Ranulf and Father Cedrick.

"Your secrets are safe with my friends," Bishop Jerome reassured him.

Anselm swallowed, his throat bobbing with the effort. "I come to tell you of all manner of mischief at Treyvaux Abbey. The fault, you see, lies with Abbess Phillipa de Claire."

"She is a respected theologian, is she not?"

Anselm's bluish lips curled with irony. "I suppose, my lord bishop, but she teaches her nuns to think independently and everyone knows a thinking woman is evil unleashed. Just the other day I heard her discussing with the abbot the marriage of Lady Margrete Trewsbury. It is not a woman's place to question the authority of a man, even if she is an abbess."

"What did you say about Lady Margrete?" Ranulf stepped forward, towering over the prior.

Anselm looked up nervously at Ranulf. "I don't remember all the details."

"Think!" Ranulf barked. "It's important."

Anselm stopped abruptly, taken off guard. This interview clearly was not going as he had planned. "Well, the abbot can speak for himself. But there is some sort of vow the lady wishes to make."

"What kind of vow?" Ranulf pressed.

"I don't know."

"God!" Ranulf cursed, whirling around and slamming his goblet on the serving table.

Jerome waved him silent. "In due time, Coz. All in due time."

"Something about chastity, I believe," Anselm added.

"Chastity?" Ranulf frowned at him as if he'd gone mad. "But she's going to be married any day."

"Today, in fact," Anselm said.

"*What?*" Ranulf's svelte body went as rigid as an arrow.

"Lady Margrete and Sir Hugh are marrying today."

"God curse them!" Ranulf cried out.

"Gently, Ranulf. Gently," Jerome said. His frown of contemplation was replaced by curiosity. "Prior Anselm, does the abbot know you are here today?"

His face drained further of color. "No, my lord bishop. He's attending the wedding."

"And so you thought to sneak out when the abbot wouldn't notice your absence."

Prior Anselm swallowed. His throat, an awkward pipe, clicked loudly. "Abbot Gregory is old. He is too weak to travel this far, but I am sure he would complain of the abbess if he could. It is not meet that an abbess should have higher acclaim than the abbot. She is teaching the sisters blasphemy. She—''

"Thank you, Prior Anselm." The bishop's decisive voice cut him to the quick.

Anselm looked to one, then the other. "You won't tell Abbot Gregory of my journey here? I came only to wish you well, and to supervise the purchase of cloth from East-ham Corner."

"Do not worry," the bishop said with a sugary smile. "I appreciate your concern for the souls of the sisters at Treyvaux."

The prior frowned, as if regretting his decision to come, then bowed and made a hasty exit. When he was gone, Jerome turned to Father Cedrick.

"Tell the abbot his sheep are in disarray. And if he can't rein them in, changes will be made at the abbey."

"The abbot does not answer to the bishop of Burnham," the steward replied, placing truth before tact, as does one who has grown comfortable with power.

"He will from now on," Jerome said, chilling the air with his frosty tones. "The Benedictines have their own rule, but I have rules as well. Things are going to change in this bishopric, I assure you."

When Father Cedrick remained where he stood, not heeding the implied dismissal, Bishop Jerome shot him a cutting look. "What is it, Father? Are you questioning my authority?"

Cedrick blinked thoughtfully. "My lord, I'm contem-plating what the prior said about the abbess. Phillipa de Claire is a great thinker and respected by the Pope. She is more intelligent than the abbot by far. Bishop Eustace re-spected her opinions."

Jerome sighed and gave him a scathing look. "But Bishop Eustace is dead, isn't he?"

Cedrick nodded with a bow. "Most certainly, my lord."

When the priest finally showed the good sense to exit, Jerome watched him leave, an unconscious sneer raising his upper lip. "It's time to put my own house in order, I see." He turned to Ranulf. "Very well, Cousin, you just might get your wish after all. Find out what sort of vow this lady has made, and if it's what I think it is, I will indeed interfere with this marriage."

"It's too late!" Ranulf shouted, throwing his empty goblet across the room like a handsome, overgrown child.

"Don't be too sure. If Lady Margrete intends to have a spiritual marriage, which is what it sounds like, the union will not be consummated. Find out which priest is conducting the ceremony and send him to me. There just may be a way for you to wed Lady Margrete yet."

Ranulf's fury began to fade and a wild exhilaration took its place. "Oh, Coz, I knew I could count on you."

"Go to Longrove Barony now and find out if the marriage is going to be consummated."

Ranulf frowned. "You have a lot of faith in me."

"You have your ways of finding out these sorts of things. If it turns out you can claim Margrete yourself, you will get to keep a third of the D'Arbereau treasure."

"And what of the other two-thirds?" Ranulf asked belligerently.

"It all goes to God, my son." Jerome gave him a beatific smile. "It all goes to God."

Ranulf smirked, admiring his cunning. "You'll never change, will you, Jerome?"

"Once a Blakely, always a Blakely."

"But enough of this cheery conversation," Ranulf said, striding for the door. "I have a wedding feast to ruin. Pray God I'm not too late for that."

"Pray God indeed," the bishop said, making the sign of the cross.

Twelve

T hat night Hugh worked his way through the festive crowd in the great hall, feeling like a king. More than a few noblemen—local barons and landed knights—slapped him on the back, congratulating him on his marriage with intimate nods and murmurs of approval, not only as if he was their equal—which he was at last— but as if he always had been. It was remarkable how much the possession of property changed the way others viewed and judged a man.

He thought he also detected a general sense of relief, as if everyone was aware of but had never openly acknowl- edged Lord Giles's incapacities.

Several merchants from the village sidled up to Hugh with deferential expressions, some even addressing him as Lord Hugh, or the new baron of Longrove. He squirmed at these courtesies, hoping Lord Giles did not overhear them. But inwardly his heart swelled with pride at the acknowl- edgments.

The only time he did not feel nearly giddy with joy was

whenever he spotted his wife amidst the milling guests. *His wife*. Lord, how strange those words sounded. Lady Margrete was his bride!

She smiled with charm and effervescent beauty as she greeted each and every guest. For the first time since he'd met her, Margrete's face was void of the lines of worry that heretofore had marked her strong yet delicate features.

When she laughed, her straight and lovely teeth flashed in the torchlight, and her blue eyes danced like sprites splashing in water. She was so clean! So graceful. The opposite of Hugh, who was naught but a rough-hewn warrior.

When she drank, she tipped up her silver goblet with graceful fingers, sipping in small measures, whereas he had to remind himself not to bend the metal in his massive hands and not to swallow the contents in one gulp. When she laughed, her delicate hands came to her mouth, and a rich peal of laughter spilled over her honeyed lips despite her modesty. And when she danced, as she did presently, she was a joy to behold.

But he should not even be noticing these details, much less cataloguing them, considering the unusual restrictions on his marriage. And that was why he hated to look at her, for he was coveting that which he could never have. She would never be his wife in any real sense. This night was a mockery—but one, he had to admit, that served a purpose. And for that, he was grateful.

"There he is! The doting bridegroom, so besotted he cannot take his eyes off his wife!"

He heard snickering laughter from afar, and turned to see his old cohorts gathered around the hearth with their customary drinking horns in hand.

"What have we here?" Hugh called out, relishing his new role as bounteous host as he strolled through the crowd. "Who invited the likes of you?"

"Your lady wife," said Keath, chortling merrily. "You must not have told her what a lot we are."

"I'm sure I did," Hugh said, joining the brawny crowd of knights errant—Keath and the other two Davids and their squires. The only one missing was Ranulf. Hugh wasn't sure if he was relieved or worried. Sometimes it was best to keep enemies close at hand.

"I warned my wife about you characters," Hugh said. "But she must not have listened to me."

"Ish the cursh of a wife," Connard said, weaving in place to keep his balance.

Hugh laughed. "Drunk as usual, eh, Connard? I can honestly say I've missed you knaves."

Keath said, "You'd have missed us altogether, but we were passing this way. Lord Buckhurst cried a tournament set for next week and we were passing through."

"Where's Ranulf?" Hugh said as nonchalantly as possible.

"Not with us, though I thought I saw him somewhere in the great hall."

Hugh's gaze darted over the heads of those milling about and dancing. A lively tune from the musicians did nothing to ease his niggling concern. "Well, I'm sure I'll see him if he's here."

"Eh, not so fast, lad," Shrewsbury cried out when a servitor passed by with two pitchers of ale in hand. He grabbed one and sloppily refilled Hugh's nearly empty tankard.

"Easy," Keath said, "the groom has a great performance yet tonight. A very *large* performance. You'll not want to quench his ardor before he *joins* his lady."

The others laughed.

"I'll drink hish share." Connard dropped to his knees

and opened his jaw. Shrewsbury obliged him and began to pour directly into his gaping mouth.

"You're wasting good ale!" cried Keath when it began to spill onto the rose petals and rushes strewn on the floor.

"Never a waste as long as it goes into one of our bellies," cried Shrewsbury, eyes dancing with delight at his own antics.

The others broke into a new round of laughter and began to clap in unison, encouraging Connard's gluttony, but Hugh did not join in. He glanced around the bustling great hall again, unable to shake the sense that the night would not be complete until Sir Ranulf Blakely made himself known.

Margrete whirled away from the dancing area when the minstrel's wild song came to an end. As the other dancers burst into exuberant applause, she sought a moment of quiet on the other side of the arches.

She'd started dancing earlier, first with Hugh, then her father and, reluctantly, Sir William. When Hugh had excused himself to attend to guests, the minstrel's songs turned bawdy and fast, until in the end what began as a circumspect dance ended in a free-form melee of skipping feet and bandied arms. Margrete had gone from partner to lively partner, hair flying, her soft gold gown sailing behind her, laughing until she had no more breath to give. She'd never danced so hard or freely in her life. It was as if she knew on some instinctive level that this was the end of her former life, and so she wanted to celebrate all that had come before. Also, since some part of her was naive enough to think the best was yet to come, she wanted to rejoice over what was to be.

And now she was breathless. She headed down the corridor that bordered the hall in the hopes of catching some fresh air outside. But before she reached the door, she caught sight of a darkly clad figure borne in shadows. He lolled against one of the archways that opened to the great hall.

"What a stunning sight," he said as she slowed her approach.

"Greetings, my lord," she said cautiously, her eyes drawn to the jagged scar on his white cheek. "You are . . . ?"

"Sir Ranulf Blakely."

He stared a moment too long, trying to quell his frustration. God's teeth, had he ever seen such a beautiful woman? And she belonged to Greyhurst! That ignorant bear. He attracted women who did not even know his stupidity, who were seemingly drawn to it for reasons Ranulf could not fathom.

When she self-consciously straightened the pleats in her gown, he saw the dazzling grace of her hands. Everything about her was smooth and perfect. He could not help noticing how snugly she fit into her deep purple undertunic and her cloth-of-gold overtunic; how tightly it gathered under her breasts and then billowed out in regal folds. Her flaxen hair was crowned with a circle of entwined purple and gold velvets.

"What a stunning sight," Ranulf said, for once meaning every word he said. "You must be the bride."

"Yes, and you must be an acquaintance of my husband's."

"Indeed, I am. I owe much to Greyhurst. He once introduced me to a fair damsel I very nearly married."

"Very nearly?"

The stranger sprang from the wall with the ease of a jongleur and came to her side, so close his hot breath bathed her neck. "She died before the marriage could take place."

"I'm so sorry." Margrete took a step back, searching his

darkly handsome face for sorrow and finding none.

"Yes, my life has been marked by one tragedy after another. What good fortune Sir Hugh has been blessed with. Would that I were so lucky. You're the fairest maiden in all the king's realm."

He took her hand and drew it to his lips for a courtly kiss.

She blushed. "Your flattery is undeserved."

"My flattery is inadequate."

"Your flattery just might get you killed." Hugh's deep voice was a hard growl coming from behind.

Turning, Margrete was taken aback by the fury that blazed in her husband's eyes. "My lord, you should welcome your old friend."

"Oh, I welcome him. Now he can see for himself what a fool I was to come here in search of a wife and how I'm suffering as the lord of a manor. Just as he predicted."

"No, no, you deserve it all," Ranulf said with good grace, then added with a mirthless smile, "and you should have it. You'll need a place to rest your old and weary body. Are you still crippled, Greyhurst?"

Hugh flushed, his scalp prickling with fury. When he took a threatening step forward, Margrete grabbed his arm.

"Gently, my lord. This is a night for merriment."

Hugh swallowed with difficulty and forced a thin smile. "Very well."

"I'll leave the blushing bride and drooling groom," Ranulf said, "but not before I hand over a missive of goodwill which my cousin the bishop of Burnham has sent to the baron of Longrove."

"The bishop is your cousin?" Margrete said, her mood brightening. "Did you hear that, Hugh?"

"Oh, I've heard it, believe me. Who hasn't?"

"That's wonderful!" Margrete looked at Ranulf with

new appreciation. "Why, perhaps we can meet with him. If you could talk to him and tell him that Hugh and I have a grave matter to discuss with him. We want to take vows of—"

"Margrete!" Hugh's loud voice cut her short.

She blinked in surprise. "What is it, my lord?"

"We can discuss that with the bishop in private."

"What is this about a vow?" Ranulf asked, all innocence.

"Nothing," Hugh pronounced.

Ranulf eyed him speculatively, then shrugged. "Very well, then, here is my cousin's message." He pulled from his tunic a small scrolled parchment. Unwinding it, he handed it to Hugh with a smirk on his face. "Go ahead, my lord, read it so your bride can hear as well."

Hugh hesitated, glowering at the parchment. Then he grabbed it and stared, scanning the words, but there was no recognition in his face. And in the long heartbeats that followed, when sweat sprang on his brow and he swallowed as hard and as loud as humanly possible, Margrete knew. He couldn't read.

"I'll take that, my lord." She gently took the parchment from Hugh's massive hands. When their gazes brushed in the transfer, hers was warm and his was grateful. She turned to Ranulf with a forced smile. "It was a pleasure to meet you, Sir Ranulf. Please join the others. Meanwhile, I will give my father this important message."

She sailed off, deftly ending the discussion. Both men watched after her. Ranulf whistled low.

"Enchanting," he said, turning to Hugh as both men watched her round the corner. "So what is it about this baron of Longrove? Quite the recluse, is he?"

Hugh crossed his arms and returned his focus to his enemy. "You might put it that way."

"He wants to keep his treasure close at hand, is that it?"

"His treasure?" Hugh frowned. "You mean Margrete?"

Ranulf's eyes darted back and forth between his. "Is that what I mean?"

"What other treasure could you be referring to? I have no illusions of wealth and power, Ranulf. I'm just grateful for what I have. I didn't give a damn what she looked like, and she turned out to be the most beautiful woman I have ever seen. You all mocked me then. I see you've changed your tune."

"The bed will be rocking tonight, I avow," Ranulf said.

Hugh chafed at the crude implication, the sneer in Ranulf's voice, and sadly the irony that nothing could be further than the truth. He would not tell his ex-compatriot that his would be a chaste marriage. He'd be the butt of too many jests to count. Oddly, Hugh did not feel particularly lacking in this moment. He could only think about how lucky he was to be leaving this crowd behind.

Later, when only the hardiest of guests still remained, Margrete stood numbly in the middle of her father's solar, knowing what was supposed to happen next, unsure of which way to turn. A fire crackled and sizzled at the hearth, shooing away the chill of the early spring night. She said little as Edith, her only lady-in-waiting, prattled and fussed, undressing her between bursts of infectious laughter.

"Oh, my lady, you were the loveliest bride I've ever seen!"

"Thank you, Edith," Margrete said, touched by her gushing sincerity.

She did not point out that Edith was scarcely the best judge of beauty. Her eyes had been crossed since childhood. The strawberry-blond maiden was the daughter of a simple knight who had scraped together the money to buy her a few pretty gowns to serve at Longrove Barony. Longing for marriage herself, Edith was a hopeless romantic who fell in love with every man in sight, including, Margrete suspected, Hugh's squire.

Margrete had seen Edith staring at Brian in the crowd tonight, moon-eyed as well as cross-eyed. Margrete only hoped that Brian would not break her heart. He was an exceptionally handsome and ambitious lad, and Margrete doubted he would have enough depth to see beyond Edith's visual impediment to appreciate her dear, sweet essence.

"And Sir Hugh was a regular Lancelot," Edith added dreamily.

"He is just a man with all the faults that men are wont to have. Now where is my gown? I want to be ready for bed before Sir Hugh arrives."

"Just a moment, my lady, let me light a torch."

Margrete looked up just in time to see her lady-in-waiting touching a candle to the curtain next to a wall sconce. Flames caught in the material and licked upward.

"Edith! No!" Margrete cried out, dashing to her side. "You'll burn the castle down!"

Margrete tamped out the flames with the gown she was to wear to bed. She looked down at the blackened garment and sighed.

"Is it ruined?" Edith fingered the fine white linen, feeling for soot. She couldn't quite see the damage.

"I'm afraid so." Her voice was laced with frustration.

"Oh, my lady, I'm sorry! Normally I compensate for my . . . my poor sight. But I'm so . . . excited tonight."

"There, there, not to worry." Margrete smiled gently, then took control of the candle. "Don't worry about lighting a torch. The less Sir Hugh sees tonight the better. The firelight will do. And I have another gown in that trunk there."

Edith hurried to the trunk, trying to make up for lost time. She had just tugged the gown over Margrete's head when they heard the approach of stomping feet, shouts of male voices, and guttural laughter.

Edith gripped her arm. "They're coming, my lady! The men are bringing Sir Hugh to your bed. You'd best get in quickly."

"Heaven forebear!" Margrete muttered. She'd never even thought to prepare for this ritual. Never felt the need. Hearing the pounding on the door, she jumped, nearly through the roof, it seemed, then scrambled into bed, pulling the covers to her chest. Just then the door flew open and a mass of bodies singing a ribald song squeezed through the doorway with Hugh sprawled on their shoulders.

"Here he is, Lady Margrete," David Shrewsbury said. "Your stud horse."

Everyone guffawed, save for Hugh. He stood alone, looking uncomfortable. And she suddenly realized how humiliated he would be if the others learned that he would not be consummating his marriage. No wonder he had been so quick to silence her in Ranulf's presence.

She decided in that moment that if she would give Hugh nothing else, she would spare him embarrassment on this night. So when the laughter died, replaced by awkward silence, Margrete reached out to him, mustering what she hoped would be a seductive wink.

"Come, my lord," her naturally sultry voice growing husky, "your brood mare is waiting."

His eyes shot to hers in disbelief.

"There's a good wife," he said, reaching out and taking her hand.

He sat on the edge of the bed and warmth kindled between them, and something more precious that she couldn't quite name. Familiarity? No, something greater than that. Trust?

She was merrily imprisoned in his gaze, shyly pleasuring at the touch of his hand, oblivious to the jests and bawdy repartee that flowed around them, until she felt someone else staring at her almost as intensely as Hugh. She turned to identify the burrowing eyes and found Sir Ranulf, apart from the others, arms crossed, leaning against the wall, just waiting. But for what? He wanted something from her. He wanted to know more about her than a man should want to know. And he knew something about her that he would use against her. But what? And why?

Eventually Edith shooed everyone out and shut the door after giving Margrete a none-too-subtle farewell wink.

Hugh watched the latch lift and fall back into place with something akin to dread. As the click of metal rose in the silence, he stared at the door, not sure what to do next. There was no one to distract them any longer—no wedding plans to occupy them, no servants to bustle about. No more excuses to keep them apart. The night was theirs for the taking. The fact that they would not take it, that they would lay still while other lovers thrashed in the darkness, that they would keep awkward distance while intimacy blossomed for other newlyweds in other bed chambers, left Hugh feeling empty.

"Well, that's that," Margrete said with an unmistakable quiver in her voice.

Hearing it, knowing she was as much at a loss as he, Hugh turned and swallowed his trepidation. "So we are married."

"Indeed." She looked down at her hands, which were clutched together in a white-knuckled grip.

"Thank you for . . . pretending in front of the others."

A blush stained her cheeks. "I did not want to embarrass

you. I know how knights prize their conquests.''

Hugh chuckled morosely. ''So what do we tell them on the morrow? Will we pretend evermore? Shall I cut my arm and let the blood spill on your sheets so that I can pretend that I took your virginity?''

She frowned. ''That would be dishonest.''

''Yes, but it would spare me a cartload of mockery.''

''You must be strong.''

''Is that all it will take to withstand the judgement of others?'' He gave her a sardonic smile that was also laced with appreciation. ''Sometimes I do wish I had your faith, lady.''

''My lord, I hope that one day you, too, will see the benefits of a celibate marriage, that your spirit will grow stronger in faith. But until then you must be content with more immediate rewards. This barony will soon be yours. Think what good you might accomplish as lord of a barony. I can think of no other man I'd rather have at my side.''

The distance between them seemed to vanish. Here was an ally like none he'd ever had. A sense of gratitude settled over him so intensely that he shivered. He moistened his lips and gazed squarely into her eyes.

''Very well. I am content. For now. Where shall I sleep?''

''The great hall will be filled with guests staying the night. Father is sleeping there as well. He insisted on giving us his chamber. You'll have to stay here tonight. Tomorrow we can move to the manor and find separate rooms.''

''Thank you,'' Hugh said when the door clicked shut. ''Twice tonight you have protected me from the judgment of others.''

''It does not matter what others think of our marriage,'' she said. ''Only God's opinion matters.''

At the mention of God, he blinked hard and looked down. "I will find another place to sleep."

"There is no other place."

He raked her with a skeptical gaze and ran one broad palm over the loose tangle of his hair. Rising, he tugged down on his floor-length tunic and went to the embrasure, staring sullenly at the moon.

"I suppose I should sleep on the floor."

"No, that's not necessary. I would not be so selfish. We can share the bed, but . . ."

"Keep my clothes on?"

When he turned her head his way, his rugged profile outlined by moonlight, a hot wave washed over her. Dare they sleep in the same bed? Could she trust him that much? Could she trust herself?

He returned to the bed and sank down wearily. "What a wonderful feast."

He stretched out beside her and she stiffened, unused to the feel of another beside her. He was so *big*—long legs and thick arms, a chest that rose high. A great mass of masculinity. What would it feel like to be held by that strength?

Pushing aside these thoughts, she snuffed out the candle by the bed and watched the dance of firelight on the ceiling.

"Do you want me to bank the fire?" he said.

"No, I want to see the shadows playing. They amuse me."

It was a lie. She didn't want to see anything, most especially not him. But more than that, she didn't want the darkness to rule them. Some brides, she supposed, were eager to snuff out the light, to hide their bodies out of modesty. But Margrete feared the darkness. She didn't want to know what might happen if they couldn't see each other, if in the darkness she forgot herself, if she had dreams again. Lord, what if she did something foolish—reach out to him, kiss him, touch him? What if she lost control?

If she did, it would be the devil's work. But who would have thought the devil capable of tempting a maiden with something so divine?

Thirteen

t dawn, Hugh woke to the comforting sounds of horses snorting and whinnying in the stable, a cock crowing, and the wind fluttering gently through the narrow, arched window cut deep into the thick castle wall.

He woke, but did not stir, for when he rolled over, he saw Margrete kneeling before the window. Dressed for the day, she was unaware of him, lost in her world of prayer.

Lying on his side, pretending to be asleep, he had a perfect view of her profile. She was so utterly feminine. The first rays of dawn splashed yellow on her pink complexion. At the insistence of the breeze, her golden hair flowed over her shoulders like clouds in a free fall—full and wavy, womanly and disorderly. Her flawless brows were gathered in consternation, her eyes shut tight. She pressed her moving lips to her folded hands as she silently mouthed the words of some private prayer.

She was a saint. A damned saint. How could he ever think of despoiling her? It would be like luring an angel from heaven for his own pleasure, only to leave her to live out the rest of her days in a world too clumsy and soiled for her seraphic soul.

But what was she praying about? Was she asking God to conspire some accidental death for this new husband she clearly did not want? No, Hugh thought, greatly comforted by his own conclusion, she needed him even if she would never want him physically.

Was she praying in the way that holy people prayed—instinctively—the way that Hugh had never understood? He'd been a warrior who never felt much kinship to God, and though most knights prayed as fervently as priests on the eve of a battle, Hugh was never so hypocritical. If God did not already know that Hugh regretted his sins and wanted to survive to an old age, then He wasn't as great a God as the priests claimed. Besides, a man doesn't want to do often that which he doesn't do well. And Hugh had never prayed well, always stumbling over words that made no sense, that seemed designed to forestall every dastardly eventuality.

Watching Margrete excel at it, he felt a hot river of emotion swell around his heart, making him ache in a part of his body he'd thought long dead; in the only place he'd thought himself incapable of further injury—his heart. He didn't need a woman, merely wanted to use her, or so he'd thought. Now his hurting chest told him otherwise. He wanted her. He wanted to feel her skin smooth over his own. He wanted her to take his wildness and break him. To tame his hunger.

She turned to him then, as if hearing his thoughts. They blinked in unison.

"How long have you been awake?"

"Not long," he lied. He propped himself up on an elbow. "Actually, for a while."

She nodded, getting used to the notion of being watched. "I hope you slept well . . . husband."

"I did . . . wife." He sat up, then felt the sudden onset of a headache. "Though I drank too much ale, methinks."

She smiled. "I doubt that you are alone." She rose to her feet and glanced out the window at the men who were mounting up for an early departure. "Your friends indulged in a great quantity as well."

"My friends," Hugh said ironically. "Fine description."

"Some of them are already leaving."

"They travel well with pounding headaches and queasy guts."

She blinked and looked at him anew. How rough his life must have been. "Are you happy to be staying, my lord?"

He blinked hard. "Yes. I am content to stay."

"Good. I will bid our guests farewell."

When she started for the door, he called out, "My lady . . . my wife." She looked over her shoulder. "I should like to see your . . . our . . . barony today."

"I'll have horses saddled. I'll show you myself. You'll need to see every nook and cranny from here to the outskirts. You are lord and master now."

"Do you mean that, Lady Margrete? Methinks you enjoyed being chatelaine of this barony. How can you so easily give up the reins?"

She looked down at her folded hands and the heaviness returned to her brow. "It is God's command." She smiled wanly. "You are now my lord and keeper. I must do as you command."

In all matters save one, he thought with irony. He frowned and nodded, but when she was out of the chamber, he broke into a broad grin. An entire day with the Lady Margrete. Perhaps there was a God after all.

• • •

After Hugh dressed and broke his fast with a piece of bread and ale, he found Margrete waiting for him at the stables. She stood by the mare she would ride, feeding it a carrot. He was so delighted to be joining his wife for a tour of his barony that he forgot all past misfortunes and strode toward her with an unabashed smile. That is, until he saw her frowning at his legs.

"How long have you been injured?" she said quietly when he came to her side.

He patted the neck of her black mare. "You just noticed my . . . weakness?"

"It is no weakness to suffer from an honest injury."

Hugh stroked the horse's soft muzzle. "I've had problems with this leg for too many years to count. I exacerbated the injury seven months ago during a joust." He looked down at her earnest face. "But you're a little late noticing. You can't back out of the marriage now."

"I did notice before and I didn't care," she said archly. "Only now did I wonder how much it pains you, that is all."

"Not much. Less so every day that I stay away from the lists."

She sighed with relief and her sweet lips parted in a smile. "Good. I don't want you to suffer."

He breathed easier and smiled in return.

"We'll be riding with Peter," she said, changing the subject. "You haven't met him yet. I sent him to London to pay the king scutage and overdue taxes. He returned late last night. Though he is of humble birth and uneducated, I couldn't do without him. Peter is a loyal servant who acts as porter, chandler, constable, and de facto steward. But I call him my castellan."

Hugh's cheeks dimpled with a winning smile. "Sounds like a man I should get to know."

Moments later the castellan exited the stable, marching squarely on short, muscular legs. He was a few years older than Hugh, but seemed somehow ageless with his wiry crop of brown hair and unwrinkled face.

"Peter," Margrete said after making introductions, "show your new lord his barony, won't you?"

"With pleasure, my lady."

They rode at a fair pace throughout the hundreds of acres that comprised Longrove Barony. Peter first took them to the manor house not far down the road, which servants were busily cleaning and airing out for the newlyweds' imminent arrival. The square stone house boasted a tower and a great hall. Though sturdy and timeless, it had been empty for some time and bore all the signs of neglect—overgrown weeds, dust, and cobwebs.

Margrete blinked at the building with some trepidation. So this would be her new home. It seemed a demotion after running Longrove Castle for so long. But marriage necessitated change. She could no longer live by her own wits and will. Hugh was in charge now, a role he readily assumed.

"Margrete, I would have thought the manor house ready by now," he said, scarcely masking his disappointment.

"It has been long neglected, my lord," she replied.

"Too long," he said, still gazing at the house, unaware of her exasperated, sidelong glance. "I want it ready by tonight."

It had been years since she'd taken orders, and it would take some getting used to. Peter seemed to sense her irritation and came to her rescue.

"The manor will be ready tonight, my lord," he said. "It won't be perfect, but there will be a clean place to sleep."

Hugh nodded and a smile of satisfaction reached his eyes

as he regarded Peter with approval. "See to it."

Margrete realized in that moment how strong a lord Hugh would be. For the rest of their tour she saw everything from his point of view. She looked at familiar sights which had heretofore been acceptable and found them wanting. A strong barony was filled with tenants—villeins and freemen, knights and burghers. But for all her efforts, Longrove was scarcely peopled. Too many fields were fallow; too many huts and houses abandoned. Why had she been so complacent? Was it merely because she had been overwhelmed by her duties? Or had her judgment been lacking, too?

Moving onward, they rode along the Tilmon River, where a mill produced grain for bread. There was also a ferry to transport paying customers. Hugh was heartened to see the potential to make money, though the ferry obviously hadn't been used in some time. Tall grass choked the footpath to its dock, and one corner of the boat had taken in water.

"Someone should clear this pathway," he said, motioning casually to the weeds. "Then we can get close enough to assess the damage to the dock. It's a pity to see such ruin."

Margrete bit her lower lip, saying nothing. He was right, of course. The ferry should be in service. It would be a valuable source of revenue. Why hadn't she seen to its repair? She'd been meaning to for some time.

"Yes, my lord," Peter said. "I'll have it done tomorrow."

Hugh narrowed his gaze on the castellan. "I speak and it is done. Is that what it means to be a lord?"

Curiosity and humor brightened Peter's unremarkable face. "Yes, my lord, in large part that is exactly what being a lord entails."

Hugh let out a soft rumble of laughter. "Then I shall enjoy being the baron of Longrove very much indeed."

"That doesn't mean your orders will be easily or enjoyably carried out with our meager resources," Margrete added quietly as she shifted uncomfortably on her saddle.

"No," Hugh replied, giving her an assessing and faintly challenging glance. "But my orders will be carried out one way or the other. This ferry will be very useful. Let me know when the weeds are gone, Peter."

"Yes, my lord."

Hugh tugged his reins and nudged his horse's belly with his spurs and was soon cantering away. After exchanging glances, Peter and Margrete followed, soon catching up.

They rode quickly through Longrove Village, past the village church and a few merchant stands and huts, then onto the vast farm acreage that stretched as far as the eye could see.

It wasn't until they galloped over acres and acres of fallow fields, inhaling too much dust and wasting chaff, that Hugh reined in his mount. The others followed suit. Margrete watched him carefully, knowing what he was thinking.

He frowned soberly at the neglected furrows of earth beneath his horse's hooves, and licked dust from his lips, shaking his head. His impatient steed pranced in a circle, tossing his head up and down, chomping on his bit.

"Steady," Hugh said, patting the horse's flanks. Then he turned to Margrete. "Why isn't this land being planted?"

Bubbling anger boiled over and she glared at him. "Where should I begin? You want an easy answer, but there are no easy answers at Longrove Barony."

"Not enough villeins or freemen to do it, my lord," Peter jumped in, protecting his mistress as usual. "Lady Margrete has been doing the best she can."

Margrete blinked at the hard truth, embarrassed that her record should be found so wanting under close scrutiny. She tossed her head as nonchalantly as possible in the breeze, staring intently at the stretch of woven fields, as if the pastoral scene held some secret for her to discern. Though she wasn't looking at Hugh, she could feel his frustration. How could anyone let a barony become so desperate and run-down, she imagined him asking.

"I've tried," she said, answering his unspoken accusations, her voice riddled with guilt. "All I can say, Hugh, is that I've tried to keep this barony together." She turned to him with a sullen expression. "Do you know how hard it is to keep vassals from knowing that their lord is witless? To make decisions without letting them know a woman is doing it? Outwardly, it seemed all was well and in order. But year after year little things chipped away at the heart of this barony."

"Margrete, I do not fault you—" Hugh said.

"No," she replied, interrupting. "I want you to understand what it's been like. Five years ago—and this is merely one example—five years ago a marauding band of mercenaries tore through this area, pillaging at will. Our vassals looked to my father for protection, but he could not give it. The one area in which I admit I have failed miserably was in recruiting strong knights to serve this barony, to protect our vassals and to answer the king's summons. But I could not bear to deal with these warriors who seemed to be so thirsty for blood. And even if I could have recruited them, any healthy knight in his right mind would not want to answer to a woman.

"Oh, I was clever about covering for this peculiar lacking. Instead of sending the king knights to fight his wars, as my father is required to do to fulfill his feudal obligation, I paid scuttage instead, using what little money we had to pay the king in lieu of knight's service. But I could not protect our people from the marauders. And so some of the freemen left to serve other stronger, richer barons. That is why many of the fields are fallow. The villeins, of course, can't leave, but there never seems to be enough of them.''

By the time she stopped speaking, her words were a hollow rasp. The overwhelming burden of the last few years made her sag in her saddle. No one spoke. All she heard was the wind whistling over the clumps of earth.

At last Hugh spoke up. ''Margrete.'' The single word was a demand for her attention. When she raised her head and met his gaze, his eyes were fierce with determination. ''You will never, ever worry about these matters again. I will not allow it.''

She turned her gaze back to the horizon, uncertain if she should be grateful or angry. Or both. Yes, indeed, Hugh de Greyhurst would change her life. For better or worse.

While Hugh and Peter lingered at a small stream that wended by the castle, discussing plans for a possible second bridge, Margrete continued on through the gatehouse, eager to get on with the day's chores. She dismounted at the stable and wandered to the curtain wall behind the beehives, where sunshine was curiously beaming through.

''What happened here?'' she said, pointing to a hole big enough for a man to crawl through.

An eleven-year-old child, one of three people trying to fix it, stepped forward and curtseyed.

''Oh, my lady, some of the knights errant had a brawl this morning before they left. The fat, drunk one fell through.''

''I see,'' Margrete said, dismayed that their rampart had

been so easily breached. "Then let's get busy. We can't have any marauders stepping into our mists."

Geoffrey, the eighteen-year-old son of the smith, was preparing mortar, and doing a fine job, considering he had only one arm. With such an impediment, he couldn't ply his father's trade. But he was an earnest young man and tried harder than anyone in moments such as this. She was glad to have his help.

"Geoffrey, ply the mortar and we'll bring you the stones."

"Right, my lady." He slathered on the gooey substance and Margrete lifted the first stone into place. And then another. They were heavy, and after carrying a half-dozen, she became winded. What little breath that remained she lost in a gust when Hugh came up behind her and shouted her name.

"Margrete!"

"Oh!" She cried out and dropped a stone, whirling around. "What in blazes is it, my lord? You nearly frightened me to death."

He towered over her like a father about to blister a recalcitrant child. "What are you doing?"

"Repairing a hole put here by one of your friends."

"You mean to tell me you labor like a common villein in your own castle?"

She compressed her lips as the heat rose in her cheeks. "When necessary, yes. I thought I'd made that abundantly clear during our tour of the barony."

"You should not be laboring so. Let these servants do the work."

At this, she wiped sweat beading on her brow with a backhand, caught her breath, and looked at her helpers.

"These servants, as you describe them, my lord, consist of one eleven-year-old girl, who is Peter's niece, a boy of five, who is the son of our falconer, and a young man of eight and ten, who has but one arm with which to commend himself, his enthusiasm notwithstanding." She sighed and put her hands on her hips. "I would have waited for Peter to take charge as usual, but I feared to leave our wall breached without any men to defend us."

"My lady, I will take over now," Peter called, jogging over from the stable. He immediately began lifting rocks back into place, and ordering his young helpers about, his wiry muscles easily handling the task.

Margrete reached for another stone.

"My lady!" Hugh shouted.

She paused, resisting an urge to drop the stone on his foot, but tamped her temper and continued about her business. Hugh stepped forward with lightning speed and grabbed the rock from her hands, his own shaking with anger. He stomped to the wall, put it in place, then returned to his weary wife and gripped her arm, leading her away from the others.

"Margrete, you are my wife. I will not allow you to burden yourself like a pack animal."

"Another thing that you will not *allow*?"

"I don't want you to blister your hands or hurt your back. God knows what you were forced to do to survive before, but now that I am your husband, you will take your proper place."

"My proper place?" she nearly shouted. "And where is that?"

"In the keep, carding wool with your lady-in-waiting."

"Oh, yes! Lord knows that is all I'm capable of handling." Her voice rang out with scathing sarcasm.

He stared at her in astonishment. This was a side of her he'd never seen.

"Before I retreat to my gilded cage, my lord, I hope I

have your permission to say a prayer in the chapel. I must ask God for the strength to keep myself from strangling you!''

He watched her go in amazement and scratched his head, unsure if he should order her back. Wasn't that what a husband did? Didn't she want to obey him now? He must be seen by the servants as master here. But in truth, he did not so much want to conquer her as save her. Didn't she understand that? Didn't she understand that she deserved a better life than the one she had been living, that she'd been working too hard for too long?

He paced, angry at himself, frustratingly uncertain, until resolve spurred him in her path. By God, she may never love him, but she would understand him. She would listen to what he had to say. When he reached the chapel moments later, he pulled the door back with a bang.

''Margrete!'' He blinked at the darkness that slapped his eyes. ''What are you doing?''

''I am praying,'' she snapped at him from the shadows that cloaked the altar.

He stepped inside and blinked until his eyes grew accustomed to the dim light. She was kneeling and turned her head over her shoulder. Light spilled through stained-glass windows, and her face was streaked with red and blue. But the brilliant colors could not mask the long-suppressed anger that flamed in her cheeks.

''You're praying?'' he returned in a surly tone. ''Is that all you ever do?''

She spun around and rose in astonishment. ''I do much more than that. Isn't that obvious? Isn't that what angered you?''

He could not argue there.

''But of all the things I do, praying is the most important. I am sorry for you, Hugh de Greyhurst, that you have no inkling of what ecstasy a soul can experience in prayer.''

"You might pity me for many things, lady, but not that. I do not mourn my distance from God.''

"You should.''

"And you should learn how to be a wife.''

"Why, in God's name? I thought for a while that you might actually care about my plight. That you might want me to have a spiritual marriage. But all you want is control. Control of a barony and the pawns who live within its borders. And to be master of the woman who gave it to you in the first place.''

"And I thought for a while that you might want a husband as a mate who could help you, who could lift your burden. But you don't want to share anything. Not your bed, not your authority, and least of all not your heart.''

"My heart?'' Her voice quavered as if he'd thrust a dagger into that very organ.

"I'd once thought a maiden's heart was something to cherish. Now I see it is like an icicle, so cold and hard to the touch it could burn the hand of a man who tries to hold it.''

When she said nothing, when it seemed in the heavy silence that she had even ceased to breathe, a stab of remorse twisted in his gut. He ran a hand through his hair, wishing he could take his cruel words back.

"Margrete, I only want to protect you.''

"And what of your heart? If it's so full of benevolence, goodly sir, then come join me in a prayer. You know how important it is to me. Please, share that if nothing else.''

She couldn't believe she was inviting him to intrude in her sanctuary, but there was something about this gently complex, yet stubbornly simplistic man, that made her want to share something. He was right—she had given him little save for a title, and that was hollow when all the other trappings of life were missing.

"Come pray with me," she entreated more gently.

"No." The word oozed with stubbornness.

"Why not?"

"I can't."

"Why not?"

He sighed, the air flaring through his nostrils. "I don't remember how."

"You can't pray," she said bitterly. "And I can't stop. Did two more dissimilar people ever bind themselves together?"

"No."

Without another word, he turned and marched back to the broken wall, which would be far easier to mend then the gulf that lay between him and his wife.

Fourteen

At the end of the day, Hugh thought about his impasse with Margrete. Frustration burrowed in his belly. They'd only been married a day and already they had locked horns royally. He would find it humorous if he wasn't so concerned about their differences. Lord, a lifetime with a woman who did not love him would be a long time indeed. He was just glad that he didn't have to spend another night alone with her.

As the sun retreated into distant rims of gold and azure, Hugh hurried down the corridor that bordered the castle's great hall, eager to depart. He wanted to spend the night in the manor house and had hoped to be there before dark.

He had almost made it to the door when a boisterous voice hailed him from the high table. Hugh paused long enough to see who it was through one of the archways that bordered the corridor.

"There he is," Lord Giles called. "What ho! my son. Don't fly so quickly."

Hugh crossed his arms and grinned at Giles. He sat in a

drunken heap next to Sir William. Both had obviously been imbibing for some time.

"Greetings, my lords," Hugh hailed in return, then started off again. "I wish I could stay longer, but it is late. I must away to the manor."

"Not so fast!" the baron protested, rising from his throne-like chair. "Come hither, lad. I insist."

Hugh sighed and stopped, his nearly overwhelming urge to visit his new home succumbing to his desire to be respectful to the man who had given it to him in the first place.

"What is it, my lord?"

Hugh strode to the high table, dodging scurrying wenches and pages who carried out empty platters and spent pitchers. He cautiously overstepped a slumbering hound sprawled before the blazing fire in a pit in the center of the room and stopped before the dais.

"Here, here, my boy," the inebriated baron said. "Join us for a cup of wine."

"I thank you for your hospitality, my lord," Hugh said, crossing his arms and enjoying the clear merriment of the old and carefree men. "But I would travel to the manor tonight to ensure it is ready for Margrete's arrival on the morrow."

"And leave your bride alone on your first full day of marriage?" Lord Giles said, raising one furry silver eyebrow in astonishment.

"If it were me, mon, I'd never have left the lassie's bed this morning," Sir William said. He smacked his lips together for emphasis and reached for his goblet.

"Aye," Lord Giles said, staring at the few sprigs of hair left on his friend's otherwise bald head. "That's true, William. How will I get my grandchildren if they don't get to work?"

William let out a raspy, suggestive snort of laughter, and the old men then turned their twinkling eyes to Hugh.

He cleared his throat and looked down at his feet. Had Margrete not told her father their marriage would be celibate? He thought Lord Giles knew about her wishes. Hugh rubbed his brow, biding time.

"What is it, my son?" Giles said. "You're not red-faced about something so natural as swiving your wife."

"Well, my lord," Hugh began, looking up with a miserable expression. "You see . . ."

"Aye, laddie, I know, ye don't want to be abraggin' aboot yer lady wife," William avowed sagely. " 'Specially not afore her father."

"It's not that . . ."

"It wouldn't bother me," Giles said innocently. "The servants are already talking about the noises that bellowed out from the solar last night."

Hugh's jaw dropped. "They are?"

The baron chuckled and his many chins jiggled beneath his long beard. "Don't be embarrassed, my son. You must enjoy your conjugal rights."

"Did I ever tell ye," Sir William said as he snatched his friend's arm, "that on me wedding night I bedded me wife ten times?"

Stabbed by envy, Hugh shifted his weight. "I think I'll take you up on your offer of wine." He poured himself a goblet brimming full of burgundy liquid and took a swallow of the biting liquor.

"Ten times, I say! Ten times! Did I ever tell ye?"

"Did you ever tell me?" Giles returned, winking at Hugh, then smiling tolerantly at his friend. "You've told me ten times at least, you old braggart. I'll tell you one better. The first night I lay with my lady we coupled only once."

"Only once?" Sir William's wizened face wilted. "What a pity."

"But it lasted six hours."

"Six *hours*?" The decrepit knight's eyes widened like two trenchers as he imagined this scenario. "I've new respect for ye, mon."

"My lords," Hugh interjected. When the old men turned to him, clearly expecting him to tell a tale that would top this feat, he sketched a short bow. Taking one last sip of his wine, he put it back on the table. "I beg your leave."

Hugh turned but had not taken two strides before Lord Giles's voice ran out with unexpected clarity.

"Go no farther, young man!"

Hugh halted immediately, feeling as if he'd just been reprimanded by his father. He turned slowly and studied the man before him. The baron's eyes were uncommonly lucid; his frown piercing.

"The manor house is not ready for you."

"But Peter said—"

"Peter was wrong." Lord Giles shrugged under some unseen weight and swilled his wine. He turned to Sir William and gave him a sound shove. "Wake up, Mac-Gregor."

"Hmmm? What?" the startled knight said.

"The manor house is not ready. Is that not so?"

"Nay, it's not ready. How could it be?"

They looked to Hugh, as if daring him to disagree.

Of course, he would not. After all, the manor house wouldn't be his to call home if not for the generosity of this man. But he could not squelch the sense that Lord Giles was once again leading him into temptation, just as he had when he'd ordered a bath for Hugh the night of his first visit.

Hugh folded his arms and stroked the stubble of a day-old beard with one hand. "My lord, what year is this?"

"What year?" Lord Giles said, and repeated the question again, clearly stalling for enough time to figure it out.

"What year?" MacGregor frowned at Hugh as if through a fog. "What sort of question is that? Naturally, it's—"

"Please, Sir William." Hugh held out a palm to silence him. "I asked Lord Giles."

"Why, it's twelve hundred and ninety-nine in the year of our Lord."

"No, my lord. This is 1313. Who is the king, my lord?"

"Richard Lionheart, of course."

"Wrong again. King Edward II sits on the throne. One more question, Lord Giles. Did you not recall your daughter telling you that . . . What I mean to say is, didn't your daughter mention that when she married she wanted to . . ."

When Hugh fell silent, Lord Giles leaned forward. "That she wanted what, my boy?"

Hugh squeezed his eyes tight and rubbed his forehead. So what if the baron was confused and had forgotten? So what if Margrete hadn't even told him about her desire for celibacy? These old men would mock him for it time and again. He'd never hear the end of it.

"Nothing, my lord." Hugh sighed with resignation. "That is something for Margrete to tell you, if she so desires."

"She's quite a shrew, isn't she, laddie?" Sir William said, giving him a conspiratorial wink. "I told ye. But ye wouldn't listen."

"On the contrary, Sir William, she's as far from being a shrew as a woman could be. And that's what's making this all so damned miserable."

The old men looked at each other in confusion.

"Miserable, did he say?" Lord Giles muttered. "Did he say *miserable*?"

That was Hugh's opportunity to escape. But not to the manor house. Lord Giles may not know the difference between a horse and a hound, but he clearly wanted Hugh and Margrete to spend another night together in the castle. And Hugh would not disappoint him. At least not outwardly. Though he be an idiot, Lord Giles had already shown Hugh more love than Jervais de Greyhurst ever had.

Clearly, there was a vast well of love here at Longrove. So why did Hugh increasingly feel like he was dying of thirst?

Goose bumps rose on Margrete's arms at the touch of ivory teeth on her scalp as Edith smoothed the comb through her hair for the umpteenth time. And each time the comb touched her temple, or crown, or nape, Margrete shivered.

Perspiration trickled between her breasts and down her slender belly. And though she was a devoted virgin, some strange heat seemed to be warming that secret place that would never be breached. She swallowed thickly, fearing what dreams the night would hold.

"What is it, my lady?" Edith said as she lifted her mistress's hair away from her neck and let it drop down her back. "You seem uneasy. Oh, but of course," she added with an embarrassed little laugh. "You're expecting your lord any time now."

"Yes, I am. Surprisingly."

Margrete was stunned when her father told her before supper that Hugh had pulled him aside earlier in the day to say that he was eager to share the solar again with his new wife. It was so unexpected. She'd thought he'd merely been tolerating her. Thinking otherwise sent shivers scrambling from her head to her toes.

"Do I look all right?" she said, spinning around and jumping up from her stool. She went to her father's full-length mirror. All her life she'd avoided looking at her reflection, choosing modesty over vanity. Her mother had gazed into this looking glass often, and what did her beauty get her in the end but a brutal rape and murder? But yesterday, Margrete had dusted off the glass and stared long and hard, scrutinizing herself for the first time through the eyes of a man.

Was there too much sun on her cheeks? Were her eyes too colorful, too much like sapphires? Were her lips too complex, too full? Were her hands too strong? Her waist too narrow? Her breasts too full?

"Edith?" she said, her gaze never wavering from her reflection.

"Yes, my lady?"

"I trust I can ask you this without hearing it repeated outside this chamber. . . ."

"Of course, Lady Margrete," the freckle-faced damsel said, coming up behind her and looking at Margrete's reflection. "What is it?"

"What do you think of my breasts?" Margrete strained a little to let their outline be seen through her gown.

Edith smiled broadly, a twinkle in her eyes, which crossed at a harrowing trajectory. "Your breasts? Why, they're lovely, my lady. All four of them."

Margrete stared at Edith's reflection, nonplussed.

"Of course I know there's only two," Edith hastened to add. "But I see four."

Margrete turned to her and hugged her. "You poor dear. I can't imagine how you cope with seeing doubles."

"Not at all, my lady," Edith said, drawing back with a cheerful grin. "When I see a handsome man, I get two times the pleasure."

Margrete laughed. "Edith, I wish I shared your easy outlook on love. My husband is coming to this bedchamber soon and all I can think about is whether he finds me adequate. I'd thought he'd married me perfunctorily. But now that I know he might feel something for me, I . . . I see the world differently."

It wasn't that she wanted him to ravish her. Far from it. But she'd felt terrible ever since their dispute in the chapel. After Hugh had left in a fit, she'd turned cold with fear that he might actually leave her. She'd been forced to acknowledge to herself how important he had quickly become in her life. Needing a man, and not knowing if he needed or wanted you in return, was terrifying. But if Hugh walked through that door tonight, then she would know her father had been telling the truth—that Hugh still cared.

A knock sounded.

"There he is!" Margrete blurted sotto voce.

"Oh, my lady!" Edith cried out with a start. "You certainly are jumpy tonight."

"May I come in?" Hugh's voice, definitely gruff, penetrated the thick oak door.

Edith turned to her mistress with a questioning look.

"Let him in, and then you may go," Margrete whispered, hurrying back to the table. She sat and grabbed the comb, pretending she had been nonchalantly sorting through the tangles in her hair.

She heard the door open, Hugh's heavy steps cracking brittle rushes on the floor, Edith's hastily mumbled farewell, and the click of the door latch.

"Undress me," Hugh said, his voice weary. He flung himself down in a chair by her table and gazed at her with jaded eyes. When she remained mute, stunned by his order, he frowned. "I said undress me."

"My lord . . ." Her voice shook. She laid the comb down with trembling hands. "Please, do not—"

She stopped, suddenly remembering her own promises

to him before their wedding. In a flash of inspiration, she dashed to her clothing trunk, flung it open, and began to dig furiously. "I nearly forgot. I have a hair shirt in here somewhere. I promised to make myself plain and undesirable and here I am traipsing about in a flimsy gown." She found a heavy veil and pulled it over her head, clasping a delicate metal circlet on her head to hold it in place. "Now that I'm married I should be plaiting my hair and wearing a veil. Now where is that hair shirt? It's in here somewhere."

She continued to dig, apologizing as she went. "Forgive me for being so insensitive. I shouldn't tempt you anymore than a man is already naturally tempted. Not that I think I'm tempting, mind you, but men are rather like rutting stags and sometimes it doesn't take much. Oh! Here is an undertunic that buttons to my throat. That might do just as well as the hair shirt, though it won't be as unpleasant to the touch. I'll just slip this on and—"

"Margrete!"

Her hands froze at his thundering voice. She turned. "Yes, my lord?"

"I said undress me, not ride me like a whore from here to Babylon. I'm tired and I want to go to bed. If I was at the manor, where I wanted to be tonight, my squire would help me undress. You don't need to clothe yourself like a nun, for God's sake. Just get on with it."

Her shoulders sagged with relief. "Oh, I thought . . . I mean, I was led to understand . . ."

"Margrete, please stop prattling and tug off my boots. My feet are aching. You said you wanted to be a helpmeet. So help me."

She pulled off her veil and pushed down the jumbled array of clothing and accoutrements, shutting the lid of the trunk. She went to his side and began to tug on a boot, her initial relief turning to unexpected and illogical pique. So he wasn't tempted after all. After looking in the mirror, she'd thought he might find something to desire. And her father had apparently lied. Hugh did not want to spend this evening with her. Angry, she gave his boot a good twist.

"Ow!" he muttered.

Her gaze shot up to this face in time to see a wince of pain. "Serves you right. You shouldn't be here if you wanted to be elsewhere. And when are you going to do something about this leg? It's still hurting you."

"What do you know about my leg?" He gave her a pinched look.

"I know it hurts and it makes you limp. Especially today. I saw you lurching through the bailey."

"It's going to rain," he growled. "It only hurts when it's going to rain."

"I don't know what you're talking about." She motioned to the embrasure. "The sky is perfectly clear. There's not a single cloud in front of the moon. You just won't admit you're less than perfect."

When she looked up, she bit her lower lip and said no more, for the hard glaze in his eyes told her exactly how much his pain troubled him and how insensitive she was being. Men were so blasted proud. To them, pride was never a sin. It was an attribute.

She pulled off the second boot, and Hugh stretched out until his body was nearly a straight plane, groaning with satisfaction.

"Thank you. That feels much better."

His hose was torn at the toes and worn at the heels. Margrete sank on her knees as she wistfully recalled rubbing her father's weary feet. As a child, he had been remote, never one for kisses and cuddles, but after the accident, the baron had craved affection. And she'd been eager to give him what he needed, for she knew at last that her father really did love her, even if he did so only because he was witless.

She licked her lips and stole a glance at Hugh. His mind was far away. With his hands clasped behind his head, he didn't even seem to remember she was in the room.

Defying better wisdom, Margrete gripped one of his feet and began to rub the callouses on his heel.

"Oh, Lord, that is exquisite," he said, shutting his eyes.

"Good," she replied, putting more muscle into the effort.

"Ow, that hurts."

"Shall I stop?"

He opened his eyes and smiled. "No, it's a good kind of hurt."

She smiled shyly and continued, and when a comfortable silence enveloped them, she began to wonder what boundary she had crossed. Was it possible for them to develop a platonic love, like brother and sister, that would allow for a healing touch? For it was a woman's duty to take care of the health of her husband and vassals. She was the one they turned to for herbs and physiques, for a consoling touch or advice about a nagging pain.

Or was she merely inviting confusion by reaching out to him at all? A moment ago she had been panic-stricken at the notion that he wanted to make love. Now that she knew he did not even want her, touching was safe, perhaps even necessary. He would never be able to use his leg fully if he didn't relieve his aching muscles. Touching was all a matter of intent, she realized. And trust.

She put his foot back to the floor and rose. "What else can I do to help you undress? Lift off your tunic?"

"No, my lady, I think that is too much to ask. I can finish undressing myself." He gripped one of her hands.

"Please forgive my ill-tempered words. I was merely angry that you'd not yet told your father the conditions of our marriage."

"But I did tell him," she hastened to clarify, pulling up a chair next to his. "He knew that I wanted a spiritual marriage the first night you came to our castle. He has simply forgotten."

Hugh rolled his eyes. "He needs reminding."

"If I continually remind him, he will continually be sad over not having grandchildren. Wouldn't that be cruel? He doesn't have long to live. . . ."

Hugh rose abruptly, rubbing his head with a hand in obvious pain.

"What is it, my lord? Something I said?"

He whirled on her, his soulful eyes flashing like two swords in battle. "You are rightly concerned about your father. But what of me? Do I deserve no consideration? What of my desires, Margrete? And don't assume that panicked look of yours. I'm not talking about . . . about conjugal relations. What about my desires for a family? I never thought much of it till now, but I want a son to carry my name, to inherit this barony. I want a daughter to adore. And I can never, ever have these things."

She held his gaze. "It's one of life's ironies, Hugh, that the very arrangement that gave you this barony in the first place will deny you its passing to the next generation."

He blinked in slow defeat. "You're right. I know you're right. But I still don't like it." He focused through the hazy torchlight on her soft white gown. The oval collar was embroidered with delicate red flowers. And he thought he saw below that the outline of her nipples. She nervously smoothed a hand over her luscious hair and then folded her arms, hunching over a bit. God, she was lovely. He could imagine making love to her ten times in a night with no trouble at all. Six hours would not be enough time.

That was another of life's merciless little ironies, that he should be bound to a woman he could never touch in a carnal sense and yet whose femininity exceeded that of any other woman he'd ever bedded. Her innocence was his salvation, and her beauty his curse. His groin pulsed with desire and he turned away, ambling to the open window, wishing that somehow they could have met under different circumstances. He pushed open the window and welcomed a sharp, cool breeze that stroked his hot cheeks.

"It's starting to rain," he said, inhaling the silvery scent. Big drops splattered the edge of the embrasure.

"You knew," she said slowly. "You knew it was going to rain."

He heard the wonder in her voice. She was so guileless, trusting, and pure. All that his mother had never been. All that he had ever desired in a woman.

Staring at the hypnotizing rain, he could feel Margrete's presence. It was as if there was no distance between them. In an odd way, she had erected no walls to protect her innocence. With her it would be all or nothing. And though he might never hold her, he could easily imagine it.

He could imagine her body pressed to his, naked and sleek—the slope of her hips, the pillowing of her breasts against his ribs, the offering of her lips, their gentle parting, the crucifying pleasure of her tongue flicking against his, their sighs, the melding of skin, the parting of thighs, the . . .

He groaned quietly, quelling the ache that squeezed his heart and guts. He stood there for some time, staring at but not seeing the sheets of rain that battered the ground below, lulled and soothed by the drumming sound. The wind shifted, and a light spray flew against his leathern cheeks. It felt good. A natural anointing. Nature was something he could count on and trust. Sometimes he thought he would have made a better pagan than a Christian.

So why in God's name had he married a saint?

"Come to bed, my lord."

He was startled by her voice. He'd almost forgotten she was there. She would always be there, close but never close enough. He turned at the gentle entreaty and found her in bed, sheet pulled high around her neck. Wordlessly, wearily, he began to undress. He pulled on a sleeping shirt she'd lain out for him and climbed in next to her.

He was more relaxed this time, for he'd shown her anger and she had not wilted. At least she would accept him for what he was. No need for pretenses.

"What troubles you so, Hugh?"

He bent his arm and tucked it under his head, turning on his side to face her. She lay on her back, but turned her head to watch him. He could see the reflection of the moonlight in her sea-blue eyes. He could breathe in her breath, warm and sweet.

"I've always measured my manhood by my ability to . . ."

"To couple with a woman," she offered.

He nodded, hair rustling against the pillow. "How will I measure my worth now? How will I stand up to the mockery that will surely come from other men, even graybeards like MacGregor and your father?"

"God will show you how."

"Oh, Margrete," he groaned in exasperation.

"He will. Trust Him."

Her eyes were so wide, so full of hope and faith. He wanted to believe her. But he was so damned cynical.

"Pray with me, my lord."

"No, I'll not give you that," he said petulantly, rolling onto his back. "Good night, Margrete."

Ever persistent, she began to whisper a prayer.

His eyes grew droopy as she said the rosary. And just before he fell asleep, in that moment when logic gives way to the fantastic, that second before sleep descends, he mumbled an amen, sounding almost as if he meant it.

Fifteen

*P*erhaps I would be the best person to comment on this difficult journey upon which our hero and heroine have embarked. After all, I have enjoyed the conjugal delights of marriage as well as the peace of monastic celibacy. It may be hard to imagine, as cherubic in comportment as I am, that at one time I counted the long hours spent in the arms of my wife as among the happiest of my life.

Conversely, I now enjoy the benefits of chastity. There is no compulsion to please another or consider another's wishes. Now I am wrapped in the peace which only God in his infinite wisdom can bestow. The peace that passes all understanding.

The early church fathers knew better than I that Christ would come again. St. Paul, after recovering from the fall from his horse on the road to Damascus, held that the time left us before Christ's return was short, therefore intimacy was a waste of time. Yet, verily, here we are many centuries later, still waiting for

*the return. Not every good Christian has refrained
from procreation in the intervening years. Life goes
on, even as we wait, leaving us to wonder what God
hoped would come to pass between men and women
in the meantime.*

*What, ultimately, is the meaning of that which we
call love? Is it an embrace? Is it a look of winking
affection? Is it shared prayer, a communion of spirits,
or is it a celebration of that which is base, that is to
say our carnal selves?*

*Perhaps you can decide. Read on, dear pilgrim. For
initial discomfort now turns to shared visions.*

Hugh's third night as the husband of Lady Margrete
Trewsbury was very different from the first two, for he was
finally sleeping in *his* home, not Lord Giles's. And, at last,
he had a sense of being master of his own destiny.

At dusk he ate a light meal in the manor's great hall with
Brian, Peter, and Margrete. They'd all been working ex-
haustively to finish what the servants had begun—throwing
down new rushes on the floors, chopping down weeds, putting up tapestries to keep air from seeping through cracks
in the stones, and clearing cobwebs from roof beams. In
addition, they had their regular chores and duties to attend
to at Longrove Castle. And so, having worked up enormous
appetites, they ate with relish—pigeon stuffed with herbs,
delicious marrow tarts, and honeyed wafers cooked especially in celebration of this new venture.

They concluded the repast with cheese, nuts, and fruit
and had a third round of watered-down mulberry wine,
mulling over the days events.

''What we need,'' Hugh said, popping a nut in his mouth
and chewing while he formulated his plan, ''is more

knights to fill the baron's other empty houses. How many are there?''

Peter blinked and scratched his square jaw. "If you count the decrepit shack on the east side, four. Three are built of wattle and daub and have thatched roofs, and one is a solid stone, though much smaller than this manor."

Hugh's eyes glittered as if he'd just discovered a treasure chest. "Let's say we fill them all. Each knight, upon accepting his tenancy, would have to pay a knight's fee of one hundred shillings. Add to that revenue from taxes and tolls and we would have some much-needed money."

"In truth, my lord, you have three fiefs available, not four," Peter amended, "for Sir William occupies the fourth. And he shows no signs of moving out."

Hugh wagged his head. "You're right, Peter. We cannot dislodge Sir William."

"As much as you'd like to," Brian murmured under his breath.

Hugh gave his squire a wry smile, but said no more on the subject. "If we grant fiefs to healthy warriors they will fight for the baron's land in order to protect their own."

Hugh looked at the others to measure their enthusiasm. Peter was nodding his head as he poured more ale into his tankard. Brian smiled as he wiped his hands on a hot towel brought by a page who stood in the shadows. Normally it was a squire's duty to serve his mentor at meals, but Brian had quickly taken on a more important role. He was learning the intricacies of estate management. He had already shown himself to be an able organizer, and so Hugh had been including him on planning sessions.

As for Margrete, she frowned dubiously as she sipped her wine. Hugh supposed that she would be reluctant to embrace any ideas that weren't her own. It would take some time for her to give up the reins of power.

"And if we repair the ferry," he added, "we'll have another opportunity to increase the barony's income. What do you think?"

"Sounds like a right fine idea to me, my lord," Brian said.

"Sir Hugh," Peter said, shaking his head as he straightened his shoulders, "these are good ideas, one and all. But there could be no greater boon to the barony than the return of Kilbury Hide. That is the richest, most fertile farmland in all of Christendom. If you could but reclaim that land from Lord Richard, and at the same time assert your authority over the freemen who are plowing the land on Richard's behalf, then this barony's fortunes would change mightily for the better, I avow."

"Hmmm," Hugh said, rubbing his square jaw with a hand. "That would take a fight."

Brian's ears pricked up at this. "You mean going to battle? With the earl of Ludham? Then I could earn my spurs at last?"

"Yes, yes, and yes," Hugh replied, breaking into a slow grin. "You bloodthirsty cur."

"Go to battle with Lord Richard?" Margrete leaned forward, searching Hugh's hardened features. "Are you mad? We have no weapons, no foot soldiers—"

"You have villeins working the fields," Hugh argued.

"And what will they fight with? Plows and sticks?"

"If we raise some revenues," Hugh reasoned, "we can buy weapons and hire mercenaries. If we recruit strong and loyal knights, they will owe us forty days' knight's service. And if we arm them well enough, God willing, we will not even have to do battle. Lord Richard will be intimidated and back down."

"What about the bishop?" Margrete persisted. "He has laid claim to the land as well."

"Has he ever fought for it?" Hugh said, raising a challenging brow.

"Bishop Eustace did not, but who's to say which way the new bishop will lean?"

"You have a point there." Hugh leaned back in his chair and frowned at the single candle that illuminated the tabletop with a golden circle of light. "Considering he's Sir Ranulf's cousin, we can expect trouble from that quarter. But let's not worry about that now. We must first recruit knights. I will give that some thought and consider my old acquaintances as possible candidates."

"What of the scutage we must pay to King Edward?" Margrete said. "We're behind in our payments. When Peter went to London he was loaded with excuses as to why he couldn't bring the king all the gold due him."

"We'll hold a fair." Hugh broke into a gloating grin, as if he'd solved all the world's problems with that simple solution.

"A fair?" Peter's eyes lit up.

"I'll seek a charter for a fair from King Edward," Hugh said confidently. "We'll make the village a center of commerce. We will tax merchants for the privilege of selling their wares."

"A center of commerce?" Margrete stared at him as if he'd just sprouted a third eye. The idea was so preposterous she pitched back her head and let out a trill of laughter.

"You find my ideas humorous, my lady?"

"You've seen the village. There are scarcely three hovels there."

"But one beautiful church, and a perfect plot of land for booths and tents. That reminds me, Peter, if worse comes to worst we will claim the church's tithes as our own as a feudal obligation."

"The new bishop won't like that," Peter said.

Hugh grinned wickedly. "No, he wouldn't, would he?"

Margrete frowned at him, trying to fathom the depth of his confidence, and then fairly squirmed with a piercing jab of jealousy. "Hugh, you cannot save this barony with grandiose plans and half-hearted dreams. Be truthful, good sir. Without a miracle, you may very well have to sign this estate over to the king. At least then you will have use of it for the duration of your life."

She said no more, but Hugh could read between the lines. If he didn't voluntarily surrender the barony, he might lose it outright and be at the king's mercy. Whereas if he gave the monarch the barony, Hugh could at least live out his days here. And since he would obviously have no heir, there would be no need to keep the land for future generations. The prospect left him with a sick, cold feeling in his gut.

"Never." He pounded the table. "I will never give this barony away. I'm shocked that you would even suggest such a thing, considering your loathing of the king."

"My lord," Margrete said in a more conciliatory tone, "if the problems were so easily solved, I would have done it myself long ago."

He reached across the table and gripped her hands. "Margrete, I will accomplish what I say. I am a man. I can do things that you can't. This is my life's work." His features screwed into a mask of quiet fury. "Do you doubt me?"

She went utterly still. She was face-to-face with the bear of a man who had bested some of the strongest knights in the realm. Feeling his power, imagining what it would be like to face him in battle, she shook her head and blinked slowly. "No, I do not doubt you."

"I will meet with the king and ask directly for the charter for a fair. And if I have strong men owing me knight's service he will listen, for he needs as much military service as my vassals can give him for his campaigns in Scotland. I can entice some of my fellow knights to settle here, and by God," he growled, "I will fight any vassal who chooses to forget his oath of fealty."

She glanced at Peter to see the effect of Hugh's impassioned speech. The castellan's face glowed with pride and hope. Already her vassals were looking to their lord for leadership, forsaking the lady who had single-handedly kept this barony running for so long. As well they should. Here was a man who would fight for all of them. No one had done that since her father's accident.

She felt light-headed, as if a great weight had been severed from her feet, and she was now floating up to queasy heights. Strangely disembodied, she rose unsteadily.

"If you will excuse me, I need some air." Margrete did not wait for a response, but hurried out of the great hall and didn't stop until she reached the edge of the yard. She looked at the fields that surrounded the manor, and it seemed as if she didn't know where she was. Everything was new. Her whole world was topsy-turvy. The rules had changed. Her purpose in life—to survive and protect her father—had disappeared overnight.

She was no longer the one solely responsible for this barony. She didn't have to worry over every detail. She didn't have to lay awake at night wondering if the king's sheriff would ride in any day with orders to vacate the castle. She was free. Truly free at last.

And she hated it.

"Margrete."

She spun around and found Hugh gazing at her with compassion.

"Margrete, you must step aside now. You must give in to me. Trust me. I will protect your estate, and most especially you. I swear I will not let you down, but you must trust me.''

She loved the way his hair danced on his shoulders in the soft breeze. She loved the steadfastness that burned like a low, undying fire in his eyes.

''I do trust you,'' she whispered. ''That is what amazes me most. I do trust you.''

When she smiled with simple acceptance, he chuckled softly in wonder. ''You are a kind soul, Margrete.''

''Am I?''

''Yes. You hate that I'm taking over your domain, and yet you'll accept it because it's your duty.''

Her fair cheeks broke with button-sized dimples, and her wholesome teeth flashed in the waning light. ''No, it's more than that. I deserve someone like you. I want protection. But old habits are hard to break. I scarcely know how to let go the reins I've clinched so long.''

''One day you'll thank me for doing this. One day soon, I avow, when you realize that you've worked too hard.''

''I know that to be true already. And frankly, I am relieved.'' She breathed in the loamy air and squinted at the gathering shadows. ''But what will I do with myself?''

He reached out and gripped one of her wrists, raising her bent arm. Then he took the flat of his other hand and pressed it to her raised palm. ''You can pray.''

She looked from the unusual sight of their praying hands, from his great palm that easily dwarfed hers, to his somber expression.

''I can?'' she whispered.

''You must.''

Tears filled her eyes. She'd never had a man to care for her needs.

''Now don't cry or I shall change my mind.'' He switched hands and wrapped his fingers around hers, tugging them playfully. "Come on. I want you to see something."

He strode off with wide strides, giving her arm an enthusiastic yank when she did not immediately follow.

"My lord, where are we going?" She took two steps for his every one, trying her best to keep up.

"Look at this!" he thundered, flinging a hand out as he led her through a gate in the stone fence that bordered the yard. He tugged her into a nearby field, where the ground was brown and littered with straw and hard clumps of earth.

She gave him an ironic smile. "You know, I've seen this field before, Hugh."

"But not with my eyes."

He stopped when they were deep into the land. The sun was a rich and soul-satisfying bronze, spilling its dazzling hue across the darkened horizon. The air was pure and startlingly fresh. And the man before her, strong and vibrant, determined and noble to the core, took it all in with an acuteness that sent shivers scurrying down Margrete's spine.

"Look at it!" he insisted, blinking back what she would have sworn were tears. "Have you ever seen anything more beautiful? Have you?"

His cheeks were red from a day in the wind and sun. He bit his lower lip, struggling with emotion. He blinked rapidly, and when a teardrop betrayed him by trailing down a wind-burned cheek, he angrily swiped it with a hand and swallowed hard.

"I mean have you ever seen land that held so much promise?" His voice broke and he frowned. He reached down and grabbed a clump of earth. It exploded in his grip and loose grains spilled through his fingers. "You speak of God, Margrete. To me this is where God lives. In the earth that gives us food. In the sky that gives us rain. In land that nourishes our bodies and our hearts.'' He pointed to the horizon, squinting one-eyed over his extended arm like an archer. ''God lives in a color so pure, so rich, no illuminator could replicate it.''

He drew in a long breath and shivered. ''God is here, Margrete. My life, my future is here, and all because of you. You have given me this.''

She watched in amazement as his arms swooped down around her and he lifted her body against him as snugly as a swaddled child. He lowered his face to her shoulder and breathed in her scent. His cheeks were rough with half a day's growth of beard. Shivers crept down her arms at the heat of his breath on the valleys of her shoulder.

''Margrete,'' he muttered, and lowered her to the ground, freeing her. ''Dear Margrete.''

With earth-stained hands, he tilted her head back, stroking her cheek, and she wished with all her might he would lower his head to her neck again, that he would draw her close so she could feel his uncommon heat. Inhaling the earthy dust that clung to his fingers, her mouth parted, awash in a sea of senses.

''Thank you, my wife. Thank you for all you have given me.''

Moved by his heartfelt gratitude, she shut her eyes. Therefore she did not know he was going to kiss her until it was too late, when she felt his lips cover hers, until her own betrayed her by melding against his. For one astonishing, mind-boggling moment, they were one.

She gripped his tunic, rough against her knuckles, inhaled his manly breath, the scent of leather that clung to him, felt the hard, threaded muscles that wove his body into a tight yet inviting mass of brawn. There was nothing between them, no air, no heartbeat, not conscience, no qualms, only a great and terrible, sweet meeting of flesh upon flesh. Heart upon heart. Mind upon mind. The power of it knocked her hard. She staggered away, and forced her eyes open.

My God, she thought, *he kissed me.* She would never be the same.

Sixteen

wo days later, Margrete sat next to her father in the great hall, drumming her fingers on the high table and nervously tapping a foot beneath it, waiting for the manor court to convene. She had cut short the last hearing in a fit of pique and several vassals had been patiently waiting for justice. When Hugh heard of their concerns, he called for another session, eager to establish his authority in all matters affecting the barony.

The court was to have started on the hour, but Hugh was late. As the moments ticked by, Margrete's eagerness turned into anxiety. How would her new husband deal with her father's vassals? Would he even show up, or was he having second thoughts about his new authoritarian role? If Hugh did come, would he be a good judge? Would he be accepted as such by their vassals? And would he be fair to all parties? Margrete sensed that he would, but she had no idea how he would react to her presence here. They hadn't been alone together since The Kiss. By unspoken mutual agreement, and out of simple embarrassment, they'd been avoiding each other.

So as a small crowd of freemen and villeins sat on the benches below the dais, waiting for their grievances to be heard, Margrete twiddled her thumbs, her heart rising higher in her throat with each passing moment.

"What are we waiting for?" grumbled Lord Giles.

"Patience, Father. We're waiting for Sir Hugh."

"You usually handle these matters, Margrete."

"Yes, but the reason you wanted me to marry Sir Hugh is so that he could take over. Remember?"

"Oh, yes!" The baron's look of boredom turned to one of pride. His cherry-red cheeks puffed up as he grinned broadly. "I know how to pick them, don't I? I knew he'd be a good husband. Yes, indeed, I know how to pick them!"

"Papa, you hadn't even met Hugh before you agreed to the match," she replied drolly.

"Yes, but it worked out perfectly nonetheless. Somehow I knew he'd be a gem. I've got good instincts!"

The double doors at the end of the hall opened. A mighty creak rent the silence. Daylight spilled into the hall, shattering shadows. Margrete's heart began to race. Though she'd been avoiding Hugh, she couldn't wait to see him again. She felt like a sot who couldn't quite understand why she craved yet another cup of ale.

"Sir Hugh?" her father called out, squinting to see across the distance. "Is that you?"

"Ach, no, mon, it's I. MacGregor."

"Heaven forbid," Margrete muttered under her breath as the tension in the hall momentarily deflated.

"What is it, old friend?" Lord Giles said.

"No, Father," she whispered, gripping his forearm. "Don't encourage him."

"I'm glad you asked, Giles," MacGregor called out. His spindly shanks carried him the length of the hall with remarkable speed. He stopped at the front of the dais and cleared his throat. "Now, aboot the portions of ale I receive a—"

"Enough!" came a forbidding voice from the arched hallway.

Gooseflesh rose on Margrete's arms. Like everyone else, she started and strained to see the source of the bass voice. When Hugh stepped out of the shadows, looking resplendent in a floor-length sunset-colored tunic, she snatched in a breath and held it, mesmerized. His long sleeves were lined with gold embroidery and a gold girdle made the most of his narrow waist, which accentuated his broad chest. He was positively dashing.

He must be wearing one of Father's old tunics, she thought as he approached the dais.

"Where did he find that clothing?" Margrete said to herself and was startled when her father answered.

"They're mine," Lord Giles said, his eyes misting over. "I gave my finest tunics to Hugh the other day. He is, after all, the son I never had. And he is the baron now in all but name. I can see that much. I used to wear that cloth-of-gold at . . . at . . . where was it?" He bit his lower lip and scowled. "I can't remember. Why can I never remember?"

"You used to wear that outfit at court, Papa." Margrete put an arm around his shoulder and gave him a gentle squeeze. "And I don't know who looks better in it, you or my husband."

"He cuts a fine figure, daughter," Giles whispered impishly as Hugh reached the dais. "Not even you can deny it."

"Sir William," Hugh said in a commanding voice as he stepped up onto the platform and stood beside Lord Giles. He frowned down his nose at MacGregor. "Do not trouble the lady of the castle. She has been more than generous with your ale, else you would not fall asleep so oft in your chair at meals."

"But . . ." MacGregor began.

"An extra portion will be added on Sunday, because it pleases Lord Giles to do so." Hugh gestured respectfully to the baron. "Now I believe the matter is settled."

Somehow Hugh managed to be commanding and kind at the same time; his voice was firm, but not strident. Margrete looked up at his profile in wonder at this feat, and his proximity made her skin tingle all over.

"Sir William, I wonder if you would be so kind as to help Brian," Hugh said, taking a different tack. "He is in the dovecote and needs your experience and wisdom to solve a dilemma."

MacGregor tugged on his collar, primping at the praise. "Why, Sir Hugh, it would be an honor." He bowed and then scurried out of the hall without another word.

Margrete watched this miracle, mouth agape, then turned back to Hugh. He broke into a closed-mouth smile, cheeks dimpling, and she smiled back, no longer embarrassed by The Kiss. Not when they could share a silent joke with such ease and pleasure. Was this the sort of intimacy her father and mother had enjoyed? That a husband and wife enjoyed?

"Now then," Hugh said. "Let us call the court to order."

Over the next hour Hugh listened carefully to each complaint. He charmed, cajoled, and otherwise convinced everyone present that he was a lord to be reckoned with. And somehow he always managed to include Lord Giles, if only nominally, in the decisions. Frequently he turned to Margrete and listened closely to her advice and warnings. In the end, there seemed to be present in the great hall, for the first time in years, a sense that all was right with the barony. Finally there was a lord present who could deal with kings as well as troublesome knights, who could be fair and yet firm, and who could relieve a burden from a lovely maiden who had sacrificed her childhood to carry a weight that even the most seasoned baron would find burdensome. That feeling pervaded in the hall, brightening the faces of all, until Thomas Gibbons aired his grievance.

"What is your complaint?" Hugh said, leaning forward with confidence, hands folded leisurely on the table.

"Well, my lord," the freeman began, rising from the bench and drawing his hat off his head. "It's like this, ye see. I've been plowing the fief south of the river all my life. But John Plowman now claims that he has the right to work the land. He says his father made a deathbed will claiming the land had been granted to him by Lord Giles's father."

"Is John Plowman here?" Hugh inquired.

A stocky man with a scruff of black hair and bushy black eyebrows rose from the bench. "Here, my lord."

"Is this true?"

"Aye, my lord. I am claiming the land and me father did say it was his to give. He died a fortnight ago, ye see."

"Then why did your father not assert this right while he lived?" Margrete said.

"He said he was too sickly and poor to fight fer it while he lived. And he didn't want to cause you no trouble, Lady Margrete, as how you already had enough worries of yer own." The burly plowman looked furtively to Lord Giles, then his sunburned cheeks turned rosy. "No disrespect meant, ye see. But when me father died he said the new lord had come and he could sort it out. And so I'm claiming what's mine. Simple as that.''

"Do either of you have proof of your claims?" Hugh said.

"I do," Gibbons quickly asserted. He pulled from his shirt a small scrolled parchment and stepped toward the dais. "Here, my lord, see for yourself. This is a benefice drawn up by Lord Giles's father. It even bears his seal.''

Hugh took the document and leaned back, staring at it as if it were a snake coiled in the palm of his hand. Margrete's eyes widened as she recognized his dilemma. He turned to her with an odd look that she alone knew to be desperation. Her heart ached with compassion. She longed to take the document from him, to save him the embarrassment, but to do so would signal his ignorance for all to see.

Hugh licked his lips, his mouth parting, but no words came. He turned his gaze back to the scroll and swallowed hard. Then he unrolled it. Holding the top and bottom so they would not curl back together, he stared hard at the parchment and the maze of letters etched in ink. Soon sweat was beading on his brow and upper lip.

"What is it, Sir Hugh?" Lord Giles said. "Is something wrong?"

Everyone in the great hall waited with baited breath.

"Read it, my son," Lord Giles entreated.

"No need to read the document now," Margrete quickly added. "Sir Hugh can study it at his leisure and then make a decision. All these men care about is your good judgment. Isn't that so, my lord?"

Hugh cut her a bitter glance. "Is it, my lady?" Placing the document on the table, he rose and glared sullenly at the small crowd. "My wife is right. I need time to consider this case. Go now. I'll call you back when I've rendered my judgment.''

· ''But my lord,'' Gibbons pleaded, ''the benefice clearly states . . .''

Hugh brushed past the freeman and stalked off, leaving everyone to gape after him in confusion.

''My lord!'' Margrete called out, rising from the table, then she sank back down after he departed. She should have anticipated such a predicament. She should have considered that someone might bring a written document. They were rare but not unknown. How thoughtless of her not to have prepared Hugh. How utterly thoughtless.

Hugh brought his axe down hard on a log. *Thwack!* The sound of wood splitting did his soul good. Sweat trickled in his eyes. It burned. That felt good, too. He raised his axe again, over and over until sweat coated his chest, until the soreness in his arms superseded that which rankled in his belly.

How on earth did he ever think he could be the lord of a barony? He couldn't even read the simplest document, for God's sake. The memory of that humiliating incident made him feel as if his very veins were bursting with roaring anger. Damnation and hell! Seeing the looks of dismay on the faces of everyone in the great hall, he had quickly departed, returning to Longrove Manor to take out his frustration on wood waiting to be chopped.

It was as if everyone, from Lord Giles to the lowliest villein, had seen through his fine tunic to what he truly was underneath—the boy who had been stricken from his own father's home, falsely called a bastard and condemned to a life as a quarry worker. An untutored pack animal.

He scraped his fingers over his forehead, regretting with new ferocity the loss of the education he might have had if his life had gone as it should have. As a child, sitting of an evening in his foster parents' hut, all huddled around the fire burning on the earthen floor, eating porridge and watching smoke channel up through a hole in their thatched roof, Hugh would try to remember the lessons he'd had at Greyhurst Castle. He'd been able to read a little when his father sent him away. But without further study and no books and living in the home of simple folk who could not read themselves, the letters he'd memorized soon became a blurry memory, the lessons forgotten, his mind a blank.

He loathed that ignorance. It was exactly what his father had wished for him. Lord Jervais had sworn that Hugh would amount to nothing. How could Hugh overcome that damning prediction when he didn't have the knowledge that other noblemen used without effort? Shame he had not felt in years rose like bile in his throat.

Thwack! He chopped with more fury than before.

When Margrete returned to Longrove Manor, she was surprised to see Hugh chopping wood in the yard that bordered the manor house. Hugging a book to her breasts, one she hoped she could use to teach him how to read, she quickened her pace, eager to apologize. But when she drew closer, something made her stop so that she could regard him without his knowledge. Something that had nothing to do with her desire to educate her husband.

He wore no shirt—merely breeches, hose that hugged his muscled calves, and leather boots. The sun beat down hard on him, nearly as hard as he pounded the wood with his axe. Each stroke was a masterful and succinct blow. He'd gotten himself a rhythm, and every muscle in his broad chest tightened and loosened in a steady beat. His chest was sunbaked bronze, as if he'd been a wood chopper all his life. His amber hair frolicked loosely in the soft, spring breeze, exposing now and then the cords of muscles that bound his neck. He was like a great rock, finely carved, chiselled by battles, polished by life itself.

Thwack! She took a step closer. *Thwack!* She inhaled chipped, green wood; a touch of lilac blooming nearby; Hugh's manly scent. She watched with fascination the web of muscles that stretched to the breaking point from shoulder blade to shoulder blade. His waist was narrow and tight. He was a stallion. A purebred. And he was hers. A burning sensation crawled through her insides, hurting with its pleasure. It was pride, pure and simple. *And desire.* But why, oh Lord, did these sins have to feel so good?

He turned then. Seeing her, his faced clouded over. She was leaning on a fence not thirty paces away.

"My lady, I did not hear your approach." He wiped a sheet of sweat from his brow with the back of one hand and rested the other on the handle of his axe.

"Why are you chopping wood?" she asked, shifting the weight of her book from one hip to the other.

"Because it is something I can do well." His eyes— infernos of sarcasm—flamed in the sunshine.

"Surely your skills and leadership are needed elsewhere."

He shook his head and bent to set up another log on the stump that took his blows. "Oh, most assuredly. You saw how valuable my skills were in the court."

"Indeed I did," she said, coming closer until he raised his axe in the air and brought it down hard. She jumped back a half-step. "You were masterful in the great hall. You had everyone convinced that life was going to be better now that an intelligent and reasonable man was in charge of the barony."

He paused a moment to catch his breath, drawing it in his throat with a winded rasp as he watched her. Then he wiped the sweat from his brow with a forearm, tossed the split wood aside, and reached for a new log.

Just when she thought he would turn her away with a sullen word, he heaved a sigh, dropped the axe, and put his hands on his hips. Surrender quenched the fire raging in his eyes.

"I have been laboring long on naught but a crust of bread and a tankard of ale, my lady," he said. "Would you take dinner with me?"

She heard the well-timed rumble of her hungry stomach and agreed at once. "That would be wonderful. I'll have the cook pack some food and we can eat down in Long Grove. It's time you enjoy my favorite spot in the entire barony."

Less than an hour later they arrived at a towering and charming gnarled oak tree in the heart of the lush grove. As Margrete spread out a blanket, she was keenly aware of Hugh's every glance, every gesture cast her way from where he stood by the tree. She noted with tender pleasure how he hugged himself with quiet intimacy and scanned the verdant beauty, taking in the sight of a scattering of ash trees, whose sooty black buds were blossoming into tight russet clusters. Elsewhere, budding alders and birch branches etched the cloud-white sky in a delicate web, like pink veins on the cheeks of a fair-skinned girl.

In the secret inlets of the wooded grove, primroses blossomed with quiet determination after winter's long and deathlike sleep, dotting the grass with pale yellow petals faintly tinged with green, a subtle harbinger of a more brilliant spring showing to come.

Hugh sniffed at their ethereal perfume and sighed away a world of trouble. This was his. The thought still left him reeling with gratitude and hope, despite his glaring weaknesses and failures.

"I'm sorry I let you down," he said.

She flattened out the last corner of the blanket and sank down on her knees, cocking her head sideways as she regarded him. "Whatever do you mean?"

"I should have told you I could not read."

"But I knew that. I'd figured that out long ago. It is I who must beg forgiveness. I should have remembered, then I wouldn't have put you in that embarrassing position."

"You deserve a husband who has been educated."

"Nonsense," she argued. "I received the tutelage that should have been yours by birthright. I will do all the reading for you. And you in turn will give me peace of mind by making the decisions that have burdened me nearly my whole life."

When he remained frowning, she smiled with hope sparkling in her eyes. "Isn't that what the best wives do? Support their husbands?"

"Is it?" The question wasn't rhetorical. He hardly knew how a man and woman could bind themselves in kindness. And he realized the time had come to tell her about his past, the reason why he had never been educated, though he was the son of one of the most powerful lords in the realm.

He sat down on the blanket, hardly even wincing, for his leg had healed much now that he was no longer fighting. In fact, he was able to cross his legs for the first time in ages with relative ease.

Margrete poured him a cup of wine. He took a sip and began. "My mother was unfaithful to my father for as long as I could remember. The very first memory I have—I must have been only three—was walking into my parents' solar and finding a naked stranger on top of her. There was never a time when she didn't take her lover to her chamber when my father was away, fighting abroad. She was very discreet," he added with a rueful smile. "Somehow managing to keep her infidelities a secret. Except with me. I was her confidante. I was the one who made excuses for her, who helped her lover escape unnoticed from my father's castle after every assignation. And when my father was home from his crusades and battles, beating my mother regularly not because he knew of her unfaithfulness but simply because he enjoyed beating women, I was the one she would come to for consolation. I would hold her hand while her handmaid put poultices on the welts and bruises left by my father's fists or sewed together the flesh that was torn by his monstrous insignia ring."

He took a deep breath and let it out slowly, and in the silence the birds around them sang cheerfully. Hugh continued with the matter-of-fact tone of one who had long ago ceased to feel pain.

"Eventually my mother must have grown careless, for I believe the castle priest became suspicious of her. One day when I was nine I went to confession and Father James pressed me to speak about her. Weary of bearing so many secrets and believing my confession would be confidential, I unburdened my soul and told Father James about my complicity in my mother's affairs. He assigned me penance and reassured me the secret would be ours. And then he went to my father and told him everything."

"How terrible," Margrete whispered. "What did your father do?"

Hugh took a sip of the tart wine. "Jervais went on a rampage. First he went after me for betraying him by keeping my mother's secrets. He chased me up to the top of the tower and after beating me senseless he threw me over the ramparts."

"He threw you off the tower?" Margrete said incredulously. "It's a miracle you survived."

"Fortunately, our marshall was a drunkard. He'd failed to have the grooms move the hay into the stalls that morning and a big pile of it broke my fall. But this leg," he said, slapping the one that had been reinjured in the joust against Sir Ranulf, "plagues me still. It twisted badly, and though I recovered, I was always able to predict rain by the pain in my joints."

"What happened after your fall?"

"Angry that I had survived, but by then too calm to try to murder me again, my father claimed that I was the result of my mother's adulterous unions and dismissed me as a bastard. He sent me to be fostered in the home of some of his poorest vassals, a quarry worker and his wife. My education ceased that day, as did my dreams of being a lord like my father."

Margrete could no longer hold back her tears. They tumbled down her cheeks, though she was too thunderstruck to weep. She wiped them with her hands and sniffled. "I'm so sorry. I can scarcely imagine what happened to your poor mother."

Hugh stretched out his legs, wincing at the effort. He might be able to cross his legs, but keeping them in one place for any length of time took its toll. He leaned back, propping himself up with his arms, and watched the clouds skitter across the sky.

"My mother was imprisoned in the tower. I never saw her again, but I'm told she spent the rest of her days looking at the world through the bars crisscrossing her embrasure. She was allowed to do embroidery, but that was her only pleasure. She spent ten years in the tower. When my father lost his memory and his wits in the final years of his life, he forgot she was there. And so no food was sent up. In the end she starved to death. When my father died and my brother opened the tower prison, he found her fully-clothed skeleton sitting in a chair, head slumped on the table, as if she were merely taking a nap."

Margrete shivered at the image. "Why didn't your brother come to her aid in secret?"

Hugh sat up straight and finished off his wine. "John? He was too weak to do anything that might risk my father's anger. He worshipped Jervais and at the same time lived in terror of his wrath. Ironically, John was the bastard, not me. My mother told me that my elder brother, her firstborn, was the son of her lover. And my father died never knowing that fact. He even used to say how much John looked like his side of the family."

"You mean your brother inherited your father's estate and he was a bastard?"

Hugh nodded with a rueful chuckle. "Yes. I technically was Jervais's firstborn son."

"Why didn't you tell him? You would have inherited everything."

"I couldn't, Margrete. I was the strongest, you see. My brother could not have survived being cast out by my father. It would have killed him. Besides, I didn't want to put my mother in any more jeopardy by confirming my father's suspicions."

Margrete stared at him for a long while, just stared, trying to comprehend the depth of his sacrifices. Then she inched closer and reached out, stroking his noble forehead, his jutting cheekbones, and the savvy curves beneath. His aristocratic features, which signified a birthright he could never claim, were muted by the earthiness of his nature. Every feature was soft and hard at the same time.

"Oh, Hugh, I wish I could have been there," she whispered. "I wish I could go back in time and be there for you, for the boy you were. I would have protected you."

She had never wanted to console another as much as she

did now. She felt the breeze rustle through her flowing hair, felt the sunlight toasting her cheeks, but what she wanted to feel was Hugh. How could you truly brush away a sorrow without touch? Is that why God had given them hands? To brush away a tear? To nurture a scraped knee? To staunch the flow from a wounded heart? How could she tell Hugh how worthy he was without touch when words were so laughably inadequate?

Compelled by a force that was greater than her mind and will put together, she wrapped her arms around his waist and brushed her mouth against his. Her tingling lips lingered a moment too long, for soon she found herself being pushed down on the blanket. It was like sinking into quicksand. With his hands pinning her shoulders, she could not rise if her life depended on it. She blinked up at the puffs of clouds skittering by, saw the shadow of him looming over her, and still had no urge to flee.

He leaned down and kissed her hard, his mouth raking over hers, then returning for a longer draw. It wasn't gentle. It wasn't nice. He was angry, perhaps for needing a healing touch, she thought. And somehow she instinctively knew that the raging ache of a man was like a storm to be endured. If she surrendered, it would blow over, leaving her with greater wisdom. Her bruised lips would heal, but what of his heart? That would take some time.

The turbulent kiss ended abruptly. He raised himself up on his knees and wiped the taste of her from his mouth with the back of his hand. "Why did you come? Not for this. You do not want this."

"I . . . I wanted to console you."

"Pity." His lips twisted as if the word tasted of rue.

She pushed herself up, knowing he would be lost to her forever if she did not scramble. "This was not planned. I . . . I came to teach you to read."

"Charity." This word clearly tasted worse than the last.

"No, not charity," she said firmly. "I need you, Hugh. I do not need a husband who can read, but if that is what it will take to make you feel like a lord, then let's start the lessons now. Right here."

His velvet amber brows collected in a tumult of thoughts as he sank down. He drew his knees up in the lock of his arms and scanned the hilly horizon. "I'll be damned." He turned to her wonderously, the first glimmer of limitless possibilities dancing beneath his sooty lashes. "I'll be damned."

Taking this as the most enthusiastic response she'd likely get, she quickly reached for the tome.

"Where to begin?" She flipped open the cover, revealing a beautifully illuminated manuscript page. "This is a copy of a great work by the German Abbess Brigitta of Ansfelden, a mystic who had visions from God. This volume was copied by one of the monks at Treyvaux Abbey, Brother Edmund. He has an especially skilled hand. You see how beautifully the letters are rendered."

Hugh moved closer and looked over her shoulder. His breath came in hot, smooth bursts on her skin. She shivered, then shut out the sensation with effort. She forced herself to read, reciting one of the abbess's poems extolling the virtues of virginity.

"Oh, maidens of the true spirit, your souls shine bright in heaven. . . ."

So it was, through the goodness of his wife who gave without making the gift seem a burden, that Hugh de Greyhurst began to learn his letters, reading about virgins and other such anomalies.

Seventeen

Lady Margrete truly did praise my work with the quill, lest you think that was pure invention on my part. My copies of the works of Abbess Brigitta of Ansfelden are highly prized here in England and abroad. I am renown for the precision of my letters, and unlike most other scribes I also do the artwork, as you can see with this manuscript. The first letter of every page is enlarged and brightly illuminated with madder crimson and azure. The shafts of the letters are decorated with floral infilling, and the roots fan out in delicate trefoils of leaves—all painstaking work.

But I humbly beg your forgiveness for boasting of my God-given talents. It's simply that writing as I just did about Hugh's strengths and weaknesses, I find myself pondering my own. I realize that as much as I treasure my ability to make beautiful books, I prize above all the love I gave my wife when she was alive.

Yes, love is budding for our hero and heroine, just

as the red primroses bordering this page are bursting
forth with great promise. But, alas, while the floral
patterns etched onto this page will bloom an eternity,
true love, like the tenderest blossom, vulnerable to the
vagaries of the earth, is not always as enduring.

The next day Hugh remained at the manor house to attend matters there while Margrete went to the castle. Her
father had had another one of his spells and once again had
been revived only by the good grace and quick thinking of
William MacGregor. Margrete had a premonition that her
father was not long for this earth, and so she wanted to
spend as much time with him as possible.

In the morning, she walked the short distance to the castle with Lady Edith after waving good-bye to Hugh, looking back with one last warm, sweet smile. He watched her
until she was out of sight, and like a besotted young pup
he sighed with sorrow, wishing he would not have to wait
until sundown for her return.

He wandered back into the house, unaccountably melancholy. Ever since he'd talked to Margrete about his family it seemed his heart had been rent open and was now
subject to all sorts of unwelcome emotions he hadn't felt
in years.

Sloughing off his uneasiness, he headed for the great hall
in search of Peter. Hugh wanted to survey Kilbury Hide
again before meeting with Lord Richard. But when he
passed by Margrete's bedchamber—the only one in the
manor—he paused outside her door. He hadn't been inside
this room since they'd moved in. Hugh had been slumbering in the great hall with the others. But now that he knew
his wife better than before, he felt an overwhelming urge
to look at her possessions, to see how they were arranged,
how sweet and feminine they were.

Feeling like a thief, he creaked open the heavy oak door, heart pounding, and surreptitiously glanced over his shoulder, scouring the shadows of the hallway, but no one was there. He needn't be so wary, he told himself. He was, after all, the lord of the manor. But he and Margrete both understood that this was her chamber, a place she would never invite him to enter.

Stepping inside, he inhaled the scent of her, a fresh blend of daisies and sunshine, and felt a cool finger of heightened awareness drag down his spine, making him shiver at the intimacy of this woman's world, this secret place of glass hearts and gentle laughter.

Standing stock-still, he scanned every detail. The rushes on the floor—reeds scattered with violets. The dried roses in the embrasure—a bouquet from a summer past. From a suitor? he wondered, his gut clutching with unexpected jealousy.

No, she wanted no man. He had to remember that. It wasn't merely that Hugh was unworthy of her that kept him from her bed. It was that she was too worthy for any man. She was heaven-sent. An angel. No discarded wings lying about, he mused as he stepped more fully into the chamber. Passing by her small table, he saw an ivory comb entwined with blond hair. *Her hair.* He reached down and pulled a strand free. How he would love to run his fingers through her mane, tangle it, grip and pull in need, whispering the secrets of his heart in her ear.

He let the strand drop to the ground and moved on.

A mourning dove cooed outside the window. A breeze floated in, along with untarnished sunshine. The rays lit up a clothing trunk in the corner. *Her clothing trunk.* She must have shut it hastily, for a piece of lace hung over the edge. A bit of lace that had, perhaps, rubbed against her skin, as his fingers would if given half a chance.

With his breath coming in ever shorter snatches, he lifted the lid and peeked into her soul. The lush scent of dried roses plumed in his face. He dipped his hands into a swirl of softness—cool silk, fleshy velvet, soothing linen. Finding the source of the lace, he tugged and pulled out a gown, white and delicate, and pressed it to his nose, breathing in her scent.

It smelled clean, and also of something more intimate—a husky womanly scent. She'd worn this recently. Perhaps even last night. In bed.

Hugh shuddered with longing for her and dropped the item that led to this temptation back into the trunk, closing the lid with a determined thud. He glanced around again, this time noticing the illuminated manuscript from which she had read to him yesterday. It sat on her table like the inanimate object it was. But to Hugh it seemed to shimmer with life, like the Emerald Tablet, a tome treasured by alchemists which contained all the secrets of how to turn base metals into gold.

Margrete had read to him a series of poems about virgins. But what else did the good Abbess Brigitta of Ansfelden have to say? Did she have some advice for a poor fool of a husband who had entered a spiritual marriage against his better judgment? he wondered as he crossed the room and reverently fingered the cover of the book.

"My lord, I've been looking all over for y—"

"God's teeth!" Hugh blurted out, spinning on his heels at the jarring sound of his squire's voice. "Good God, have you not heard of knocking?"

"The door was open," Brian replied defensively, standing in the doorway, brash and handsome, full of youthful indiscretion. "What is that book you're holding?"

Hugh started to answer, then an idea he'd had earlier in the day clicked into place. "You read, do you not, Brian?"

"Yes, Sir Hugh. I once thought to be a cleric and learned to read Latin and English."

Hugh crept to the door, looked out surreptitiously, then, tugging Brian inside, quietly closed it. He put an arm around the lad and urged him to sit at the table. "Read to me from this book."

Brian looked askance at his master. "I'm a bit rusty, my lord."

"No matter."

Brian opened the great volume and whistled. "Quite a treatise. Where shall I start? Here's a poem about virgins."

"Good God, no! See if there is anything written there about . . . conjugal relations."

Brian eyed him with a teasing grin. "Reading about it is better than nothing, eh, my lord?"

Hugh flushed and scowled. "Keep your opinions to yourself, if you know what's good for you."

Brian dutifully wiped away his smile and began to finger through the pages. Each parchment page was made from the tanned hide of a sheep. So an entire book represented the sacrifice of an entire flock, which meant it was a very expensive and very treasured possession.

"Let's see. Perhaps this—no, that won't do. Ah, here we are. This might be something you're interested in."

Hugh listened with rapt attention as Brian read Brigitta's admonitions that husband and wife are to be of one flesh just as Adam and Eve were, not for the satisfaction of lust, but out of desire for children. It was the very affirmation that Hugh needed. This great religious thinker, whom Margrete admired, could acknowledge the supremacy of virginity, and yet at the same time affirm the righteousness of holy matrimony.

Hugh listened closely, occasionally rubbing his hands together with palpable glee. Eventually Brian grew weary of reading aloud. He began to flip pages, looking for an excuse to shut the book.

"Ho-hum," he muttered, but then paused at a particular page and whistled low.

"What is it?" Hugh said, sitting up straighter.

"My lord, listen to this!" He began to read aloud. " 'A husband will instinctively feel the impulses of his carnal nature as surely as a bee will flit to a flower to suck its nectar. Like the bee, the husband will press his stinger in the virgin blossom in moist, ecstatic union. And like a flower, the wife will sigh and wilt with pleasure.' "

There was a long pause, punctuated by a low whistle from Hugh. "A nun wrote that?" he asked incredulously.

Brian shrugged. "So it says here."

"Margrete either doesn't know of such passages, or she avoided reading them to me. What else does this abbess say?"

Brian scanned the text, running a finger along the sentences as he skimmed. "Hmmm. Well, my lord, I think what she's trying to say is that conjugal relations should be engaged for procreation alone, but it's understandable if a man and woman take pleasure in the meantime." Brian impatiently snapped the book shut. "My lord, end your misery. Take Lady Margrete as you please. It is your right and her duty to submit to you. I do not know how you've lasted this long."

Hugh crossed his arms and strolled to the embrasure, contemplating this assertion. His father would certainly never have cared so for a wife's feelings. But Margrete was more than a wife. She was quite the most extraordinary woman he'd ever met. No, he would have to take a different approach if he were to bed his lovely wife. An approach that matched the gentleness of her soul.

"Read the words to me again, Brian. The part about the bees."

"Why ever?"

"I want to commit them to memory." He pinned the youth with a cunning glare. "Just in case I need to argue my case."

Brian did so reluctantly. It seemed a waste of time. He knew what Hugh needed even if he did not. And Brian knew just where to get it. He would solve his lord's problem without his permission. For a man hungering for a woman sometimes didn't know which way to turn, or where to sink his aching need.

The perfect cover for Brian's mission of mercy presented itself the next day when the cook bemoaned her shortage of spices. Brian listened closely to her list, made mental notes of directions to the nearest spice market, which was in nearby Brisby Village, then set off at once.

The dirt road leading into Brisby was lined by a cluster of thatched huts and timber buildings, where spice and cloth merchants operated open-air stalls next to a stable, an inn, and an alehouse. At the other end of the strip of civilization was a whorehouse.

It wasn't far, and so Brian left his mount at the stables. He bought saffron and pepper from the merchant along the way—enough to keep the cook from raising an eyebrow over the quantity. Then he pocketed the rest of the money, tucked the spices into his tunic, and set out on foot to buy the services of a good whore.

The whorehouse was a shabby wattle and daub building, whose shutters were askew and where weeds grew green and tall against the soiled whitewashed exterior. When the door opened a few seconds after his knock, Brian gasped and took a step away from the woman who greeted him.

"Greetings, young cock. I'm Magdalene. What do you want, lovely lad?"

Magdalene adjusted her sagging breasts against the bulge of her belly, hiking up the sagging flesh, then letting it drop back down like a string of pearls. She pursed her red-painted lips, which created a web of wrinkles around her mouth. Her teeth were nearly all black and she smelled of garlic. Brian stifled a gag.

"Well, sir knight, speak yer peace or leave. What will you have?"

"A whore," he said, then turned crimson for stating the obvious.

"Well, yer come to the right place, laddie," Magdalene said, cackling. "What did you think this was, a mews?"

The worn-out prostitute waved him in. When Brian hesitated, her eyes hardened into dark beads.

"What, we're not good enough fer the likes of you? Leave then, little boy."

Brian knew he shouldn't let such an outcast goad him one way or the other, but her sarcasm served to strengthen his resolve, and he stepped into the foul-smelling place.

A few women, clearly prostitutes, though none as old and hideous as Magdalene, were playing a game of dice at a table. They looked up speculatively at the sound of Brian's footsteps. One winked invitingly. Another tugged on her bodice, pulling it lower to expose more of her abundant breasts. All the women wore the badge of prostitution, which was required by law.

The room reeked of an unidentifiable exotic scent, and he imagined some Knight Templar coming here to break his vow of chastity, bringing gifts of incense and myrrh from the Holy Land.

The entire setting evoked dueling feelings of repugnance and desire. It had been some time since he'd lain with a woman. He was too particular—always wanting the prettiest damsel—and too ambitious to debauch his life away. He wanted to be a lord one day and did not want to come to a noble wife with a whore's disease, or a cartload of bastards trailing in his wake. And yet, he did not know how long he could resist such comfort.

S'blood, he thought, poor Sir Hugh. He must be nearly mad with frustration. Reminded of his purpose, Brian stepped in closer and focused on a girl sitting in the corner. Her face was somehow fresh, her soft brown eyes wounded, not hard like the others'; her thin brown hair was plaited down her back, stray wisps spreading over her chestnut-colored gown. Her lips were moist and parted, and even in the shadows he could see the flash of white teeth.

"I'll take that one," he said quickly, pointing to her, then turning to the old and haggard pimp. "What is her name?"

"Ruth," Magdalene said with a sour twist of her blood-red lips. "Though she'll not pleasure ye much. She lays there like a stick and whimpers no matter how hard and pleasure-giving be yer manroot."

The old bawd limped to the other side of the gaming table and grabbed the arm of a plumper, more experienced prostitute. Her cherub-soft lips were naturally puckered and swollen. She smiled as Magdalene grabbed her chemise and yanked it down to expose fully her bosom. Two overly ripe breasts bulged out completely. Her hard nipples were as large and purple as plums. Much to Brian's surprise, he found this offering distasteful.

He thought of Edith, Lady Margrete's lady-in-waiting, who had been flirting with him shamelessly from the start. He had not pursued her for, though she was of humble means and cross-eyed to boot, she was a lady and could not be despoiled without consequences. She was charming and devoted and quite lovely if you did not stare too hard into her crossed eyes. Brian wished her well. She would make someone a fine wife one day. A fine wife, he thought, suddenly ashamed to be here.

"She is too . . . too plump for my tastes," he said to Magdalene who waited expectantly at the whore's side. "Now how much do you want for Ruth?"

Magdalene let go of the chemise and it popped back in place. Then she set about bartering with Brian for the girl who would lie there like a stick. When all the arrangements were complete, it was understood that Ruth would come to Longrove Manor on Magdalene's donkey the very next day. She would not under any circumstances let herself be seen by the lady of the manor, and she would not tell Sir Hugh who had sent her.

Brian sighed with relief as he left the brothel and stepped out into the sunshine, inhaling a much-needed breath of fresh air. It felt so good that his lungs tingled. He stifled a nagging doubt about his plan, reassuring himself that Sir Hugh would thank him in the end. He would be happy with Ruth. She had an air of innocence not yet beaten out of her by the roughest clients. Hugh would like that. Brian saw how he looked on his innocent wife with something akin to shocked adoration. Yes, he would like Ruth very much.

Everything was working out perfectly. Or so Brian thought until he felt iron fingers close on his shoulder, spinning him around.

"What have we here?" Sir Ranulf said, crossing his arms and tossing a sly glance at his ever-present companion, Sir David Keath. The curly-haired knight came up to Ranulf's sleek side and surveyed the squire from head to foot.

"Well, he still has on his hose and, presumably, his braies as well," Keath said, a smile adorning his well-crafted face, though his eyes as always were a pale green void.

"His clothes are on, but I did see him departing that brothel, didn't you, Keath?"

"Indeed, Sir Ranulf. A pity when such a fine-looking youth has to pay to spill his seed. He should have stayed on the circuit with us. There's young women aplenty willing to act like a whore when they see iron men jousting. A pity you stayed with that womanly master of yours, Brian. You'd have gained your spurs and lost your virginity by now."

"I did not pay for the services of a whore!" Brian shot back, anger replacing his initial foreboding. "And I'll have you know that I have plenty of willing women available to me."

"For a price," Ranulf snorted.

"I once knew a merchant who couldn't make his manroot rise no matter how hard a woman flailed at it," Keath said. "He went to a brothel to prove himself, and came away with the realization that it wasn't a woman he wanted at all. He buggered a young man and was killed in the town square with a hot poker placed where he wanted something else put."

Brian shuddered, then his face flamed as he realized what Keath was hinting at. "I am not a sodomite, and you know it!"

Ranulf stroked his long, bold chin. "Brian always was unnaturally devoted to Sir Hugh."

"Sir Hugh isn't a sodomite either," Brian countered. "He desires a woman as much as any other man. Why do you think I went to the broth—"

Brian stopped short, biting his tongue till it hurt. Damnation, he could not tell Ranulf the details of Hugh's marriage. Such a foul figure would only use such knowledge to cause trouble.

"You went to the brothel on Sir Hugh's behalf?" Keath said, exchanging a look with Ranulf like two cats who'd cornered a mouse with no possible escape.

"I didn't say that."

"But you would have if you'd finished your sentence," Ranulf pressed. He placed those iron fingers on Brian's right shoulder again, dipping his head so he could better see the youth's eyes. "Be honest, Brian. God will curse a liar. Just ask my cousin, Bishop Jerome. You know I have connections with the church. Cross me and I'll see that you pay for every sin. Cooperate, and I'll make sure you get all the indulgences you could hope for. Are you telling me Sir Hugh is so dissatisfied with his new wife that he is already seeking the beds of other women?"

"No," Brian said in all honesty.

But Ranulf was far too clever for him, and Brian felt as if he were a fly that had flown into a complex and sticky web of deceit and ill will. Sweat began to pour down his chest.

"He hasn't bedded her at all, has he?" The nefarious knight's black eyes snapped with certainty. "That's it, isn't it? That's why no one else would have her."

"No!" Brian said. "She never wanted to marry. Her father is witless and she did as she pleased."

"Oh, this grows more interesting by the moment, wouldn't you say, Keath? A witless baron is hardly fit to rule, especially not when he's trying to lay claim to Kilbury Hide."

"I didn't mean that! Lord Giles is . . . is more than fit," Brian sputtered. "He's—"

"So Hugh hasn't consummated his marriage," Keath said, thrusting his thumbs in his girdle. "Either she's as cold as a dead fish in January, or she's a holy maiden who has no plans to do her duty."

"Yes," Ranulf said, his handsome face kindling with excitement. "Jerome told me about such unions."

He threw back his head and laughed richly, then focused on Brian with a look of genuine gratitude. "Thank you, Brian. You have helped me more than I can say. Let us hie away, Keath. Bishop Jerome is waiting for us."

When the knights abruptly turned, a flash of panic nearly buckled Brain to the ground. "Wait! Where are you going? Aren't you still tourneying with the other knights errant?"

Ranulf turned and cocked one brow, pausing as he so often and so eloquently did for effect. "I am no longer a knight errant. I am now acting as Bishop Jerome's steward. Keath is his new bailiff. One day—perhaps very soon—I will become a baron in my own right. And when I marry you can be sure my wife will give her husband his due."

There was something, not in the words, but in his tone of voice that made Brian shiver.

God's wounds, how had he let so much private information slip in front of such a wicked man? He cursed himself for a knave, and tried to reassure himself that Ranulf would be too busy tending to his new post to bother Sir Hugh and Lady Margrete. But a nagging voice in his head told him the trouble had just begun.

Eighteen

That night as Brian laid out two sleeping pallets in the great hall, as was his custom, Hugh went about his ablutions. He would sleep in his breeches and hose as usual, but removed his shirt to wash his neck, arms, and face in a bowl of warm water. As lord of the manor he used the water first, and the servants followed.

For the first few weeks he'd endured the pitying stares of those who could not understand why the lord was sleeping with those beneath him and not with the lady of the manor, as was meet. But everyone took his presence in stride now, scarcely even lowering their voices to gossip. Hugh supposed that some couples who chose celibacy shared a bed chastely. But Hugh's willpower wasn't that strong, and there were no other bedrooms to be had in this old manor. Soon Hugh would have the servants clean out the attic for him, but for now he wanted to be near Margrete, to protect her.

On this particular night Hugh was especially weary. He mumbled good night to Brian and laid down on his pallet while his squire banked the fire. Eager for sleep, Hugh rolled on his side, tugging a light blanket over his shoulder, only to find two unnaturally white eyes glaring at him not a foot away in the darkness.

"Greetings, mon, how's our dear laddie?" a voice croaked.

"MacGregor!" Hugh barked in irritation, sitting up and glaring at the bundle next to him. "I thought you were one of the servants. God's teeth, MacGregor, what are you doing here?"

The old man sat up, grinning from ear to ear. "Ach, mon, I'd as lief you'd give an old mon a warmer welcome."

"Why aren't you at the castle?"

"I told the baron I'd see how ye were progressing. He wants to know if Margrete is with child yet, that he does."

Hugh groaned, raked his hands over his head, then laid back down in defeat. "Obviously she is not."

MacGregor's hand shot out of the darkness and clutched Hugh's massive upper arm. "What are ye waitin' fer? The second cooming? The baron, he's not long to live, ye see. He wants some wee bairns. Get going, mon."

Hugh squeezed his eyes tightly together. "You don't understand."

"All I know is that on me wedding night, I—"

"Yes, I know, I know." Hugh pulled the bony fingers from his arm and flung them away. "I've heard your boasting before."

"Then go in there, mon, and take what's yers."

"No."

"And if she turns ye away, give her the back of yer hand. And if she cries oot, cover her mouth with yer'n and soon she'll warm up to ye!"

Hugh stared up at the rafters of the hall, focusing on the banners that hung like black clouds from the beams above.

Although he disliked violence against women, Hugh knew MacGregor was right about him needing to be the master. And as long as he agreed to a spiritual marriage, there would be no wee bairns, nor satisfaction, nor true intimacy. It was his right, damnation take her. And she wanted him. He'd felt it in her kiss. She simply didn't know it yet herself.

Sitting up, he thought of his mother, what a slave she had been to Eros, and how happy her affairs had seemed to make her, until Hugh's father had imprisoned her for her infidelities. His mother had proven that a woman could receive as much pleasure, if not more so, than a man. If Margrete knew that, truly knew it, would she change her mind? Would her aspirations turn from heaven to earth? But how would she know if someone did not show her?

A fly buzzed by and Hugh swatted at the air. The humming reminded him of a bee, flitting to a flower, stinger poised for the union.

Hugh tossed back his blanket and rose.

"Where are ye going?" MacGregor asked.

"Where I belong."

"Ach, there's a good mon. Show her what she's been missing!"

Hugh strode through the hall, heart pounding, groin pulsing, never so certain in his life of what he wanted as he was now. Life was for the taking, wasn't that what he had learned? That women wanted to be taken, to be commandeered. They wanted to know the force of a man, to feel the immortality that a moment of passion evokes. God help him but he wanted it, too. He would have it.

When he reached the door, lust cowed but not slaked by his conscience, he hesitated but a moment, fingers itching to lift the latch. Then he gave in to his desire and pushed the door open, harder than he'd meant to.

"Margrete." He could see her lithe form beneath the sheet. What next? He would yank back her covers, swoop down beside her, scoop her into his arms, and melt into her skin. He would kiss her brilliant eyes, and her elegant nose, and her divine lips. He could trail his fingers over the porcelain of her neck, gripping more firmly as he encompassed her breasts, and when she was fully aroused, he would fill her with his aching need, threshing her with his pounding hunger.

"Margrete," he said, starting for the bed.

"Oh, no!" she cried out.

He halted. She tossed her head on the pillow, back and forth. "No," came a muted cry. "Do not . . . do not kill her. No! Get off her, you beast. Please. Help!"

Hugh's body went from hot to cold in an instant. The sound of her forlorn voice sent a shiver racing up his spine. Lust was replaced by concern. Was she ill?

"Margrete?" He went to her bedside, but not in the way he had envisioned. He loomed over her, a mighty oak shading a reed. Moonlight spilled from a crack in the shutters over her face, making her fair skin blue and haunting.

"Please, please don't!" she cried in the breathy voice of a half-lived dream.

Her hair spilled around her shoulders like cream on carved ivory. Her neck, taut with fear, was slender and delicate. He reached to smooth her forehead, but her head twisted back and forth too fast.

"Margrete," he said forcefully, then sat on the edge of the bed, placing his palms on her shoulders, giving her a firm shake. "Wake up. You're having a nightmare."

At this her eyes flew open, and she took in a shivering breath. "No!" she cried out, then flung herself upright, pounding his shoulders. "You will not kill her, you beast!"

"Margrete!" he shouted and gave her a good shake. "You're still asleep. Wake up!"

She went still, her eyes searching his face, at first with confusion, then recognition. Then her taut arms slackened in his hands and she slumped forward. She laid her head on his shoulder, but he knew it was no invitation to make love. She began to weep softly.

He held himself utterly still as her mewling sounds cut a clean path through the remaining armor protecting his heart. He had comforted women before—namely, his mother. But this was different. This was Margrete, a perfect soul, strong yet fragile. And she needed him now.

"Margrete," he whispered into her hair and encased her with his arms. "Why do you cry, my gentle lady?"

"Because I cannot forget."

"Forget what?"

"What was done so long ago by a man like you."

He frowned into the shadows of the chamber. "You mean the man who killed your mother?"

"Yes."

She blamed him, and yet she held him all the tighter. Why was it that the very kind of strength that had destroyed her happiness was now here to comfort her like no one ever had? She wanted to curl into his lap and never leave. Oh, Lord, let him hold her a while. Let her curl her head into his neck as she did now and inhale his warmth. Let him hold her tight with these muscles of his that were as entwined and as tight as the ropes that anchored the greatest sailing vessels. And in that security she would sail away from care and sadness.

"Margrete, there is a difference between strength that is used for good and strength that is bent on destroying. Perhaps if you tell me what happened that night I can understand your fear of warriors."

She tightened her grip on his shoulder, digging her fingers into his bare flesh. In her mind's eye, she tiptoed into that death chamber and then skittered back with a horrified gasp.

"Shhhh," he crooned, stroking her hair. "Take your time, Margrete. It has been many years between then and now."

She grabbed the corner of her sheet and touched it to her eyes to sop up the tears poised on her lashes. Still leaning into him, she blinked at the darkness as the colors, the dreadful sights and sounds, came rushing back.

"I awoke the night of the raid to the sounds of screaming women. I recognized my mother's voice. At first she screamed in outrage, that a lady of her ilk should be ill-used by a ruffian warrior. Then her rich voice turned thin as fear replaced indignation. I ran from the women and children's bower as fast as I could, dodging into the shadows of the corridor whenever an enemy soldier ran by, pillaging along the way."

She sat up, pulling herself from the comfort of Hugh's arms as the memories came reeling in. He let her go, but held one of her hands tight. It was the reassurance that enabled her to speak of that which she had kept to herself these many years.

"When I reached the great hall, the door was ajar. I stepped in and stopped in horror at the sight that greeted me. A knight was on top of Mother, heaving into her like a battering ram. His chain mail and plate armor clanged and rattled with each violent thrust. His hand was clapped over her mouth. Her eyes were wide, filled with terror and loathing, but she no longer screamed.

"At the time I did not know exactly what he was doing, but I understood that he was hurting my mother and it sickened me.

" 'Stop!' I cried, but the grunting warrior did not hear, or did not heed. When his ugly thrusts quickened and he let out a strangling cry, he pulled himself off her, unsheathed a dagger, and slit her throat with a clean slice. A necklace of blood formed on her white throat, then spurted in his face."

Hugh brought her hand to his lips and kissed it consolingly. The gesture was so tender in comparison to what she was remembering that a single tear coursed down her cheek. She swept it away with her fingertips and continued.

"I cried out to Mama and lunged forward, as if I could protect her! The knight, wiping the blood from his beard, turned to me and said 'Ah, so there's a wee lass to be had, too, eh?' The ignorant beast grabbed me as I tried to fly past him. He clutched me around the waist with one arm while he fiddled with his braies. I scarcely noticed, for I was batting my arms at him like a windmill in a tempest. I was biting, scratching, doing anything to free myself so I could aid Mother. But I was a tiny bird in the talons of a terrible falcon. He threw me to the floor like so much down, then lowered himself on top of me."

She shuddered and dropped her face into her hands. That, more than anything, had cemented her loathing of intimacy. That single, disgusting moment. If only Hugh could have been there, then he would understand why she had robbed him of his conjugal rights.

"He did not take you, did he?" Hugh rasped in the darkness.

"No. Almost. But then Father entered, sealing his fate as well."

"He was . . . he had his wits then?" Hugh asked.

She chuckled morosely. "Oh, yes. He was a stern and remote father, the perfect baron who was fair and discerning. Until that night." She took a deep breath and let it out slowly. " 'What in God's name have you done?' he roared at the mercenary who was attacking me. 'I'll kill you for this!' he bellowed and raised his great sword high above his head. The mercenary knight jumped to his feet and staggered back as my father strode across the room. The warrior had dropped his dagger and scrambled for a weapon. He snatched a copper urn and heaved it at Papa. The urn landed on his head with a terrible clunk. Papa stumbled back, cracking his skull on the stone hearth, and then lay still as death.

"For one long, terrifying moment I was certain that both my mother and father had been killed in the same night. Then another warrior came trotting to the doorway.

" 'Lord Henry has been slain. Hie you hence!' he shouted. 'We must away.' And with that, the man who murdered my mother dashed off. I suppose there was no sense risking his life for a baron who lay dead in his enemy's keep."

They sat in silence for a long time. At last Hugh understood her terror. When she sniffled, breaking the heavy spell, he looked up and found her eyes in the moonlight. They were filled with life, empathy, and doubt.

"I know you are not such a man," she whispered. "But I could never . . . never even attempt to . . ."

"I know," he said.

"Kisses are one thing, but . . ."

"I know now."

He tilted her chin up and placed his lips on hers. They tasted of salty tears and sweet fruit. He breathed in the scent of her, letting his kiss be the healing touch she craved. He loved her in this moment more than he had ever loved anything. Not for what she had given him, but for what he could give her—healing, compassion, understanding, devotion. All the things he'd never known a man could give.

When she sighed with contentment, infusing him with her luscious breath, he drew back and nodded, certain about what he had to do.

"We will go to see Abbot Gregory tomorrow."

"Why?" she said.

"To make our vows of celibacy."

She burst into tears again, and he swooped her into a hug.

"Do not be sad."

"No," she said. "I am crying with happiness. I knew you were an honorable man."

He held her till she quieted, then he rose, knowing he was condemning himself to a life of sweet torture. But if anyone on earth was worth it, it was Margrete.

Nineteen

The next morning they walked hand in hand through Long Grove toward Treyvaux Abbey.

"Are you certain?" she asked more than once.

"I am certain," he would answer and give her hand a reassuring squeeze. "This is part of the agreement we made when we married. Let it not be said that Sir Hugh de Greyhurst doesn't keep his promises."

"But this will be forever."

"I understand."

"Forever is . . . forever."

He looked down at her with his uncommonly steady gaze and then cracked a smile. "How astute you are, maiden."

She giggled, tossing back her head with a newfound sense of security. "You make me say the silliest things."

"Good," he said, chuckling, "let it not be said that Sir Hugh de Greyhurst married a woman smarter than him."

Then they laughed together, not at his feeble jest, but in a rare rejoicing of the peace they'd found together. And so it was in this lighthearted humor that they arrived to make their solemn vows.

They were greeted warmly by Abbess Phillipa de Claire, who seemed pleased, and surprised, that Hugh and Margrete were actually going through with their plans for a spiritual marriage. But when Hugh said he wanted Abbot Gregory to hear their vows that very afternoon, the abbess's sparkling, intelligent eyes clouded over.

"He does not look favorably on this notion," the abbess said in warning as she led them to the abbot's chamber door.

"He does not *have* to look favorably upon it," Hugh said with quiet anger. "He is not God. It is not his place to judge. He just needs to listen."

The abbess looked with quiet irony over her shoulder. "Your devotion to your wife, and your faith, pleases me well, my son. But it will not please Abbot Gregory."

A short time later the abbess knocked on the abbot's door. When it opened, she was greeted by a pale, bony-faced monk whose eyes widened at the sight of her.

"Yes, Mother Abbess?"

"May we come in, Prior Anselm?"

For a moment, it seemed that he would deny her, but in the end he nodded curtly. "Of course. I'm sure you have important business. Just because the abbot is busy with his missive to the new bishop . . ."

"Lady Margrete de Greyhurst and her husband Sir Hugh wish to see the abbot," the abbess said evenly.

At the mention of their names, the prior seemed to go pale. His eyes sharpened on the couple like blades on a wet stone.

"What is it?" An old man's voice came from behind the door.

The prior tipped his head back behind the door. "Abbess Phillipa de Claire wants—"

"Let her come in," the old abbot groused. "How many times do I have to tell you, Prior Anselm? Never keep the abbess waiting."

"But you have been ill, Father Abbot. I care only for your well-being. It's simply that—"

"Yes, yes. Now let them in."

At last the prior opened the door to reveal a simple chamber dominated by a large writing table. Sitting behind it, dwarfed in comparison, was a gaunt old man who had a short crop of gray hair, sunken eyes, and skeletal fingers.

"Good morning, Mother Abbess."

"Good morning, Father Abbot," she said in her crisp and confident manner, sharing a genuine smile with her male counterpart. "You have visitors today."

"So I see." He closed a book and gave them his full attention. "What is this about?"

"Visitors, Father Abbot," the prior repeated.

"I heard that much already, Prior Anselm. You may go now."

At the abbot's sharp tone, the prior colored pink. For a moment he almost looked healthy. He gave a terse nod and departed.

Phillipa held out her hand to present Hugh and Margrete. "You remember Lady Margrete? This is her husband, Sir Hugh de Greyhurst."

"Ah, so he is. We met at their wedding."

"Father Abbot, thank you for seeing us," Hugh said. "I hope we are not disturbing you."

"Of course you are," he said with a wry smile. "But I trust you have a good reason."

"We certainly do," Margrete said when Phillipa took a step back, indicating that they were on their own. "We have come to ask you to speak on our behalf to the new bishop. We would like an audience so that he might hear our vows of celibacy."

"So it's come to that, has it?"

When the frail abbot exchanged a look with the abbess, Hugh realized they'd discussed this matter before, and apparently had not come to any sort of agreement.

"My wife wants the bishop to hear our vows," Hugh said. "But I wonder if you could be our witness today. Here and now."

"I'm afraid not. And I cannot recommend you to the bishop."

"Why not?" asked Margrete, dismayed.

"Though I respect your love of God, having a woman remain celibate in a marriage defies the natural order of things. It is a woman's duty to submit to her husband. Just as Christ is the head of the church, a man is the head of the family. If the woman tries to circumvent that order, then she essentially controls her own ability to reproduce. And that is playing God." He smiled placatingly at Margrete. "Dear Lady Margrete, surely you do not wish to deny your husband, and the church, their God-given dominion over you?"

She swallowed hard. "How can I be defying God if all I want to do is remain pure in His eyes?"

He shook his head as he drummed his fingers on the desk. "It's not that simple. And I can tell you the bishop of Burnham has a harsher opinion of celibate marriages. He considers them a form of heresy."

"Heresy?" Hugh repeated disbelievingly.

The abbot blinked several times, gathering his patience. "Yes, my son. As you know the heretical group known as the Cathars believe that there are two mighty powers in the world. The power that is good is associated with spirit, and the power that is evil is associated with the physical world. Therefore, the Cathars believe, engaging in conjugal relations is essentially evil. These heretics also desire celibate marriages.''

Margrete's jaw dropped as she tried to follow this logic. ''But I am not a heretic. Quite the contrary. I love God.''

''My child,'' the abbot said, ''if you loved God with all your heart, you would have joined this monastery. Instead you're trying to have the best of both worlds—piousness as well as the benefits of marriage. You can't have it both ways. That is form of greed.''

''But I could not join this abbey! My father would not permit it.''

''Then you should obey his will.''

''Did God give woman no will at all, my lord abbot?'' Hugh's voice filled the room with its force.

''No, my son,'' the abbot replied. ''Woman lost her freedom of choice when Eve plucked the apple from the tree in the Garden of Eden.''

''And you would condemn all women for that one mistake?''

''Not I,'' the abbot said archly. ''But God. God made woman from man's rib, not the other way around. And it is God who condemns a woman for her natural sin.''

''If a woman is damned whether she sins or not,'' Hugh returned hotly, ''what good is faith?''

The abbot gasped in shock and Abbess Phillipa gripped Hugh's arm. ''Go gently, my son,'' she said. ''The abbot has spoken. Let us leave him in peace.''

''If you doubt my word,'' Gregory snapped, ''then speak to the bishop yourself. He will be leading mass here at Treyvaux Abbey this Sunday. Now good day to you both.''

He turned back to his papers, not looking up as his three visitors departed. Phillipa led them out into the cloisters, and when they were well away from the abbot's chambers, she pulled them aside.

"I'm sorry. The old bishop gave his blessing to more than one spiritual marriage. I doubt the good abbot would have responded this way if it were not for the arrival of Bishop Jerome."

"Can you not hear our vows, good abbess?" Hugh said.

"A nun does not have the authority of a priest. I cannot give sacraments or hear confessions. And even if I could, Bishop Jerome Blakely is said to be jealous of his authority, and dubious of mine. I think it would hurt your cause for me to intervene in any way."

Hugh and Margrete said brief farewells to the abbess and began their walk back to Longrove Barony. Fury burned in Hugh's belly like a white, hot poker. He did not even trust himself to speak, lest he curse the name of God Himself.

"What is it, my lord?" Margrete said at length.

He glanced down at his side and realized she'd been taking two steps for his every one. "Forgive me, my lady, I walk too fast." He slowed down and took her hand in his.

"What made you so angry?"

He stopped abruptly in the middle of the meadow. "I wonder that you should ask. Did the abbot not make you furious?"

She blinked up at him and brushed aside a tendril of hair that blew before her eyes. "No, I am not angry. It is not my position to question the will of God."

"But this is not the will of God! It is the will of these men who speak for Him!" he shouted. "How can you stand here and say you accept condemnation for your desire to be pure in heart and body? How can that be a sin? The way the abbot speaks, you'd think you'd created original sin yourself!"

"Please, Hugh, I know you are suspicious of priests after your experience with Father James, but this is surely just a misunderstanding. We will seek the bishop this Sunday and ask him ourselves. Surely he will not refuse us if he knows our hearts and motives are pure."

Hugh frowned at her and shook his head. "You are too naive. Ranulf has something to do with this. And I tremble to think what hell he'll create if he's now sharing even a portion of his cousin's power. Mark my words, Margrete. We have not heard the last of Sir Ranulf Blakely."

Twenty

hen they returned to the manor house after a brief stop at Longrove Castle, Margrete went to the kitchen to supervise the midday meal while Hugh went in search of Brian. He found his squire grooming his destrier at the far end of the stable.

As Hugh strode down the hay-strewn aisle between the stalls, several horses bobbed their heads and stamped their feet in greeting.

"Brian," he called out.

"Wha—?" Brian started with a jolt at the sound of Hugh's voice and turned to him, pale and wide-eyed, as if Hugh had just risen from the dead. "My lord! What are you doing here?"

"I want you to go to Tilmon River and watch over the repairs of the ferry. You can leave this work to the groom."

"He's sick today. My lord, what are you doing here? I thought you would be in the great hall. You said you were going to look at maps of the barony today."

"I had a change of plans. I went out early with Lady Margrete to Treyvaux Abbey."

"But you didn't take horses?"

"No, we walked."

"And Lady Margrete?" Brian dropped the brush from his hands, then scrambled to retrieve it, leaning a hand on the big round belly of the silver stallion. "Sh-she's at the castle today, is she not?"

Hugh frowned. "No. She's in the manor house right now, readying our meal."

Brian's eyes grew even rounder, then he cleared his throat and gave Hugh a weak smile. "Oh, how thoughtful of her. I-I suppose the cook is ill with whatever is ailing the groom."

"Perhaps," Hugh replied distractedly as he patted the flanks of his destrier. He actually missed riding on the lists now and then. But not enough to mount up again. "You can be spared here. Go to the ferry and see how the workers are progressing."

"Yes, my lord," Brian said, hurrying to put his brush away, and he was out of the stables before Hugh could say another word.

"What was bothering him?" Hugh muttered to himself. He turned his attention to the destrier and retrieved the brush that Brian had put away. Hugh smoothed it over the bristly coat, dragging the brush from the beast's withers to its tail, over and over until he was sure the horse's coat would gleam in the sun like a polished coin.

"Good boy," Hugh crooned, and the horse whinnied contentedly in reply.

"Sir Hugh?" A small, feminine voice called from the entrance to the stable where sunlight spilled on piles of yellow-green hay.

"Yes? What is it?"

The woman said no more. Instead she walked with calm precision along the stalls, clutching what appeared to be a handful of daisies. Was she a servant? Not one that he had ever seen. As she drew closer, her slender form took shape in the shadows and Hugh could make out more details. Her hair was an undistinguished brown color and was pulled back into a sloppy braid. Her lips were full and had been stained with berries; her eyes, somehow innocent and jaded at the same time, gazed upon him without timidity. It wasn't until she took one last step into the light that fell down from an overhead shutter that Hugh saw the badge sewn to the breast of her low-cut garment. *A prostitute.*

"Are ye Sir Hugh?" she inquired, her flat brown eyebrows forming a little question mark on her forehead.

"Yes."

"I thank ye, my lord, fer sending fer me."

"What do you mean? Who are you?"

"Ruth." The prostitute began to loosen the girdle swathed around her straight waist. Then, to Hugh's amazement, she reached down and pulled her gown up over her head, tossing it on the ground in a crumpled heap. She stood before him wearing nothing but a thin chemise. "I was waiting fer ye in the great hall, but yer squire said I should come here instead and take ye to the loft above the horses."

"My squire!" Brian, that whelp. Hugh would blister his arse but good when he got his hands on him. "There has been a mistake. I did not send for you. I—"

Hugh stopped short when Ruth suddenly pulled her chemise over her head, tossing it aside without a jot of embarrassment. She was now utterly naked—her breasts full and plump, her hips thin, a triangle of dark hair hiding what she was readily offering.

Hugh swallowed hard. In the past he would not hesitate

to avail himself of such a woman. He would have pleasured himself without a second thought. But now he was married, and he had promised Margrete he would take a vow of celibacy. To couple with a whore now would be a complete betrayal to his wife.

Ruth stepping toward him. "Ye already paid fer me. And handsomely. Ye shouldn't let Magdalene take ye so next time. Tell yer squire."

"There won't be a next time, Ruth, just as there won't be a this time." Hugh reached to turn her out, but she grabbed his hand, placing it on her right breast. He froze at the softness in his palm.

Margrete approached the stables with William MacGregor hot on her trail. He'd been begging for more ale, and she'd turned him down, saying he'd have to wait until the meal. But, as usual, that did little to stop his complaints. Margrete was hoping Hugh could divert him. By the time she reached the stable entrance, MacGregor had caught up to her and was tugging at her sleeve.

"You must admit, Lady Margrete, that I've saved yer father's life more than once. And lassie, he depends on me to keep oop his spirits. All I ask is fer some spirits in return."

"I know that well enough, Sir William," she said over her shoulder as she stepped into the shadows of the stable. "And I am grateful. I simply think you can wait until the meal is served. Talk to Lord Hugh about it. I saw him headed this way earlier. He's here somewhere. It's time he came in to sup."

She saw Hugh at the end of the stalls and hurried toward him. "Here he is!"

At the sound of her voice, Hugh looked up with the most peculiar look of horror she'd ever seen.

"What is it, my lord?" she said, laughing. "You look as if you've seen a ghost. I—"

Margrete came to a profound stop when she realized Hugh was not alone; that he was, in fact, standing next to a naked woman. Moreover, one whose breast he held in his palm. Sir William, who was slow to react, ran headlong into Margrete.

"Ach, lassie, ye don't have to be so rude. If ye don't want me here ye should just say . . ." Sir William ceased his rants when he spied Hugh and the prostitute. A grin spread slowly across his wizened face. "Ach, mon, there's a lad! I have new respect for ye."

"Sir William!" Margrete chastised him.

"Once ye get started on these matters ye can't stop, eh, laddie? Why, on me wedding night, I had me wife ten—"

"Silence, old man!" Hugh shouted, pulling his hand away at last, looking at the appendage accusingly as if it alone were responsible for this mess. "Margrete, this is not what it would seem."

"No, I'm sure it is much more than it would seem. William MacGregor, come to the kitchen and I'll get you another cup of ale. And then . . . I'll have one myself."

Hugh watched her storm off, then turned slowly to the prostitute, who seemed thoroughly unmoved by the scene she'd witnessed. Apparently she'd been through this before.

"Get dressed," he commanded.

"But my lord—"

"Get dressed! You and I are going to explain this to Lady Margrete. You're going to tell her that my squire paid you for this visit. And then I'm going to send you on your merry way."

Ruth, wide-eyed at the anger that seethed in his voice, nodded and began to pull her clothing back on. When she was dressed, Hugh grabbed her hand and pulled her alongside him in search of his wife. She was not in any of the usual places—not in her chamber, or the kitchen, or the dovecote, or the mews.

"Damnation take her," Hugh muttered as he and Ruth exited the manor. He was literally scratching his head in confusion when he looked up and saw Margrete in the one place he would never have imagined, doing the one thing of which he would never have guessed her capable.

"Why is she chopping wood?" Ruth asked, pointing to Margrete and frowning up at Hugh.

He did not reply, captivated as he was by the sight. His frown of wonder turned slowly into a grin of admiration. She'd picked up where he had left off at the woodpile. Raising the heavy axe with surprising strength, she brought the blade down hard. And though her strokes did not penetrate the logs with as much force as when Hugh had wielded the axe, she was making progress. *Thwack! Thwack! Thwack!* She pounded the wood over and over, a resounding testimony to her jealousy. When Hugh and his unexpected visitor silently moved toward her, she glanced up and gave them an angry sneer.

"Go away!" She flipped back the locks of flaxen hair that were falling into her eyes. Perspiration was glistening on her flushed cheeks.

"No," Hugh said, thoroughly amused. "We won't go away."

"Isn't there somewhere else"—*Thwack!*—"that you two can"—*Thwack!*—"have your tryst?"

"We were not trysting," Hugh said resolutely. "Now put that axe down and talk to me."

He took a step closer and she spun around, raising the axe threateningly in the air.

"Don't come any closer."

"You won't hurt me with that, Margrete."

"How I'd like to!"

"You're angry. That must mean you care about me."

Her eyes narrowed and simmered at this. Then she turned with a frustrated growl and brought the axe down hard on the wood again.

"Why should I care about you?" she said as she continued to chop. "You claimed to want to take a vow of celibacy, and all the while you were finding release behind my back. What a hypocrite! What a lying, dishonest, dishonorable, untrustworthy . . ."

She stopped and gasped when Hugh came up behind her and grabbed the handle of the axe.

"I'll take that," he said, giving it a tug.

She tightened her grip. "No!" He gave it a yank, but she held on for dear life. "I'll not give this up."

Not wanting to fight like children over a coveted toy, he released his hold. "Margrete, be reasonable."

"I have always been reasonable," she said, taking a step back and wiping the perspiration from her brow with a forearm. "I have been reasonable and responsible. And this is what I get for it. Did you know I have chopped wood before? I have mucked out stalls and cleaned dovecotes. I have washed clothing in the river and gathered filthy rushes after a long winter. There is probably nothing on this barony that I haven't done to keep it going. And now you come along, supposedly to help me. But you've been using me, claiming to want a spiritual marriage and relieving yourself of your lust with women like this."

She waved a hand at Ruth.

"I never said I wanted a spiritual marriage," Hugh clarified, raising a finger in the air. "But I agreed to it. And I have not violated that agreement."

"What do you call this?" Again Margrete motioned to Ruth.

"I call this a very bad decision on Brian's part. My squire hired this woman out of a man's pity for another. He naturally thought I would welcome her company." He paused and grimaced, as one pained by a sudden realization. "I did not. And I do not."

"I saw you, Hugh!" Margrete threw the axe to the ground, stepped forward, and ground the words between her teeth. "I saw you with your hand on her breast."

"That you did," Hugh admitted, sighing as he raked a hand through his hair. "Ruth tried to seduce me. God's teeth, woman! Are you so naive not to know anything about a man? I do not claim to be a saint such as you. I am but a man. And yet . . . in the end I could not do it."

He reddened. How could he tell this maiden that even touching the breast of another woman, he had not become aroused. Somehow his wife's purity had left him with no taste for casual trysts.

"I want no woman but you, Margrete. That's the way of it, God help me."

The prostitute blinked with embarrassment but managed to look Margrete in the eye. "It's as he says, my lady. His lordship's squire hired me. He said as how his master was in need of a little pleasuring."

Margrete sighed and looked at Hugh.

"It's true," he said. "This is Brian's doing."

Margrete crossed her arms and began to pace, now and then looking at Hugh, now and then regarding Ruth. At last she heaved another sigh and came face-to-face with the prostitute. "Ruth, do you enjoy coupling with men?"

The girl blinked in surprise, then blushed and shook her head, eyes cast downward. "No, me lady."

"Then why do you do it?"

Ruth shuffled her feet from side to side.

"Do not be afraid," Margrete added softly, touching her

arm for support. "I am not here to judge you. Why do you offer yourself for such base pleasures?"

"M-me father sold me to Magdalene, the whoremonger, when me family was starving."

"How old were you?"

"Eight," the girl whispered.

"You can't be more than sixteen now," Margrete said. She glared at Hugh, then turned a motherly gaze to the whore. "You're much too young to live such a hellish existence. Ruth, how would you like to be my handmaid? I've been doing without one for years. But now that my lord and master is here to reap more prosperity from the land, we can afford one."

"What?" the girl whispered, looking up in astonishment.

"What?" Hugh echoed with dismay.

"I have need of a handmaid, and you would do wonderfully."

"But the badge," Ruth said, pointing to the circle of cloth that marked her as an outcast.

"We'll burn it," Margrete said, a new tone of defiance ringing in her voice. "You will now be my servant, and I dare anyone to defy that decision."

She turned a scathing look to her husband. "Do you object?"

Hugh gave her a forlorn look. "Margrete, you can't take a prostitute into your household—"

"A *former* prostitute. And yes I can. Just watch me."

He blinked as if she was not quite in focus. He did not know this angry, resolute woman. "Margrete, what has gotten into you?"

She took a step forward and gripped his tunic with both hands. He wasn't sure if she was going to give him a good shake or a hug. Her face was blazing with defiance, but there was also a deep well of hurt in her eyes that stabbed at his heart like a pruning knife.

"You—you men—will not deny Ruth this chance. You men who condemn women as whores and then condemn them at the same time for wanting to be holy, for aspiring to something better. If we are condemned no matter what we do, then we might as well please ourselves. Isn't that right, Ruth?"

She turned her head over her shoulder and saw a glimmer of hope and a tremor of fear fly across the girl's face.

"But Magdalene, my lady, she'll beat me fer this."

"No, she won't," Margrete said decisively. "Sir Hugh will take care of Magdalene. He'll make it worth her while to let you go."

"With what, Margrete?" Hugh interjected.

"The wealth your able leadership will reap from this godforsaken barony."

"Margrete . . ."

"And Ruth will be sleeping with *me*," she said, finally letting go of Hugh's tunic. Then she added with a tart smile, "Not you."

"Don't do this, Margrete. It will only bring you embarrassment."

"I don't care," she said. "I simply don't care. There is a passage in the Bible you might find of interest. Matthew 9:13. Read it sometime."

As Margrete put her arm around Ruth and led her to the house, Hugh shouted after them. "I *will* read it. Just as soon as I learn how!"

He watched them go, flushed with anger, then he threw back his head and roared with laughter, remembering the sight of his lovely, jealous wife whacking away at the wood.

Twenty-one

"You will sleep near me on a pallet in my bedchamber," Margrete said, pushing open the door, guiding Ruth in with a hand on the small of her back.

Lady Edith sat in the corner by the embrasure, working a needle through her embroidery. "Ow," she muttered after pricking her finger.

"Greetings, Edith. I want you to meet Ruth, my new handmaiden. Ruth, this is Lady Edith, my lady-in-waiting."

"Oh, how exciting." Edith dropped the embroidery in her lap and clapped her hands together. "It will be wonderful to have another woman in the house."

She rose with a sparkling smile and came to greet Ruth with a hug. When she drew back, her crossed eyes settled on the young woman's chest. "Oh, what a lovely medallion! I can't quite make it out. Are those cherubim? Or your father's crest?"

Ruth shot a nervous glance to Margrete, who cleared her throat and glared at her lady-in-waiting. "Lady Edith, what you are admiring is a badge of prostitution."

Edith gasped and flung both hands to her mouth. "I'm so sorry. I couldn't see clearly."

"But I trust Ruth's profession will make no difference to you," Margrete continued as she led the girl to a chair. "I fully expect you to give her your warmest welcome and help teach her her duties as a handmaid. She is giving up her life of prostitution. As you know, God forgives us all our sins. We can do no less ourselves."

"B-but of course," Edith stammered, then recovered her smile. "A prostitute. How exciting!"

"In truth, my lady," Ruth said, "it's dreadful."

Edith's mouth puckered in disappointment.

"There are no knights in shining armor in whore-houses," Margrete commented wryly. "Now help me prepare this girl for castle life."

"Of course."

Since the noon meal had long passed, Margrete sent for cheese and bread from the kitchen. Ruth ate voraciously while Edith organized a bath and sorted through trunks of older gowns to find some suitable for a servant. And all the while the lady-in-waiting prattled on about her hopes for marriage, until a knock sounded at the door.

"Who is it?" Margrete called out, bracing herself for the possibility of another confrontation with Hugh. But it was his squire.

"Lady Edith . . ." Brian came to a jolting stop when he spied Margrete. "Oh, my lady! I didn't expect you here."

"Brian," she fairly growled, starting toward him. "You impudent, sinful little—"

"No, Lady Margrete!" Edith said, stepping in between them. "What is the matter? Brian wanted to take me on a picnic."

Margrete flung a hand to her chest. "And you said yes? Do you know what this young man did?"

"He hired me," Ruth said, chewing a curd of cheese as she spoke.

Edith looked down at Ruth, aghast.

"Edith, it's not what it would seem," Brian said.

"I've heard *that* before," Margrete snapped.

"I'm sure he had his reasons," Edith said placatingly. "Please, my lady, let me hear him out."

"Do so at your own risk," Margrete said icily.

"You yourself said God forgives all our sins. Therefore you must forgive Brian his faults as well."

Stymied, Margrete waved her off. "Go on, then. I will help Ruth bathe. But keep your distance from that young squire, Edith, if you know what's good for you."

Edith and Brian broke out in relieved smiles. Brian gazed on her as if she were the Madonna incarnate. My God, Margrete thought, looking at their foolish grins, they're in love! When had that happened?

"I'll be back in an hour, my lady," Edith said, hurrying after Brian, who had already made his escape. Edith paused at the door to wave good-bye to Margrete, then turned and ran headlong into the doorframe. "Oh!"

"Are you all right?"

The lady-in-waiting rubbed her forehead, then let out a rush of giggles. "Never been better!"

When Edith dashed down the hall, Margrete turned to Ruth, shaking her head. "Why on earth do women react that way to men?"

"I 'aven't any notion, me lady. Men are all pigs as far as I've seen."

"Indeed," Margrete said on a sigh.

After the kitchen scullions had brought up pails of hot water, Ruth climbed into her bath and shivered with pleasure.

"Feel good?" Margrete said with a smile as she sat down on a stool next to her.

"It's heaven," Ruth said, breaking into a smile for the first time since she'd arrived. "I've never had a hot bath before."

"Never? Oh, you poor thing. Some say they're unhealthy, but I delight in them."

Margrete scrubbed her down and washed her hair and when Ruth had toweled herself dry and donned a simple linen gown, the lady of the manor nodded with satisfaction. "Ruth, you look as fresh as a daisy."

The girl beamed at the compliment, then frowned. "But I'll never be as clean as you, me lady. Yer skin is fair and not scarred like mine."

Margrete blinked with sadness, reminded of the white blotches on Ruth's back and legs. She hadn't wanted to ask the girl how she'd gotten them. Doubtless she'd been whipped. "You look lovely, Ruth. I mean it truly."

"I wish I was as fair as you. Yer's is a pure beauty, my lady. Though yer could use a ribbon in yer hair."

"A ribbon?" Margrete smothered a smile at this unexpected bit of advice. She ran her hands under her neck and lifted her hair back over her shoulders. "You think that would look pretty?"

Ruth nodded enthusiastically. "Oh, yes, me lady. Men like pretty strips of color braided in a lady's hair."

"How do you know?"

"They told me. Lots of men told me that."

Margrete smiled with melancholy, wondering if Ruth would ever be able to forget her days in Magdalene's whorehouse. And Margrete wondered if she herself would ever be able to erase the image of Hugh touching Ruth. He might not have hired the girl, but there was little doubt that some part of him was still a slave to desire.

• • •

Early Sunday morning Hugh and Brian sat like two stiff sentinals in a horse-drawn chariot outside the manor, waiting to take the women to mass at Treyvaux Abbey.

"Why does it always take women so long to dress?" Brian asked, frowning at the sliver of sun peeking up from the horizon.

"They have secret rituals," Hugh replied, also staring at the sunrise. "They practice alchemy and magical tricks and cast spells on men. They just *pretend* that the time is being spent on making themselves pretty."

"Truly?"

A half-smile slid up one of Hugh's rugged cheeks. "No."

"Not that I'm in a hurry to see them," Brian hastened to add. "I've managed to avoid Lady Margrete for days. You don't suppose she'll box my ears in front of the bishop, do you?"

Hugh crossed his arms and rubbed his chin. "Hmmm. It's possible." When Brian gulped, Hugh grinned. "Don't worry, lad. I doubt she'll do anything to embarrass her family in front of the bishop, no matter how angry she might be over your antics. But if you see her coming after you with an axe when we return home, I'd run if I were you."

"An axe?" Brian's brashly handsome face wrinkled with anxiety.

"I'm jesting, Brian. Ah, here our ladies come now."

Margrete appeared first, looking elegant and modest in a silvery blue gown. Both Brian and Hugh looked for signs of fury in her eyes, but she was clearly preoccupied with other matters, presumably her impending introduction to the bishop.

She was followed by Lady Edith, who had drawn back her strawberry blond hair beneath a flowing veil. Her chin was swathed with a wimple, and her eyes, crossed though they were, shimmered like two priceless emeralds.

"Have you ever seen a prettier lass?" Brian crooned softly.

"She's lovely."

"Oh, I know her eyes are askew, but it matters not to me."

Heretofore, Brian had been wont to chase the prettiest skirts, but he apparently had decided to love by deeper standards. Hugh recalled the story Brian had once told him about how he'd nearly been burned at the stake because one of his eyes was blue and the other green. That experience had apparently given Brian great empathy for Edith's plight, and perhaps made him understand better than most that one must look inward to find true beauty.

"She is a lovely and vivacious woman," Hugh said. "You have chosen well."

"Oh, no," Brian whispered.

Hugh looked up to see what his squire was bemoaning, then groaned himself. Lady Edith was followed by none other than Ruth, dressed in her Sunday best. Close on her heels came Peter, who gazed at Ruth with an unusually solicitous look.

"I can't believe she'd bring a whore to church," Brian rasped in frustration. "Now I'm in for it."

"A former whore," Hugh corrected. "And I'd believe anything at this point. I'm married to the only woman on earth who takes every chapter and verse of the Scriptures to heart."

"Do the Scriptures tell you to take a whore—a former whore—to meet the new bishop?"

"Jesus said: For I came not to call the righteous, but sinners," Hugh said, quoting Matthew. "Remember? You read that to me two days ago at my bidding."

"I read it, but I suppose I did not hear it."

By now the women were nearing the cart. Brian jumped down to keep Lady Edith from walking into the harnessed horses. Hugh helped Margrete into the chariot, seating her on one of the long benches that ran the length of the wooden cart. Then he helped Ruth, whom he hardly recognized. Her face was pale and fair as any maiden's. She looked years younger without her garish cosmetics.

"Nice of you to join us, Ruth," Hugh said.

She didn't look at him directly, but nodded as Peter gently placed her next to her mistress. Margrete rewarded Hugh's compliment with a soft smile.

"Are we ready, then?" he said.

"Go to Longrove Castle and pick up my father and then we can go to the abbey."

"Is that wise? Are you sure you want the bishop to meet Lord Giles?"

She nodded with a worried frown. "He is growing weaker by the day, Hugh. The fate of his soul is more important now than the fate of this barony. If the bishop notices his confusion, then so be it. You are now the lord of Longrove. Let Bishop Jerome, and all the king's men for that matter, deal with you now."

Hugh sucked in a breath and gave her a wry smile. "I can hardly wait for that."

Her icy blue eyes thawed a bit at his gentle sarcasm. When she turned to Ruth, Hugh noticed a pale blue strip entwined in her plaited blond hair.

"Pretty ribbon," he remarked.

She snapped her head toward him and frowned in surprise, then touched her braid with one hand. "I didn't think you'd notice."

"There's nothing you do that I don't notice," he whispered, taking her hand and kissing it.

• • •

Sir Ranulf Blakely saw the chariot's lumbering approach long before its passengers had a chance to see him.

"By God," he whispered just outside the gatehouse of Treyvaux Abbey. "What Providence befalls those with wicked hearts!"

"What is it?" said Keath, dismounting and handing his reins over to a monk who tended the abbey stables on Sundays.

Ranulf pointed to the cart rounding a bend in the road. Keath squinted, then his eyes widened in amazement. "Good God, Sir Hugh de Greyhurst is bringing not only his wife but his whore as well. Where does he get his courage?"

"His wife?" Ranulf said. "Can you call a woman your wife if you've never bedded her?"

Keath rubbed his hands free of the grit from his reins. "Good question. Eh, what have you in mind, Ranulf? More trouble? I see that glint in your eyes."

"You'd have to be blind to miss it. Let it suffice to say I have my plans. And I've just decided today is the day they go into effect. I beg your pardon, but I'm off to see my cousin before mass begins. Prior Anselm tells me Lady Margrete comes to church here on the days when she doesn't attend mass in Longrove Village. But I may not get another opportunity to deal with all of them here at once."

Ranulf gave his cohort a courtly bow and headed toward the shady cloisters to the piercing sound of church bells. He found his cousin in the monks' chapter house. The bishop was fully dressed in his chasuble and alb, a mitre rising to a swollen point on his head. In his hand he held a crosier, a staff that always looked to Ranulf suspiciously like a shepherd's crook. Jerome and Abbot Gregory were sitting in two chairs, discussing church matters, when Ranulf burst into the room.

Seeing the flare of pique in Jerome's eyes, Ranulf bowed. "Forgive my untimely visit, my lord bishop and beloved cousin, but I would have a word with you before mass begins."

The abbot, a skeleton of a man, rose and tipped his head in the bishop's direction. "I will excuse myself now, my lord. We can talk further later."

Ranulf waited until the abbot departed, then he turned to his cousin with devilish glee dancing in his eyes.

"Dear Coz, we both have reason to rejoice today."

Jerome propped his chin on his fist with a look of ennui. "And why is that?"

"Because the object of my joy, the woman of my dreams, is on her way to the abbey as we speak. You will have an opportunity, from your pulpit of course, to put her foolish notions to rest."

"You speak of the lady of Longrove? What have you found out about that situation?"

"A great deal." Ranulf helped himself to a pitcher of wine, pouring a cup and sipping. "I've been dying to tell you, but you were away from your castle."

"God help me I was. I've been traveling about the bishopric meeting my flock." He looked up at his crosier with boredom. "Thank the saints this is the last stop before I return to Burnham Castle."

Ranulf went to the chair warmed by Abbot Gregory and hoisted a boot on it, leaning on his knee as he cradled the cup in his hands. "How would you like to expand your holdings with one of the richest hides in the territory?"

"Kilbury Hide?" Jerome said, pursing his lips. "You're all talk, Ranulf. I've looked into that matter and learned that I won't get that hide without a fight."

"You're wrong, it could be yours by week's end."

The bishop's eyes gleamed brighter. "Do tell."

"You were right about Lady Margrete. She wants to have a spiritual marriage. She's on her way right now to speak to you about it."

"Hmmmm."

"Forget your planned homily this morning and instead speak out against the heresy of celibate marriages. That way when I marry Margrete myself and take her virginity, no one will doubt that I am her true and legitimate husband. And while you're at it, give a rousing speech on the hell-fires suffered by prostitutes and men who avail themselves of whores."

"And what will you do to ensure that I claim Kilbury Hide?"

"I'll make sure that Margrete is my wife before the week is through, and then I'll grant you the hide, pure and simple."

"How will you get Lady Margrete away from Lord Hugh?"

Ranulf straightened and gulped the remains of his wine, licking his lips and exhaling with satisfaction. "I'll claim her in the oldest way known to man."

The bishop sat up, alarm coloring his cheeks. "You mean you're going to—"

"Shhhh." Ranulf held a finger to his lips, his eyelids at half-mast. "Don't say it, Coz, for you can't be held accountable for that which you do not know. Just leave it to me."

The bishop interlaced his bejeweled fingers and pressed them to his mouth, thinking about the ramifications. "And what of the hidden treasure?"

"The D'Arbereau treasure is hidden so well," Ranulf said with a blossoming smile, "that no one seems to know about it. When I become the lord of Longrove, my first order of business will be finding out where the Norman treasure is buried.''

''How can it be that no one knows where it is?''

''Perhaps Lord Giles is senile and has forgotten about it. Or perhaps the old fox wants to keep it all to himself. Either way, Lady Margrete and Sir Hugh haven't heard about it. And they never will, for soon it will be mine!''

Twenty-two

argrete watched the bishop closely during Mass from her place in the second pew. Hugh sat to her right and Lord Giles to her left. The other members of their household were scattered nearby.

The bishop made an impressive entrance from the back of the chapel, forging through a trail of incense, his handsome face serious and pious, as the monks and nuns sang a haunting Latin hymn from their choir stalls.

Jerome Blakely, simply put, looked like a bishop. His voice was rich and authoritative, his face handsome and dignified, and he seemed to have the presence one would expect of someone in his position. But Margrete's hopes that he might also be wise and compassionate quickly vanished when he started the homily.

He rose to the octagonal pulpit and matter-of-factly spoke his opening benedictions. Then he cleared his throat and assumed an expression of grave concern.

"It has come to my attention," Bishop Jerome said,

"that a debate over spiritual marriages has surfaced in this bishopric."

Margrete took in a tiny snatch of air, exchanging a stunned look with Hugh.

"What, you might wonder," the bishop continued, briefly meeting Margrete's gaze, "is wrong with a woman swearing eternal chastity to our God in heaven? There is nothing inherently wrong with chastity. In fact, a maiden's vow is a worthy one, an exalted one, if it's made by someone who takes the veil and lives out her days among fellow sisters who have likewise devoted their lives to God."

Hugh's hand found hers on the pew in the folds of her gown and gave her a reassuring squeeze.

"But a woman who is married," Bishop Jerome continued, raising his voice to give the full effect of his ire, "and denies her husband his conjugal rights is actually *displeasing* God in heaven."

Blood rushed to Margrete's cheeks, burning her ears.

"What is he talking about?" Lord Giles whispered.

"He's talking about spiritual marriages," she whispered in return. "Now be quiet, Papa, please."

A grin spread beneath the mass of his gray beard. "Spiritual marriages? Isn't that what you wanted, daughter? Oh, but that would never do. I need grandchildren."

"Hush, Father. *Please!*"

"How can it please God to see a woman decide her own fate?" the bishop droned on. "We all know that it was Eve who lured Adam out of paradise, tempting him with knowledge and condemning mankind to an eternity of separation from God. It was a woman who ruined mankind. Therefore, it cannot please God to see a woman who would willfully deny her husband the right to have sons. If a woman cannot multiply, as God commanded, what value does she have?

None, I say. And any woman who has the temerity to chose her own fate is a woman who needs to have the sin of pride beaten out of her with a very hard stick.''

Hugh inched forward in the pew, every muscle taut as if ready for battle, but Margrete clutched his arm, nudging him back.

"Moreover," the bishop said, eyeing Hugh with displeasure, "a woman who denies her husband, who refuses to serve her husband as the church serves Christ, in effect leads her husband down the path to sin. For would not a husband who has been denied his conjugal rights be tempted to avail himself of whores and prostitutes and the like?''

There was a gasp from the crowd. Margrete was too dazed to discern its source. It might have been Brian, or poor Ruth. Margrete looked down the pew and saw the girl shaking, hands covering her face. It was a mistake to bring her here, she now realized. She had thought this would be a good way to start Ruth's reformation. But she didn't count on the bishop being so much less forgiving than Christ Himself.

"Any woman who could cause such mayhem over her unwillingness to submit to a man," he continued, "is committing a form of heresy.''

This time a chorus of voices rose in a gasp. The very mention of heresy raised in everyone's minds the visions of people burning at the stake. The bishop must have known this, for he gave the crowd a sublime smile.

"Yes, heresy. For what is the difference between questioning the existence of God and calling into question the hierarchy of power created by God? God to church. Church to man. Man to woman. That is the natural order. The lesser, the weaker vessel, must submit! Is there anyone in this church today who questions the righteousness of this order?''

In the morbid silence that followed, Margrete's heart pounded so loudly she could scarcely hear the nervous shuffling of feet in the pews around her.

''Is there anyone,'' the bishop nearly shouted now, ''who desires to have a spiritual marriage, knowing how displeasing it is to God?''

Margrete turned to stone, or so it seemed; not like Lot's wife, but rather like one of the angels who guarded over the flowers in the abbey gardens—lifeless, frozen in time, not quite ascended to heaven and not quite belonging to the earth. She felt all eyes turn her way, waiting to see her reaction. But she returned the gaze of only one person. The only one who mattered now. Her husband.

After the bishop's unexpected diatribe, Margrete exited the church in a daze. She very likely would have collapsed on the front steps if Hugh hadn't been supporting one of her arms. Outside the bright sunshine momentarily blinded her, making a cheery mockery of the darkness she felt descending on her. Normally, she would talk with neighbors and other abbey visitors, but today no one stopped to chat. Lords and ladies passing by cast their eyes away, making it clear they wanted nothing to do with the woman who had so obviously earned the wrath of the new bishop.

On the bumpy ride home to Longrove, everyone was silent, too stunned to speak about the bishop's unexpected attack on Margrete. Only Lord Giles had the heart to protest.

''Why would no one speak to us?'' he said. ''Why did they all turn their backs?''

Margrete had no easy answers. Only Abbess Phillipa de Claire had sought her out after the bishop's stinging rebuke.

She had warmly hugged Margrete, whispering in her ear, "Fear not, God knows the righteousness of your quest."

But church politics were too complex for her father to comprehend, and so she merely patted his hand, saying, "Do not worry, Father."

"But why would no one speak to us?"

"Don't worry, Father, it's too difficult for you to understand. Wait till you're feeling better."

Unfortunately, Lord Giles understood much more about what was at stake than Margrete would have credited. When they neared Longrove Castle, he whispered to her, "The bishop will not let this matter go. He will hound you to the grave if you do not give in to his wishes."

She looked at him, astonished by his perceptiveness, but made no reply. She hoped he wasn't speaking like one of the prophets of old—men who were considered lunatics except for rare moments of uncommon lucidity when they were gripped by a fit of the sight, or by a revelation from God. Did her father see some dire outcome waiting in the future?

She shook off her premonitions and stroked one of his hands, though her gentle caresses did little to soothe his agitation. By the time they reached the castle he seemed to have aged a year.

"Why don't you rest a while, Father," Margrete said, then turned to her husband. "I will stay here at the castle if you can spare me from the manor."

"Of course," Hugh said, his sensitive eyes narrowing with concern on his father-in-law. After helping Margrete down from the cart, he embraced her and tucked a fist under her chin, tipping her head back to burrow his eyes into hers.

"Do not fear, wife," he whispered. "I am here. I would protect you from the devil himself."

She sighed contentedly when he pressed his lips to hers

in a reassuring kiss, yesterday's discord now seeming like yesteryear's in light of these new problems.

She helped her father into the castle and by the time the old man reached his solar he was complaining of chest pains. Quick to fear the worst, Margrete made him climb immediately into bed and ordered meat broth from the kitchen.

She opened a window and sang songs from her childhood as she mopped his brow with a cool, wet cloth. The old man smiled at her from the comfort of his pillows, humming along when he had the strength. Then, his eyes sharpening with rare lucidity, he studied her with a smile of wonder.

"You look so much like your mother." He reached out and stroked her face. "Rosamunde was such a beautiful wife."

By now a servant had brought a cup of broth and Margrete lifted the spoon to his lips. As her father slurped the beefy-smelling soup, she realized this was the first time he had ever spoken of her mother in the past tense.

"I was heartbroken when she died," he said, licking his lips and gently fending off the spoon when she tried to give him another portion.

"I was too, Papa."

He blinked as if seeing her for the first time since that tragedy. His eyes seemed to swim with memories, half-thoughts, and hopes buried but not forgotten. He pursed his lips and tried to form words that couldn't quite be found.

"What is it, Father?" she asked softly, dabbing at a drop of broth that had fallen in his beard.

"There was something I was going to tell you a long time ago, but I can't quite remember."

"Don't worry about it and it will come to you when you least expect it."

He gripped one of her wrists. "No, there is no more time. If I don't remember it now . . ." His pale cheeks colored with frustration. "I was going to give you something. Something of great value . . . when you came of age."

"You have given me so many things of value," she said, gripping his hand. His fingers were smooth. It seemed that time calloused a man's hands, then smoothed them out in the end.

"No," he said impatiently. "There was something . . . something of beauty. Something sparkling and bright . . . I hid it somewhere, but I don't remember . . ."

"Hush, Father," she said, soothing his brow with her hand. "It doesn't matter anymore. You have given me all I need. I love you, Papa."

"I love you, Margrete." He sighed and shut his eyes. "Perhaps I'll remember tomorrow."

"Yes, Papa, tomorrow."

There was no tomorrow for Lord Giles. He died that night in his sleep. Margrete, who slumbered on a pallet by his bed, woke up moments after it happened as if she'd been startled by the utter stillness in the room. She listened for his breathing, but heard only the tap of a tree branch on the window. She broke out in a cold sweat, the chill of absence, of loneliness, shivering along her limbs, and she knew. Her last living relative was dead.

"Papa?" she mewled nonetheless, crawling to her knees and then climbing to the edge of the bed. He looked like he was sleeping, his face peaceful and blue in the moonlight. She touched his forehead. It was still warm. Regret that she had not been awake to hear his last breath struck at her heart like a dagger.

Then she remembered what she had been dreaming: her father, young and strong, smiling at some jest, striding across Kilbury Hide, motioning for her to follow over a hill, but she couldn't keep up. She was crying, saying, "Wait for me!" But of course he couldn't, and immediately she realized how much happier he would be in heaven with her mother. The best part of him had left long ago.

Lord Giles was buried with little fanfare a few days later next to his wife in the family crypt in Longrove Chapel. Sir William wept heartily, as boisterous in his grief as he had been persistent in his complaints about his treatment at Longrove.

After the funeral mass, the old Scot fell on his knees at the chapel steps and begged Margrete not to throw him out. She assured him she wouldn't and, struggling with her own tears, she motioned for Hugh to console the knight.

"Ach, he was a good mon," Sir William said as Hugh escorted him back to the great hall for a somber funeral feast. When McGregor stumbled over his own feet, Hugh gripped his elbow and steadied him. "I tried to keep him alive."

"And you saved his life more than once," Hugh said. "You were a good friend, Sir William. Lord Giles loved you dearly."

"I just wish he'd spent his treasure while he lived. I told him a thousand times, you can't take it with you. But he never listened. He couldn't remember these things."

Hugh helped him up the steps to the great-hall doors, then paused. "Treasure, you say?"

"Oh, Giles, Giles ..." MacGregor groaned, breaking into a new round of weeping.

"There, there, Sir William. Come into the great hall and help yourself to a cup of ale."

"Ale?" the old man said, his tears drying up at the

thought of quenching his thirst. He blew his nose into a crusty old rag with a loud honk.

"Plenty of ale for the funeral feast," Hugh assured him, relieved when the old man suddenly regained his composure and hurried into the hall with jaunty steps.

Hugh watched him go with a melancholy sense of appreciation. So often it seemed the most bothersome of people loved and mourned the passing of others the most keenly. But what the devil did MacGregor mean about a treasure? He was probably speaking metaphorically. If Lord Giles had a treasure, he surely would have told Margrete about it. Or would he have?

The feast that followed the funeral services was somber and small. It saddened Margrete to realize how few people came to pay their respects. But word didn't travel very fast, and in summer a quick funeral was a necessity. To many, Giles had been a mysterious baron who kept his distance even from his nearest neighbors. Margrete had worked hard to maintain that image. Now she regretted it, for who was there to mourn the strong and able man he had once been?

With her official role as chief protector and prevaricator coming to an end, she knew she would feel very alone and purposeless if not for Hugh. Her raison d'être had ended, but new roles, new expectations were there to take its place.

That night Hugh escorted her from the chapel to her chamber in heavy silence. They held hands, each taking measure of an endless array of twinkling stars. They'd gone through so much together in the last few days that no words were needed. Margrete had been all but branded a heretic and Hugh a whoremonger. They'd learned that their desire for a spiritual marriage was not only refused but condemned. And now they had buried the dear, simple man who had given them everything they now possessed. They both felt hollow and more intimate for these shared experiences.

"If you have any nightmares tonight," Hugh said when they reached her door, "come get me."

Margrete sighed and leaned against the doorframe while Ruth turned down the covers on her bed. "Do I have to wait until I have a nightmare?"

He smiled but didn't take her question seriously. He scooped up one of her hands in his, bending over and kissing the back of it. When she sucked in a little breath and shivered, he turned her hand over with a spark of desire and placed his lips on her palm.

"Don't go," she whispered, running her free hand through his shoulder-length hair.

A shiver coursed down his spine. He did not want to read too much into this entreaty. Still kissing her palm, he paused, then righted himself, searching her face for her true desire. Even if some part of her, wild in her grief, suddenly longed for him in a carnal way, there was surely a wiser part of her that wanted the very opposite. What direction, what path should he take? he wondered as he tried to read the map of her lovely features.

Her eyes were moist, as they had been all day. A fierce and raw grief shone in them. Her nose was red from crying; her lips slightly swollen. All the markers indicated that this was a woman who desperately needed human contact of the deepest order.

Instinctively, he slipped an arm around her waist and pulled her close. She sagged against him, running her hands up the flat of his chest. He had never meant to love her. When planning this marriage the thought had never crossed his mind. It was enough that she had given him a home and hearth. It was enough that together they would keep the wolves at bay. But sometimes you get more than what you need. Sometimes you get what you didn't even know you wanted.

He reached down and cupped her cheeks in his calloused hands, admiring her humble beauty. Then he lowered his lips to hers. A bolt a pleasure shivered up his legs, turning them into steel. She molded to him with the greatest ease. It felt like he was kissing a cloud, perfectly soft and utterly malleable. He swirled his lips on hers, until they caught with invisible fire. Sighing, he wrapped his other arm around her and enfolded her completely in his arms. At the same time his tongue flicked apart her mouth and plunged inward for a passionate kiss.

Margrete met him kiss for kiss, a well of passion rising and surging in her like a tide at the will of the moon. She clutched his back with her nails. This was real, something she could hold on to, count on. This was someone who would never damn her, never doubt her. This was her husband.

He scooped her up and pushed back the door, carrying her to the bed. She scarcely noticed as Ruth scurried out, quietly shutting the door behind her. The handmaid had probably known this was going to happen even before Margrete did.

Hugh laid her on the bed, watching her by torchlight as he began to undress—unlacing his hose, tugging them off along with his shoes, unfastening his tunic, peeling it off his broad shoulders, and carelessly tossing it aside. He pulled off his shirt in one fell swoop, exposing his naked torso without embarrassment or humility. All that remained were his braies which loosely swathed his groin.

His skin gleamed bronze in the flickering light of the flame. His nipples were like two brown berries against a mat of rich brown hair. His stomach tapered down to his pelvis, the flat plain riven with muscles like the pattern of water left on the sand when a wave washes out.

"Now you," he whispered, his voice hoarse with desire.

He reached out and pulled her up from the bed until she stood but inches from him. She felt his hot breath beating on her forehead in quick pants. His broad hands reached out and clutched her hips, branding them with his hungry grip. He kissed her again, his head circling in a lover's dance as he bent at the knees, letting his hands run down the outside of her thighs. Gripping her gown, he then stood to full height, taking the material with him.

By now she was shivering. When he raised her under-tunic over her head, her breath stopped in her chest. All that remained was her chemise. He reached out and after a moment's hesitation cupped a breast in his hand, fondling the nipple through the thin material. She shuddered and closed her eyes.

He pulled the gown up over her arms until she was naked. Then he hugged her again, skin on skin. He still wore his braies, but something large and hard weeped against the material, pressing into her belly.

She realized then what he was about to do. What she wanted to do. She couldn't let her conscience stop her now, not when something inside her burned for him. She no longer feared him. And she knew that even if he had reached out to Ruth, he had really been grasping for Margrete.

He nudged her back onto the bed and climbed on top of her. All that separated them was the thin material of his braies. Propping himself up with one arm, he unfastened the garment with his other hand and tugged it down over his tight buttocks, kicking it off. Now his turgid manhood pressed against the apex of her thighs, hot and smooth.

He stared hard at her, then kissed her again, his tongue delving expertly into her depths and making her writhe beneath him. But then he drew his head back, frowning, his eyes darting back and forth between hers. His frown turned to a scowl.

"What is it?" she whispered. "What?"

He did not move, did not answer. But she felt the most peculiar sensation. The rod poised at the door to her virginity began to shrink. She felt the tension melt, the lightning charge between them ease and leave a hollowness in its wake, a void where once there had been purpose. She felt panic in its absence.

Hugh heaved a tortured sigh and rolled over, falling on his back beside her. He ran a hand over his forehead, his arm muscles bulging in silhouette.

"I can't, Margrete."

"Why not?"

"Because it's what they want."

"*They?*"

"The bishop. The Church."

"No, it's what I want!"

He turned his head toward her. "You want it now. But what about tomorrow? And the day after that?"

"What if there is no tomorrow?" she argued, raising herself up on a bent elbow. "What will I have missed then? My father has proven that life is tenuous."

"No, he lived a long life. It was time for him to go. Past time. Time is irrelevant here. You want to touch God, not me."

"No!"

"Yes, you do." Now he raised himself up on an elbow till they faced each other, their naked lengths stretched out together. He tapped her chest gently with a forefinger. "And even if you now think you see a bit of God in my eyes, you can't give in to those devils in priest robes. You can't succumb just because the bishop ordered it."

"That's not why I'm lying here naked next to you."

"No. You're doing that because you're grieving and you wanted consolation and in your grief you could not remember the principles by which you've chosen to live your life."

She groaned. "Principles won't keep me warm at night."

"And a lover won't get you to heaven."

"You're not my lover. You're my husband!"

He couldn't argue that. They were finally back where the bishop wanted them—with no reason not to consummate their relationship.

"I will couple with you, Margrete. But not until you've won the right to turn me away."

"And when will that be?"

"When someone in the Church with appropriate authority agrees to hear our vows."

"But—"

"That doesn't mean we have to say the vows. But we have to have the right to live by our consciences. I want you, Margrete, more than I have ever wanted any woman in my life. But I want you to want me because it's a choice. Not a last resort."

Margrete groaned again and fell back onto the bed, staring at the beams on the ceiling in the flickering torchlight. Her desire had started to dissipate, and she was thinking more clearly now. She suspected she would be very grateful to Hugh when the sun rose. But he had complicated her life. Now if she bedded her husband and abandoned her spiritual goals, she could not blame passion. It would be a logical choice. She would have to accept the responsibility herself. And if, in the end, she chose the spiritual path, she would have to live a life knowing just how close she'd come to ecstasy on earth.

Twenty-three

In the following weeks, Hugh fell naturally into his role as the new baron of Longrove. He'd already taken over most of the estate's responsibilities, but now people were free to deal with him as the final authority. Hugh had quickly filled his empty properties with knights and freemen and had already begun to forge a peaceful relationship with the second earl of Ludham, Lord Richard.

Much to Hugh's surprise, the earl was willing to negotiate the future of Kilbury Hide. Lord Richard said he was concerned about a dispute with King Edward and didn't want to squander resources on an old squabble with a neighbor. He wanted to discuss a fair split on the property, and without saying it overtly, he hinted that he and Hugh might join forces to fight the bishop's claim to the land. That suited Hugh just fine. While he could never challenge Jerome Blakely's authority as a bishop, he could damn well bedevil him on baronial matters.

Margrete, now far removed from the world of baronial politics, conducted battles on a far more personal level. She had taken what Hugh had said to heart and was more determined than ever to win the right to have a spiritual marriage. Though she now doubted her own devotion to that cause, she agreed that it had become a matter of principle.

After giving the subject much thought, Margrete decided that a visit to Abbess Phillipa de Claire was in order. She would ask the abbess to use her connections to the papacy to get some sort of a judgment on the matter, hopefully in her favor. The abbess was respected by the Pope. If the local church authorities would not hear her out, Margrete would go straight to the top.

It was with that purpose in mind that she set out to visit Treyvaux Abbey early one morning. She was dismayed, however, to discover upon her arrival that Phillipa was nowhere in sight. When Margrete tried to visit her private chamber, she was deftly rerouted to the gatehouse by Prior Anselm, who responded to every question about the abbess's whereabouts with the statement: "Only God in his infinite wisdom knows."

Margrete was thoroughly bewildered and confused. Surely the abbess wasn't avoiding her. Then why couldn't Margrete see her?

Puzzling over the nun's absence, Margrete wandered distractedly back through the woods toward Longrove Barony. Lost in her own thoughts, she did not at first notice the lone figure adorned in black who lolled leisurely against the magnificent and ancient oak that towered over the field of daisies in her favorite meadow.

When she finally did look up, she recognized him instantly, and the fine hair lining her nape rose to prickly attention. She stopped, unsure whether to continue.

"Do not be afraid," Sir Ranulf Blakely called out. "I mean you no harm, Lady Margrete. Did you think otherwise?"

"I know not what to think when it comes to you."

Margrete knew that her husband had always been wary of Sir Ranulf. She had once considered him a charming oddity, openly wicked, but perhaps redeemable beneath his conniving facade. Now, however, she associated him primarily with his cousin the bishop of Burnham, and deep suspicion burrowed in her heart at the very sight of him.

"What are you doing here?" she asked, resuming her progress until she met him beneath the tree. The sun was up now, winking just over the horizon. The birds sang with great promise. She forced a thin smile.

"I've been thinking about you a great deal," Ranulf said, grinning at her as he leaned against the tree, one arm hooked over a low branch. "Wondering what the fairest damsel in the realm has been doing since I last saw her."

"You seem to hold me in greater esteem than your cousin the bishop," she said with barely detectable sarcasm.

His eyes flared with appreciation for her tact. "My cousin is a devoted son of the Church. If he errs in his interpretation of Church laws or Biblical precedent, he must be forgiven."

"If only I could speak to him in person about my desire for a spiritual marriage perhaps he would see that my love for God is as great as his."

"Or greater." Ranulf cocked his head, eyeing her speculatively. "Yes, my lady, I do believe you are truly spiritual in nature. Such a shame."

"I have never thought so. Would you speak to your cousin on my behalf?"

"No need for that."

"What do you mean?" Margrete was unnerved by his cold certainty.

"You won't have a spiritual marriage." He lowered his

arm from the branch and, like the snake in the Garden of Eden, struck with lightning speed and snatched her wrist. His grip was firm, almost painful, and she knew he would not let her go without great violence. "You're going to lose your virginity, Lady Margrete. But not at the hands of Sir Hugh."

He yanked her close. His breath smelled of stale ale. Had he imbibed more than usual for breakfast to gather up his courage? She doubted it. One did not need courage when one had no conscience. He'd probably just finished bedding a maid in the nearest village and washed the taste of her out of his mouth with a swill.

"You're mine now, Margrete. I will teach you the pleasures of love." He gripped a breast then, dipping a finger below her collar and scraping it along her flesh. She shivered with disgust, shoving him away with all her might, but his strong arm did not give way. That's when the first jolt of panic riveted her, and her breath seemed to die in her lungs. She was so far away from Longrove. Even if she screamed, she'd never be heard.

"You can rape me, Ranulf, but what good will it do you? My husband will come after you and seek his revenge."

Ranulf gave a derisive snort. "You have no husband. The man you are living with has never consummated his marriage vows. So he is not a real husband."

"He swore to be my mate before a priest!"

"That priest is dead."

A frown gathered on her forehead like a storm that bruises the sky in a terrifying instant. "He's dead? Did you kill him?"

He threw back his head with perverse laughter. "If I did, I wouldn't admit it. No, he died of natural causes a fortnight ago."

Now it was Margrete's turn to laugh with sarcasm. "I very much doubt that."

"Doubt what you will, for it will not matter once your virgin's blood lies on my sheets. Then you will have no choice but to marry me or face the shame of being a whore. Who would have you after I despoil you?"

"And who would perform a marriage ceremony for us knowing I already have a husband?"

"The bishop of Burnham." Ranulf gave her a mirthless smile.

"Why? Why would he do such an evil thing?"

"Because he wants Kilbury Hide. Not to mention the D'Arbereau treasure."

She scowled at him. "The what?"

"You still don't know about the treasure your father has been hiding all these years?"

She laughed out loud. "Lord, no."

"You laugh now. But wait until I find it. When you see the gold and rubies and pearls that have been sitting idly on your barony all these years, you will wish your father would return from the dead just so you can strangle him for not telling you about it."

A voice called in the distance. Margrete strained against Ranulf's grip, trying to see if someone was coming. But she realized the voice could have been carried on the wind from a great distance, and her momentary hope of rescue faded.

Disappointment gave way to terror when Ranulf clamped a hand over her mouth and dragged her to his horse, which was tethered on the other side of the tree. He mounted, then pulled her up in front of him.

"Where are you taking me?" she rasped quickly when he momentarily took away his hand to tighten his grip on the reins.

"To a place where you'll feel very comfortable. The old abbey keep on Winslow Downs."

Margrete's mind raced. Winslow Downs. That was an obscure part of the bishop's barony. And by the old abbey he must be referring to the ruins of St. Joseph's Keep, an old monastery that was now little more than rubble scattered through clumps of grass. Dear Lord, Hugh would never think to look for her there. He didn't even know the place existed.

Old MacGregor slowly stirred from his dream with a contented yawn, stretching his legs and arms in his favorite chair by the great-hall hearth. The day had turned unseasonably cool and so a fire was lit despite the time of year. If he didn't know better he would have thought the leaves would soon be tumbling down in their showy array outside.

He blinked open an eye, wondering if a scullion had brought him another pitcher of ale. Lady Margrete had certainly been generous since her father's death. Damned impertinent filly had doubtless learned at last that her elders should be respected.

Remembering the day's odd turn of events, and Lady Margrete's uncharacteristic betrayal of her husband, he sat upright, trying to make sense of it all. He'd been sorting through the odd facts earlier just before falling asleep. Now people were racing to and fro with worried frowns, barking frantic orders, some bearing torches, others lanterns. What the devil was going on? He sat up taller and scratched his head.

"Did you check Kilbury Hide?" Peter asked, striding past MacGregor with such force he left a breeze in his wake.

"Why would she go to Kilbury Hide at this hour?" Lord

Hugh answered, coming from the other direction and meeting him in the middle of the hall.

"Well, my lord," Peter said, crossing his arms, "I've just learned from Ruth that Lady Margrete has been gone since this morning. Perhaps she traveled to Kilbury earlier and . . . and met with some misfortune."

"Hell," Hugh cursed. "Has every other likely location been checked?"

Peter nodded. "We know she's not at the manor and she hasn't been to Treyvaux Abbey since early this morning. She's not in Longrove Village and she didn't travel to the earl's marketplace, either."

MacGregor scratched his head, which pounded from too much ale. Should he speak up? Should he tell Lord Hugh that there was no use searching for his wife, that she'd run away with another knight?

"My lord," MacGregor called out, waving a hand.

Hugh did not hear him. He could hear little but the whoosh of blood hammering through his ears. There was something very wrong. Margrete would never be gone so long without leaving word.

"Go to Reed House," Hugh ordered Peter. "Tell Sir Bernard I need him to gather all his vassals. Send someone over to Lord Richard's castle and ask him to send men-at-arms to help in the search. Then—"

"My lord!" MacGregor shouted.

Hugh looked down and found the shrunken old man at his side. "Not now, Sir William!"

"But I know where Lady Margrete is."

It took a moment for the words to register in Hugh's whirling mind. Then it took another long moment for him to give them any credence. How would this old sot know her whereabouts?

"Very well, Sir William, tell me what you know. Out with it!"

"Well, ye see . . ." The old man raised a finger to punctuate his thoughts, but he merely gummed the words, hesitating.

"What is it?" Hugh angrily pressed.

"Well, ye see, she ran off with another mon."

"What did you say? Another man?" Hugh scowled at him, then at Peter.

"What do you mean?" Peter said in his patient, nononsense manner.

MacGregor looked from one to another, wounded at the echo of doubt reverberating in their voices. "That knight errant with the jagged scar on his face. I saw them ride away together from the meadow."

Hugh went pale. "Sir Ranulf?"

"Aye, that's the one. I was wandering in the grove when I heard him say he was taking her to St. Joseph's Keep."

Cold swept over Hugh, shriveling his skin into gooseflesh. He blinked slowly as the implications of this horrible news sank in. Then he turned to Peter, who answered his question before he could ever utter it.

"St. Joseph's Keep is in Winslow Downs," the able servant said, starting for the door. "It lies on the bishop's land. I'll lead the way."

"Tell Brian to follow as soon as he rallies a band of men-at-arms," Hugh said, jogging in Peter's wake. "But when we find Ranulf, I want him all to myself. It's time he paid for his sins. If God won't strike him dead, I will."

Hugh only prayed that he wasn't too late to keep Ranulf from despoiling another beloved maiden.

Twenty-four

You're shivering," Ranulf said.

Margrete did not answer. She merely leaned her head against the stone wall that dug into her back and shut her eyes, wishing she were anywhere but here.

After taking a diversionary trip to a cottage Margrete did not recognize, they'd arrived at the abandoned abbey keep before sundown. An unexpected chill snapped in the air, making the isolated spot seem even more desolate.

Ranulf pushed open a wooden door that was only half hinged in place, shattering spiderwebs and spewing ancient dust. He pulled her in and apologized for the accomodations, saying that a lady deserved better. But in truth, though the keep was a half-crumbled shell, it could have been worse. She would have been more comfortable if it had been, for Ranulf's thoughts surely wouldn't turn to seduction in an uncomfortable setting.

A single table, apparently left behind when the old monastery had been abandoned, had been wiped clean, and there was a candle burning on it, as well as a pitcher and two cups. And worst of all, there was a mattress thrown on the floor with fresh covers, looking wholly out of place, for high above it the roof was falling through and skylight could be seen.

Margrete's stomach grew queasy at the site, for it was clear that the place had been prepared for them. Ranulf had been plotting this abduction for some time. If there was an accomplice lurking nearby, Margrete would have even less of a chance to escape.

When Ranulf saw her glance at the mattress and grow pale, he blinked with an unexpected tremor of sentimentality. "That will be our wedding bed."

"Shouldn't there be a wedding first?" she tartly replied.

"Sometimes it's prudent to place the cart before the horse. Sir Hugh wouldn't know about that. He bought the horse and never did see hide nor hair of the cart."

Margrete frowned at him in the shadows as he poured wine for them both. "You hate him, don't you?" she whispered and saw his jaw muscles tick reflexively. "That is what all this is about—your cousin's condemnation of me, your desire to be my husband. You just want to hurt Hugh."

Ranulf looked up at her, black eyes blazing with twin flames of hatred. He quenched the fire by tossing back his head and taking a long drink from his cup. His subsequent sigh sounded like the rasping sizzle of a bonfire being doused with water. With cooler demeaner, he leaned down and handed her the other cup.

"I do hate him," he said, sliding down the wall to sit a few feet from her. "He succeeds where he should not. He is strong, but not clever, and yet he has outwitted me and other deft knights on the lists time and again. He is not particularly charming or even exceptionally handsome, and yet he is the one whom maidens sought. And now he is the one who is a baron, while I am a mere steward." Ranulf's assessment ended in a hoarse whisper, as if he were still trying to figure out how it had all happened.

"He has a heart," Margrete said. "And you do not. That is why he has succeeded where you have failed."

Ranulf's lifeless eyes turned her way. He stared at her for a long time. Then he cocked his head speculatively. "Perhaps. But there are ways to circumvent grace and fortune. You will be mine, Lady Margrete, before this night is through. Yes, I hate Hugh de Greyhurst. Nearly as much as I admire him. But more important, I am weary, just like he was. I want a home and hearth." He gave her a twisted smile. "Yours, as a matter of fact."

"You're taking your time, Ranulf. Aren't you afraid my husband will burst in here before you can despoil me?"

"No," he said confidently. "Sir Hugh will never know to look here. Besides, my cousin will hear our vows as soon as we are man and wife . . . in the irrevocable sense." He glanced at the mattress. "Then there will be nothing Hugh can do except challenge me. And I'd welcome the chance to kill him on the lists, once and for all."

He spoke with such frank eloquence that she had to remind herself that Ranulf was a despicable enemy that would take from her the very thing she had treasured all her life—her purity. The precious possession she had at last decided she wanted to give to Hugh.

As if his thoughts, too, had suddenly turned to that topic, he inched over the distance until he was close enough for her to smell the horse dung that clung to the bottom of his boots. He gripped her face, pinching it between his graceful fingers, eyeing her like a horse at market. Then he lunged forward and kissed her roughly. She jerked away and rubbed the taste of him from her mouth.

"You disgust me," she whispered in a quivering voice.

He glared at her, disappointment and fury out of all proportion turning his well-crafted features to stone. Then he slapped her so hard her head flew back against the wall.

Margrete stifled a groan. Her face stung and her head hurt, but she was glad. He had shown his true character at last.

"I'm sorry," he said. "But you shouldn't insult me."

She licked her upper lip and tasted blood, knowing it wasn't the last time she would bleed tonight.

Peter and Hugh finally halted their furious gallops and drew in their reins at the crest of a small hill. Hugh's heart, already thundering as fast as his horse's hooves, quickened painfully in his chest, for he could see a candle burning in a decrepit keep in the distance and could only imagine what was happening in its glow.

"You stay here," Hugh said, drawing his sword.

"No, my lord," Peter argued. "Do not go in by yourself. Wait until the others arrive. Sir Ranulf may not be alone."

"I can't wait! My wife is in there."

"Think, man! Use your head, not your heart. You have no armor. Your squire will be along with it soon."

"I can't wait that long. I have a sword. That's all I need."

Peter sighed with resignation. "Then go with stealth. Listen outside the door. If Lady Margrete is in danger you will hear it. If not, wait until you have other men-at-arms to back you."

Hugh's face was as taut as a crossbow. "Very well. But at the slightest provocation, I'm going in."

Hugh rode a short distance by himself, then tethered his mount to a tree and dismounted, walking the rest of the way behind the cover of bracken and trees. When he finally reached the keep, carefully stepping over the crumbled remains of the building—moss-covered stones and shattered mortar—he could hear voices. Ranulf's and Margrete's. It took all his willpower not to bolt in immediately.

As he listened with his ear pressed to the stone wall, sweat dripping down his temples, Hugh thought of Margrete's mother, how she had died at the hands of such a man. That would never happen to her daughter. He swore that now, in this moment, in the moonlight, to a God who had damned well better exist, that Margrete would never suffer at the hands of a knight errant.

Soon the muffled voices grew more excited. Hugh looked anxiously in the distance, but there was no sign of reinforcements waiting on the hill. His hand was itching for the door. When Margrete let out a clearly terrified cry, he flung into the door, bursting it wide open. The door ripped from its last remaining hinge and banged to the floor.

For once in his life Ranulf was ill-prepared and completely stunned. He lay next to Margrete on a mattress, naked, his long black hair hanging in strings about his sleek white shoulders, his arousal disgustingly obvious. Margrete was clothed, but she wouldn't have been for long if Hugh hadn't interceded, that was clear.

"I'll kill you for this," Hugh roared. He raised his sword to hack Ranulf in two.

Margrete scrambled to her knees, reaching out placatingly to her husband, her face white with fear. "No, Hugh, don't! He's the bishop's cousin. You can't kill him without witnesses."

In the moment that Hugh paused to consider, then disgard, his wife's entreaty, Ranulf scrambled for his dagger. Crouching in defense, he threateningly held the blade aloft, meager though it was in the shadow of Hugh's great sword.

"You hesitate," Ranulf said gloatingly, clutching his dagger with a white-knuckled grip. "Are you afraid you won't win, Greyhurst? Afraid you'll end up with a broken neck like Sir Roland?''

Hugh's skin tingled with cold fury. "Don't mention Rolly's name, you loathsome cur."

"You should have died that day," Ranulf said, slowly rising. "I told the priest to be at the Round Table at noon precisely. And I arranged for you to be up first. Unfortunately, Rolly fell when the priest leapt between you. I had thought, what with your injured leg, that you would be the one to lose balance and fall to your unhappy demise."

"You invited that cleric to interfere with the joust?" Hugh rasped, blinking hard as rage blurred his vision. "That means Roland would be alive now if not for you. Just as dear sweet Lady Alys would be alive. How many deaths are on your conscience, you damnable knave?"

"Too many to count. But should you try, you can add one more to the list," Ranulf said, leaping forward, his dagger trained on Hugh's heart.

"Die, you black son of the devil!" Hugh snarled as he rammed his sword in Ranulf's belly.

The sound of slicing flesh and crunching bones rent the air, followed by Ranulf's stunned *oof* of pain. He staggered back as blood gushed from his belly, a look of astonishment on his face. Had he actually thought he might best Hugh with a mere dagger? Hugh wondered. Ranulf's pride—just one of his many faults—was his downfall in the end.

When Hugh pulled his sword out of Ranulf's soon-to-be carcass, the knight slid gracefully down the wall again, this time to his knees. With blood spurting from his lips, he looked down at the bed that had held such promise, fell into it, and breathed his last.

There was a moment of complete silence as Hugh and Margrete stared at Ranulf. Hugh could hear only the violent beat of his heart as he savored a melancholy victory. He had vanquished an enemy, but had taken another life. More blood on his hands.

The silence was quickly broken by the snort of a horse and boots hurriedly tamping the ground. Then a finely cloaked figure appeared.

"What's this?" the man thundered in shock.

Hugh turned and found Sir David Keath standing in the doorway. His cheeks were flushed and his eyes wide with horror. He turned to Hugh, accusation narrowing his lids.

"You . . . you did this!"

"Steady, Keath," Hugh growled.

"You murdered him!"

"I was defending myself, and my wife."

Behind Keath there was a drumming of horse hooves and shouts. For a moment Hugh allowed himself to hope that Brian had arrived with enough men-at-arms to get him out of here. But when a soldier bearing the bishop's livery appeared in the doorway, followed by four more, Hugh knew it was too late for help and he sheathed his bloody sword.

"Take him," Keath ordered the men.

When they swarmed upon him, Hugh offered no fight. He would not give them any excuse to kill him.

"I hearby arrest you and order you into the bishop's custody!" Keath shouted, spittle flying from his mottled lips.

"By what authority?"

"The bishop's. He named me his bailiff and you are on his property. This is a matter for the church now."

"No!" Margrete cried, running to Keath. She gripped his tunic. He drew his head back, regarding her warily. "He won't get a fair trial from the bishop and you know it."

"He should have thought of that before he murdered the bishop's cousin on church property." Keath detached her hands from his chest and started for the door.

"Ranulf kidnapped my wife!" Hugh shouted. "He tried to rape her, Keath. I was defending my wife's honor."

"Tell that to the bishop," Keath replied coldly. "But I'm not sure he'll care. It seems there's some question about whether Lady Margrete really is your wife."

Hugh shut his eyes tight, knowing in that instant what a trial lay before them, in every sense of the word. He blinked open his eyes and scowled at his former companion. "You'll see that Lady Margrete is escorted properly?"

"I'll see that the lady of Longrove is treated as one befitting her station."

"My man is not far from here, over the hill beyond," Hugh said as the bishop's men dragged him out of the keep in Keath's wake, firmly gripping his arms. "Peter is his name. Go fetch him and he will take her back to Longrove. Do it, Keath. On your honor!"

As Keath gave orders to that effect, Hugh measured the fair-haired warrior's empty good looks and hollow grief. His sorrow over Ranulf's death would be short-lived.

"And what will you do with me?" Hugh asked as Margrete threw her arms around his waist, hugging him though he could not hold her in kind. "What is my fate to be, David?"

Sir David Keath grinned with satisfaction. "You will be held in the bishop's tower."

"For how long?"

Keath smiled, perhaps realizing for the first time the extent of his power. "Until the sheriff can charge you with the murder of Sir Ranulf Blakely."

Twenty-five

Hugh spent the next fortnight locked in the bishop's tower. His lodgings were pleasant enough for a prison and befitted a baron, albeit one suspected of murder. Hugh had argued that he had not been formally charged by the sheriff and, therefore, should not be held at all. He quickly learned, though, that a bishop was a law unto himself, and an imprisoned man couldn't lodge a complaint if his keepers turned a deaf ear.

The weeks were even more agonizing for Margrete. Hugh had quickly become her world. Without his warm laughter and measured commands, the castle seemed empty and lifeless. She found that she no longer wanted to make weighty decisions, but was forced to in his absence.

She did what she had to, but all she wanted to do was see Hugh again and express her love, not only with words, but with the bodies God had given them. She no longer cared to prove a point. She simply wanted to make love to her husband, to commune with him as fully as possible.

Her anxiety over his absence reached an unbearable level

on the day the sheriff had said he would announce his report of Sir Ranulf's death. There was no question that Ranulf had been killed, but the circumstances were in doubt. If it was a case of murder, Hugh would be tried. Otherwise, he would be freed and their lives could go on as before.

Waiting to hear the decision, Margrete barely ate her midday meal, not even nibbling at the sugar sculptures Lady Edith had purchased at a nearby fair to cheer her up. Instead, Margrete listened dutifully but distractedly as Peter rattled on about what needed to be done at the manor in Hugh's absence. Suddenly Brian burst into the great hall. He strode with mud-splattered riding breeches the long length of the hall, his bicolored eyes bright above wind-burned cheeks.

"My lady!" he called out.

She tensed and held up a hand to silence Peter. "Brian, what news?"

"I come from the See of Burnham, where the sheriff has informed the bishop of his decision in this wretched matter."

When he reached the dais, he bowed.

"Don't stand on formality, Brian," Margrete said, gripping the arms of her chair. "What did the sheriff decide?"

When he stood tall again, his reddened cheeks were a paler hue. "Lord Hugh is accused of murder."

Everyone in the great hall gasped. Margrete pounded the table with a fist, crying out, "But it was self-defense!"

"Sir David Keath claims he saw the whole thing and that Lord Hugh cut open Ranulf's belly without provocation."

Margrete shut her eyes tight, fighting a wave of vertigo. She couldn't lose control. Hugh needed her now more than ever. She rose with the coolness she'd perfected when acting in her father's stead and said, "Very well. We must make our plans. Let's away to the solar."

She led Brian, Edith, and Peter to the private chamber. Ruth hurried before them to make sure there was a pitcher of wine. After quickly straightening the solar, she turned to Peter. From the corner of her eye, Margrete saw him put a reassuring hand on her shoulder and nod with approval. Ruth curtseyed, flashed him an adoring look, and hurried out the door. MacGregor managed to slip in before it closed behind her. He scuttled to the empty fireplace, squatting on a stool as contently as a frog on a lily pad.

After her father's death, Sir William had mellowed, switching his allegiance from Lord Giles to her without missing a beat. He'd shown himself to be loyal and, surprisingly, sometimes even helpful with advice, and so she did not send him away.

"What will we do?" Margrete asked to one and all, her voice breaking.

"Hire a man of the law," Peter said, tucking two fingers in his breeches.

"With what?" Margrete returned in a sharp challenge. "We do not have any more money than when my father died."

"We'll manage, my lady," Edith said.

She stood next to Brian, her hand tucked in the nook of his arm. Even in her despair, Margrete admired them— Brian dashing and vigorous in his startlingly-green tunic, and Edith shimmering like a firefly in her yellow gown. They were the picture of youth in love, imperfections and all.

"Where will Lord Hugh be tried?" Edith murmured, fully expecting the answer to be London.

Brian cast her a gloomy look. "He will be tried in the church courts."

"But this is a felony offense," Margrete said, whirling on him with agitation. "The church doesn't deal with such matters."

"But the murder took place on church lands. That means the bishop has the right to hear the case himself."

Margrete let out a shuddering gasp and covered her face with both hands. The memories of Jerome Blakely's damning homily turned her blood to ice. "My God. We are lost."

"No, my lady," Edith crooned, rushing forward and putting her arms around her. "Have faith."

"Faith is what got us into this trouble in the first place," Margrete said jadedly. "I should have known better than to expect my love for God to be acceptable to the church."

"Don't be bitter," Edith said. "This is God's way of testing you."

Margrete sighed and hugged her warmly. "You're right, Edith. I can't let one bishop ruin my faith in the whole church."

She went to a table and poured wine for all, calming herself with the role of hostess. She took a soothing sip and said, "So where will we find a good man of the law?"

"The earl of Ludham knows a smart fellow trained at the University of Bologna," Peter said. "That's where all the best legal experts study."

"But won't he need a proctor to help him with canon law?"

"Yes, my lady. Very likely."

Margrete began to pace, a new anxiety filling her. "How will I pay these legal experts? They won't come cheaply. And they won't come without assurance of payment."

"Give them a ruby or a gold piece," MacGregor said. He'd already swilled his wine and was helping himself to more.

Margrete frowned at him, not with disapproval, but rather with curiosity. What an odd thing to say. "If only I had rubies and gold to give, Sir William, I would gladly do it."

"You do," he said, taking another swill and smacking his lips together with satisfaction.

"What do you mean?"

"The D'Arbereau treasure. Your father left it behind. It's worth a fortune."

Margrete exchanged a skeptical look with Peter, who shrugged.

"I've not heard of it, my lady," Peter said, "and I've lived here all my life."

Margrete turned back to the old knight, rubbing her hands together as she regarded him. Perhaps it was because of her desperation, but something about Sir William's comments rang true. Was she remembering something she'd heard as a child and had long since forgotten?

"Sir William," Margrete said, "my father had no treasure. He died a poor man."

"At first I thought he'd forgotten he even had the treasure." The old knight was lost in his memories. "But then I realized he just didn't care aboot it anymore. I stopped nagging him aboot it years ago. He didn't care aboot anything after your mother died."

"What are you talking about?" Brian said impatiently. "How much is this treasure worth?"

"Picture a trunk big enough fer a man to sit upon and then imagine it filled with pearls, rubies, sapphires, and gold."

"You're lying, old man," Brian said, as much to get at the truth as to dampen his budding hope.

"The hell with you!" MacGregor shouted. "I saw it with me own eyes. Lord Giles showed me in secret. It was yer lady mother's dowery. Yer father knew that such a treasure would tempt thieves, and so he kept it hidden, using it as he saw fit. He always said it was so well hidden he'd never lose a night's sleep over it.'' William chuckled, then blinked sadly. ''Though he did lose his wife fer it in the end.''

''What do you mean?'' Margrete whispered, fighting a tide of dread.

''The earl of Ludham's raid. Lord Henry came here that night to steal the treasure. Somehow one of his vassals managed to find oot aboot it, and that set the greedy earl to plotting fer it.''

''No!'' Margrete countered. ''Lord Henry attacked my father's barony for political reasons. The Prince of Wales supplied the mercenaries.''

''Only because he wanted a cut of the booty when it was all over. But Edward and Ludham never got it. Lord Henry tripped and fell on his own dagger trying to drag the trunk oot of the castle.''

Margrete frowned, remembering that, just as MacGregor said, Lord Henry had died in her father's yard that night. ''Then why didn't his son come after the treasure following his father's death? Why didn't Lord Richard raid Longrove in search of jewels?''

MacGregor snorted with satisfaction. ''He thought the D'Arbereau treasure was cursed. Being as how yer father wasn't himself after that nasty fall in the solar, I paid a little visit to Lord Richard meself. I told him the only reason his valiant father had been killed was because the jewels were cursed. Only the pure in heart, I said, could possess the treasure without coming to some bloody and gruesome death. Word must have gotten back to Edward as well, fer the Prince of Wales never funded any raids after that.''

"Is it true?" Edith said, her green eyes wide and wondering. "Is the treasure cursed?"

"Naw!" MacGregor waved her off. "I just made it up to frighten them off."

"Well, where is it!" Brian nearly shouted.

MacGregor scratched the gray whiskers sprouting on his bony chin, then shrugged. "I do not know."

"What do you mean, you do not know?" Margrete impatiently came to his side, wanting to shake the answer out of him.

"Yer father, lassie, planned to tell ye where it was buried when ye came of age. He didn't want the love of riches to spoil yer pure heart and soul while ye was young. But when he lost his wits, he never mentioned the treasure again."

"You said you saw it. Can't you remember where?" Brian insisted.

"Aye, I can. I saw it before their wedding. And never again."

"Father forgot where it was," Margrete said in a monotone, trying to comprehend the scope of her misfortune. She owned a priceless treasure that would solve all their financial problems, and the only person who knew its location had died without passing on his secret.

"Mayhap yer father fergot," MacGregor mused. "But I like to think he didn't want to remember. After all, his beloved wife died because of the treasure. She'd be alive today if Lord Henry hadn't been trying to get his greedy hands on it."

Margrete turned away. She went to the embrasure, looking out the window at this land of hers. How often had her mother looked out from this very place, treasuring life, hoping it might last forever? Had she known that night when she kissed Margrete good night, with a mother's love cradled in her eyes, that that would be their last touch before death parted them, that she would die because of the incredible treasure her wealthy parents had given her, hoping to protect her future as much as she hoped to protect Margrete's?

She hoped her mother knew that she'd given Margrete a treasure greater than any cask of jewels—her love, strength, character, faith, devotion, and tenacity. And that had been enough. Until now.

"This treasure *is* cursed," she said soberly, turning back to the others with a wan expression. "Cursed because it killed my mother. But I need it now before another tragedy befalls this family. Brian?"

"Yes, my lady?" He stepped forward.

"I want you to find the D'Arbereau treasure. Look in every nook and cranny in this castle. At the manor as well. Search the ground for markers. Do whatever it takes to find it."

"Yes, my lady." Brian swilled the last of his wine and started away. Edith followed. When they embraced at the door, Margrete turned her attention to Peter.

"I want you to contact this lawyer trained in Bologna. Promise him whatever it takes to put aside his current cases and to come here to defend Lord Hugh. Tell him money is no object."

"Yes, my lady." Peter bowed and departed immediately.

"Sir William, would you please help Brian?"

"Aye, that I will." He nodded and headed for the door on his wobbly, bowed legs.

"Edith," she said when the lady-in-waiting returned to her side. "You and I will make a visit to Abbess Phillipa de Claire."

"What for?"

Margrete took her hands and squeezed them hard. "I need one last miracle."

• • •

Miracles, it seemed, had become a rare commodity in the See of Burnham since the arrival of the new bishop. And the abbess, as it turned out, needed one herself.

Margrete found Phillipa de Claire at her desk in her private quarters during a time when she would normally be praying in church. Margrete was so surprised to see her there that she stood speechless for a moment. The whole world, it seemed, had become disordered. Why wasn't the abbess in church with the others? Then Margrete remembered that the last time she was here Phillipa de Claire had not been following her usual routine either. Clearly something terrible had happened at Treyvaux Abbey.

"Are you ill?" Margrete blurted out, still standing in the doorway. "Are you dying? Is that why you are no longer carrying out your duties?"

The abbess, who had looked up from her documents at the sound of the opening door, smiled one of her wise smiles, and for a moment Margrete breathed easy. As long as the abbess still maintained her intelligent sense of humor there was hope.

"No, my child, I am not ill. But come in and I will tell you all that has come to pass. Please, come and sit with me by the window."

Margrete readily did so, shutting the door behind her and settling in one of two chairs splashed with sunlight. In the tranquility of this ancient and quiet chamber, the sound of monks and nuns chanting floated in on a soft breeze. Abbess Phillipa sat with her usual straight-backed dignity, her big bones filling her habit like a female warrior for God.

"Things have changed here at Treyvaux Abbey," she said matter-of-factly.

Margrete nodded, her stomach growing queasier than it

already was. She didn't like change. "What has happened?"

"Bishop Jerome has asked me to remove myself from the day-to-day operations of the abbey."

"Why?"

"He doesn't approve of my writings. He thinks my books about mystic visions and the special status of virgins are . . . unacceptable."

"What does it matter what he thinks? The Pope holds you in high esteem."

"But the Pope is far away, and Bishop Jerome is very near. It would violate my oath to God to defy someone as blessed as Bishop Jerome simply for my own gratification."

"But this is a Benedictine Abbey. You live by the Rule of St. Benedict. You are not subject to the local bishop."

"No, not technically. But he can intercede when members of the order are living scandalously. The bishop thinks it's scandalous that a woman should share her thoughts with the religious community at large."

"You? Scandalous?" Margrete said increduously. Then she began to laugh, letting out pent-up anger in a wild giggle.

The abbess sobered at her unnatural trill. "You are troubled, my child."

When Margrete had calmed herself, she leveled the abbess with a flat, uncompromising stare. "I am deeply troubled to see a woman of your stature, noble birth, and great intellect being dismissed by an evil man just because he wears a bishop's robe. You cannot give in to him!"

"I am not," Phillipa said evenly. "I am merely obliging him for the time being. He has raised questions that some of the monks and nuns themselves have thought but dared not voice. I thought it best to confront these lingering doubts once and for all. An abbey can't function properly when sisters are questioning the wisdom and authority of their abbess. I have not relinquished my title. I have simply handed over my duties to the prioress. And then only until I hear from the Pope. I have written to him asking for his intercession. I trust that he will write the bishop and remind him that the Benedictine Rule is independent of his authority and speak out in support of my writings, which the Pope himself, as you know, considers enlightened.''

Margrete nodded, mollified that the abbess was being more the diplomat than the martyr. ''What does Abbot Gregory have to say on this matter?''

''He thinks I should defy the bishop vociferously. While he supports Bishop Jerome in other matters, the abbot is quite jealous of his authority. If the bishop dares to challenge a great abbess, what's to keep him from questioning the domain of the abbot? I haven't seen Gregory quite so angry in some time. And I see it is a disease that has infected you as well.''

''If anger is a disease,'' Margrete said, ''then I am gravely ill.''

She began to tell the abbess about Sir Ranulf's attack and his subsequent death; about Hugh's imprisonment and the charge of murder. During her tense and furious diatribe, she began to pace, so that when she had ended her tale of woe, it was as clear to Margrete as it was to the abbess that her soul was troubled indeed.

''What can I do?'' Margrete implored, sinking down in her chair in defeat, no longer hoping for a miracle, but willing to settle for any bit of advice that would calm her fears.

''You are doing all that you can. And I hope you are not forgetting to pray.''

Margrete nodded, admitting to herself that she had not

sought as much solace in the castle chapel as she should have.

"Meanwhile, my child, there is something I can do for you. I will write to the Pope and ask him to intercede on your behalf. Clearly, the bishop cannot rule objectively in this case since the victim was his own cousin."

"I would hardly call him a victim."

Phillipa nodded. "I will explain Sir Ranulf's crime fully. I will also ask the Pope to speak up on your behalf regarding your decision to remain celibate."

Margrete blushed. How could she tell the abbess she had changed her decision on that matter? But there was no need, for Hugh doubtless still wanted that victory over the bishop, perhaps now more than ever.

"Thank you," she whispered.

"Now go back home and pray for God's intercession. That is the most important thing you should be doing right now."

"Thank you, Abbess. God bless you."

Forgive my intrusion, but I must hasten to add what happened next, since it involved me directly. After Lady Margrete departed, the abbess called me to her chamber and asked me to act as scribe.

I carefully wrote down what she dictated, and then I rewrote it with a more steady hand in the scriptorium. I presented the document, decorated with a few flourishes in the margins, to the abbess for her signature and then I bound it carefully and sent it with a messenger who was heading immediately to the Continent. As you well know, the Pope at that time lived in Avignon, France.

Neither I nor the abbess remarked upon that which

I know we both were thinking—that it would take weeks at best to receive a response from His Holiness. And weeks might be too long to save Lord Hugh de Greyhurst.

Twenty-six

t was another fortnight before the bishop allowed Hugh to have any visitors. Margrete was admitted to the tower two days before his trial was to begin. When the sentry unlocked the door, she momentarily blinked at him as if he were a ghost. It took but a moment for her to head instinctively into his embrace. When he folded his powerful arms around her, she relaxed for the first time in a month.

"My lord," she murmured into his soft cambric shirt.

He stroked her cheek, then tipped up her chin. Even through a blur of tears she managed to make out his best features—intense eyes; a strong, finely chiseled jaw and cheeks; tumbled amber hair. His lips touched hers, and she flung an arm around his neck, pulling him closer.

She fairly melted in his embrace, not so much from heat as from sheer bliss. She had never touched or tasted anything so exquisite. Was it possible that she might never love him fully—would he be found guilty and sentenced to die? Or if he were freed would she somehow be unable to overcome her fear of intimacy? That did not seem possible. Not when she wanted him so much.

He pulled away at last and cupped her cheeks. "I've never seen anyone so beautiful or welcome in my life."

"Ahem." An erudite-looking man standing in the doorway cleared his throat.

Margrete turned to him and blushed. "I'm sorry. I quite lost my head. I didn't realize you'd be here so soon. Hugh, this is Guillaume de Berry, a man of the law who will act as your advocate in the church court tomorrow. He is the son of a French lord and has studied at the University of Bologna."

Hugh held out a hand in greeting. "Thank you for coming."

"My lord," the lawyer said with only a slight and undefinable accent, "your wife made a most compelling case. I am pleased to represent you."

Hugh glanced at her and frowned in silent question. To a lawyer, a compelling case was defined as one for which he'd be paid handsomely. Had she made false promises on that score? If there was one thing Hugh was quite sure his wife would never do, that was to tell a lie.

"I'll explain it all later," she said, sensing his curiosity.

"Shall we begin?" Berry asked, setting his satchel on the small table that dominated the chamber.

"Yes, certainly." Hugh nodded and studied the lawyer as he organized his documents.

He wore a light cloak edged with fur, even though it was quite warm outside, and his floor-length tunic was made of the finest silk. His small spectacles amplified his earnest brown eyes, giving him a studious look. His hair was cut squarely around his head, fanning over his unwrinkled forehead which, like his hands, was smooth and untested, indicating that he'd never known a day of labor or battle in his life. Which he probably hadn't. His manner, as one might expect of his profession, was dispassionate and precise. In short, he was all that Hugh was not.

"He'll do fine," Hugh whispered to Margrete, and her eyes glittered with satisfaction.

"May I remove my cloak?" Berry asked Margrete.

"Of course."

He put it on a chair, then sat behind the table, spreading out his documents. "Let me be frank. This is a difficult case. It is not often that a baron is accused of murdering the kin of a bishop on church land."

"And it is not often," Hugh said, crossing his arms and leaning against the stone wall, "that a bishop is as black-hearted as Burnham, with a cousin who was even worse."

Berry looked up over his spectacles but did not reply until he shuffled through more documents. "Your defense, of course, will consist of calling forth witnesses who will speak of your good character and swear to your innocence. Your wife and I have made a list of those we thought best suited to the task."

He handed the list to Hugh, who then passed it to Margrete without even glancing down. Though he had made some progress with his letters, he could not read names he had not seen before and, in any event, could scarcely make out Berry's terse handwriting.

"There is Peter, my lord," she said, "and Sir William McGregor, and Sir Bennet, the new knight you recruited to Longrove, and Lord Richard, who offered to speak on your behalf."

"The earl of Ludham?" Hugh said, pleased.

"Yes, he volunteered. And," Margrete added in conclusion, "myself."

"No!" Hugh's reaction was instantaneous and sprang from deep in his gut.

"Hugh, I am the only one who witnessed the murder."

"No! I won't have you reliving that horrible event. Once was bad enough."

"My lord . . ." Berry began.

"No! I will not allow it. That's final."

Berry cast Margrete an irritated look. She glanced away, knowing how stubborn Hugh could be.

"Well then," Berry said, "if your wife can't speak on your behalf, do you have more friends, Lord Hugh? Any relatives? Parents?"

Hugh shook his head and looked away. "No. None that I trust."

Berry raised his brows. "Well, then. We'll have to make do. Your wife has gone over the night of Sir Ranulf's death in great detail. But there are a few things I would ask of you both. Is there anything I need to know about your . . . circumstances? Anything unexpected that the bishop might bring up tomorrow?"

Margrete and Hugh exchanged wary glances, then she cleared her throat. "Have you ever heard of celibate marriages?"

Berry's smooth brow furled with concern. "Go on."

She took a deep breath and slowly paced as she apprised the lawyer of all that had come to pass between them and the bishop regarding the status of their marriage.

Berry listened carefully, lips pursed, an owlish frown carved above his spectacles. When Margrete completed her tale, he let out a breath of air that billowed his cheeks like sails.

"Well, then. It's even worse than I'd realized." He folded and unfolded his hands, pressing them flat on the rough-hewn table as he mustered an indomitable smile.

"Anything else I should know about?"

"Have you heard of the papal ban against jousting?"

Berry blanched. "Don't tell me . . ."

"I wasn't the only one who violated the ban. The bishop's cousin, Sir Ranulf, did so as well. And I am given to understand that the bishop looked the other way."

"Still, my lord," the flustered lawyer argued, "canon law is clearly on the bishop's side in this matter. I may be able to keep your head off the block, but I won't be able to keep you from being excommunicated."

"That's the least of my worries at this moment," was Hugh's droll reply.

At this blasphemous comment, the lawyer lowered his spectacles down his nose for a better look at his client. Then he rose abruptly. "I will need use of a proctor to guide me through the intracacies of canon law. I've already arranged for someone to be with us tomorrow. I'm given to understand that that is acceptable."

"Yes," Margrete was quick to answer. Hugh frowned at her again. She held up a hand of reassurance. "Whatever it takes. We can afford it."

"I will do the best I can." Berry gathered up his documents and cloak and gave a half bow. "Until tomorrow. Fare you well."

She watched him go out the door and when it creaked shut, she turned to Hugh. "Do not question my means, husband. We can afford Guillaume de Berry, his proctor, and a host of canon lawyers if need be."

"How?" he asked simply, coming to her and rubbing her arms affectionately. "Are you an alchemist, changing base metals into gold?"

She put her arms around his waist, feeling like herself again. "If you'd like to put it that way, yes."

"How, Margrete? Have you raided a neighboring baron?"

She bit her lower lip, debating whether to tell him. But

it would sound too far-fetched. He would doubt whether the treasure could be found and would worry unecessarily.

"Trust me, Hugh. We will find the means. It's just a matter of time."

He nodded, too concerned about life-and-death issues to be bothered by trifling matters such as debts. And too drawn to his wife to speak more. He'd rather use his lips for kissing, and did. Her mouth molded to his, succumbing like a flower to a bee. He dipped his tongue into the nectar waiting to be drawn, her own tongue swirling artfully against his.

But then a rude knock came and the sentry threw open the door. "None of that in the bishop's tower. Out with you, then."

She did as she was told, but turned back once with an intimate look that told Hugh there was much more of that to come. If only he survived this trial.

It began on a gloomy morning when the rain pelted Burn-ham Cathedral in pulsing waves, sheets of it splattering the narrow stained-glass windows that crawled like bejeweled fingers up the walls of the nave.

The trial was being held in the chantry, a small chapel attached to the main cathedral. Margrete sat in the first pew next to Abbess Phillipa. Brian, Edith, and Peter were scattered behind them, along with other witnesses and observers.

Hugh sat sullenly next to his lawyer at a table in front of the first pew. The wooden and marble statues of a half-dozen martyred saints scattered about all seemed to be looking down on him—some forlornly, some accusingly. He didn't give them a second glance. Nor did he pay much attention to two burly apparitors who stood on either side of the foot of the altar to keep order, or the officious, bloodless-looking notaries and scribes who would record everything from their vantage at a side table. It wasn't until the prosecutor entered the chantry that Hugh's dull anger started to seethe.

The prosecutor in this case was a priest named Father Markham. Dressed in multiple layers of white robes, with shortly cropped gray hair and soft oblong bags that drooped beneath his eyes, he bore an uncanny resemblence to Father James, the priest who had betrayed Hugh to his father. While both gave off an air of paternal congeniality, Hugh knew just how cunning they could be.

Father Markham's smooth and matter-of-fact demeanor indicated his confidence in his case. Thank God trial by ordeal had gone out of fashion, Hugh thought, for he had no doubt this man would use any technique necessary—including dunking—to get the verdict he sought. Then again, a guilty verdict was all but assured since Bishop Jerome was acting as judge.

The trial would consist of a series of witnesses who would speak of Hugh's nature and character, and based on their assurances of Hugh's guilt or innocence the bishop would decide on Hugh's fate. The actual circumstances of the crime itself were almost of secondary importance.

The first witness was Sir David Keath. When Father Markham called him forward, Keath rose and smoothed out the wrinkles in his tunic. He swaggered with self-importance from the pews to a chair placed at the foot of the dais below the bishop's throne.

"Sir David Keath," Father Markham began after going through all the initial formalities, "what can you tell us about the murder suspect, Lord Hugh de Greyhurst?"

"I can tell you he's an untutored brute who regularly defied the papal ban on jousting and encouraged others to do so as well."

"He defied the papal ban?" Father Markham raised his bushy eyebrows as if they might reach the vaulted ceiling; as if his good nature could not quite grasp such an effrontery.

"Yes, he's the one who killed Sir Roland in that Round Table near Longrove."

"So killing is nothing new to Lord Hugh?"

Keath tossed his chin up, narrowing his vacuous eyes on Hugh as if in disgust. "No, he was little more than an animal on the tournament circuit. All brute force and little conscience. I heard there were times when he would sneak in a steel-tipped lance, instead of using the usual blunted weapons, and I suspect he killed Sir Ranulf out of wounded pride."

"Pride is one of the many sins inspired by tournaments and jousting," the priest said, casting a sweeping gaze to those sitting in the pews, playing to his audience, though the bishop was the only one he needed to convince. Steepling his hands, he paced back and forth. "How does the sin of pride play a part in Sir Ranulf's murder?"

"Greyhurst was angry because Ranulf beat him seven months before on the lists. Greyhurst lost his best charger and armor. Such a thing can fester in a man till murder seems the only way to *lance* the boil." Keath smiled at his own pun.

"My lord bishop," Guillaume de Berry said, rising abruptly from his chair. "If Sir Ranulf won Lord Hugh's armor and horse it was because Sir Ranulf was violating the papal ban himself."

"The victim's character is not under scrutiny here!" Bishop Jerome shot back, his jowls shaking with the force of his indignation.

Berry grit his teeth and looked to the proctor he'd hired for advice—a gluttonous old canon lawyer with a cherry-red nose who had used his considerable knowledge of the church courts to see his way into the finest feasts in England. The proctor waved his pudgy fingers downward, and Berry sat with obvious frustration.

"What else can you tell us about the character of Lord Hugh de Greyhurst?" Father Markham prompted Keath.

"He is a cold-hearted man."

"And what makes you say that?"

Keath swallowed hard. "I saw the look in his eyes before he thrust his sword through Ranulf's belly."

A murmur rose from the pews. One of the apparitors rapped a staff on the ground to draw silence. Hugh gripped the arms of his chair, wishing his hands were instead wrapped tightly around Keath's neck. The bishop fidgeted, his face flushing with color.

"Proceed," he said, overcoming his distress.

"You say you saw Lord Hugh kill Sir Ranulf?" Markham said.

"That I did. I saw the whole thing. I'm the bailiff at the bishop's castle, you see." Pride oozed through Keath's words, though Father Markham did not seem to disapprove of it in this context. "I followed Lord Hugh, wondering what he was doing on the bishop's land, and I watched as he thrust his sword through his unarmed victim."

The proctor whispered in Berry's ear. The uptight lawyer then rose. "My lord, I beg you leave to question Sir David myself."

The bishop stroked his neatly trimmed beard. "What more can Sir David say? He has spoken to Sir Hugh's character. That is all the information I need."

"But he has mentioned the circumstances of the murder, and since that subject has been raised, I would ask a few more questions about the details. I beg you, most gracious lord."

Bishop Jerome waved him on with a flick of his fingers.

"Sir David, why was Sir Ranulf alone with Lady Margrete at Winslow Downs? And why was he naked at the time of his death?"

"The reason does not matter," Keath sniffed. "A man has been murdered." He turned to the bishop. "That is what matters most."

"Yes, but the reason Ranulf was alone with Lord Hugh's wife," Berry said, pushing his spectacles up his nose, "might speak to a motivation for the killing."

"Greyhurst's motivation does not matter," the bishop said in a slow, gravelly voice. "Murder is a mortal sin no matter what the reason."

"My lord," Berry said, coming out from behind the table to face the cleric more fully. "I would argue that Hugh had two legitimate reasons for killing Sir Ranulf Blakely. First, this was clearly a case of self-defense. Sir Ranulf was about to stab Lord Hugh with his dagger."

"That's not what happened according to Sir David," Bishop Jerome drawled.

"No, but Lord Hugh's wife was there. She saw everything. In fact, she says Sir David did not appear until moments *after* Sir Ranulf had been slain."

"You would hardly expect Lady Margrete to be a reliable witness. She is a woman and, therefore, unable to sort fact from fiction, and no doubt biased in favor Lord Hugh."

"But she *saw* what happened," Berry reasoned.

"Just as Eve saw the apple in the Garden of Eden. Do you think that means her judgment could be trusted? No, of course not!"

"My lord," Berry said quietly, taking a steadying breath, "if that argument does not sit well with you, I would have you consider the other reason Lord Hugh was justified in killing your cousin."

It was the first time in court that anyone had stated the obvious relationship between the judge and the victim. Jerome narrowed his eyes, but did not rebuke the lawyer. "Go on with your spurious arguments, Guillaume de Berry."

"Lord Hugh was defending the honor of his wife. Surely you would not begrudge a man who protects his own wife from being raped by another man."

A gasp went up in the crowd. The lawyer nodded with satisfaction at the impact of his statement.

"Yes, my lord bishop," he continued with more confidence, "Sir Ranulf Blakely was about to rape Lady Margrete. Lord Hugh stopped this terrible crime before it occurred. Then Sir Ranulf reached for his dagger and attacked Hugh de Greyhurst, leaving him no choice but to defend himself. That is when Sir David Keath appeared, too late to see what had come to pass."

All eyes in the court turned from Berry to the bishop. Hugh sat at the edge of his seat, hoping against hope that the cleric would dismiss the case in the face of such obvious reason.

"A very interesting theory, Berry. Except you are wrong on one fundamental point. Lord Hugh de Greyhurst," the bishop said, each word gaining in intensity and volume as he spoke, "has no wife. For you cannot have a wife unless she submits to her conjugal duties. And if you have a wife who does not give her lord and master his due, then there is no marriage. And you cannot excuse a murderer for defending a wife he doesn't have!"

The crowd of witnesses and visitors broke into a flurry of whispers and gasps. The apparitor rapped his staff on the marble floor in a vain attempt to restore order. Hugh shut his eyes with resignation. The trial was over. And he was doomed.

Twenty-seven

I t is a conundrum and one that vexes me greatly, I will admit. A woman is cherished most when in a virgin state. And yet a woman who marries is considered arrogant, odd, and unnatural if she does not willingly and graciously surrender her maidenhead to her husband.

St. Paul himself in 1 Corinthians 7 wrote that a wife and husband should submit their bodies to each other, but only to prevent uncontrolled passion. Paul saw marriage as a necessary evil for those who cannot control their lusts. And while the Virgin Mary is looked upon in her purity as the apotheosis of her gender, a woman who aspires to such purity in marriage is suspected of arrogance at best and heresy at worst. Such a complicated stew!

With the benefit of hindsight, I now understand what truly motivated the bishop's objection to the notion of chastity in Lady Margrete's marriage. His real concern wasn't based on the Bible, nor was he spurred *by his greed for her land, as was his cousin. What truly bothered Jerome Blakely most was the very idea that a woman might choose her own fate. For a woman who abstains from sex is unencumbered by children and, therefore, free to live her life as she pleases. This lack of submission was most unacceptable to the bishop, and many others in the church hierarchy.*

But I digress. Our heroine was not contemplating church politics at this bleak moment. Nor was I, for that matter. As I watched the trial quietly from one of the back pews in the chantry, I was worried about the weather. A newly arrived mendicant friar had informed me that terrible storms were wracking the channel. Few ships were able to make their way between France and England. I doubted very much whether that breathlessly awaited missive from the Pope would arrive safely across the sea in time to save Sir Hugh.

And I wondered what, if anything, I could do to help him.

"My lord bishop," Father Markham said when the court reconvened the next day. "I would like to call the next witness."

Margrete dug her fingers into the wooden pew. What now? What absurd account would the bishop hear next? Everyone around her seemed to be wondering the same thing; a current crackled in the air as surely as if lightning had struck the chantry, for that is the effect the bishop's diatribe the previous day had had on those gathered for Lord Hugh's trial. Even the unflappable abbess, who sat next to Margrete, bore a grim expression as she tersely fingered her rosary beads.

"Proceed," the bishop said. He shifted to a more comfortable position in his great chair.

"Certainly, my lord bishop," Father Markham said, giving his superior a glib smile. "I would like to call before the judge the prostitute known as Ruth."

Margrete swooned. "Oh, Lord!" she whispered. Edith put an arm around her and gave her a reassuring hug. Both turned at the ominous sound of slippers on stone as someone walked up the aisle toward the dais. It was Ruth, forlorn and scared, marching reluctantly beside an apparitor who gripped her arm. The bishop had apparently sent the apparitor to Longrove to summon her. If only Margrete had anticipated this possibility she might have prepared the poor girl. When her burly escort handed her over to the prosecutor, she cringed in fright.

"There, there, Ruth," Father Markham said, patting her back, "do not fear. Sit here, if you will."

Ruth did as she was told. Answering the prosecutor's perfunctory questions, her voice was as small as a mouse's, her face as plain and doleful as a child's.

"Ruth," Father Markham said, not ungently, for he had already shown in his manner of questioning that he could be kind, even charming when it suited him, "I want you to tell me when you first met Lord Hugh de Greyhurst."

She looked down at her white knuckles and dug her nails further into her palms.

"Do not be afraid," Father Markham said. "Just tell me when you met the suspect."

"I-I met Lord Hugh when I came to Longrove Barony."

"And why did you come to his castle?"

"To . . ." She broke off and looked forlornly at Margrete, then slumped down further in the chair and continued in a softer voice. "I went there to bed him."

Another gasp arose in the chantry, so that Margrete wondered in irritation if the entire assemblage had come down with some respiratory illness. Was there no end to their shock? She, too, had been astonished by Ruth's unexpected appearance, but now shock turned to hard-boiled anger. The prosecutor was clearly trying to make unlucky circumstances seem like nefarious plots, in order to blacken Hugh's reputation.

"So you came to Longrove Castle to have sexual relations with the lord, even though he was newly married and it can be assumed that he was newly sated as far as his physical needs were concerned?"

"Huh?" Ruth stared at him in blank confusion, utterly still save for a hand that pulled a fallen wisp of hair out of her eyes.

The priest looked at her dumb expression and gave her a patronizing smile. "Let me put it more simply. Did it not strike you as odd that you would be hired by a man who was recently married and who, presumably, had recently bedded a new and lovely wife?"

"I didn't think about it, Father," Ruth said. "I was paid and aimed to do me work."

A round of laughter trickled through the chantry. Margrete bristled.

"You were paid and aimed to do your work," the priest repeated slowly, pointedly. "My lord bishop, clearly the suspect was venting frustration of a sexual nature in an act which was curiously absent from his own marriage."

Hugh leaned over and whispered in his lawyer's ear. Berry stood as Father Markham went back to his table.

"Bishop Jerome," Berry said, "I have questions for Ruth as well. I would ask her if she was able to carry out her mission. That is to say, did she ply her trade with Lord Hugh as she had so professionally intended to do?"

Ruth looked questioningly to the bishop and he nodded

his permission for her to respond. "No, my lord. I did not bed Lord Hugh."

"And why not? Could it be that Lord Hugh turned you away?"

"No, my lord."

Berry blinked, nonplussed. He pursed his lips. "Then why did you not perform your duties?"

"Lady Margrete interrupted us."

A few more snickers arose around the room. Margrete blushed to the roots of her hair.

"You did not have relations with Lord Hugh then, when you were interrupted, nor any time after that, even though Lord Hugh would have had plenty of opportunities to do so if he had chosen to. Isn't that true?"

"Yes, that's true."

"Even though Lady Margrete generously took you into her castle as a personal servant? Even then you did not have relations with Lord Hugh, though there were plenty of opportunities?"

"Even then I did not."

"Very well, Ruth, I have no more questions. You may go."

"Take her to the tower," the bishop said with a lazy yawn.

"What?" Margrete blurted out.

Ruth gave her a terrified look, like a doe awaiting the splitting point of an arrow. The apparitors came to her side and started dragging her away.

"My lord bishop," Margrete cried out, jumping up from the pew, "Ruth is my handmaiden. She must go to my castle, where she attends my needs."

"She is a prostitute," the bishop replied.

"But no more," Margrete argued. "She has given up her former profession."

"The only way for a prostitute to give up her life of sin is to marry a man or join a convent."

"But . . ."

"There are no exceptions," the bishop said. "Take her away."

"My lord bishop—"

"Enough!" he shouted. The chantry fell silent, except for Ruth, who whimpered as the apparitors hauled her out of the cathedral like a sack of down. "I will have no speaking out of turn, not even from the wife of a baron."

During this exchange, Barry had been consulting with Hugh, so when order had been restored, he was prepared to call a new witness.

"My lord bishop, I call Lord Hugh's squire, Brian, forward."

Margrete watched Hugh watch Brian come to the dais. She had no doubt that all three were thinking the same thing—the squire held his lord's future in his hands.

Brian sat, pale and perspiring, but with determination glinting in his blue and green eyes. While the lawyer verified the squire's identity and status at Longrove Castle for the bishop's edification, Edith clutched Margrete's hand. A pulse pounded in the lady-in-waiting's alabaster throat.

"Brian," Berry said, "tell me what you know of Lord Hugh's character."

"He is the best and most honest man I have ever known."

"High praise, indeed. What leads you to say such an extraordinary thing?"

"I have seen him behave honorably on the lists," Brian said, then blushed, realizing his error. "That is, before the papal ban."

"Yes," Berry said tightly, casting a doleful look to Hugh.

"And he has saved numerous friends from danger. He respects the rights of others."

"You know your sponsor well, Brian. Did he hire Ruth to indulge in carnal intercourse?"

"No," Brian whispered, looking down at his feet with a sore frown.

"So Lord Hugh did *not* hire a prostitute?"

"No."

"Well, if he did not, then who hired Ruth?"

Brian swallowed. "I did."

"You hired Ruth to pleasure your lord and sponsor?"

"Yes."

"And he had no knowledge of it?"

"No, for he would not have approved of such business. He is too good-hearted."

Berry flashed a brief smile of victory. "Very good, Brian, I have no more questions."

"But I do," Father Markham said, raising a hand in the air as he came around from behind his desk. "Brian, why did you hire a prostitute for Lord Hugh?"

The squire turned red, slowly but surely.

"Go on, then, speak up. Why did you feel it was necessary to hire a prostitute for your lord?"

"It was not *necessary*—"

"Perhaps not, but something inspired such an odd transaction."

Brian glared sullenly at the floor.

"Is it not true, good squire, that you hired a joy-woman because you knew that your lord was being denied his conjugal rights and you did not want him to suffer unduly?"

"No, I merely—"

"And if it is true that Lord Hugh has not consummated his marriage, as St. Paul instructed husbands to do, then

Lord Hugh is not truly married in the eyes of the church, is he?''

''But we were married before a priest!'' Hugh shouted, pounding his table. Berry gripped his forearm to stay him.

''Yes, but the priest did not know the conditions that you had set for your marriage,'' Father Markham countered. ''That it would spiritual in nature.''

''Can that be wrong in the eyes of God?'' Hugh came back, louder than before.

''It is wrong,'' Markham shot back, ''when you are defying the holy order of nature.''

''A wife can expect to remain chaste,'' the bishop clarified, ''only if she has a change of heart and enters a monastery soon after her nuptials. Otherwise, the conjugal debt must be paid.''

''You had no marriage, Lord Hugh de Greyhurst,'' Markham added, ''and therefore you could not have justifiably killed Sir Ranulf Blakely defending the honor of your wife. As the bishop has said, you had no wife.''

''God's teeth,'' Hugh roared, staggering to stand and pounding his fists on the table. ''You will not humiliate my wife any further! I will not have it. God curse you all, you villainous, pious fools!''

Hugh lunged for Father Markham, knocking over his chair and overturning the table.

''See!'' Keath shouted from the pews, ''he's nothing but an animal. A vicious beast!''

''No, Hugh!'' Margrete cried out, jumping up.

The apparitors came after him like dogs in a bearbaiting, clinging to his powerful arms. Hugh threw one of the men off with a violent shove, then smashed a brawny fist in the other's face. The man wobbled and fell to the floor, blood spurting from his nose.

When Hugh reached for him again, Margrete cried, "No, wait!"

Somehow, despite the fury that had nearly turned him deaf and dumb, Hugh heard her voice and his heart responded. His anger fled as quickly as it had come. He turned to his wife, saw the tears streaming down her fair cheeks, and his heart ached for her. He would do anything to avoid hurting her further.

"My lord bishop," she called out with a quavering voice, her eyes never leaving Hugh. "I would like to testify myself."

Yet another phlegmatic gasp went up. All eyes turned to Margrete.

"What could you tell us that would not be suspect?" Bishop Jerome said, waving her off.

"I would tell you the truth about my marriage."

"No," Hugh groaned. "Spare yourself."

"Only I know the truth about my marriage," she persisted.

The bishop frowned, narrowing his eyes with suspicion. "And what truth is that?"

"Simply put, my lord, I am *not* a virgin."

Twenty-eight

t seemed that an eternity passed before anyone spoke. Margrete felt disembodied, as if she were above herself, looking down with the same thunderous shock with which everyone else regarded her. For a while, it seemed no one would respond—that they would all stare at her evermore—until Hugh rubbed his hands over his face, shaking his head.

"No. No, Margrete," he said in a low voice. "Don't—"

"Yes," she answered quickly, holding up the flat of her hand to stop his denial. "I must speak the truth."

He gazed at her with sad, honey-colored eyes.

"Don't worry, husband," she said sweetly, sending him all the love in her heart. "It is for the best."

"You may proceed to the chair," the bishop said. Margrete excused herself as she left her place next to the abbess and Edith. She felt her lady-in-waiting's confusion and fear, but could not take the time to reassure her. Margrete knew it was just a matter of time before her taut nerves snapped and failed her. She had to speak quickly.

"My lady," Berry said when she was seated, taking over when the dumbfounded prosecutor merely stared at her in blinking wonder. "You say you are not a virgin. What do you mean by this extraordinary statement?"

"I mean that my husband and I have consummated our marriage. I did not think a witness was required on my wedding night," she added tartly, looking at Father Markham, "but I surely would have invited one into our solar if I thought something so private would be of such interest to others."

"She's lying," Father Markham said, leaning ominously over his table. "My lord bishop, her words can't be trusted. She's lying to save her husband!"

"I thought you said she had no husband," Berry retorted, one eyebrow cocked high.

Ignoring the lawyer, the priest pointed an accusing finger at Margrete. "She is not telling the truth. I know it. If she wants us to believe she's no longer a virgin, there is only one way to prove it. A physical examination."

"That won't be necessary," came a deep and measured voice. Margrete searched the pews, as did everyone else, to see who had spoken. Abbot Gregory rose from the fourth pew, looking gaunt and weary in his black robes.

Though his back was stooped and his skin pale and translucent, there was no mistaking the strength of will that emanated from his eyes. He stared the bishop down. "I have heard Lady Margrete's confession and I know that she speaks the truth. She is no longer a virgin. There is no need to examine her. That is, my lord bishop," he added with thinly veiled hostility, "unless you doubt the word of the abbot of Treyvaux Abbey."

The abbot cocked his head, focusing on Father Markham. "Well, prosecutor?" the abbot said. "Do you still insist on examining the lady of Longrove?"

"My lord bishop!" came another voice, this one bearing a suspiciously familiar Scottish accent.

Margrete paled, then her worst fears were confirmed when a short, decrepit old knight rose from the pews.

"I can avow she's no virgin," MacGregor offered unbidden.

"Sir William!" Margrete hissed to no avail.

"She lost her virginity long ago, that she did," the knight prattled on. "Everyone at Longrove Castle knows that. Why, they coupled ten times on their wedding night! They—"

"Silence!" the bishop bellowed. "I will have no more witnesses speaking out unless they are called. Father Abbot, I accept your testimony most prayerfully and with the greatest respect. And therefore I will accept Lady Margrete's statement as the truth. Still, a murder has been committed and—"

"My lord bishop!" yet another voice rang out.

Jerome Blakely sighed, exhaling pent-up anger and frustration. "What is it now?"

Margrete squinted in the shadows of the chantry as a rotund monk hurried toward the dais. It was Brother Edmund! When she saw what he bore in his hands, her heart joyfully skipped a beat.

"My lord bishop, I bring tidings from the Pope!" Friar Edmund said excitedly, his voice raspy for want of air, as if he'd run all the way from Treyvaux Abbey.

Margrete sought the abbess's reaction and saw that she was equally surprised and hopeful.

"What's this? You bring tidings from the Pope?" Jerome asked, nervously stroking his short black-and-grey beard. "What sort of tidings?"

"A decretal," Edmund said, as if that would be obvious to anyone but an imbecile. He pressed a hand to his chest to catch his breath. His eyes, bright with excitement, seemed particularly white against his florid cheeks. "A decretal regarding spiritual marriages."

Bishop Jerome scowled and snatched it from the fat monk's hands. "Let me see that."

The bishop unscrolled the parchment and, seeing the Pope's insignia, his dubious frown vanished and he nodded. "It looks legitimate. I recognize the Pope's seal."

As he perused the message, a new frown gathered, this one blacker than its predecessor. Muscles in the bishop's jaw and temples pulsed with anger. Then he handed the decretal back to Edmund, glowering at the monk as he reconciled himself with painful resignation. "Read this for the edification of the court."

"Yes, my lord bishop." Edmund turned to face those in the pews and began to read with an unmistakable tone of victory ringing in his voice.

" 'Greetings to the Right Reverend Jerome Blakely, bishop of Burnham, from His Holiness Pope Clement V. Dear brother in Christ, it comes to my attention that you are trying the case of one Lord Hugh de Greyhurst in the most contentious of circumstances. Taking into consideration your proximity and relation to the victim, I hereby relieve you of the case, dear brother, and commend you for your good stewardship thus far. But considering the circumstances and the recommendations of our most esteemed Abbess Phillipa de Claire, I rule that Lord Hugh should be acquitted.'

" 'Regrettably, your cousin was about to commit a heinous crime for which I know God in His mercy will forgive his soul. Lord Hugh could be expected to do aught but protect his wife.'

" 'Regarding the controversy over spiritual marriages, let this case be gently put aside as God sees fit. I mean to take this matter to heart when I have more time and will make my position known after closely considering what has been written on this subject by previous theologians and church scholars. Until then, I give leave to Lady Margrete to follow her heart and God's will as she sees fit.'

" 'As for the status of the abbess herself, you know that I hold her in the highest esteem. Not only do I hope she thrives in her position as abbess, I entrust you to turn to her for advice should the need arise.'

" 'I hope that you will take my words to heart, dear bishop and brother in Christ, for I have high hopes for your future and wish you all of God's blessings. Signed, Pope Clement V.' "

Profound silence enveloped the chantry. A ray of light had wrestled through the stormy sky and beamed through a stained-glass window. The bishop seemed to be watching the play of sunlight on an enormous garnet ring that graced the middle finger of his right hand.

Edmund quietly scrolled the document, handed it to the prosecutor, and joined Abbess Phillipa in the front pew.

"My lord," Father Markham said in a reedy voice, wiping the bags beneath his eyes with a thumb and forefinger. "I beg you leave to dismiss my case against Sir Hugh de Greyhurst."

"So done," Jerome said, turning hateful eyes on the abbess. "This court is finished."

No one moved until the bishop and the prosecutor swept down the aisle and out of the chantry. Then slowly the others began to rise. Hugh came straight for Margrete. She wrapped her arms around his waist and relished his embrace. The world was safe again. And for once, sense had reigned over mayhem.

The abbess, abbot, and Brother Edmund joined them, each offering congratulations. Margrete released her hold on her husband and turned to the abbot. She owed him much. He had lied for her, just as she had lied for her husband.

"Thank you," she said, but stifled the question she was dying to ask: Why?

He offered no explanation. Words would only give form and substance to their deception. They had colluded in the face of evil and injustice. All they could do now was pray that God would understand and forgive.

"How providential that a decretal from the Pope should arrive," Hugh said to the abbess. "The timing couldn't have been more perfect."

"Yes," she agreed, "it is curious that word reached the Pope so quickly and that he was able to get a missive to the bishop despite the terrible weather ravaging the channel."

Phillipa de Claire turned to Brother Edmund, a trace of admonition winking in her eyes. "Don't you find that curious, Brother Edmund?"

He flushed crimson and stammered, "Well, I—I suppose it is curious. But one might also say it is miraculous, Mother Abbess. Clearly it was God's will. And as we all know," he added with a mischievous smile, "God works in mysterious ways."

He sobered again and bowed his head. But as he turned, Margrete would have sworn he winked at her.

Twenty-nine

Hugh led the Longrove entourage home, with Margrete riding on a beautiful black mare beside him. A fine mist of rain sprinkled their faces, and he thought he'd never felt anything so refreshing in all his days.

Of all the possessions that he might have had, had lost, or now possessed, freedom was the most precious. The freedom to love, to fight for his land. The trial had proven that if nothing else, he was still free.

His new life would begin this day. There was only one question that nagged his thoughts: Why had Margrete lied to the bishop? Was she wishing they had made love, or was she merely trying to protect Hugh? If the latter, their marriage would continue as before—chastely. They had won that right.

But for all his present sense of satisfaction, the thought of a celibate marriage left him hollow inside as it never had before.

• • •

By the time they straggled into Longrove Castle, the sun had set. Margrete was both weary and exhilarated. She felt something she had never known before—unfettered hope. Hope born of hard work, faith, and luck, for which, it seemed, the world rejoiced with her—at least, the world that was Longrove Barony.

When she and Hugh arrived at the stable, they were warmly greeted by Peter, who had ridden ahead at a hard and fast pace. He had wanted to prepare the great hall for an impromptu feast and celebration.

"My lord and lady, welcome home," Peter said. His earthy, earnest features brimmed with pride as he led the horses over to the groom. Then he bowed low.

"Oh, Peter," she said and hugged him as soon as he had risen. "Do not bow before us, but dance if you will, for I have never been so happy in all my life."

He was the first to pull away, always mindful of his lower status, even though he had been her invaluable right arm for so many years.

"I am happy, my lord," he said, clasping Hugh's hand, "to know that there is justice in this world."

"I am happy, too," Hugh said, grinning ear to ear. "Happy and amazed."

The two men laughed and walked to the castle with their arms wrapped around each other's shoulders, trading jests. Soon Brian and Edith pulled into the stable. They'd ridden on the same horse and had traveled at a slower pace.

Margrete smiled to see them so close. It was as if an invisible thread connected their hearts, for whenever one strayed more than an arm's length, the other looked about anxiously until their eyes met again and twinkled with a shared smile. The kind of smile that was reserved for lovers, and Margrete realized they had probably coupled in love.

"Congratulations, my lady," said a beaming Brian.

"Yes," Edith added. "It seemed you got your miracle after all. No one deserved it more."

"Thank you for your kind words and support throughout this ordeal." Margrete smiled. "After all that has come to pass, good and bad, I see now that I am the luckiest person in the world. Sometimes it just takes perspective to realize it."

"And patience," Brian said.

"And faith," Edith chimed in.

"What will happen to you now, Brian?" Margrete gently steered the conversation away from herself. "Will you stay with Lord Hugh as he rebuilds this barony? Or will you go off seeking battles to win your spurs and knighthood?"

Edith cast her eyes downward, and Brian put an arm around her shoulder. "That's something I would like to talk to Lord Hugh about. Tonight."

Margrete nodded, hoping he would not deliver bad news on such a joyful occasion. If Brian were to announce his departure, Edith would be crushed.

"Very well," Margrete said. "Hie you to the great hall. I'll be along soon. I hear a horse, the last of our party trickling in. I want to welcome him home properly."

Brian and Edith strolled toward the keep, arm in arm as well. Watching after them, Margrete sighed with satisfaction. It seemed harmony had never blossomed with such vigor at Longrove Castle.

To test this idea, the last member of the Longrove party entered through the gatehouse, his nag nearly staggering with weariness.

"Hail! Greetings and joy!" shouted William MacGregor. The knight drew in his nag at the stable and slid from his saddle, landing with a brief wobble next to Margrete.

"Greetings, Sir William." She was feeling so joyful and

magnanimous that she reached over, placed her hands on either side of his head, and planted a smacking kiss on his forehead.

He frowned, rubbing the spot, eyeing her suspiciously. "Ach, young filly, don't start what ye don't plan to finish."

She let loose with a round of giggles. "Oh, Sir William, don't take offense. I just happen to love everyone today. Even you."

He tugged at his tunic, blushing. "Why me?"

"Because you told us about the D'Arbereau treasure. I might have lived my entire life never knowing about it."

"Ach, but ye don't have it in yer hands yet, do ye?"

She crossed her arms and grimaced. "No, you're right. But it's got to be here somewhere."

He waved her off. "Learn a lesson from yer father. He said he'd never lose a night's sleep over it. Nor should ye."

She smiled sardonically. "The only reason my father said that was because he knew where the jewels were hidden. But let us not worry about that tonight. We have to celebrate. Let's go sup with the others."

"Not so fast, lassie." MacGregor looked toward the gatehouse. "I picked up a fellow traveler along the way. He should be here any moment."

Soon the sound of horse hooves rose from over the wall, and another rider came through the gatehouse, reining in at the stable.

"Here is our man!" MacGregor said, slapping him on the back when he dismounted. "A jongleur traveling to Lord Richard's castle. I enticed him to perform for us tonight."

"You are most welcome, then," Margrete said, introducing herself.

The jongleur, a stringy man with bright parti-colored hose and a garish orange and red tunic, greeted her with extravagant and overwrought praise, then hurried, with lute in hand, to the great hall to sing for his supper.

The evening promised to be a joyful and entertaining celebration. But, Margrete wondered, butterflies whirling in her stomach, how would the night end?

After supping on a hastily prepared but delicious feast, Margrete and Hugh sank back into their chairs, pushing aside their trencher plates to enjoy a fine sweet claret and another equally intoxicating song from the jongleur. He had performed throughout the evening, doing flips and acrobatics, singing lively dance songs and melancholy love ballads. Through it all the members of the household had danced and caroused and sometimes even wept. And now a contented weariness settled about them. It was late and long past bedtime. But Margrete didn't want the happiness to end, and so she requested one more song.

As the jongleur strummed his lute and sang out sweetly, his throat trembling with an enchanting vibrato, Margrete leaned against the tall back of her chair, savoring the touch of her husband's hand on hers. His strong fingers encased hers on the arm of her chair.

"Margrete," he murmured, leaning close so she alone could hear, "I think fortune is finally smiling upon us."

She turned her head, meeting his burning gaze in the smoky torchlight. "Yes, my lord. We have everything that we've ever wanted."

He smiled, his rugged cheeks dimpling with a sexy smile. "*Almost* everything."

A shiver ran up her spine, for his husky voice spoke clearly that which his words merely implied. And, just in case there was any doubt about his meaning, he touched her chin with a crooked finger and tipped her chin up. Leaning forward, he covered her lips with his own. Fire spread over her body, searing her to the spot as his lips plundered hers, as his tongue boldly sought her own, as her nipples hardened then burned like tiny flames. Indeed, she knew then this night was far from over.

The song ended, as did the kiss. A smattering of applause greeted the jongleur who was clearly pleased. His overly expressive face, previously clownish, was now the picture of romance, and was lit with pleasure as he bowed.

"My lord!" Brian called out, coming from one of the arches where he had been listening to the musician. He tugged Edith by the hand until they stood before Hugh and Margrete on the floor below the dais. "I would like to speak to my future."

"So would I," Hugh returned with a quick smile. "If you meet him on the road, bid him welcome."

Laughter pattered around the hall. Brian raised his brows in mock surprise. "My lord, you have a sense of humor. Was that the last lesson I was to learn from you before earning my spurs?"

More laughter rippled about.

"Yes," Hugh shot back, "and you'd have learned it sooner if you weren't always spilling soup in my lap at feasts, and handing me swords that had grown rusty for your lack of care."

"Mea culpa," Brian said, sighing and placing his hands over his heart. "What a terrible squire I have been. But if I am no longer angering you at every turn, that can mean only one thing. I've outlived my usefulness to you."

MacGregor and the smith's son, drinking together by the cold fireplace, laughed at this. But their guffaws stood out awkwardly, for Margrete and Hugh quickly sobered, as did Peter and, above all, Edith. She regarded her lover with her sweet, crossed eyes, her face, already as fair as a white summer blossom, turning a paler hue.

"You will never outlive your usefulness to me," Hugh said, studying the glimmer of light on his goblet as he slowly twirled its stem in his fingers. Then he regarded Brian with a mix of melancholy and affection. "I would have you at my side forever if I could. But I will understand if you are ready to move on. You have always wanted to be a great warrior. I told you when I came to Longrove Barony that you should find a more bloodthirsty knight to train with."

"My lord," Brian said, brushing a finger down his straight nose in a nervous gesture, "the recent months have given me much to think about. I have considered what is most precious in life and have decided I can't be your squire any longer."

Hugh nodded sadly. "I understand."

"I'm not sure you do, my lord. You see, I no longer want to seek my fortune as a warrior. For I will soon have a wife to care for. That is," he added, turning at last to Edith, "if Lady Edith will have me."

Margrete bit her fist to stifle a cry of joy as Brian took Edith into his arms for a long, passionate kiss.

When the lady-in-waiting finally pulled back for a gasp of air, she blinked in astonishment, then shouted, "I do!" with such glee that everyone cheered and applauded.

Hugh stood and raised his cup high. "I toast the most valiant and able squire in the realm, and his beautiful bride-to-be."

"Hear! Hear!" Peter and MacGregor intoned.

Two servants hurried around the room, refilling cups.

"What will you do if you do not plan to be a soldier?" Hugh asked, taking Margrete by the hand and leading her off the dais to join the happy couple. She hugged Edith joyfully, then took Hugh's hand in hers.

"I was hoping," Brian cautiously replied, "to stay on at

Longrove Barony. With a fief of my own I could feed and clothe my wife and be a loyal vassal to you.''

"You? A farmer?" Hugh scowled good-naturedly. "I need your talents elsewhere. If you won't fight for me, then be my steward. I plan to oversee every aspect of my barony. I'll need someone to record accounts and organize the details of the barony while I keep a host of new knights and vassals in line and attend matters at court. I expect more trouble in Scotland. That means I'll probably have to answer the king's summons to fight. You can run the barony in my absence. And you can live in the manor house.''

Brian blinked in complete shock. "The manor house? Are you sure? It is such a grand place.''

"If you don't want it . . ." Hugh shrugged, giving him a look of doubt that all but Brian recognized as a jest.

"No, no, it's not that I don't want it. It's just . . . I'm a second son. I never . . . never thought such fortune would come my way.''

Hugh slapped a hand to his neck and gave him an affectionate shake. "Believe it. You deserve as much as any first son who ever lived.''

Brian flung himself into Hugh's arms for an embrace, then drew back, frowning. "But what about Peter?''

Everyone knew that Peter, though not of noble birth and without official title, had done the brunt of the work required to keep the barony running.

Hugh waved the able servant to his side and placed a hand firmly on his square shoulder. "Peter has asked me for a fief of his own. He wants a home and plans to take a wife as well.''

"You plan to marry?" Margrete said in pleasant surprise.

Peter turned red and exchanged a private look with Hugh.

"Go on," Hugh said softly. "Tell her."

The simple and bright man cleared his throat and found her gaze. "I want to marry Ruth."

"Ruth?" Margrete said.

"She won't ever be free of her past until she marries. I hate thinking of her imprisoned by that black-hearted bishop. She wants to start a new life. She's young, I know, and I'm twice her age. But I'll take good care of her. But only if you approve, my lady. I have served you for many years and would not want to displease you."

"I can't think of anything that would please me more." She regarded him through tears. "You're a good man, Peter. Salt of the earth. I know you'll be a splendid husband."

"And he will be an important tenant," Hugh said with a beaming smile. "I'm granting him a large fief south of the river, which includes a portion of the land in Kilbury Hide that Lord Richard and I settled over. After all, in spite of my wife's great courage and ample skills as a chatelaine we might have lost this barony long ago were it not for Peter's able assistance. We owe him a great debt."

"If you will excuse me, my lord and lady," Peter said, "I would travel back to the See of Burnham to fetch Ruth. I'll leave first thing in the morning and need to rest."

"Of course, Peter," Margrete said. "God bless you."

The new tenant smiled with complete satisfaction. "God already has."

"Yes, indeed," Margrete said to herself as he left the great hall. She turned to her husband and saw in his eyes that he, too, felt blessed. And more than ready for bed himself.

Thirty

argrete went to the solar alone. Hugh, ever the responsible lord of the castle, said that regrettably there were just a few matters to attend to before he joined her. She laughed and teased him, saying he just couldn't accept the fact that the barony had survived without him for a month. His handsome face flared with the obvious desire to return her gentle barb with one of his own, but he merely said he wouldn't waste any more time on words and to expect him in the solar sooner than she thought.

When she arrived there, her heart aflutter with excitement, she found Edith turning down the covers on the canopy bed.

"Edith! What are you doing here at this hour?"

The lady-in-waiting gave her an impish smile. "You thought I would have other plans for the evening?"

Margrete chuckled. "It wouldn't surprise me."

"I thought I would help you ready the solar for your

husband, since this will be only his third night here since the wedding."

Margrete crossed her arms and cocked her head musingly. "How did you know he would be sharing my bed tonight?"

"I just knew. I saw the way you looked at Lord Hugh tonight. I ordered a bath a while ago."

"Oh, bless you! Hugh will be grateful as well."

Soon there was a soft knock on the door and scullions from the kitchen filed in with pails of hot water, pouring them into a tub that Edith had placed by the embrasure.

When they departed, Edith helped Margrete undress, leaving her in her thin chemise after a quick good night. And so it was that Margrete stood at the embrasure, staring through the open window at the full, round moon, waiting for that which should have happened long ago.

The moon was so large, so blue and enchanting, that Margrete began to tingle all over. She'd been so busy before Hugh's arrival she'd scarcely noticed nature's miraculous beauty. Had she ever been more alive than she was now? Had she ever felt so deeply the senses God had given her?

It was doubtful. She had had to risk loving someone, then risk losing him, in order to truly feel the depths of her own humanity.

"Thank you, God, for this night," she whispered to the moon. "Thank you for this life, for this love, for my ability to feel, both the good and the bad."

The latch lifted quietly and the door creaked softly. She heard his footsteps but did not turn. She wanted one long last look at the moon, at the unknown. At the infinite.

"What are you smiling at?" he asked, coming up behind her and wrapping his arms around hers.

"I'm smiling at . . . everything. Everything is new to me now. Because of you."

He let out a short gust of air. "I thought I was the only one who felt that way."

She turned in his arms until they were face-to-face. "I once thought life to be a cage, and it is. But one full of miracles. All it takes to set them free is love."

"And I once thought myself to be unworthy. Until I held a maiden's heart, pure and true, in my trembling hands. Now I am whole. And you have made me so."

He gripped her neck and kissed her with all the gentleness, all the goodness in his soul. He loved her. God, how he loved her.

"I love you," he whispered in her ear.

She pressed his head close to her cheek, wishing they could melt into each other. Perhaps then he could know just how deeply she loved him in return.

"Love me," she whispered, meaning something else altogether.

His heart skipped a beat, and his groin jolted with desire. But he had one last surprise for her before they got down to the serious business of consummation.

"I want to read something to you first." When she pulled away, regarding him with quizzical blue eyes, he laughed. "Don't look at me as if I'm mad. I just found something in your tome by Brigitta of Ansfelden you may not have discovered. I think you'll find it *very* interesting."

She crossed her arms and watched with absolute amusement as he retrieved the book from her table and flipped through the pages.

"Ah, here we are," he said, smiling up at her like a schoolboy eager to please his teacher. He cleared his throat and began to recite. " 'A husband will instinctively feel the impulses of his carnal nature as surely as a bee will flit to a flower to suck its nectar. Like the bee, the husband will press his stinger in the virgin blossom in moist, ecstatic union. And like a flower, the wife will sigh and wilt with pleasure.' "

He pressed his tongue against the inside of his right cheek, stifling a grin of victory, watching her reaction closely.

"Well," she said archly, wandering to the table. She turned the book toward her and scanned the page. "I didn't know that Abbess Brigitta was so . . . graphic."

He sat on the table, taunting her with a brash smile. "You didn't know, or you pretended not to know? Why did you never read that part to me? Instead you made me endure hours of poems about virgins."

She returned a cunning grin of her own. "I don't care to answer that question, my lord prosecutor, for fear of incriminating myself in the church court. But let me ask *you* a question. How long have you been able to read so well? You didn't stumble over a single word."

Hugh shrugged as if it were a skill too insignificant to acknowledge. Unconvinced, Margrete flipped through the book and turned it back his way. "Read this. It's one of my favorite poems."

"About virgins, no doubt," he said, frowning at the words. "Hmmmm. I can't quite make out the letters. Must be the poor lighting."

"Shall I light another candle?"

"No, that won't be necessary."

"Oh? And why is that?"

He sighed in resignation. "Very well. I confess. I wasn't reading at all. I memorized that passage about the bee and the flower. Though I do plan to return to my studies now that I am a free man."

"Why did you memorize that particular passage?" she said, tickling his ribs playfully.

"Because," he replied, squirming as he tried not to laugh, "that's exactly what I've wanted to do to you since the day I first met you."

"I bathed you that first day," she said coyly, tugging him toward the tub. "Do you remember?"

"Do I remember?" he said sarcastically, submitting to her as she unfastened his garments. "How could I forget? I had to sit in the bathwater until it was cold before I could leave without embarrassing myself."

"Oh, poor man," she murmured as she loosened his tunic and untied the laces that attached the garment to his hose. He tugged the hose off his legs by yanking on the leather soles while she continued to unfasten his tunic down the front. When both their tasks were complete, she slipped a hand through his remaining shirt with a groan of approval. "Oooh. You're so . . . warm."

"Hot is the word you're looking for, I believe," Hugh said on a quivering breath when her fingers brushed over his nipples. Her hands crawled through the hair matted on his brawny chest. He tugged her closer, pressing her hips to his so she could feel the effect her caresses had on him.

"Do you need another cold bath?" she asked coyly.

He laughed. Was this the prim wife he had married such a short time ago? This temptress with her flowing blond hair and her eyes the color of sapphires? Whoever she was, saint or sinner, virgin or whore, he wanted all of her.

He tugged off his tunic and whipped off his shirt. Barechested, he pulled her close. She stroked her fingers down the thick muscles woven over his chest, combed them through the mat of hair, then glided them along his neck and over his face, as if she were blind and still wanted to see every bit of him, every secret place, every nuance. Then she pressed her cheek to his chest and hugged him tightly.

He knew in that moment, if he had ever doubted it, that she loved him. For Margrete would never hold in her arms anything she did not already hold in her heart.

"I love you," she murmured. "I think I loved you from the moment I saw you. From the moment you stopped to comfort that child." She blinked in the candlelight, seeing the past, seeing him striding down the hall with his injured leg and wounded pride. She breathed in his musky, manly scent and let out a shuddering sigh of relief. He'd stayed, and she was so glad. "I think I knew how good you were even then. And somewhere deep inside I knew I deserved you. I needed you. I wanted you."

She tossed back her head, her flaxen locks trailing down her back like a waterfall as she looked up into his face. "Kiss me, please. Kiss me like you've never kissed me before."

He stroked her hair as a wry grin inched up his cheeks. "I thought I'd done my best by you, my lady. But I could be wrong. Let's find out."

He slowly lowered his head till all that parted their lips was a breath of air. Looking deep in her eyes—two enormous, gleaming blue gems—he saw the reflection of his own soul. He saw the limitless depths of his own goodness and love. He would never truly have known himself were it not for her.

Grateful, soul-trembling, he shut his eyes and lowered his head until their lips fused, making them one. He breathed her in, her honeyed scent, her sweet breath, and felt the ecstasy of utter satisfaction.

"I love you," he murmured against her cheek. "This is what my life was for. This moment. You are my world. You are my home."

"Then come inside," she whispered, "where it's safe and warm."

He lifted her up, scooping an arm beneath her legs and carrying her to the bed. It was an ornately carved canopy with curtains dangling at the four corners. The mattress was big and fluffy, filled with soft down. When he lowered her to the bed, she sank like an angel in a cloud. With her blond hair curled against the pillow, sultry eyes gleaming blue as the sky, rose-pink lips slightly parted, her skin as creamy as a pearl, he was sure he'd never seen such pure femininity.

"You're still clothed," she complained, a sad pucker on her brow. Her gaze lowered. "Your braies. . . ."

"Gladly." He pulled off the linen that swathed his groin and sat by her. "Better?"

"Hmmmm," she murmured in approval, eyes feasting on his tan, hard, naked body.

"Now your turn." His eyes simmered like two burning cauldrons. He slipped a hand beneath her chemise and let his fingers crawl up a leg, his thumb caressing the sensitive inner thigh.

She sucked in a breath and shut her eyes tight, wondering where he would go next. Sweetly torturing her, he moved on, smoothing his hand over her pelvis, skimming higher until he cupped a tingling breast. He squeezed the nipple and bent down for another kiss, this one plundering and deep. Soon she was squirming and clutching his shoulders, digging her nails in his flesh as she pressed her breasts to his chest, begging without words.

He drew back and gave her a dark smile. "Very well. Take off your chemise."

She knew what he was after. He wanted her to be the one to lift the last defense. He wanted her to know beyond doubt that this was her choice. And it was.

She sat up and pulled the thin gown over her head. The air was cool on her breasts. Her nipples puckered into beads. She tossed the chemise aside and sat there, letting him look at her, his eyes flicking over her as erotically as if he were using his tongue. He blinked languidly, eyes not quite in focus, seeing her on a level that did not require vision.

Like a wave pulled inexorably to shore by the subtle, persistent tug of the moon, he rose up on one knee, pushed her down, then crashed on the shore, spreading over her, sinking on her. He pressed against the moist inlet at her thighs, the tributary of life, the dam of her maidenhead. It was the place where his seed would be watered with her maiden's blood, giving birth to a life that would sanctify their love.

He spread her arms out on the bed like an angel's wings, pinning her wrists with his hands. Still poised at her threshold, he spread her ankles apart with his legs. There was only one last move to make.

"Are you sure?" he whispered.

She nodded and exhaled a shuddering breath.

He was the seventh wave. The one that crashes in harder than the others. The one that has been building in the ocean deep, urged on by some unknowable primal force.

He slid in with deceptive force, as gently as possible, past the barricade she'd guarded so carefully for so long. When that fine sheath was torn, she made a small noise, half pain and half sorrow: the last unexpected sob of a woman saying farewell to the girl. Then she crawled fearlessly and without remorse out to sea and rode the wave home.

Making love was very much like being in water. In Hugh's arms Margrete's body had no form, no limitations, every motion was poetic and slow.

When that first burst of exquisite pleasure came, and it came quickly, it surprised her with its uniqueness and force. With her womanhood gripped in exotic little spasms, she flailed her arms, clawing in half speed as would a drowning person. But there was no fear, for she was drowning in love and never wanted to come up for air, never wanted to breathe normally again.

His skin slid over her with each potentially explosive thrust, sweat making him glide on her, the musky scent of sex rising like steam from a warm pond after a rain. It infused her head, and she laughed giddily, overwhelmed with the utter pleasure of her body.

"What?" he asked, so skillful in his loving that he could talk, even study her, as his turgid strength throbbed in her, controlled but threatening a great unleashing. "What is it?"

She wrapped her legs around his waist to take him more fully. "Alchemy," she whispered, tasting the salt of her own sweat. That was all she could utter as she began to groan in unison with his powerful thrusts. This was some kind of alchemy, turning normal flesh into a song, a high-pitched vibration that shot straight up to the stars.

It was a special gift from heaven. How had she been so blind to it? How had she resisted it for so long?

Thirty-one

They made love ten times that night. Ten or eleven. Hugh lost count. He would fall asleep out of sheer exhaustion, sometimes even as an "I love you" spilled over his lips, only to be awakened an hour later by the instinctual pulsing of his own hips. Even in sleep he would seek relief in the sweet place his body knew it would find it.

And so, half awake, he would crawl onto her, or pull her onto him and slide in, waking her, and they would make love until they were both sated, until eventually neither could feel a blasted thing, so numb and swollen did their faithless bodies become.

And in the morning, when he'd rested a few hours, he made love to her again, loving the smell of their mingled scents, the woozy softness of her plundered lips, the sunshine on her chafed skin—his whiskers had done some damage. He'd never felt so much a part of someone in his life. They truly were of one mind, and now one body.

"I love you," was the first thing she said when her eyes

blinked open, finding him, then glowing with adoration.

"I know," he replied, watching her as he laid on his side. "I love you, too."

He trailed a finger from her collarbone down between her breasts where the breastbone rises, down the flat plane of her belly to the apex of her thighs, then back up again.

"What are you thinking about?" she murmured.

His gold eyes found hers and he smiled distractedly. "How fortunate we were that the Pope's decretal arrived so promptly. I'm not used to such Providence." She smiled whimsically and he laughed in mock indignation. "You find my brush with death humorous?"

"I don't think Providence had anything to do with your salvation. I'd wager that missive from the Pope was a brilliant forgery executed by none other than dear Brother Edmund."

"A forgery?" Hugh scoffed. "Why would he do something so fraught with danger?"

"Because he was capable of pulling it off. He's undoubtedly seen the Pope's seal dozens of times on missives sent to Abbess Phillipa. Edmund is an artist. He could easily reproduce the insignia in wax and forge Clement V's signature."

"But why should he care enough about me to risk his own career in the church?"

"Because like the abbot, Brother Edmund loathes injustices committed in the name of God. He probably hates seeing men like Jerome Blakely give religion a bad name."

This last was said concurrent with a deep yawn.

"You're sleepy. Didn't you sleep well?" he murmured, tracing the outline of her face with a forefinger.

"Did I sleep at all?" she said, laughing lushly, leaning forward and kissing the bristly hairs on his cheek. "How did you fare?"

"What little sleep I did get was disturbed by this." He pressed the down mattress with a fist. "There's a terrible lump right here in the middle of the bed."

She frowned in mock horror, but a slip of a smile betrayed her sense of humor. "Yes, I felt it, too. But it was a small price to pay for so much pleasure."

"What do you suppose it is? You aren't storing any tomes about virgins under the bed, are you?"

She pressed down and felt a distinct point. "No, it's too hard and small for that. It must be a clump of goose down."

Hugh poked down, feeling the cone-shaped hardness. "No, it's too solid. How did your father sleep on this mattress so many years?"

"He never complained. And I never noticed it until last night."

He grinned, eyes twinkling. He slapped the bed. "Yes, indeed, this old bed was well used by us. But even though your father slept alone, he was heavy. His weight surely brought him in contact with this unwelcoming lump."

Margrete sat up, not in the least bit modest about her body. How could she be, after sharing every intimate secret the night through?

"My father used to say he slept soundly." Margrete frowned, trying to recall something that tickled her memory. "What did I hear recently?"

"Something about the bed?"

"About his sleep." She blinked, then stared at Hugh as realization dawned.

"What?" He sat up, frowning now himself. "What is it? You look as if you've seen the ghost of William the Conqueror."

"Sir William recently told me that my father used to say he'd never lose a night's sleep over the D'Arbereau treasure because it was so well hidden."

Hugh had learned of the treasure on the trip back from Burnham. He narrowed his eyes as he stroked his chin. "And Brian has looked everywhere for it? To no avail?"

Margrete nodded. Their eyes locked. Certainty clicked. And like two rehearsed dancers they both leapt off the bed at once.

"Let's slide the mattress this way." He went to the foot of the bed and gripped the bottom, tugging as Margrete shoved from the other end.

Hugh jogged backward until the enormous mattress flopped on the floor. Then Margrete gasped.

"What is it?" he said, coming to her side. Then he focused on what she was gaping at. "God's wounds, who would have guessed?"

There was a flat panel of wood at the base of the wooden frame. In the center someone had carved out a rectangle. In that hole sat an ornately painted wooden trunk, which was topped with a decorative cone encrusted with glittering jewels.

"So *that's* what was digging into my back all night long," Hugh said.

"Do you know what this is?" Her voice was a hushed monotone.

"A pain in the back?"

She gripped his arms. "No! Don't you realize what this is? *This* is the D'Arbereau treasure."

He tossed back his head with a laugh. "I was jesting, Margrete. I've already guessed what it is. Go ahead. Open it."

She reached over and lifted a latch on the trunk. Hugh helped her flip back the lid. Then they stared at the contents, gaping and speechless.

There were strands of pearls, ruby-studded goblets, bracelets of gold filigree, emerald rings, an amber-studded belt, and a dagger dripping with jewels. And those were just the items visible on top.

"Holy Mary and Joseph," Hugh said at last. "Why didn't Giles tell you about this?"

"I think he forgot," Margrete replied, tucking her hand around his waist. "He'd planned to tell me about it when I grew up, but by then he had lost his memory."

"How could anyone forget something like this? I would think that some things are so incredible they would survive the loss of memory."

"Perhaps Sir William was right. Maybe Father didn't want to remember. Or maybe he knew what I only last night discovered. That the greatest treasure is buried right here."

She pressed her hands to her heart. Hugh's own heart thudded sweetly at this. He pressed a hand over hers and drew her closer with the other, giving her a lingering kiss, knowing she was right. Knowing beyond doubt why he loved her so.

They managed to pry themselves out of the bedchamber before noon. Hugh had business to attend at Kilbury Hide, and Margrete wanted to help Edith plan her wedding. When their tasks were complete, they all gathered at dusk for a simple meal in the great hall. The minstrel had stayed an extra night and entertained them with gentle ballads that made everyone wistful and grateful for the love in their lives.

Holding Margrete's hand at the high table, Hugh was certain he'd never known such contentment. Margrete was more than a wife to him. She was a miracle. And the importance of finding the D'Arbereau treasure, he could honestly say, came a distant second to her importance in his life. They'd told no one about their discovery, but as they rose to retire for the evening, Hugh called Brian aside.

"I have a mission for you. Your first as my new steward."

"Yes, my lord?" Brian looked up expectantly. When Hugh placed a plum-sized ruby in his palm, he gasped. "Good Lord!"

"Give this to Guillaume de Berry as payment for his services. Tell him I am most grateful."

"Dear saints in heaven! You found it!" He shot Hugh a victorious and brilliant smile. "Where? Where was it?"

Hugh's brow curled and his eyes glinted cunningly. "Where did I find what?"

"The D'Arbereau treasure!"

"As far as the world is concerned, I haven't found it. And I never will. Do you understand?"

Brian's eyelids flickered as understanding washed over him. "Oh, I see. Yes. It's best that way. It will remain our secret. I don't want anyone coming here after it and raping our wives."

Hugh nodded. "I knew you'd understand."

"Where was it? I looked everywhere."

Hugh thought before he answered, then grinned sardonically. "Let's just say it's so well hidden I'll never lose a night's sleep over it."

Hugh didn't sleep much that night, but he couldn't blame the lumpiness of the bed, which had been restored to its original position. Nor could he blame his excitement over the discovery of the D'Arbereau treasure, which he and Margrete agreed they would use as much as necessary to restore the barony and save the rest for their children, if they should be so blessed.

No, the blame for his sleeplessness lay squarely with his

wife. She was too beautiful to resist. And it wasn't her looks that drove him over and over again into her arms. It was her heart. Her beautiful maiden's heart. Now, richer still, the heart of a woman, beating with love eternal.

Epilogue

So, kind pilgrim, you may now rest your weary eyes and gently close the leather binding of this tome. Do not mind if a plume of dust rises to make you sneeze, for it may well be that this tale is not oft read. I cannot say what will become of this manuscript, if it will stand the test of time, if it will survive the officious and prim judgment of the monks who follow in my place. I write this final note many years after the first pages were penned, and I do not know how long I will live to protect this work of art. It does not matter. I have told my story. I have done my best. The rest is in the hands of God.

I am humbled when I think of the sacrifices Lady Margrete and Lord Hugh made for each other—she her innocence, he his freedom. Their very union was an act of faith. And I am happy that I have lived to such an age (yes, I am now old, though still not gaunt!) that enables me to see the rewards and fruits of their sacrifices. Longrove Barony is now a polished *jewel, the envy of kings and earls alike. And the happy couple proudly boasts five children and three grand-children, with many more sure to follow.*

Though the intervening years have left their marks upon the lovely face of our heroine, and have stooped the shoulders of our hero, their affection for one another still burns bright, for love is timeless. Remember that, gentle pilgrim. Love is a timeless and priceless gift. A precious gem to be treasured whenever and wherever it is found. So go now and love as you will, and may God bless you on your journey.

> *Brother Edmund*
> *Treyvaux Abbey*
> *1343*

Turn the page for a preview of
JILL MARIE LANDIS'S
latest novel

Blue Moon

Coming in July from Jove Books

Prologue

he would be nineteen tomorrow. If she lived.

In the center of a faint deer trail on a ribbon of dry land running through a dense swamp, a young woman crouched like a cornered animal. The weak, gray light from a dull, overcast sky barely penetrated the bald cypress forest as she wrapped her arms around herself and shivered, trying to catch her breath. She wore nothing to protect her from the elements but a tattered rough, home-spun dress and an ill-fitting pair of leather shoes that had worn blisters on her heels.

The primeval path was nearly obliterated by lichen and fern that grew over deep drifts of dried twigs and leaves. Here and there the ground was littered with the larger rot-ting fallen limbs of trees. The fecund scent of decay clung to the air, pressed down on her, stoked her fear, and gave it life.

Breathe. Breathe.

The young woman's breath came fast and hard. She squinted through her tangled black hair, shoved it back, her fingers streaked with mud. Her hands shook. Terror born of being lost was heightened by the knowledge that night was going to fall before she found her way out of the swamp.

Not only did the encroaching darkness frighten her, but so did the murky, silent water along both sides of the trail. She realized she would soon be surrounded by both night and water. Behind her, from somewhere deep amid the cypress trees wrapped in rust-colored bark, came the sound of a splash as some unseen creature dropped into the watery ooze.

She rose, spun around, and scanned the surface of the swamp. Frogs and fish, venomous copperheads, and turtles, big as frying pans, thrived beneath the lacy emerald carpet of duckweed that floated upon the water. As she knelt there wondering whether she should continue on in the same direction or turn back, she watched a small knot of fur float toward her over the surface of the water.

A soaking wet muskrat lost its grace as soon as it made land and lumbered up the bank in her direction. Amused, yet wary, she scrambled back a few inches. The creature froze and stared with dark, beady eyes before it turned tail, hit the water, and disappeared.

Getting to her feet, the girl kept her eyes trained on the narrow footpath, gingerly stepping through piles of damp, decayed leaves. Again she paused, lifted her head, listened for the sound of a human voice and the pounding footsteps which meant someone was in pursuit of her along the trail. When all she heard was the distant knock of a woodpecker, she let out a sigh of relief. Determined to keep moving, she trudged on, ever vigilant, hoping that the edge of the swamp lay just ahead.

Suddenly, the sharp, shrill scream of a bobcat set her heart pounding. A strangled cry escaped from her lips. With a fist pressed against her mouth, she squeezed her eyes closed and froze, afraid to move, afraid to even breathe. The cat screamed again and the cry echoed across the haunting silence of the swamp until it seemed to stir the very air around her.

She glanced up at dishwater-gray patches of weak afternoon light nearly obliterated by the cypress trees that grew so close together in some places that not even a small child could pass between them. The thought that a wildcat might be looming somewhere above her in the tangled limbs, crouched and ready to pounce, sent her running down the narrow, winding trail.

She had not gone a hundred steps when the toe of her shoe caught beneath an exposed tree root. Thrown forward, she began to fall and cried out.

As the forest floor rushed up to meet her, she put out her hands to break the fall. A shock of pain shot through her wrist an instant before her head hit a log.

And then her world went black.

One

oah LeCroix walked to the edge of the wide wooden porch surrounding the one-room cabin he had built high in the sheltering arms of an ancient bald cypress tree and looked out over the swamp. Twilight gathered, thickening the shadows that shrouded the trees. The moon had already risen, a bright silver crescent riding atop a faded blue sphere. He loved the magic of the night, loved watching the moon and stars appear in the sky almost as much as he loved the swamp. The wetlands pulsed with life all night long. The darkness coupled with the still, watery landscape settled a protective blanket of solitude around him. In the dense, liquid world beneath him and the forest around his home, all manner of life coexisted in a delicate balance. He likened the swamp's dance of life and death to the way good and evil existed together in the world of men beyond its boundaries.

This shadowy place was his universe, his sanctuary. He savored its peace, was used to it after having grown up in almost complete isolation with his mother, a reclusive Cherokee woman who had left her people behind when she chose to settle in far-off Kentucky with his father, a French Canadian fur trapper named Gerard LeCroix.

Living alone served Noah's purpose now more than ever. He had no desire to dwell among "civilized men," especially now that so many white settlers were moving in droves across the Ohio into the new state of Illinois.

Noah turned away from the smooth log railing that bordered the wide, covered porch cantilevered out over the swamp. He was about to step into the cabin where a single oil lamp cast its circle of light when he heard a bobcat scream. He would not have given the sound a second thought if not for the fact that a few seconds later the sound was followed by a high-pitched shriek, one that sounded human enough to stop him in his tracks. He paused on the threshold and listened intently. A chill ran down his spine.

It had been so long since he had heard the sound of another human voice that he could not really be certain, but he thought he had just heard a woman's cry.

Noah shook off the ridiculous, unsettling notion and walked into the cabin. The walls were covered with the tanned hides of mink, bobcat, otter, beaver, fox, white-tailed deer and bear. His few other possessions—a bone-handled hunting knife with a distinctive wolf's head carved on it, various traps, some odd pieces of clothing, a few pots and a skillet, four wooden trenchers and mugs, and a rifle— were all neatly stored inside. They were all he owned and needed in the world, save the dugout canoe secured outside near the base of the tree.

Sparse but comfortable, even the sight of the familiar surroundings could not help him shake the feeling that something unsettling was about to happen, that all was not right in his world.

Pulling a crock off a high shelf, Noah poured a splash of whiskey in a cup and drank it down, his concentration intent on the deepening gloaming and the sounds of the swamp. An unnatural stillness lingered in the air after the puzzling scream, almost as if, like him, the wild inhabitants of Heron Pond were collectively waiting for something to happen. Unable to deny his curiosity any longer, Noah sighed in resignation and walked back to the door.

He lingered there for a moment, staring out at the growing shadows. Something was wrong. *Someone* was out there. He reached for the primed and loaded Hawken rifle that stood just inside the door and stepped out into the gathering dusk.

He climbed down the crude ladder of wooden strips nailed to the trunk of one of the four prehistoric cypress that supported his home, and stepped into the dugout *pirogue* tied to a cypress knee that poked out of the water. Noah paddled the shallow wooden craft toward a spot where the land met the deep, dark water with its camouflage net of duckweed, a natural boundary all but invisible to anyone unfamiliar with the swamp.

He reached a rise of land which supported a trail, carefully stepped out of the *pirogue* and secured it to a low-hanging tree branch. Walking through thickening shadows, Noah breathed in his surroundings, aware of every subtle nuance of change, every depression on the path that might really be a footprint on the trail, every tree and stand of switchcane.

The sound he thought he'd heard had come from the southeast. Noah headed in that direction, head down, staring at the trail although it was almost too dark to pick up any sign. A few hundred yards from where he left the *pi-*

rogue, he paused, raised his head, sniffed the air, and listened to the silence.

Instinctively, he swung his gaze in the direction of a thicket of slender cane stalks and found himself staring across ten yards of low undergrowth into the eyes of a female bobcat on the prowl. Slowly he raised his rifle to his shoulder and waited to see what the big cat would do. The animal stared back at him, its eyes intense in the gathering gloaming. Finally, she blinked and with muscles bunching beneath her fine, shiny coat, the cat turned and padded away.

Noah lowered the rifle and shook his head. He decided the sound he heard earlier must have been the bobcat's cry and nothing more. But just as he stepped back in the direction of the *pirogue,* he caught a glimpse of ivory on the trail ahead that stood out against the dark tableau. His leather moccasins did not make even a whisper of sound on the soft earth. He closed the distance and quickly realized what he was seeing was a body lying across the path.

His heart was pounding as hard as Chickasaw drums when he knelt beside the young woman stretched out upon the ground. Laying his rifle aside he stared at the unconscious female, then looked up and glanced around in every direction. The nearest white settlement was beyond the swamp to the northeast. There was no sign of a companion or fellow traveler nearby, something he found more than curious.

Noah took a deep breath, let go a ragged sigh, and looked at the girl again. She lay on her side, as peacefully as if she were napping. She was so very still that the only evidence that she was alive was the slow, steady rise and fall of her breasts. Although there was no visible sign of injury, she lay on the forest floor with her head beside a fallen log. One of her arms was outstretched, the other tucked beneath her. What he could see of her face was filthy. So were her hands; they were beautifully shaped, her fingers long and tapered. Her dress, nothing but a rag with sleeves, was hiked up to her thighs. Her shapely legs showed stark ivory against the decayed leaves and brush beneath her.

He tentatively reached out to touch her, noticed his hand shook, and balled it into a fist. He clenched it tight, then opened his hand and gently touched the tangled, black hair that hid the side of her face. She did not stir when he moved the silken skein, nor when he brushed it back and looped it over her ear.

Her face was streaked with mud. Her lashes were long and dark, her full lips tinged pink. The sight of her beauty took his breath away. Noah leaned forward and gently reached beneath her. Rolling her onto her back, he straightened her arms and noted her injuries. Her wrist appeared to be swollen. She had an angry lump on her forehead near her hairline. She moaned as he lightly probed her injured wrist; he realized he was holding his breath. Noah expected her eyelids to flutter open, but they did not.

He scanned the forest once again. With night fast closing in, he saw no alternative except to take her home with him. If he was going to get her back to the tree house before dark, he would have to hurry. He cradled her gently in his arms, reached for his rifle, and then straightened. Even then the girl did not awaken, although she did whimper and turn her face against his buckskin jacket, burrowing against him. It felt strange carrying a woman in his arms, but he had no time to dwell on that as he quickly carried her back to the *pirogue*, set her inside, and untied the craft. He climbed in behind her, holding her upright, then gently drew her back until she leaned against his chest.

As the paddle cut silently through water black as pitch, he tried to concentrate on guiding the dugout canoe home, but was distracted by the way the girl felt pressed against him, the way she warmed him. As his body responded to a need he had long tried to deny, he felt ashamed at his lack of control. What kind of a man was he, to become aroused by a helpless, unconscious female?

Overhead, the sky was tinted deep violet, an early canvas for the night's first stars. During the last few yards of the journey, the swamp grew so dark that he had only the yellow glow of lamplight shining from his home high above the water to guide him.

Run. Keep running.

The dream was so real that Olivia Bond could feel the leaf-littered ground beneath her feet and the faded chill of winter that lingered on the damp April air. She suffered, haunted by memories of the past year, some still so vivid they turned her dreams into nightmares. Even now, as she lay tossing in her sleep, she could feel the faint sway of the flatboat as it moved down the river long ago. In her sleep the fear welled up inside her.

Her dreaming mind began to taunt her with palpable memories of new sights and scents and dangers.

Run. Run. Run, Olivia. You're almost home.

Her legs thrashed, startling her awake. She sat straight up, felt a searing pain in her right wrist and a pounding in her head that forced her to quickly lie back down. She kept her eyes closed until the stars stopped dancing behind them, then she slowly opened them and looked around.

The red glow of embers burning in a fireplace illuminated the ceiling above her. She lay staring up at even log beams that ran across a wide, planked ceiling, trying to ignore the pounding in her head, fighting to stay calm and let her memory come rushing back. Slowly she realized she was no longer lost on the forest trail. She had not become a bobcat's dinner, but was indoors, in a cabin, on a bed.

She spread her fingers and pressed her hands palms down against a rough, woven sheet drawn over her. The mattress was filled with something soft that gave off a tangy scent. A pillow cradled her head.

Slowly Olivia turned her aching head, afraid of who or what she might find beside her, but when she discovered she was in bed alone, she thanked God for small favors.

Refusing to panic, she thought back to her last lucid memory: a wildcat's scream. She recalled tearing through the cypress swamp, trying to make out the trail in the dim light before she tripped. She lifted her hand to her forehead and felt swelling. After testing it gingerly, she was thankful that she had not gashed her head open and bled to death.

She tried to lift her head again but intense pain forced her to lie still. Olivia closed her eyes and sighed. A moment later, an unsettling feeling came over her. She knew by the way her skin tingled, the way her nerve endings danced, that someone was nearby. Someone was watching her. An instinctive, intuitive sensation warned her that the *someone* was a man.

At first she peered through her lashes, but all she could make out was a tall, shadowy figure standing in the open doorway across the room. Her heart began to pound so hard she was certain the sound would give her consciousness away.

The man walked into the room and she bit her lips together to hold back a cry. She watched him move about purposefully. Instead of coming directly to the bed, he walked over to a small square table. She heard him strike a piece of flint, smelled lamp oil as it flared to life.

His back was to her as he stood at the table; Olivia opened her eyes wider and watched. He was tall, taller than most men, strongly built, dressed in buckskin pants topped by a buff shirt with billowing sleeves. Despite the coolness of the evening, he wore no coat, no jacket. Indian moccasins, not shoes, covered his feet. His hair was a deep black, cut straight and worn long enough to hang just over his collar. She watched his bronzed, well-tapered hands turn up the lamp wick and set the glass chimney in place.

Olivia sensed he was about to turn and look at her. She wanted to close her eyes and pretend to be unconscious, thinking that might be safer than letting him catch her staring at him, but as he slowly turned toward the bed, she knew she had to see him. She had to know what she was up against.

Her gaze swept his body, taking in his great height, the length of his arms, the width and breadth of his shoulders before she dared even look at his face.

When she did, she gasped.

Noah stood frozen beside the table, shame and anger welling up from deep inside. He was unable to move, unable to breathe as the telling sound of the girl's shock upon seeing his face died on the air. He watched her flinch and scoot back into the corner, press close to the wall. He knew her head pained her, but obviously not enough to keep her from showing her revulsion or from trying to scramble as far away as she could.

He had the urge to walk out, to turn around and leave. Instead, he stared back and let her look all she wanted. It had been three years since he had lost an eye to a flatboat accident on the Mississippi. Three years since another woman had laughed in his face. Three years since he had moved to southern Illinois to put the past behind him.

When her breathing slowed and she calmed, he held his hands up to show her that they were empty, hoping to put her a little more at ease.

"I'm sorry," he said as gently as he could. "I don't mean you any harm."

She stared up at him as if she did not understand a blessed word.

Louder this time, he spoke slowly. "Do-you-speak-English?"

The girl clutched the sheet against the filthy bodice of her dress and nodded. She licked her lips, cleared her throat. Her mouth opened and closed like a fish out of water, but no sound came out.

"Yes," she finally croaked. "Yes, I do." And then, "Who are you?"

"My name is Noah. Noah LeCroix. This is my home. Who are you?"

The lamplight gilded her skin. She looked to be all eyes, soft green eyes, long black hair, and fear. She favored her injured wrist, held it cradled against her midriff. From the way she carefully moved her head, he knew she was fighting one hell of a headache, too.

Ignoring his question, she asked one of her own. "How did I get here?" Her tone was wary. Her gaze kept flitting over to the door and then back to him.

"I heard a scream. Went out and found you in the swamp. Brought you here—"

"The wildcat?"

"Wasn't very hungry." Noah tried to put her at ease, then he shrugged, stared down at his moccasins. Could she tell how nervous he was? Could she see his awkwardness, know how strange it was for him to be alone with a woman? He had no idea what to say or do. When he looked over at her again, she was staring at the ruined side of his face.

"How long have I been asleep?" Her voice was so low that he had to strain to hear her. She looked like she expected him to leap on her and attack her at any moment, as if he might be coveting her scalp.

"Around two hours. You must have hit your head really hard."

She reached up, felt the bump on her head. "I guess I did."

He decided not to get any closer, not with her acting like she was going to jump out of her skin. He backed up, pulled a stool out from under the table, and sat down.

"You going to tell me your name?" he asked.

The girl hesitated, glanced toward the door, then looked back at him. "Where am I?"

"Heron Pond."

Her attention shifted to the door once again; recollection dawned. She whispered, "The swamp." Her eyes widened as if she expected a bobcat or a cottonmouth to come slithering in.

"You're fairly safe here. I built this cabin over the water."

"*Fairly?*" She looked as if she was going to try to stand up again. "Did you say—"

"Built on cypress trunks. About fifteen feet above the water."

"How do I get down?"

"There are wooden planks nailed to a trunk."

"Am I anywhere near Illinois?"

"You're in it."

She appeared a bit relieved. Obviously she wasn't going to tell him her name until she was good and ready, so he did not bother to ask again. Instead he tried, "Are you hungry? I figure anybody with as little meat on her bones as you ought to be hungry."

What happened next surprised the hell out of him. It was a little thing, one that another man might not have even noticed, but he had lived alone so long he was used to concentrating on the very smallest of details: the way an irredescent dragonfly looked with its wings backlit by the sun, the sound of cypress needles whispering on the wind.

Someone else might have missed the smile that hovered at the corner of her lips when he had said she had little meat on her bones, but he did not. How could he, when that slight, almost-smile damn had him holding his breath.

"I got some jerked venison and some potatoes around here someplace." He started to smile back until he felt the pull of the scar at the left corner of his mouth and stopped. He stood up, turned his back on the girl, and headed for the long wide plank tacked to the far wall where he stored his larder.

He kept his back to her while he found what he was looking for, dug some strips of dried meat from a hide bag, unwrapped a checkered rag with four potatoes inside, and set one on the plank where he did all his stand-up work. Then he took a trencher and a wooden mug off a smaller shelf high on the wall, and turned it over to knock any unwanted creatures out. He was headed for the door, intent on filling the cook pot with water from a small barrel he kept out on the porch when the sound of her voice stopped him cold.

"Perhaps an eye patch," she whispered.

"What?"

"I'm sorry. I was thinking out loud."

She looked so terrified he wanted to put her at ease.

"It's all right. What were you thinking?"

Instead of looking at him when she spoke, she looked down at her hands. "I was just thinking . . ."

Noah had to strain to hear her.

"With some kind of an eye patch, you wouldn't look half bad."

His feet rooted themselves to the threshold. He stared at her for a heartbeat before he closed his good eye and shook his head. He had no idea what in the hell he looked like anymore. He had had no reason to care.

He turned his back on her and stepped out onto the porch, welcoming the darkness.

National Bestselling Author
JULIE BEARD

__ROMANCE OF THE ROSE   0-425-16342-3/$5.99

Lady Rosalind Carberry is determined to rule Thornbury House—her inheritance—as a free and single woman. But when her childhood nemesis, the handsome Drake Rothwell, returns to claim the estate as his rightful inheritance, the Rose of Thornbury is ready to fight for what is hers...

__FALCON AND THE SWORD   0-515-12065-0/$5.99

People whispered about Ariel. For a young woman in the Middle Ages, she was anything but common. She was beautiful, independent, and the most skilled falconer anyone at Lonegrine Castle could remember. Still, she longed for something she'd never known...When a Knight Templar appeared at the castle seeking the healing powers of Lady Lonegrine, Ariel realized he was the most powerful and fearsome-looking man she had ever seen...

__A DANCE IN HEATHER   0-515-11873-7/$5.99

Lady Tess Farnsworth bitterly accepted the royal decree to wed the man whom she detested above all. The gloriously handsome Earl of Easterby had failed her in a desperate time of need, and her only solace in wedding him was the promise of vengeance. So, Tess plotted to seduce the Earl. Too late, she realized that the man she sought to seduce was himself a master of seduction...

__LADY AND THE WOLF   0-786-50015-8/$4.99

Lady Katherine swears to her dying brother that she will spend the rest of her life in a convent. But her father betroths her to cold-hearted Stephen Bartingham, the son of an earl. She embarks on a journey to join her future husband, determined to remain chaste. When her path crosses that of a rugged stranger, Katherine realizes that the compelling man she thought a peasant is, in fact, her betrothed...

Prices slightly higher in Canada

Payable in U.S. funds only. No cash/COD accepted. Postage & handling: U.S./CAN. $2.75 for one book, $1.00 for each additional, not to exceed $6.75; Int'l $5.00 for one book, $1.00 each additional. We accept Visa, Amex, MC ($10.00 min.), checks ($15.00 fee for returned checks) and money orders.   Call 800-788-6262 or 201-933-9292, fax 201-896-8569; refer to ad # 701 (2/99)

Penguin Putnam Inc.	Bill my: ☐Visa ☐MasterCard ☐Amex_____ (expires)
P.O. Box 12289, Dept. B	Card#_____
Newark, NJ 07101-5289	
Please allow 4-6 weeks for delivery.	Signature_____
Foreign and Canadian delivery 6-8 weeks.	

Bill to:

Name_____

Address_____ City_____

State/ZIP_____

Daytime Phone #_____

Ship to:

Name_____	Book Total	$_____
Address_____	Applicable Sales Tax	$_____
City_____	Postage & Handling	$_____
State/ZIP_____	Total Amount Due	$_____

This offer subject to change without notice.

AWARD-WINNING NATIONAL BESTSELLING AUTHOR

JODI THOMAS

__THE TEXAN'S TOUCH 0-515-12299-8/$5.99

Nicole never forgot the man who'd evoked powerful new feelings within her. And months later, she was sent to the Texas frontier to ask for his help once again. But could she also hope for love from this handsome Texan?

__TWO TEXAS HEARTS 0-515-12099-5/$5.99

Winter McQuillen had inherited a sprawling Texas ranch not far from the one room cabin Kora called home. But the only way he could claim it was if he found a wife *that night*. Kora knew she needed every bit of comfort marriage would provide. What she didn't know was that Winter needed *her* even more...

__TEXAS LOVE SONG 0-515-11953-9/$5.99

As a beautiful widow and a fallen soldier risk their lives to save children in the middle of the Indian War, danger and desire lead them to take the greatest risk of all—falling in love.

__FOREVER IN TEXAS 0-515-11710-2/$5.99

When Ford Colston is caught kissing Hannah Randell, the minister wants the two to marry at once, but Hannah refuses. Ford begins to fall in love with his reluctant bride, and now must convince her that they belong to each other.

Prices slightly higher in Canada

Payable in U.S. funds only. No cash/COD accepted. Postage & handling: U.S./CAN. $2.75 for one book, $1.00 for each additional, not to exceed $6.75; Int'l $5.00 for one book, $1.00 each additional. We accept Visa, Amex, MC ($10.00 min.), checks ($15.00 fee for returned checks) and money orders. Call 800-788-6262 or 201-933-9292, fax 201-896-8569; refer to ad # 361 (2/99)

Penguin Putnam Inc.	Bill my: ☐Visa ☐MasterCard ☐Amex _____ (expires)
P.O. Box 12289, Dept. B	Card# _____
Newark, NJ 07101-5289	
Please allow 4-6 weeks for delivery.	Signature _____
Foreign and Canadian delivery 6-8 weeks.	

Bill to:

Name_____

Address_____City_____

State/ZIP_____

Daytime Phone #_____

Ship to:

Name_____	Book Total	$_____
Address_____	Applicable Sales Tax	$_____
City_____	Postage & Handling	$_____
State/ZIP_____	Total Amount Due	$_____

This offer subject to change without notice.

> "Kurland out-writes romance fiction's top authors by a mile."—*Publishers Weekly*

National Bestselling and Award Winning Author

LYNN KURLAND

THE VERY THOUGHT OF YOU
__0-515-12261-0/$5.99

A medieval map leads corporate exec Alexander Smith on a journey back in time...where a beautiful woman helps him rediscover his own chivalrous—and passionate—heart.

THIS IS ALL I ASK __0-515-12139-8/$6.50

Set near the Scottish border, this is the breathtaking story of two lost souls who find in each other a reason to live again, to laugh again, and to love for the first time...

Also available by Lynn Kurland:

A DANCE THROUGH TIME
__0-515-11927-X/$6.50

STARDUST OF YESTERDAY
__0-515-11839-7/$6.50

ANOTHER CHANCE TO DREAM
__0-515-12261-0/$5.99

Prices slightly higher in Canada

Payable in U.S. funds only. No cash/COD accepted. Postage & handling: U.S./CAN. $2.75 for one book, $1.00 for each additional, not to exceed $6.75; Int'l $5.00 for one book, $1.00 each additional. We accept Visa, Amex, MC ($10.00 min.), checks ($15.00 fee for returned checks) and money orders. Call 800-788-6262 or 201-933-9292, fax 201-896-8569; refer to ad # 739 (2/99)

Penguin Putnam Inc.	Bill my: ☐ Visa ☐ MasterCard ☐ Amex _____ (expires)
P.O. Box 12289, Dept. B	Card#_____
Newark, NJ 07101-5289	
Please allow 4-6 weeks for delivery.	Signature_____
Foreign and Canadian delivery 6-8 weeks.	

Bill to:

Name_____

Address_____City_____

State/ZIP_____

Daytime Phone #_____

Ship to:

Name_____	Book Total	$_____
Address_____	Applicable Sales Tax	$_____
City_____	Postage & Handling	$_____
State/ZIP_____	Total Amount Due	$_____

This offer subject to change without notice.

National Bestselling Author
JILL MARIE LANDIS

Experience a world where danger and romance are as vast as the prairies and where love survives even the most trying hardships...

__Wildflower	0-515-10102-8/$6.50
__Sunflower	0-515-10659-3/$6.50
__Rose	0-515-10346-2/$6.50
__Jade	0-515-10591-0/$6.50
__Come Spring	0-515-10861-8/$6.50
__Past Promises	0-515-11207-0/$6.50
__Until Tomorrow	0-515-11403-0/$6.99
__After All	0-515-11501-0/$6.50
__Last Chance	0-515-11760-9/$5.99
__Day Dreamer	0-515-11948-2/$6.99
__Just Once	0-515-12062-6/$6.50

__Glass Beach	0-515-12285-8/$6.99

Elizabeth Bennett was in paradise. Her loveless marriage was at an end, and now she was blissfully alone to raise her young daughter on their lush Hawaiian estate.

Then everything changed when a dark, handsome stranger appeared on her doorstep. He was her husband's illegitimate son. And he made her heart beat with a passion she'd never felt before...

Prices slightly higher in Canada

Payable in U.S. funds only. No cash/COD accepted. Postage & handling: U.S./CAN. $2.75 for one book, $1.00 for each additional, not to exceed $6.75; Int'l $5.00 for one book, $1.00 each additional. We accept Visa, Amex, MC ($10.00 min.), checks ($15.00 fee for returned checks) and money orders. Call 800-788-6262 or 201-933-9292, fax 201-896-8569; refer to ad #310(2/99)

Penguin Putnam Inc.	Bill my: ☐Visa ☐MasterCard ☐Amex _____ (expires)
P.O. Box 12289, Dept. B	Card#_____
Newark, NJ 07101-5289	
Please allow 4-6 weeks for delivery.	Signature_____
Foreign and Canadian delivery 6-8 weeks.	

Bill to:

Name_____

Address_____City_____

State/ZIP_____

Daytime Phone #_____

Ship to:

Name_____	Book Total	$_____
Address_____	Applicable Sales Tax	$_____
City_____	Postage & Handling	$_____
State/ZIP_____	Total Amount Due	$_____

This offer subject to change without notice.